Cast Adrift

Book One of Reaching out of the Shadows
by Mannah Pierce

Clink Street

Published by Clink Street Publishing 2015

Copyright © Mannah Pierce 2015

Cover image was commissioned from Curtis Hamilton

ISBN: 978-1-910782-35-4
Ebook: 978-1-910782-06-4

1

Jax had to trot to keep up with his escort. The big man's stride was smooth and effortless but deceptively quick. Jax recognised it as one of the many features that dissuaded the honourable from challenging and the dishonourable from attacking.

Other, equally intimidating, characteristics were his height, his muscular bulk and the knife scar that ran down his left cheek.

He wondered what the man's name was. He would not ask, just as he had not asked the other five men who had escorted him over the last three days. They would not remember him; the forgetting pills would see to that.

So this was Carrefour Station. Jax recalled the models of spacestations that his tutor had insisted he study. This type of corridor, ten paces wide with its walls lined with advertisements, was typical of throughways in residential sectors. They passed a media screen. On it was displayed the person Jax used to be; a towheaded, green eyed boy in a velvet jacket. It was a shock. None of the simulations had suggested that his uncle would throw the net this wide this soon.

The reward for useful information had been raised to five thousand credits and the cover story of a kidnapping would be more believable out here than at home.

Suddenly the corridor was wider and lined with shops. Jax realised that they were closing on their destination; the margins of the spacer quarter were where residents sold and spacers bought. Reflected in one of the shop windows was a small, cloaked figure trotting beside a large spacer. Peering out from inside the hood were dark eyes and Jax could see wisps of brown hair.

His eyes and his hair; his mother had made temporary changes and then reprogrammed his nanobots to maintain them.

He blinked back tears. He would never again hear her voice or feel her touch.

There was no time for such sentiment. As his mother had made him promise; he would escape and survive until he could challenge the usurper and reclaim his inheritance.

This day was critical; he had to go through an open recruitment fair and yet end up with the correct crew.

They slowed. The change in pace refocused Jax on his surroundings. The shops had gone, replaced by stalls. Now almost everyone around them was a spacer, identified by their long hair, short jackets and tall boots. Instead of their path being direct, it swerved this way and that; residents scuttled out of a spacer's way but spacers avoided each other.

Then their route was blocked by people standing with their backs to them; the rear of a crowd.

His escort's hand grasped his shoulder and pulled him close. It was a shock to be manhandled; Jax had to stop himself twisting away. No one other than his mother, his father or his trainer had been allowed within touching distance for as long as he could remember.

The crowd was not uniform; it was made up of groups with gaps between them. Jax realised the groups were crews and that they must weave their way carefully between them. Touching a spacer without permission was dangerous; it could easily precipitate a challenge.

His escort made Jax walk before him, a large hand on either shoulder.

Then they were out the other side of the crowd and into the Killing Square. Jax's eyes went immediately to the empty floor around the cross.

It was clean; no blood had been shed since it had been scrubbed at station's dawn.

They joined the queue that contained the younger boys; a few were alone but most had adults with them.

These were those wishing to be cabin boys. Most crews did not recruit cabin boys; they were considered more trouble than they were worth. It made more sense to stick to cats, who were bigger, stronger and old enough to help relieve sexual tensions amongst the crew.

That was how his tutor had put it; relieving sexual tensions. The other men in the household had been much blunter; cats sucked rod and, once they were old enough, spread their rear cheeks for anyone who was interested in poking a hole.

Jax would not think about that. He was pretending to be twelve, which was too young. He would be a cabin boy and not a cat.

Two ahead of him in the queue was a very small boy.

"Age?" asked one of the two recruiters seated at the table.

"Twelve," the boy squeaked.

"Not a chance," the other man said. "Be off with you."

"I'm a hybrid," the boy replied. "It's not my fault I'm this size."

Jax was intrigued. He had never seen a hybrid close up; his father disapproved of them. He moved so he had a better view between the adults in front of him. The boy did not seem to have a tail, which was a disappointment.

He did, however, have whiskers. He also had fangs, which he was displaying to the recruiters.

"You been tested?" the first recruiter asked.

"No," the boy admitted, "but I've got the fee."

Jax wondered where the boy had got the gold credit that he put on the table. There was a silence; apparently the recruiters were similarly surprised.

"Fine," the second recruiter decided. "Name?"

"Ray," the boy replied.

"How do you spell that?" the recruiter asked.

Jax doubted the boy could spell but he answered, "R, A, E," and the man tapped the information into the tablet strapped to his forearm.

Then the gold credit was exchanged for a token and the boy was directed to one of the booths at the side of the square.

The next boy, like Jax, had his test results. The man with him, maybe his father, passed a tape to the first recruiter, who checked it in a portable viewer before taking the boy's details, giving him a token and directing him to the pen.

They suggested that the adult accompanying the boy wait in the crowd until the end of the fair, which was worrying. Jax had thought the adults handed the boys over and left. Certainly his escort would not stay.

Jax was next. His escort pulled down his hood as they reached the table. The two men looked at him with approval, which was more than they had done when faced with the previous two boys.

"Age?"

"Twelve," Jax answered. Neither man queried it. It was as his mother had said; a well-nourished boy of eleven could easily pass for twelve.

"Name?"

"Jax."

"Test?"

He handed over the tape and watched, heart thumping, as they checked it. The last thing he wanted was for them to insist on a retest; the data on the tape had been heavily edited.

"Fine." The second recruiter turned his attention to Jax's escort. "We accept responsibility for the boy Jax until he becomes a member of a certified Traditional crew."

Jax realised it was a compliment. It meant that they were certain he would be placed with a crew.

Then his escort was gone and Jax was walking towards the indicated pen clutching his token.

When he got there he took off his cloak, folded it carefully and strapped it to the outside of his pack. Once he had slung his pack across his back, he stood up straight and risked looking at the crews, hoping that one of the men would give him a signal he recognised.

Tre lurked by the ship's airlock and fought the urge to check the chronometer. It was already out of character to insist that the Willow divert to Carrefour so that they could check out the recruiting fair. Worrying about being tardy would get his crewmates wondering where the real Tre had gone.

It was a problem he could see reoccurring. For the last decade he had been the Willow's enforcer. He had appeared content living the itinerant life of a Traditional spacer crew: laid back to the point of laziness; only piqued into action when the spacer code was broken or the Willow was threatened.

His mission had always been there but was never overt. It was about the long game. This person was recruited; that one was persuaded to leave. The Willow got remarkably good deals on weaponry or upgrades. They always managed to find a load, even when other crews were struggling.

Now it was here; without warning and three standards earlier than he had expected.

He could feel himself tensing at the thought; in response he forced himself to lean nonchalantly against the bulkhead.

"I thought we weren't in any rush to recruit," Vic commented from the other side of the loading bay.

Tre shrugged.

"Carrefour always has cabin boys. You do realise that? Ean will go all maternal on us, like he did when we ended up with Obe," Vic grumbled.

Tre was relying on it.

He was saved from having to reply by Captain Mel sliding down the ladder. He stopped precisely one rung from the deck and stepped off to join them. "Tre, Vic," he acknowledged. "Let's get her opened up. Ean assures me the others will be along soon."

"Aye, Cap'n," they replied and Vic started cycling the small airlock. Carrefour had pressurised docking bays, so they could open both doors and exit as a crew. Normally they would have to leave in twos or threes or use the big airlock, which took forever to cycle.

Unasked, the processor inside Tre's head accessed his implanted data crystal array and informed him of the relative risks of each route.

The others arrived in quick succession as Vic opened the inner door; Ben and Art, followed by Cas, Obe and, finally, Ean. Tre found himself studying Art. He had intended to lever him out of the crew over the next three standards, even if it meant losing Ben with him.

He would have to keep a close eye on him.

They opened the outer door. Tre went first. They had paid for a secure docking bay so it should be deserted. He felt his scanners activate without him making a conscious decision.

It was a symptom of nervous anticipation, like the unwanted stream of data from his array. He felt as if he was about to enter combat. Trouble was, the task ahead required diplomacy and negotiating skills, not the ability to eliminate an enemy as effectively as possible.

Ean was looking askance at him. Tre's gut twisted; he should have never allowed an outsider so close.

He signalled the all clear. They exited the Willow and stood in formation while Vic sealed the airlock and the Captain locked the ship. While they waited, Ean lectured Obe, emphasising yet again how important it was to stick close to the senior members of the crew.

Art rolled his eyes and made some comment that would have been inappropriate on the ship and was unacceptable off it. Ean ignored it, choosing to concentrate on Obe.

Thankfully, the captain did not let it go. He cleared his throat and then favoured Art with one of his sternest stares. "Do we need to have words, navigator?"

"No, Cap'n," Art replied, but Tre did not need augmented senses to hear the resentment in his voice.

Tre agreed with Ean; Obe was well trained but they rarely visited a big spacestation like Carrefour. There would always be crews who would prefer to challenge for another crew's cat, or even steal one, rather than pay the recruiters' fee.

Finally the ship was secure and the crew of the Willow was ready to Walk.

With his adrenalin levels so high, there was no way Tre could switch off his processor or dial his senses back to ordinary levels. He had the schematics for the whole station laid out in his mind and he could hear people corridors away.

He hoped no one challenged them or, worse, attacked them. Explaining how he had slaughtered their opponents within seconds would be difficult.

No, this level of control was unacceptably low. He had not used any of his enhanced abilities in divs, probably standards; he had been too focused on keeping them a secret. Somehow he would have to engineer opportunities to train so he was switching them on and off rather than the level of adrenalin in his system.

They moved as a unit. Obe, as cat, and Ean, as queen, were at the centre with the captain directly behind them. Tre had point. Art, who for all his other faults was an excellent fighter, was rearguard. They walked without incident down the spur until it joined one of the wide corridors that ran through the spacer quarter.

The few non-spacers clung to the walls, wary of impeding the progress of the crews. The crews themselves walked down the middle unless they met another crew coming in the opposite direction. Then the trick was to deviate as little as possible to the left whilst not coming within three paces of each other.

Colliding was unacceptable; a challenge invariably resulted.

At least Carrefour followed the Code and the spacer quarter was well-run. Only station security was allowed laser pistols or rifles and the guards stayed in their posts unless there was trouble.

The crew of the Willow reached the Killing Square without incident.

Today any formal combats would have to wait until the recruiting fair was over. Tre scanned the square, checking for anything out of the ordinary. The area had been divided in the standard way, with desks for the recruiters and roped off pens for the cats and the cabin boys. The rest of the space had divided into two, with crews looking for recruits on one side and qualified spacers looking for berths on the other. Between the two were a collection of floozies who could be looking for a crew or just touting for business. Over the far side were a few anxious-looking adults; probably the parents of some of the boys.

They were late; the queues were gone and most of the desks were deserted. Some crews had already paid the basic fee and had been given tablets containing information about each youngster's test results. There were even crews at each of the pens and although most were looking over the cats there were too many gathered around the cabin boys for Tre's liking.

He could only get a direct line of sight on a few of the boys. Even his augmented sight could not see through bodies.

"Let's just look over the lads," Ean decided. Tre could have hugged him. Ignoring Art's complaints and Vic's sighs they made their way over.

Tre only needed a glimpse. Even with entirely the wrong colouring, the boy was unmistakeably his father's son. On looks alone he was, by far, the best boy in the bunch, something that had not escaped those surrounding the pen.

Three of the crews with tablets were already negotiating with the recruiters.

He was late; he was horribly, horribly late.

"That one looks worth having," Captain Mel stated.

Tre looked at him in surprise and met an unexpectedly candid gaze.

"Ean, I think he would be an asset," the captain continued. "See what you can do to prolong the negotiation while I pay the fee and get a tablet."

Jax was accustomed to being the sole focus of attention. This time was different. He wished the crews were paying attention to the other boys.

None of the men gathered around the pen, nor any one of those he could see in the crowd, had offered the prearranged signal.

The queens of three of the crews were well into a ruthless nego-tiation with one of the recruiters over who should claim him.

In a bizarre way they reminded him of his mother, which was crazy because they were male and ugly while his mother was female and beautiful.

Perhaps not ugly; different. All three were thin. Their long hair was dyed, their jackets embellished and their faces painted. To Jax's eyes, their pants were too tight, their heels too high and their chests too exposed.

If no one gave the signal, he would end up going with one of these men.

"It's up to you," a voice whispered.

It was the hybrid boy. Jax twisted around and looked at him.

"The recruiter gets a cut, so he wants them to bid each other up, but the rules say you choose. That's why you have the token."

Jax had forgotten that. He looked back at the three queens. He didn't want to go with any of them. He scanned the crowd around him, his gaze darted from man to man, hoping to see the signal.

Another voice, this time soft and pleasant. "My name is Ean; I am queen of the Willow."

Jax looked around and up. It was a young man with kind brown eyes.

"What's your name?"

Jax knew it was in the information on the tablet but the young man, Ean, was not holding one. "Jax," he replied.

Ean smiled and Jax felt himself smiling back.

"Excuse me," one of the queens interrupted in a tone that said, "Get away from him."

The recruiter was beginning to look anxious. "Please stay away from the boys unless you are serious about making an offer."

Ean turned to face the queens rather than the recruiter. "I am Ean. I am queen of the Willow. We are interested in the boy Jax."

"You are too late," one of the other queens hissed.

"Have you registered an interest?" the recruiter asked, much more politely.

Someone walked up behind Ean and handed him a tablet. Jax moved a little so he could see better; it was an older man with a captain's insignia.

"Yes," Ean replied. He turned back to Jax. "The Willow is a small, strictly Traditional crew. Our song goes back centuries. Over a thousand spacers have begun their new lives with us. With us you will learn what it means to be a spacer."

"Six thousand credits," squawked one of the other queens.

The sheer magnitude of the offer stunned the other queens into silence.

Ean recovered first. "It is not about credit," he continued, still only speaking to Jax. "I know that you get three-quarters of the fee, I know that four and a half thousand credits seems a lot, but what you could get from being cabin boy and cat on the Willow is beyond price."

One of the other queens snorted with derision and another laughed outright.

Jax had already decided. Something had gone wrong. The man he was meant to be meeting was not here. He either chose a crew or walked away with his test tape and his token. The latter was not an option. A boy of eleven would not last a single night in a spacestation without protection.

If he was going with a crew, he preferred Ean's.

"Can I meet the rest of your crew first?" he asked Ean.

Ean smiled again. "Of course you can."

One of the other queens groaned, turned and walked away. The other two were slower to accept they had lost but they faded into the background when Ean's crew came to stand around him.

There were Ean, the captain and five others: four with knives and a cat.

Then another man appeared at Ean's side and, suddenly, Jax could not look anywhere else.

He was a cyborg. Jax had been trained to recognise them. What was a cyborg doing spacing? Converting a man into a functional cyborg cost...Jax discovered that he did not know how much; enough that even his father could afford only a few of them.

Then the cyborg's fingers were moving and Jax recognised the signal.

It all fell into place. This was the man: the one his father had ordered to prepare a crew for him; the one who had held him as a newborn and pledged his life to him.

That his father should allocate one of his precious cyborgs to the task was unexpected. Perhaps his father had cared more about him than he had ever shown. Jax's eyes prickled with tears but he willed them away. He would not cry. Only the weak cried.

Ean was introducing the crew. "…Captain Mel. This is Vic, our engineer, Art our navigator, Ben our pilot and this is Cas." He did not introduce the cat, which Jax recognised as proper space etiquette. Then he turned to the cyborg. "This is Tre."

Jax held out his token.

"I see you have worked your usual magic, Ean," the engineer, Vic, commented. He was the oldest other than the captain. Of course the cyborg could be older; if you were paying for cybernetic enhancements you would not skimp on nanobots and age retard.

The captain looked towards the recruiter. "We will give you an honorarium of two hundred credits."

The recruiter managed to look grateful for the payment, even though it was scant compensation for missing out on over seven times as much commission.

Ean's fingers closed on the token and Jax gave it to him.

It was over. He was safe. Jax had thought he would feel better than this. Instead, he was convinced he had missed something important.

He found himself looking back, toward the hybrid boy. What was his name? Rae.

The boy gave a grin, which showed his fangs and lifted his whiskers.

He seemed more pleased that Jax had found a crew than he was worried about no one showing the least interest in him.

"Is that your friend?" Ean asked.

One of the crew, Jax thought it was Vic, groaned.

"Yes," Jax heard himself answer, which was weird because he didn't have any friends. Neither his father nor his mother approved of friendship.

"Ean," the captain warned.

"But…" Ean began.

"One is more than enough," Art complained. "Let's go."

"Wait," the cyborg, Tre, ordered. He was looking at the tablet; presumably at Rae's details. "You, Rae, come here."

Rae came over. Suddenly Jax was aware that the boy was grubby and probably stank. Worse, he was a hybrid. What had possessed Jax to claim him as a friend?

"Put your hands this far apart," Tre instructed him.

Rae's whiskers twitched in what Jax guessed was suspicion but he did what he was told.

"I'm going to drop a coin. I want you to catch it. No moving your hands until you see it drop."

Jax squirmed. It was impossible; Rae was being set up to fail. His hands were too far apart; no one's reaction time was that good.

The coin dropped but there was no clink of the coin on the metal floor. Rae's left hand had moved so fast that all Jax had seen was a blur.

"By the Lady," Ben murmured.

"We'll take this one too," the captain said immediately.

The recruiter looked over. He obviously had not seen the outcome of Tre's test. "The hybrid?"

"Rae," the captain clarified.

Rae's chin came up. "Maybe I don't want to go with you."

Ean frowned slightly. "We are a good choice, Rae. If…"

"As if you have anywhere else to go," Art interrupted, which Jax thought was rude. Ean was queen; Art should be treating him with more respect.

"I've survived on my own this long," Rae replied. "I've a choice. It's up to me."

"Yes, it is," the captain agreed.

Rae paused for a moment and then held out his token and the coin to Tre. "I'll join because you thought I would pass your test. No one ever thought I could do anything before."

Tre nodded and took both. He handed the token to Ean and the coin back to Rae. "You won it."

Rae pocketed the coin and grinned.

Jax got his first close-up look at Rae's fangs. They were long and impressively pointy.

What had he done?

2

To Ean's relief they made it back to the Willow without incident. All the way he had been thinking about the three other crews' interest in Jax. One of them might resent missing out and challenge for him.

Tre would win, Ean knew that, but the less conflict the better.

That was how the Willow operated: be ready for a challenge but try to avoid one; never expose the ship or the crew to unnecessary risk; think situations through carefully before acting.

Which was why he was more than a little surprised that both Tre and Captain Mel had encouraged him to acquire two cabin boys without even a crew meeting.

For once Ean sympathised with Art; he had a perfect right to be pissed.

Art managed to wait until they were inside the ship with the outer door closed.

"We didn't even discuss it," he complained.

Ean gave him a look that meant "Not in front of the boys", but he knew it would not work. Art was too annoyed.

Vic shepherded everyone through the airlock and closed the inner door.

"It was too good an opportunity to miss," Captain Mel replied. "Sometimes there is no time for discussion."

"But…" Art argued.

"Let's vote now," the captain announced, which was so outrageous that Ean wondered for a moment if he had taken some stuff. "The proposal is that we take Jax and Rae on as cabin boys for an honorarium payment of two hundred credits. Ean?"

Ean smiled at the boys, hoping that they were not too upset by the thought that Art might not want them. "I vote in favour."

"Tre?"

"I vote for the proposal."

"Vic?"

There was a resigned sigh. "Aye."

"Art?"

There was a pause. Ean hoped Art would do the right thing. With Vic voting in favour, the proposal would be passed even if Art, Ben and Cas voted against. When he finally spoke he bit out the words. "In favour, but I want it on record that I object to the lack of discussion beforehand."

"It will be entered into the ship's log," the captain assured him. "Ben?"

"In favour."

"Cas?"

"For the proposal."

"Obe?"

"Aye."

Captain Mel nodded. "As captain I vote in favour of the proposal, which means it is passed unanimously. So it will be entered into the ship's log." He smiled at Jax and Rae. "You have been members of the crew since the moment you gave and we accepted your tokens, but now all the loose ends have been knotted up and tidied away." He looked towards Art. "Why don't you and Ben go out and about for a bit? Ben will enjoy it and it will give Ean space to induct the boys."

"I'll go with you," Vic added. "Cas, do you want to come?"

Cas nodded, obviously pleased to be included.

"Tre?" Vic queried.

Ean waited. Normally Tre would jump at the idea of avoiding the crewroom while Ean fussed over youngsters but today none of Tre's behaviour was normal. So far today Tre had been impatient, nervy and keen to recruit cabin boys. Today Tre was not behaving at all like Tre.

"I'll stay here," Tre replied. "Look after them, Art. Cas, keep your wits about you."

The four of them left and then Tre started securing the ship from inside with Obe observing him. The captain studied the two boys.

They both stood straighter under his gaze, which was a good sign.

"When a boy joins our crew, we don't make any assumptions," Captain Mel began. "We have taken you on because of your potential, not your experience or what you know or even your skills.

"This is the Willow. She will be your home for at least the next four standards. I am the crew's captain. Although we try to make decisions as a crew, like the vote you just saw, if I give an order it must be obeyed. It has to be that way because space is a dangerous place and in dangerous situations a few seconds' delay can mean someone dies. A good captain is careful about issuing orders and I try to be a good captain.

"Ean is queen of the Willow. He is the most senior member of the crew other than me. You, as cabin boys, must obey his orders just like you must obey mine. He will be looking after you. Over the next four standards Ean, with help from the rest of us, will turn you from a boy who has potential into a spacer who has his knife and who is capable of making his own decisions." He looked from Jax to Rae and then back to Jax. "Do you understand?"

"Yes, Captain Mel," Jax answered promptly.

Rae smiled, which lit up his face in the most endearing way. "Aye, aye, captain," he piped.

Ean could see that the captain was struggling not to smile in return. "That is a good start." He turned to Ean. "I shall be in my cabin."

Ean nodded.

The captain began climbing the ladder. Tre had finished securing the ship and had melted away in the way only he could;

Ean suspected he was somewhere close by listening in. Obe stood to one side. Ean could see how excited he was by the prospect of no longer being the most junior member of the crew.

He was probably looking forward to ordering them about. Ean did not see him having much success with that. Jax had the air of someone who was more accustomed to giving orders than receiving them.

As for Rae, that smile was a formidable weapon.

He cleared his throat, which drew the boys' attention away from gazing up the ladder shaft after the captain.

"First things first. We will get you settled in. Obe will show you the way to the crewroom." He looked to Obe, warning him to behave. "I shall follow along. I have to get a few things on the way."

Obe set off up the ladder with Jax following him. Ean noticed that Rae waited a bit, as if not wanting to be too close to Jax's boots. Ean recognised the signs; Rae had been on the receiving end of a kick far too often.

Rae's foot-coverings, they did not qualify as shoes, were in the most appalling state. Ean sighed. He doubted that they would have anything in the closet small enough to fit him.

Clothes could be altered or even made from scratch; boots were another matter.

Above him he could see Rae stepping off the ladder and joining Jax and Obe in the corridor beyond.

"This is the galley," Obe announced. "That's what we call a kitchen on a ship. We walk through it to get to the crewroom."

Ean stepped from the ladder onto the floor of the corridor and headed for the store cupboards. Opening the one where the smallest clothes were, he began searching through the neat piles.

No, there was nothing small enough for Rae; he would need to get busy on the sewing machine. He picked out a selection from the shorts and the short-sleeved shirts so at least they would not be too long in the leg and arm. Placing them in a basket, he added similar clothes that would fit Jax, underpants, towels, grooming tools, bed linen and two lockboxes.

Then it was to the crewroom before Obe had time to start probing the boys' sore points with his characteristic mixture of curiosity and crassness.

He was showing them their room. "Cabin boys live in here," he informed them.

It was perfect timing for Ean to observe the difference in their response: Rae's amazement at having a room with a bed and Jax's horror that he was going to have to share.

"Thank you, Obe," Ean acknowledged. Interestingly only Obe jumped; both the others knew that someone was behind them. "Please go and prepare lunch. Leave the foods on the table or in the coolbox as appropriate. Then you can check if the captain has any jobs for you."

Obe glanced at Jax and Rae as if considering suggesting that they could assist.

Ean frowned slightly.

"Yes, Ean," he replied and was gone.

Ean placed the basket on the shelf that ran the length of a short side of the tiny, trapezium-shaped cabin.

"As Obe said, this is your room. You are too young to live in the main part of the crewroom. At the moment it is set up for one." He pointed at the single narrow bunk high up on the opposite wall. "So we will be adding another bunk."

Jax relaxed a little, obviously relieved.

"I expect you to be sensible about the way you share the space, including the storage," he warned them. "Through here is a shower." He slid open the door to reveal the triangular shower stall that they had crammed in when Ean had caught Von perving at a newly-recruited Obe.

Von had left soon after that. The Willow was a Traditional crew; anyone under fourteen was strictly off-limits.

Ean crossed the room, which was all of two paces wide, and slid open the door to the left of the one leading to the crewroom. "Through here is your head." He stood to one side, hoping that the equipment would be familiar enough for him not to have to explain. "You will be expected to keep your cabin, your shower and this head clean and tidy." He waited.

"Yes, Ean," Jax responded, followed quickly by Rae.

Managing the different needs of the two of them was going to be tricky but Ean liked a challenge.

"Good. Jax, I want you to use the head and the shower and then dress in the clothes I lay out for you. Meanwhile Rae and I will do a few chores. Then you will swap over."

Jax nodded. He took off his pack, placed it on the shelf and took out a small bag. He vanished into the head.

Ean put out a towel, underpants, shorts and a top for Jax. He then smiled at Rae. "We are going to get that second bunk."

The spare bunks were in one of the storage cupboards that lined the corridors. Like everything on the ship, they were made of lightweight materials. Even so, a bunk was too heavy and too unwieldy for one person to handle easily.

If Rae could not manage to help, Ean would call Obe.

As he had suspected, Rae was a great deal stronger that he looked; unnaturally so for a boy of that size. Inhuman strength, like superhumanly fast reflexes, was a characteristic of high-function hybrids.

Not that there were many of those. Most free-living hybrids had something wrong with them. All the ones that worked properly were owned.

Ean wondered about Rae's story; where he had come from. Not that he would ask. Spacers never asked personal questions.

As they carried the bunk into the cabin Ean could hear the sound of the shower; he looked at the shelf and saw that the towel and the underpants had gone, replaced by a neat pile of carefully-folded clothes.

Jax's boots stood side by side on the floor under the shelf.

It was only a minute's work to get the bunk fastened onto four of the wall sockets so that it was beneath the one above. Ean watched as Rae experimented folding it up against the wall and then down again.

"Nice," he observed.

Ean collected the basket before sitting on the newly-installed bunk and gesturing that Rae should do the same.

Rae sat well away from him. Ean suppressed a sigh. He hoped that Rae trusted another child more than he did adults; otherwise there could be problems with the two of them sharing such a small space.

He employed his best smile. "When I joined the Willow I only had the clothes I was wearing," he began, "and a little pouch this big…" He demonstrated with his hands. "…that carried a few precious objects."

Rae's whiskers twitched.

Ean realised that he did not have any experience of interpreting whisker twitching. It was a skill he would have to develop.

"Every spacer needs a lockbox," he continued. He reached into the basket and brought out a wooden box. It had been the nicest one in the store cupboard. He opened the lid and displayed the key on its chain that lay inside. "It's for your precious objects."

Another whisker twitch.

Ean waited.

"What if I haven't got any?" Rae asked.

"You will," Ean promised. "What about the coin Tre gave you?"

Rae thought about it and put a hand to his mouth. Ean realised that he had been storing the coin in his cheek.

Ean opened the hinged lid and held the box out. Rae dried the coin on his shirt and swapped it for the key. Ean shut the box so that Rae could lock it.

"Most of us wear our keys around our necks," he hinted.

Rae hesitated but followed the suggestion. Ean handed him the box and Rae stroked it.

"What's it made of?" he asked.

"Wood. That's a material people get from trees."

"Heard of wood," Rae admitted. "Seen pictures of trees. Didn't know the two went together." He looked up at Ean. "Is this for me to use for now?"

"No, it is yours. If you ever decide to leave the crew you can take it with you. Now, I want you to use the head and the shower and dress in the clothes I put out for you. I am afraid they will be a bit big." He paused and then decided to say it. "I want you to take your time and get really clean. Can you do that?"

Rae nodded.

"And will you ask me if you don't know how something works?"

This time there was a whisker twitch. "If I can't figure it out," he agreed.

Rae had finished in the head and was ready for the shower by the time Jax emerged. Jax was wearing the underpants Ean had put out for him and had the towel draped around his neck. He was carrying the small bag from his pack and his hair was neatly combed.

Ean felt a breeze as Rae grabbed a pair of underpants and a towel and darted into the shower; he was going to have to get used to someone moving that fast.

Jax took the towel off from around his neck and looked around for a place to hang it to dry. Ean saw him spot the rail before stepping across and neatly draping his towel over it. Then he turned to face Ean.

He was magnificently healthy; Ean could not see even the smallest scar or deformity.

"I did bring some clothes," he said.

Ean could sense that Jax was making an effort to keep his tone neutral. What he really meant was, "Why do I have to wear these old clothes that don't fit properly rather than the much better ones I have in my pack?"

"For now, I want you to wear those," Ean replied, pointing at the shorts and top. "Can you think why?"

Jax opened his mouth to speak and then closed it again while he thought a bit longer. Ean waited patiently for him to speak.

"Rae is too small for the clothes you have. You don't want him to feel out of place, so you have picked similar clothes for us to wear. Like a uniform."

It was a much better answer than Ean had anticipated or even hoped for. He decided to push further than he had intended. "What did you think of Rae's answer when Art said he had nowhere else to go?"

Jax considered. In its way, his behaviour was as strange as Rae's reflexes and strength. No boy of twelve Ean had known had ever thought so carefully before he spoke. "If he can survive on his own in a place like Carrefour, he must be tough."

Ean waited, hoping for more.

"And resourceful," Jax added. There was another pause and this time it was as if he was reluctant to admit what he was going to say. "I couldn't do it. I wouldn't last a single night."

"Good." One more push and then he would stop for now. "Why am I praising that answer?"

Jax looked at him. "I am recognising the strengths and abilities of others." His chin came up slightly. "I am acknowledging my limitations."

Who was this boy? Was he the reason that Tre had pushed so hard to get to Carrefour in time for the recruiting fair?

Ean did not have any answers, either for that question or any of the hundreds of others he had asked himself about Tre over the last nine standards.

"That was an excellent reply," he acknowledged. "Now get dressed and help me make up the two bunks."

When Rae emerged from the shower he had scrubbed himself so hard that he was glowing pink. Ean could see raw patches where scabs had been rubbed off as well as an impressive assortment of bruises at various stages of healing.

He was holding on to the waistband of his underpants; it was obvious that they would drop around his ankles as soon as he let go.

Ean reached for his nécessaire and extracted two safety pins; at least the shorts had a drawstring. He placed them on the shelf. "Rae, you finish getting dressed and join us in the galley."

Rae nodded and scrunched himself into a corner so that Ean and Jax could get past him.

The way Rae's eyes lit up when he saw the food confirmed Ean's suspicion that he was not accustomed to eating regularly.

"Lunch is at ship's noon," Ean explained, pointing at the chronometer on the wall of the galley. "That's when the pointer is down, like now."

Rae looked at the chronometer and then back at him, as if querying why they had not started eating. Before he could explain Obe arrived from taking the captain his tray, followed by Tre.

Once everyone was seated, Ean reached for some bread and told the boys they could eat.

Watching Rae eat was fascinating. He was obviously trying to model his table manners on those around him but he was so desperate for food that he kept forgetting. Ean noticed how he went straight for the high protein foods; the nuts and the cheeses.

After a while even Tre, who had started the meal pretending not to study Jax, was mesmerised by it.

Obe cracked first. "Wow, where are you putting it, Rae?"

Rae stopped; a piece of cheese halfway to his mouth. His eyes went to Ean.

"Hybrids eat far more than purebreds," Tre stated. "We can expect Rae to eat twice as much as you or Jax, perhaps even more while he is growing."

Ean was grateful for the information, even if he was astonished that Tre had intervened. "Eat all you want, Rae, but stop before you make yourself ill. There will be another meal this evening."

Rae nodded, finished the cheese, and reached for another helping of nuts.

Finally even Rae stopped. Ean made coffee while Obe showed the boys how to clear the table. He was doing a good job of it, so Ean decided to take the captain's coffee himself rather than interrupt him.

The captain stood up when he realised who had entered.

"Ean," he acknowledged.

"Obe is showing the boys how to do something," Ean explained, placing the tray in its usual place on the small side table next to Captain Mel's chair.

"Going well?" the captain queried.

Ean considered. "Yes. Running expenses may rise for a while. Nothing in the store cupboards fits Rae and Tre says that hybrids eat large amounts."

The captain waved a hand. "Cabin boys are an investment in the future," he insisted. "What about Jax? What do you think of him?"

"I am surprised that a boy like that was put through an open recruiting fair," Ean admitted. "I would have expected his family to use an agency or even to approach suitable crews directly. Consider his boots, they were obviously made for him from the best leather by a skilled cobbler and they will only fit him for a handful of divs before he outgrows them. It suggests that his family has funds to spare."

"Maybe he is from a planet where leather is cheap and cobblers are plentiful," the captain suggested with a smile. "Or maybe his grandfather is a master cobbler."

Captain Mel had always done that; he made Ean consider alternative explanations. However, this time Ean was certain he had been on the right track; Jax was from a wealthy family.

When he returned to the galley Tre was still at the table sipping his coffee. Everything had been cleaned or tidied away. Obe was telling Jax how to make tea and Rae was blinking owlishly as if he was going to fall asleep on the spot.

"All his blood has gone to his digestive system," Tre pointed out in a low voice as Ean sat down. "You had better tell him to go to his cabin before he just curls up in the nearest corner."

"Rae, go and have a nap in your bunk," Ean instructed.

He did not need any more encouragement. Ean watched him leave. When he turned back, Jax was bringing him a tray bearing the pot, a cup and saucer from his best teaset.

Ean frowned. Surely Obe had pointed out that no one but Ean himself was allowed to touch that particular set? He was about to say something but Tre tapped the pot as soon as Jax put the tray on the table.

"Nice choice, Jax. Why this one?"

"The others are not of the correct material for the tea to brew properly," Jax replied. He stood there, as if waiting for something, and then poured Ean's tea.

It even looked different. As for the taste; Ean had not known that tea could taste that good.

"Thank you, Jax, that is delicious."

For a split moment Jax seemed upset but then the expression had gone.

"Why don't you go and have some time in your cabin?" Ean suggested. "I shall knock on the door when I need you."

He was about to watch Jax leave but decided to study Tre instead. Sure enough, his eyes were fixed on the boy as he left the galley.

Ean had never known Tre to show such interest in anyone or anything.

What was going on?

3

Rae stayed very still when he woke. It was safer to check what was happening before moving.

Then he remembered where he was; on the Willow.

Joining a crew, becoming a spacer, had started off as a dream. Every boy he had met talked about it, whether they were a corridor rat or a purebred child at the orphanage. If you could make it onto a crew it didn't matter that you had no family and no prospects. It didn't even matter if you weren't purebred.

None of the others had worked to make it happen. They didn't eavesdrop on crews to work out that a small, Trad crew was a better place to be than a big, non-Trad one. They didn't find out about the different ways to get onto a ship and discover that small Trad crews used recruiting fairs. They hadn't staked out the recruiting fair two standards ago and one standard ago so that they knew what happened.

They hadn't spent over two standards earning that gold credit penny by penny.

Only it hadn't worked. Not one of the crews had looked at him. They wanted big, healthy, purebred boys like the one with the pack.

For a few minutes Rae had allowed himself to be disappointed. Then he had pulled himself together. He now had a test tape and a token. Armed with those he could approach any crew.

It would be riskier. Crews had to be properly Trad and have a good rep before the recruiters would deal with them. Rae would have to make the judgement himself rather than let the recruiters do it for him.

So he had been eavesdropping on the crew of the Willow to find out what a good crew sounded like. It was then that he heard the Willow's queen ask his question and the boy with the pack, Jax, give his answer.

Rae had no idea why Jax had claimed him as a friend.

In Rae's world you didn't question little bits of luck that came your way; you grabbed them.

Then the scary spacer had focused on him and it had been all he could do not to bolt. Tre didn't smell right. He made every hair on Rae's body stand up, which was a sure sign that someone or something was dangerous.

Terrifying or not, he had set a test that only Rae could pass and it had led to him being here, in a safe place enclosed by another safe place.

It had given him the future that had only been a dream.

Rae stretched and then curled up into a ball. He had made it. He was in a crew. Better still it was a small, Trad crew. Best of all, it was the kind of crew that a boy like Jax chose.

Ean, the ship's queen, was nice. Rae had met other people that nice but not many and not often. Ean looked nice, he sounded nice, he smelt nice and he did nice things, like give him the box and the pins to hold his underpants up.

Captain Mel was nice too, but in a more distant and sterner way.

Obe was... He would have to think more about Obe. Normally Rae would ignore him. He wasn't dangerous or interesting or particularly nice. Rae wasn't drawn to him or repelled by him.

Not like Jax; he was drawn to Jax.

Jax was in the bunk below him now. Rae could hear him and smell him. He was sleeping.

Rae listened. He always heard a lot, far more that he could take in, but to hear detail he had to concentrate. He had to listen to that sound and ignore the others.

The other members of the crew were back. Maybe their arrival was what had woken him. There were two people in the crewroom but they weren't talking much. More people were in the kitchen, the galley. Rae concentrated, blocking out the closer, louder sounds and compensating for the muffling effect of the closed door.

"Lady knows what she thought." It was a young man's voice; perhaps Cas. "Vic told her they were for a cabin boy but I don't think she believed him."

"It was really thoughtful of you." That was Ean. "Are you sure they will fit?"

"They scan them when they do the test." It was a low rumbly voice, not the captain, most likely Vic. "I took the measurements off the tablet. Told her to build in lots of growing room. Got these as well."

"Vic." Ean sounded......soft.

"He's part of our crew now. Can't have him looking like a corridor rat. Also, you saw what Jax's things were like."

Had Vic bought him something? Vic hadn't wanted one cabin boy, never mind two.

"Where are they?" That was the young man again.

"Having a nap," Ean replied. "You can imagine how stressful this morning was for them. They've had long enough. I'll go knock."

Rae heard chair legs scraping on the floor. He decided to wake Jax. He poked his head down over the side and gave a softer version of his usual alarm call.

✳ ✳ ✳

Jax woke because of the strange sound. It reminded him of a coyote, which brought back memories of being at the ranch in high summer.

It took him a moment to realise where he was and the source

of the sounds. It was Rae, whose face was upside down. He grinned and Jax felt himself smiling in return.

It felt odd, as if his face had forgotten how to arrange itself that way.

"Ean's coming," Rae warned and vanished.

Sure enough, there was a knock on the door.

Rae was out of his bunk and at the door in a trice. Jax tensed but made himself relax. He would just have to get used to how fast Rae could move. They were together on a team; it was an asset.

A backwards look and a whisker twitch; Jax interpreted that as 'Should I open the door?' and nodded.

Ean smiled through the gap. "You are both awake, good." A basket was passed through to Rae. "Get dressed and come to the galley. Shoes rather than boots."

The door slid shut and Rae was standing there, staring at the contents of the basket. Jax sat up on the edge of his bunk. "What is it?"

Rae thrust it at him and Jax took it. On top were a pair of boots that were obviously for Rae; they were far too small for Jax. Underneath appeared to be some folded clothes.

Jax put the basket on the mattress and handed the boots to Rae. "These must be yours."

Rae took them and then stood staring at them. It was like he had never seen boots before.

"You could put them next to mine," Jax suggested, pointing at where his boots were under the shelf.

While Rae did that Jax investigated the clothes. There was a top and a pair of pants to fit him and another of each to fit Rae. Underneath there were three pairs of underpants for Rae.

Jax took that as permission to wear the underpants he had brought with him.

At the bottom of the basket were two pairs of soft, leather shoes with laces. The smaller pair looked new.

They dressed in the new tops, pants and shoes. Jax would much have preferred to wear the shoes he had in his pack, but he remembered what Ean had said.

"Do you think they bought all these?" Rae asked, waving a hand to encompass his outfit and the boots.

Jax doubted the clothes were new. "Your boots and shoes," he agreed. "Ean or Obe probably altered the others to fit you while we were asleep."

Sewing was women's work but Jax knew it was different for spacers. There were no female spacers. Well, maybe a few, but none in a Traditional crew like the Willow's. Instead some of the men took the women's roles.

It had been one of the things his father had chosen to explain to him. Jax had sat on the small chair next to his father's large one and listened carefully, as he always had when his father put aside time to speak with him.

"When you are a cat, Jax, you will have to experience all aspects of spacer life. Even the womanly aspects. You will have to clean and sew and cook. You may even have to warm a man's bed, like a wife warms her husband's bed."

At the time Jax had not been sure what that meant but he knew it was something to do with what adults did in their big beds. Now he knew. It was about sucking rod or letting someone poke your hole.

"You will do all parts of a cat's duty well, as befits my son. Then, when you get your knife, you will concentrate on the manly aspects of spacer life because those will prepare you to fulfil your duties as my heir. Do you understand, Jax?"

Men did their duty and protected their family. Jax had nodded and answered, "Yes, Papá."

"Some spacers continue to concentrate on the womanly aspects of spacer life. While some of these men are weak and wayward, others are strong. They are dedicated to doing what is best for their crew. Such men become the queen of their crews. Being a queen is not for you but it is an honourable and important role. The queen of a crew must be treated with respect."

Now that Jax had met Ean, he understood what his father had been saying.

Something was moving in front of his face; Rae's hand. As soon as he had Jax's attention he was at the door. Again there was the whisker twitch.

"I'm coming," Jax assured him.

Art and Ben were in the crewroom. Ben was sitting on the edge of a bunk. Jax noticed that the bunk was a lot wider than his and had curtains, which were half drawn. Art was standing close to him.

"At least the rat looks half decent now he has some proper clothes," Art observed, as if he were speaking to Ben but loud enough to be heard by Jax and Rae.

It was unnecessary and cruel. It was Art's third black mark in the tally Jax was keeping; the first had been when he had been disrespectful to Ean and the second when he had objected to the manner in which they had been recruited.

"Art," Ben objected, which put some distance between them in Jax's mind.

He did not miss Art's response; the pull towards a kiss that was more about shutting Ben up than affection.

A fourth mark; Jax disliked bullies.

A small, interrogative yip from Rae reminded him that they were meant to be on the way to the galley.

Obe, Cas, Vic and Ean were sitting around the table.

Rae piped up as soon as they were over the threshold. "Thank you for the boots and the shoes and the clothes."

Vic smiled. "You are welcome, Rae."

Jax realised that he must have been responsible for getting the boots and the shoes.

Ean told them that they would be shown around the ship but separately.

"It will work better that way," he explained. "You will ask more questions and you will each learn different things that you can then share with each other."

Jax was impressed. Ean reminded him of his best trainers at home, the ones that focused on Jax learning as quickly and effectively as possible. Not like his tutor; who had been most interested in impressing Jax's parents with his teaching.

"Vic will be taking you, Rae, and Tre will have you, Jax."

Jax wondered for a moment where Tre was but then he was there in the doorway to the corridor. Jax went over immediately and they set off for the further of the two shafts.

"She's a standard 14-hex-eight-6," Tre began. "Can you explain what that means?"

Jax was ready. "The Willow has fourteen gravitational field generators, each set at six gee, arranged in a planar hexagonal array with the generators eight mets apart."

Tre nodded. "And the consequence of that?"

"There is one level on each side of the array where we will experience normal or near-normal weight, particularly close to the nose-to-tail axis of the ship. At levels closer to the array, the gee force will be higher and further away it will be lower. It will also be lower in some places at the periphery of the ship."

"And at the moment?"

"We are within the gravitational field generated by the station so the ship's gravitational field generators are turned off." He considered. "We have rented a mooring with near-normal gee."

Tre nodded, which Jax chose to interpret as approval for his answers. He pointed up the ladder. "Go to the top. What do you expect to find there?"

"The control room," Jax answered and started to climb.

The control room was set out in the usual way. Tre pointed at the navigator's chair and Jax sat on it. He took the pilot's position.

"By this time Rae will be on his way to the engine room and everyone else is in the crewroom or the galley," Tre began. "We can talk freely because I am certain we cannot be overheard and I know that there are no monitoring devices on this ship. You will always have to be careful about Rae. He can probably hear through closed doors and maybe even between levels."

Jax nodded.

"Do you know who I am?"

Jax knew the answer to that. "Until I am an adult, you are the man whom I should respect and obey as I would my father."

Tre stiffened. "Yes. Do you know anything else about me?"

"You are a cyborg living as an ordinary man." He tried to interpret Tre's expression and failed. "Nothing more."

"The mission was triggered almost three standards early," Tre stated. "What happened?"

Jax hoped he could say it without his voice shaking.

"My father was murdered. My uncle has usurped his position."

"Your Uncle Gil?" Tre checked.

"Yes," Jax confirmed. "My mother had me spirited away." He blinked back tears and raised his chin. "I am to prepare to remove the usurper and claim my inheritance."

There was a short silence that Tre broke. "We will need to build a team around you, which will be difficult without access to the usual resources. We will have to use our initiative and accept that it may be necessary to be unconventional. You will have me. It is a start."

"Rae has potential," Jax insisted. "He is incredibly fast." Then he felt like a fool. "You know that. You thought of testing him."

Tre gave him a reassuring smile, which was a surprise. Jax had never seen a cyborg smile.

"I want you to say what you think, even if you believe I already know it. It is always best to check. Yes, if we are lucky we will be able to develop Rae into a formidable fighter."

His father would not approve, Jax knew that; Rae was a hybrid. However, Tre was correct, when resources were limited you had to compromise.

"We will need others." Tre told him. "The next step is to find someone who can fulfil the same function as an Advisor."

A fully qualified Alexandrian Advisor was as expensive as a cyborg and, according to his mother, a better investment. You contacted the guild on Alexandria and applied for one. A request from a clan like theirs was invariably accepted and an

Advisor would be despatched to serve the contract holder for a decade.

Trouble was, the contract was non-transferrable. By now his father's Advisor, an elderly man who rarely spoke, would be on his way back to Alexandria. Worse, the clan would probably be blacklisted; the Advisors' Guild did not approve of assassinations, coups or anything else that exposed its members to danger.

"I have a solution in mind," Tre informed him. "Again, it may require some flexibility. We shall discuss it at another time. We should begin our tour. Tell me about what you see."

Rae was happy to go with Vic, who was not scary and who had bought him boots. They went to the shaft Rae had climbed up last time while Jax and Tre headed for the other.

"You know anything about ships?" Vic asked.

Rae had been concentrating too hard on getting into a crew to worry much about their ships. He shook his head. "Crews use them to go between planets or spacestations."

Vic chuckled. "That's the basic idea. We're going to start back at the airlock where you entered the ship."

He was soon there, waiting for Vic to catch up.

"You're quick," Vic acknowledged. "Now stand there and listen. Animals like humans and dogs and cats started off living on planets."

Rae had never heard anyone say that humans were a type of animal. Usually it was humans in one group, animals in another and hybrids put with the animals.

"Are you listening to me, Rae?"

He nodded and focused.

"Planets have air and planets have gravity. We need air to breathe and gravity gives us weight. Do you understand?"

"I get the air bit," he answered.

"Good. There is no air in space so we have to carry it around with us. Ships are made to keep the air in. Rae, have you ever been anywhere in Carrefour where you felt heavy, or so light that it was easier to jump?"

Rae thought about it. There were some places in the tunnels where it felt like you were carrying a heavy pack and, once, he had climbed up a shaft to a place where he felt floaty. "Yes."

"That's gravity. At the moment we are using the station's gravity. Once we separate from the station we will need our own gravity."

Rae remembered the floaty feeling. "Why?"

Vic looked puzzled and smelt a bit frustrated.

"Why not just be floaty?"

"Oh, good question. We don't work that well without gravity. Our guts play up and, after a long time without it, our muscles and bones get weak. Spacers who spend too much time without gravity can't stand up when they go to a planet or a spacestation with gravity."

Rae could see that would be a problem. "So ships keep the air in and make gravity."

"Exactly." Vic paused. "The machines that make the gravity on a ship have to be small, because they have to fit on a ship. That means the gravity they make varies more than in a spacestation." He stopped again and thought for a bit. "You know, I think we'll leave that for a bit. We've got the station's gravity for now."

Rae soon realised that the ship was bigger than he had thought; over half of it was below the level where they had entered. They went a long way down to the engine room and then worked their way up. There were cargo holds, two different places to take exercise, rooms where they were growing food in big swinging baskets and more storage.

It was a lot to take in and it all looked different from the bits of the spacestation Rae knew.

Vic stopped at a small airlock and opened both doors. "This is a gun turret. Once in a while we have to protect ourselves. We have seven of these turrets. Given your reflexes, you may have what it takes to be a gunner."

Part of Rae liked the idea of being a gunner. The rest hated the idea of his safe place being threatened.

Then they were back at the airlock where they had entered the ship.

"There are three levels above this," Vic told him. "For now we'll only worry about the upper two. In the nose of the ship is the control room and below that is our living level, with the crewroom. Climb up to the top."

The control room was full of machines that hummed, buzzed and flashed. Vic tried to explain, but all Rae heard were noises that he guessed were words.

He was relieved when they went down a level.

As well as the crewroom and the galley there was a laundry and an infirmary. Then Vic opened a door to a small room. It was full of more machinery, like the control room but darker and more crowded.

"This is a simulator." He started to explain but Rae was lost after the first few words. He stopped. "Will you trust me, Rae?" he asked.

Vic had bought him boots. Rae nodded.

Vic fiddled with some controls. There were whirrs and clunks. Then Vic pulled a handle up and the top of the machine opened like the lid of his lockbox.

Rae peered in. There was a chair.

"I have set it for as small as it will go," Vic said. "Sit inside."

He crawled in and settled into the chair.

"Have you ever seen a story vid?" Vic asked.

Rae had. They used to have them at the orphanage on feast days. He nodded.

"Well this is like a story vid where you get to take part. You have to wear a helmet and gloves. Until the story starts, you may feel closed in. In you want to stop and get out, just say so."

It was scary. It was dark and he felt trapped. Rae was not used to trusting people but Vic was crew and Vic smelt right.

Then the story started.

There were baddies; pirates. They had lots and lots of little flying things that were chasing the ship. If the ship made it somewhere called the gate they would be safe. He was the gunner and he could destroy the little flying things if he hit them right in the middle. At first he only controlled one gun but then he worked out how to use two at once and then three.

Three was tricky.

When they made it to the gate the game was over. He was about to push 'start' and go again but the lid of the machine opened and Vic was lifting his helmet off.

Behind Vic, in the open doorway, were Tre and Captain Mel. Rae wondered if he had done anything wrong but Captain Mel and Vic were smiling and even Tre looked pleased.

"Did you enjoy that?" Captain Mel asked.

Rae nodded. "It was great."

Then Ean came up behind them.

"What is going on?"

Vic and Captain Mel jumped. It reminded Rae of a teacher catching boys misbehaving.

"Just showing Rae the simulator," Vic replied.

"Oh, and that makes a good spectator sport does it?" Ean queried in that way that adults did when they weren't really asking a question.

Captain Mel and Tre faded away, leaving Vic to take any blame that was going.

"Rae, go and sit with Jax in the galley," Ean instructed. "I shall be along in a moment."

Rae walked slowly; he was pretty sure Ean and Vic would be talking about him.

"Well?" Ean asked.

"He's bright. He asks good questions. I think he can read, at least a little, because he looked at all the notices. Other than that, you will be starting from scratch. He's never been on a ship before. At least he has lived on a spacestation. What about Jax?"

"Well-educated and from a family that prepares their sons to space."

"A spacer clan?" Vic sounded surprised. "What's a lad from a spacer clan doing at an open recruitment fair?"

"Might not be an actual clan," Ean suggested but he did not sound sure.

"We both know that Tre is up to something," Vic pointed out. "You're the only person who has a hope of finding out what. He shares your bunk."

"He won't if I start asking questions," Ean replied and Rae could hear his voice changing as he turned to start walking along the corridor.

Rae sped up so that he would be sitting in the galley by the time Ean got there. His mind was churning the information he had overheard. Did Ean and Tre 'sharing a bunk' mean what he thought it did? What was Tre 'up to'? What was a 'spacer clan'?

Through the open doorway, he spotted Jax sitting at the table. Jax looked up at him and made some sounds, "¿Estás bien?"

Rae guessed Jax was asking if it was all right, so he nodded and went to sit beside him. Just being close to Jax made Rae feel different: a tiny bit safer; a touch happier.

He agreed with Vic and Ean; there was something special about Jax.

4

Tre stole some time alone before supper. One of the advantages of the Willow was the number of cargo holds; there was always somewhere to go when he needed some solitude.

The boy, Jax, was......a relief. Tre had feared he would be more like his father; not that he had any idea of what Oro had been like at eleven. Perhaps he had been like Jax. Maybe four decades of shouldering the burden of clan leadership carved a boy like Jax into a man like Oro.

The crisis was over. The boy was safe. As an unexpected bonus, Rae had potential and Jax had displayed none of his father's prejudice against hybrids.

Tre smiled as he remembered Vic's response to Rae handling three gun turrets on his first attempt.

Then there was Ean's response to the boys. Tre had wanted a queen for the crew who would create a calm, ordered environment; too many queens were obsessed by status and wanted the people around them fighting for their favour. For standards Tre had worried that he had overshot; Ean was unnaturally sensitive to others and so caring that it was more a need, like food or water, than a mere characteristic.

He was perfect for a boy of eleven who had been torn from his home and family.

Tre considered opening one of his hidey-holes and pouring himself a shot of whisky to celebrate. There would be that brief, pleasant buzz before his nanobots sprung into action and neutralised the poison.

Only, somehow, Ean would know. His brow would pucker and there would be that unique mixture of sympathy and curiosity in those soft, brown eyes. He would say nothing but, later, when they were alone and Tre's defences were down, Ean would ask if there was anything worrying him.

Which would be fine if Tre did not always have a brief but urgent urge to respond.

So far he had managed to resist. Instead he would reach for a kiss and Ean, being Ean, would not insist on any other answer.

He consulted his internal chronometer; time to make an appearance before Ean sent Obe or asked Cas to look for him.

Ean had very definite ideas about supper. The door to the crewroom was shut and the captain invited to eat with the crew. Shirts and shoes had to be worn. Everyone was expected to be on time. Each person had his place, with Captain Mel at the head of the table and Ean opposite him.

Obe had been moved across the table to sit between Cas and Ben. Jax and Rae had been put between Tre and Ean with Jax next to Tre and Rae next to Ean.

The food was in covered serving dishes and everyone sat patiently until the captain pronounced, "Let's eat."

Even then, they were expected to behave themselves rather than dig in. Woe betide anyone who reached out with his fork to spear a tasty morsel rather than using a serving spoon.

Just why someone raised in a whorehouse was so fussy about table manners was beyond Tre.

It was easy for Jax, whose manners were immaculate. Rae would have struggled but Ean served him and kept topping up his plate. Tre noted how he would tense every time Ean's hand came too close to his meal only to dip his head in submissive gratitude when the serving spoon delivered more food. At least he was managing without making too much of a mess, helped by his determination that every scrap would end up in his mouth.

Tre took the opportunity to check each of the others. Vic and Captain Mel were, as Tre had anticipated, pleased. Despite Vic's grumbling, they liked having a cabin boy in the crew. One of the biggest problems with spacing was the boredom; having Rae and Jax around would alleviate that.

It helped that Jax had chosen their crew over many others and that Rae was so likeable.

Obe was delighted. Tre imagined him thinking of all the things he would be able to do now that the focus of Ean's attention was elsewhere. Of course he was mistaken, but Tre saw nothing wrong with Obe enjoying his illusion while it lasted.

Cas seemed vaguely intriguely intrigued and a little disappointed. Tre wondered if he had been hoping that they would recruit someone older. Obe was talking to him and Cas was pretending not to listen; the same younger and older siblings' roles they had played for the two and a half standards.

Tre looked at them in a different way now that Jax was here; allowing them to develop slowly was no longer an option.

Then there were Ben and Art. Ben looked like his normal self but the analysis Tre was running on his processor told another story. The tension in Ben's muscles, his breathing rate and his eye movements suggested a high level of anxiety; a sure sign that all was not well.

Tre turned his attention to Art and, immediately, his targeting systems activated.

It was a very bad sign; his programming was categorising Art as an enemy. Tre forced himself to concentrate on his food: on the taste and the texture; on anything other than ways to kill Art.

Two involuntary activations in a single day; Tre had not experienced such poor control since his first few standards as a cyborg. He turned from analysing the crew to evaluating his own state of mind.

He should feel calm. The crisis was over. Jax was where he should be, in Tre's care.

Had his instability been triggered by the confirmation that Oro was dead? Or the news that Gil had been responsible? Both were irrelevant. Tre's duty had been transferred from

Oro to Jax as soon as the tiny newborn had been placed in his arms and he had taken the oath.

Maybe that was it. The baby was now a boy and that boy was here, on the Willow.

The boy he lived for; the man he would probably die for.

He told himself that his systems would settle once he became accustomed to Jax's presence. Only what if they didn't? Tre imagined a blood-soaked crewroom, Ean's dismembered body and a terrified boy who had realised that his protector was a monster.

No, it was not worth the risk. He needed a check-up, possibly some maintenance. Tracking down his substitute Advisor would have to wait.

Instead he would have to come up with an excuse to visit Mercy Station. Maybe something relating to Rae's hybrid nature; there was a good chance that might work.

Most people had cleared their plates, with the exception of Rae, who was putting away what was either his third or fourth portion. Tre could see that Ean was eating more slowly than he usually did, so that Rae would not be last.

There was no question of the dishes being cleared before everyone had finished; they all knew better than to even suggest it.

Captain Mel cleared his throat, attracting everyone but Rae's attention. "I have found us a cargo," he told them. "I followed up on a lead Cas gave me."

Cas managed to look both surprised and blank.

"The crippled freighter," the captain reminded him.

"What was it carrying?" Ean asked.

"Nut butter," the captain replied. "You can sell nut butter almost anywhere. I had to buy a whole container, though."

Art and Ben's eyes widened and Vic choked on whatever he had been swallowing. Tre's processor obliged with how much of the load would not fit into their cargo holds.

It was a lot.

"Perhaps we could sell on half," Ean suggested.

"We'll fit it in," the captain insisted. "I've even found a buyer for the container, provided it is empty by station's dawn the day after tomorrow. The stevedores have agreed to let us take the Willow into the cargo hold and I have managed to sell on the balance of this berth."

There was a short silence only broken by the sound of Rae eating.

"When are we leaving?" Ean asked. His voice could have frozen water at ten paces.

The captain flushed slightly. "We have to be out of here by midnight," he admitted. "We can move directly to the cargo hold."

Tre wondered how big the bribe to the stevedores had been; presumably a lot less than they were getting from the crew that wanted the berth.

"The cargo bay is not pressurised and the station's gravitational field will be negligible?" Ean queried.

Tre's watched the captain's gaze go to the two new recruits as he realised that Ean had been planning on covering the basics of shipboard life before they moved into an environment where a careless error could kill someone.

There was a noise from Art, as if he been going to speak but had decided against it. A sideways glance at Ean confirmed that Art had been transfixed by Ean's best 'I dare you' stare.

"I am sure Jax has experience of ships," Vic pointed out, "and I am sure that Rae will do exactly as he is told."

Everyone looked at Rae, who stopped chewing, twitched his whiskers and nodded.

"Part of being a successful crew is taking advantage of opportunities that present themselves," Ean conceded. He turned to Rae. "Have you finished, Rae?"

Rae looked at little wistfully at the few streaks of sauce that were left on his plate but nodded.

"Obe and Jax, please clear the plates and the serving dishes," Ean instructed.

Jax did not hesitate for a moment; to Tre's relief there was no hint that he had been raised surrounded by servants. Ean stood up, went to the oven and returned with what Tre knew from the smell was an apple crumble and a large jug of custard sauce.

They did not get apples very often; Cas or Ben must have picked some up at the market.

Even though the crumble was twice as large as usual, every scrap was consumed.

As usual, the cat and the cabin boys cleared the table. Rae did manage to stay awake until everything was piled on the counter but he was moving more and more slowly as his digestive system kicked into top gear.

In the end Ean ordered him to go and sit on one of the couches in the crewroom before he dropped something.

Ben volunteered to make coffee and Cas helped by scrubbing the pans while Obe showed Jax what went into which recycler and how to operate the crockery and cutlery cleaner.

Then they went to join Rae while the older members of the crew enjoyed their coffee.

Not that Tre did. Real coffee beans were rare and expensive; far beyond the Willow's provisions budget. Unfortunately, or fortunately, depending on how you looked at it, Tre had been raised on a planet that grew and exported coffee.

Ean bought the best substitute they could afford and Tre did not have the heart to tell him that it fell so short that he would have preferred not to drink it.

They usually tried to avoid talking about work during or after supper but the change in plans meant they had to make an exception. They talked though the move to the cargo bay and agreed to meet in the planning room afterwards to discuss the logistics of loading twice as much nut butter than would reasonably fit.

At least it was in catering packs. Tre imagined a tanker-sized container filled to the brim with the stuff and shuddered.

Once the coffee was gone, the captain excused himself and Ean went to add the cups and saucers to the cleaner. The others went through to the crewroom but Tre lurked, waiting for Ean.

"How old do you think he is?" Ean asked.

For a moment Tre thought Ean was querying that Jax was twelve, but then realised that he meant Rae. "Does it matter? Hybrids develop at different rates and different times to purebreds. Anyway, he's far better off with us than living as a corridor rat."

Ean relaxed. "True," he acknowledged and started the cleaner. "Jax's table manners are perfect. In fact, they remind me of yours."

Tre's heart sped up. Of course he and Jax would have behaviours in common; they had been raised on the same planet and spent time in the same household. He settled for a shrug and went for a distraction. "I was thinking. The dia-doc won't work for Rae and some of the stuff in the medico kits might kill him rather than cure him. I'm not even sure if we could tank him or pod him safely."

Ean paled and Tre had to ignore the guilt that made his gut clench.

"We could swing by Mercy Station," he suggested in what he hoped was a casual voice. "I've got a contact there. He might be able to give us some ideas about who to ask."

Some colour returned to Ean's face. "Even Mercy Station needs nut butter."

"Indeed," Tre encouraged, slipping an arm around Ean's waist.

Ean smiled but twisted away as Tre had known he would. "Let's join the others."

After supper the crew usually spent some time sitting on the couches in the centre of the crewroom. There were four. Art and Ben usually sat on one of the two shorter ones; Ean and Tre on the other. The other three members of the crew sat wherever they fancied.

The short couch where Ean and Tre usually sat was occupied by Rae. He was curled up in a ball on his side, fast asleep.

"I'll move him," Tre decided, moving towards the sleeping boy.

"I wouldn't," Vic warned.

Rae growled in his sleep. His upper lip curled up in a snarl exposing his fangs.

"Poke him with a stick," Art suggested, which earned him another of Ean's disapproving looks.

"I'll wake him," Jax volunteered.

He had moved into range of those teeth before Tre could decide if it would look odd to stop him. There was no growl, just a whisker twitch.

Jax reached out, placed a hand on Rae's upper arm and shook him gently.

There was a small whimper. Jax sat down beside him and shook him a little harder. Rae responded by crawling onto

Jax and then shifting about until he found a comfortable position.

Tre was reminded of the dogs at home, how they would turn around and around on the spot before lying down.

Rae settled and went back to the serious business of sleeping. He was straddling Jax's lap, chest to chest and with his head pillowed on Jax's shoulder.

Jax's perplexed expression was a picture. Even Ean laughed.

"Do you think you can lift him, Jax?" Vic asked.

Jax considered and nodded. He slid forward to the edge of the couch, leaned forward so that their combined weight was over his feet and then straightened his knees.

At least Jax did not have to worry about supporting Rae because the little hybrid's legs had automatically coiled around his waist.

Rae showed no signs of waking up as Jax tottered towards their cabin. Ean went with them to open the door and then returned alone.

"Rae trusts him, I wonder when they became friends," he commented as he took his usual place on the couch next to Tre.

So did Tre; he could not imagine that they had met before the recruitment fair.

"We had better be sharp tomorrow," Vic pointed out. "We'll need to be on our toes. You know what stevedores are like."

Tre did; they had their own code but it did not stretch to being accommodating to spacers. He hoped that the captain had offered them a big enough bribe and was paying it in instalments.

Short moves across a spacestation were always tricky. The captain, Ben, Art and Vic were in the control room. Tre was in one of the simulators, which he had switched to act as an interface for the defence and security systems. Ean stayed in the crewroom with Obe in case the ship's movement or the fluctuations in the artificial gravity field disturbed the boys. Cas was in the other simulator, observing.

Vic had not reset the simulator quite right after Rae had been in it. Tre spent a few minutes adjusting it; if Rae was going to use it regularly he would have to activate the memory and store their individual settings.

It was one of the many simulators' functions he did not use; he did not want to alert the others to the fact that they were built to a much higher specification than normal.

So much so that they had cost more than a complete refit of the Willow's gravitational field generator array.

Tre sighed. If Vic did not already suspect, he would soon, joining the captain and Ean.

Mel had always known that Tre was more than he seemed; it would have been impossible for Tre to prepare the ship and the crew without the captain's support. Given Mel's behaviour at the fair, he had recognised that Jax was important to Tre's plans.

As for Ean, Tre had no idea how much he knew. He was frightened to ask. If Ean answered, Tre would have to decide what to do about it.

The move went without a hitch; they ended up neatly tucked in a corner of the cargo bay with their container of nut butter beside them. That done, they met to discuss the plan for the next day.

It was decided that all the adults but Cas would be transferring the nut butter from the container into the ship. They would depressurise the ship with the exception of the top two levels and hydroponics to make the process easier. Cas would monitor the situation from the control room.

The captain had suggested that Ean and Cas swap roles; Ean could continue inducting the boys and Cas needed more experience working in a suit at near-zero gravity. However, they decided against it. Given the limited time they had to empty the container, they would need Ean's strength and experience.

Once the meeting was over, the captain left for his cabin and the others for the crewroom. Ean hung back. Tre recognised the invitation.

If Tre left, Ean would accept that Tre wanted to sleep alone. Common sense told Tre to walk away. His systems had been showing the strain; he should be increasing the distance between him and Ean, not strengthening their relationship.

On the other hand, it had been a stressful day; a dose of Ean would be the perfect antidote.

He walked over, stood close and stroked Ean's back.

Ean turned and smiled up at him. It was that small, intimate smile that went straight to Tre's groin and, although he was loath to admit it, his heart. It transformed Ean's ordinary, plain face into something beautiful.

They decided to check the bathroom but as they entered the crewroom, Tre could hear that it was occupied; it sounded like Art and Ben.

Ean would suggest a shower and Tre was not in the mood for anything so practical. He swept Ean off his feet and carried him over to the bunk.

"Tre!" Ean complained but there was no edge to it.

Tre smiled; now there would be no showers until the morning.

5

Jax had put Rae on the lower of the two bunks. There hadn't been another option. He couldn't lift Rae high enough to get him onto the top bunk and asking Ean to help didn't seem like a good idea; not after the way Rae had growled at Vic and Tre.

Trouble was, the lower bunk was his and the upper bunk was Rae's.

He had thought about sleeping in the top bunk but it didn't seem right. Rae hadn't chosen to sleep in Jax's bunk; Jax had put him there. He would be choosing to invade Rae's private space.

So, instead, he slept in his bunk with Rae curled up at the foot end.

In the morning he had gone. Jax could hear the shower. Still half asleep, he listened as the sound of the spray was replaced by the blowers and then silence.

Rae shot out of the shower wearing just underpants and jumped up to the top bunk. There were a few rustles and then he landed on the floor fully clothed except for shoes.

He twitched his whiskers and looked towards the door.

"You go," Jax suggested. "I'll be along in a minute."

Rae looked disbelieving.

"Five minutes," Jax amended, which must have satisfied Rae because he was out the door in a flash.

Jax wasn't even out of bed when Rae was back for his shoes.

By the time he reached the galley, Rae was tucking into his breakfast. The only other person around was Obe and Jax remembered that everyone but the three of them and Cas were loading nut butter.

"You are to stay on this level," Obe reminded them. "Ean will be cross if you don't do what you are told."

Rae stopped eating for a few seconds, twitched his whiskers and glanced at Jax with a look that said, "He doesn't think we'll do what he tells us unless he mentions Ean. Interesting."

Or that's what Jax thought it meant. He sat down at the table and began spooning food into a bowl; equal portions toasted grains, rehydrated dried fruit and yoghurt.

Many people, including his father, had warned him that food aboard ship was poor. Obviously none of them had been on a ship run by someone like Ean.

Rae spooned the last of his current bowlful into his mouth and reached for the chopped nuts.

"Maybe you shouldn't eat so much that you fall asleep," Jax suggested. "We probably have work to do."

Rae looked at the chronometer, as if assessing how long it was until the midday meal, and then nodded.

"Ean said you could have meal bars midmorning if you got hungry," Obe volunteered.

Rae replied with a smile that, judging from the way Obe shrank back, was a bit too toothy for comfort.

They were impressive teeth. Jax could see that they fitted together like a coyote's. If Rae bit into something it would be sliced rather than crushed.

"What does Ean want us to do?" Jax asked.

Obe sighed. "Clean. Ean is obsessed with cleanliness." He perked up. "Later they will send some of the nut butter up here and we are to find places to put it."

Apparently they were responsible for cleaning their cabin, the galley and the corridors. They began with the galley with Obe standing over them describing how Ean liked things done.

Jax remembered what his father has said; on a ship the womanly tasks were shared and it was the younger members of the crew who did most of them. It could be worse. Obe gave good instructions and showed them when they did not understand.

Rae was quick but Jax was thorough; Rae often had to do a task three times over before Obe agreed that it was completed to Ean's standards.

They were moving onto the corridors when Cas called down from the control room.

"Ean is on his way up. We are going to transfer some of the nut butter up the shaft to this level and the easiest way to do it is to switch off the ship's gravitational field."

Rae looked at Jax. This time his eyebrows went up at the same time as his whiskers twitched and Jax formed the impression that he was asking for a translation.

"There won't be a downwards pull. We'll be weightless."

"All floaty?" Rae queried.

Jax thought about explaining the complexities of interacting forces. "Yes."

Rae smiled at that, which left Jax wondering what he had done.

Cas checked the control room and Ean the crewroom. Jax explained to Rae that everything had to be fastened down or put away in case it floated away. As he did so he could hear his tutor's voice in his head, scolding him for reinforcing Rae's misconception that things would float upwards when the gravitational field generators were switched off.

Then Ean and Obe fastened nets across the doorways and at intervals along the corridor.

"For safety," he explained.

Rae looked at Jax with the combination of eyebrow-lifting and whisker-twitch. Jax tried to explain about momentum and inertia but he could tell that Rae did not get it.

"The two of you will stay on the galley side of the net," Ean ordered. "You can watch. This first time I want you on safety lines. It is a precaution until we have had time to assess whether you can handle yourself at zero gee."

Jax wanted to complain. He had been on ships and, every time, his trainer had made sure he put in time in the zero gravity gym. Then he remembered Rae. This was like the clothes. It was about not making Rae feel inadequate.

So he put up with wearing a safety belt and being clipped onto the doorframe with a short length of line.

Obe had been sent up to the control room with strict instructions to call someone if anything happened. Cas came down to work with Ean.

Ean and Cas had obviously worked together at zero gee before.

The way they handled the myriad cuboid containers of nut butter was amazing. They created carefully ordered stacks that would be far too heavy to move under normal conditions. Then they put a board against the vertical face of the stack and pushed gently.

The stack moved slowly along the corridor and they followed up. When it hit the net they stopped it bouncing back with the board.

Every so often they moved a net. Soon the entire corridor was filled with nut butter, with only a narrow path between the immense floor to ceiling stack of containers and the corridor wall.

It was a lot of nut butter.

He looked around to see whether Rae was as impressed as he was but there was only an empty belt floating on the end of the safety line.

Jax froze. What should he do? Unclip and go find Rae or follow orders and stay where he was?

There were some excited yips from beyond the galley, in the crewroom. As he watched, Rae shot across his line of sight, moving from bottom left to top right.

Tre had said that Rae could hear across levels and through closed doors. Jax was about to try calling softly when he realised that Ean and Cas were behind him, on the other side of the net, wondering what he was looking at.

Rae flew across the open doorway with more yipping.

Ean unhooked the side of the net and held it up for Cas, who pulled on the doorframe to accelerate himself through the gap.

"Can you handle yourself at zero gee?" Ean asked Jax.

Jax nodded and Ean unclipped his line from the doorframe.

The three of them pushed off and drifted at a safe and controlled velocity to the opposite wall of the galley. Jax had to use a foot to correct his path so that he missed the table but otherwise he managed fine.

Cas and Jax stopped themselves on the wall while Ean used the doorframe.

Jax peered through into the crewroom.

Rae rebounded off a wall, somersaulted upwards, ran along the ceiling, pushed off with his legs, performed a perfect high-velocity flip and landed on the floor.

It was as if he had practised in a zero gee gym for divs.

Jax looked at Ean. He could see that Cas was doing the same.

Ean looked stern and disappointed but the impact was compromised by the way his eyes were sparkling with mirth and one side of his mouth kept twitching upwards.

There was another volley of delighted yips as Rae tumbled though the air and ricocheted off two of the bunks.

Then he saw Ean.

He froze and his eyes widened and his mouth formed a perfect circle. Trouble was, he was still travelling at speed.

Ean launched himself into the crewroom to save him but Jax could see that he would not get there in time.

By luck Rae hit one of the couches rather than anything hard and Ean was able to hook a foot around a table leg and grab him before he could bounce too high.

Rae cowered and gave a whimper that made Jax feel a bit sick. It was as if he expected Ean to hit him. Would Ean? Did queens beat errant cabin boys? At home boys were often beaten for their misdemeanours.

Not Jax; only his father punished Jax and the last time it had happened he had been at an age to receive a spanking rather than a caning.

Instead Ean sat Rae on one end of a long couch.

"Stay there," he ordered and sat beside him but with some distance between them. He looked towards where Jax and Cas were watching from the doorway. "Shut the door please and wait in the galley. I will be there in a few minutes."

Cas slid the door shut and signalled that they should move away. Jax waited and then followed as Cas drifted across the galley, snagged a table leg with his foot and pulled himself down onto a chair.

"Don't look so worried," Cas advised as Jax came to rest on a chair. "Ean isn't even cross. He only gets angry if one of us gets hurt. Anyway, he's got a real soft spot for Rae."

Jax knew that but it did make him feel better to hear someone else say it. He looked towards the shut door, wondering what was happening.

Rae sat still and resisted the urge to run away and hide, like he had managed to resist the urge to bite Ean when he had grabbed him. It had helped that Ean didn't smell scary, that it hadn't hurt and that Ean had let go of him quickly.

Then the door to the galley slid shut, cutting him off from Jax.

Ean fixed Rae with his scarily direct gaze. "Rae, I told you to wear the safety belt and stay clipped to the door frame. Did you understand?"

Rae deciding that pretending to be stupid was worse than admitting that he had disobeyed. He nodded.

"So why did you undo the belt?" Ean asked.

There were lots of answers to that. Watching people stacking boxes was really boring and Jax finding it so fascinating had made it worse. Then there was being tied up. Rae hated that. It made him think of dark, cold places where he was always hungry.

He decided to use the answer he had prepared in advance; the one that had always worked on teachers in the orphanage.

"I needed to pee." The teachers had thought about having to clean up a puddle of piss and let him get away with it.

Ean didn't smell convinced but, to Rae's relief, he accepted it. "And?"

Rae decided to try the truth, "Being floaty was fun."

"Sometimes fun has to wait. You should have told me or Cas that you needed to use the head. You can experience zero gee when there is someone to supervise you."

Rae thought he had done pretty well on his own.

Ean frowned at him. "You will go to your cabin and stay there until I come and get you."

Rae told himself that being in his cabin was better than being on the tether. He tried moving about but it wasn't as much fun as it had been in the crewroom. He ended up stretched out half way between his mattress and the ceiling, floating in the air.

How long would he be here? Would he get fed?

He wondered what Jax was doing.

There were steps coming towards the door, a knock and then Ean's voice.

"May I come in, Rae?"

Rae considered saying no but only for a moment.

Once inside, Ean stayed upright, floating a handbreadth from the floor as if he was standing.

"I know it is difficult for you, Rae," he began. "You aren't used to having someone tell you what to do. For all I know the people in your past who told you what to do may have hurt you."

Rae didn't remember the people who had hurt him; it had been too long ago. It was mostly the teachers at the orphanage who had told him what to do and he had only obeyed them when he had wanted to.

Ean was looking at him in that way that made Rae squirm. "You joined our crew, Rae. You accepted my authority like you did Captain Mel's."

Rae wasn't sure what 'authority' meant.

Ean sighed. "Rae, we made a deal."

A deal? Rae understood about deals.

"You do what we think is best for the next four standards. We turn you into such a good spacer that crews will be falling over themselves to recruit you."

It was the deal that Rae had wanted, the one he had worked so hard to make happen. He nodded.

"Good. Now I want you to really try to do what you are told. If you are struggling, I want to know. We'll work something out."

That was the kind of thing the teachers said and they had never meant it.

There was another sigh. "Rae, tell me why you took the belt off. The truth this time."

Rae decided to give it a go. "I was bored and I don't like being tied up."

Ean considered and nodded. "If you had told me you didn't like being tied up I would have made the tether much longer. If I had known how easily you get bored, I would have given you something to do."

It wouldn't have been as much fun as careering around the crewroom but it would have been better. He nodded.

"Good," Ean acknowledged. "Now that I know that both you and Jax can handle yourselves just fine at zero gee, you can help Obe and me find places for all that nut butter."

It turned out that all the boxes piled up in the corridor had to be stored on that level. They started by moving other stuff up in the store cupboards and putting the boxes at the bottom.

That only dealt with about one-third of it.

Next they had to find places that could be made into temporary storage cupboards, like under bunks, shelves or tables. Once the boxes were packed in, they had to wedge the piles so that they couldn't move and net the exposed sides.

If there weren't well-placed hooks on the walls, floors or ceilings for the nets they had to stick ones on.

It was hard work and to Rae's surprise it wasn't boring. It was a challenge. The pile in the corridor got smaller and smaller. Finally it was gone.

Ean was really pleased; Rae could smell it. He went to a panel on the wall and pushed a button.

"This is Ean," he said and his voice, or parts of it, came back from all over the place. "*This is Ean.*"

"That's the intercom," Obe informed him. "We use it to communicate within the ship."

"We have finished storing all the nut butter on the crewroom level."

There was a click; another voice came from everywhere. "*This is Vic. All of it? Already?*"

Ean smiled and pushed the button again. "This is Ean. Yes, Jax and Rae helped. How close are we to being able to turn on the gravitational field generators?"

There was a pause and then another click. "*This is Tre. We have packed all the levels affected by the ship's gravitational field.*"

"*This is the captain. We will activate the gravitational field generators, have lunch and then load the rest into the lower storage holds this afternoon.*"

Rae was disappointed, it had been fun moving in zero gee, but then he smelt the bread Ean was crisping up in the oven and decided it wasn't so bad.

He decided not to eat so much that he fell asleep. If he got hungry he could ask for a meal bar; the ones Ean made were much more tasty than the ones he had been able to get cheap at the market.

After they had finish eating, the captain, Tre, Ben and Art went back out to load the rest of the nut butter and Cas returned to the control room.

Once they had tidied up, Ean brought out a large sheet of thin white plastic. On it was a diagram that Rae guessed was the ship.

He pointed at some large red dots. "These show the gravitational field generators and they pull everything towards them."

Rae looked from the diagram to Ean and then back at the diagram. He was confused. If you were above the red dots you would be pulled down but what happened if you were below them?

Ean smiled. "I think you are one of those people who learn better by doing, Rae. Let's go."

They climbed down the ladder towards the airlock where they had entered the ship. Ean went first with Rae, Jax and Obe following.

"Under ship's gravity, the downward pull gets less as we get closer to the airlock," Ean explained. "You may also experience a sideways pull."

Rae could feel it. It was like he was crawling backward. By the time they were gathered at the airlock the wall opposite the airlock was definitely the floor and the airlock was in the ceiling.

"Now we climb up the ladder the other way," Ean told them, heading towards what had been down when they had been using the station's gravity.

It was like scrambling along the top of monkey bars that curved upwards to make a ladder. Soon they were climbing up towards hydroponics.

When they got there, Rae could see why all the plants were in baskets. Before they had been like huge cradles swinging between two big floor supports. Now the supports were from the ceiling but the cradles were still the right way up. He understood this time why the lights were in the walls and the floor and ceiling were mirrored; it meant you were never walking on the lamps.

There was a lot of mess on the floor that had been a ceiling.

"No matter how careful we are, stuff always escapes from the baskets when we change the direction of the gravitational field," Ean explained. "Obe will show you how to clean up and then teach you the basics of looking after the plants. Then you can pick some berries and tomatoes. Try not to eat them all."

They had to clean the ceiling with sponges on long poles, so that it would reflect more light down onto the plants. Then they had to mop and polish the floor.

Obe explained about the water supply, which Rae understood, and then started to go on about nutrients and media, whatever they were.

Jax seemed to understand; Rae might ask him later.

The small, red berries were sweet and delicious; Rae had to stop himself eating every one he picked. He was less sure about the tomatoes but he knew that they cooked up to make good food.

"This is a very sophisticated hydroponics set up for such a small ship," Jax observed as they selected the ripest fruit and put it in a basket.

Rae just looked at him. Obe was doing the same. Probably Obe, like Rae, had never been on another ship. Obviously Jax had.

"Ean is very keen on fresh food," Obe replied. "He says it's better than pills for keeping people healthy."

As Rae fell asleep that evening after another delicious meal, he could not have agreed more.

6

Ean sighed as he poured himself tea. Packing the entire ship with nut butter had its drawbacks. What had been spacious accommodation for eight was now cramped conditions for ten. They had even had to fill the storage hold that they usually used as a gym.

It was three divs to Mercy Station with only two stops on the way. Even if there was a glut of nut butter at their first port of call, Ean was determined to get rid of a third of the load.

Unfortunately they had to survive over a div until they had that option.

The only person who appeared unaffected was Captain Mel, which was possibly because Ean had not stored any of the boxes in his cabin or, more likely, because he refused to admit that buying a whole container of nut butter had been a crazy idea.

Ben came through from the crewroom, collected a tea cup from the cupboard and sat beside him. Ean filled the cup from the pot.

"Thank you," Ben acknowledged. "Only another forty-two days."

Ean grimaced. It was easier to think about it being the next stop rather than forty-two days away.

"We could dump some of it," Ben suggested.

It was tempting but Ean knew they would end up voting against it. Spacers did not dump potentially profitable loads.

"Tre missing his gym?" Ben queried. "It's difficult to miss that he's compensating with his other favourite form of exercise."

Ean flushed. Tre was, indeed, insatiable. It was the main reason Ean was in the galley this early. Not that it was not enjoyable, but by the time they were finished all Ean would want to do was curl up in his bunk and sleep.

"How many times was it in the bath yesterday evening? And in the shower yesterday morning?" Ben reminded him.

Ean knew he was a deep red but Ben was his closest friend and, as such, was allowed to tease.

Ben had been sixteen when Ean had been recruited nine standards ago. He had taught Ean about space and how to survive on a ship, getting Ean through a difficult transition when Tre and even Captain Mel had been convinced that they had made a mistake.

Then, three standards ago, Art had bought in. It was just after Ean had become queen and three crew members had left in quick succession; Rex and Sam had retired and Eli had bought out because he had opposed Ean's being made queen.

It had left them short-handed and strapped for funds. Art had been by far the best of those who had wanted to buy in and he was a navigator, which they desperately needed. Also there had been chemistry between him and Ben from the moment they had met.

Ean could still remember it. They had been clubbing with half an eye out for suitable talent. The handsome navigator had not been able to pull his eyes away from Ben.

They had finished negotiating the buy in three days later.

Ben loved Art; Ean knew that. In his way Art loved Ben but it would never be an equal relationship. According to their natures, Ben gave and Art took.

Not that Ean was in any position to criticise. Ben and Art had exchanged love rings. Ean had accepted long ago that he and Tre would not. Tre would never acknowledge that anyone had a claim on him.

Or that was what Ean had thought until they had recruited Jax. Now he wondered. The boy was special to Tre. In retrospect it was obvious that Tre had been desperate to be at the fair in Carrefour to recruit him.

Ean suspected they were from the same home planet but spacers did not ask other spacers about their backgrounds.

"Rae obviously respects you," Ben said.

The comment chased all thought of Tre from Ean's mind. "What do you mean?"

Ben smiled. "He makes sure that you are well out of the way before he does something naughty."

Ean supposed that Ben was right; it showed that Rae respected his authority. "What is he up to this time?"

"I think he needs lots of exercise, probably more than Tre does," Ben pointed out.

"Ben!" Ean objected, his mind boggling.

"I'm only telling you because I'm afraid Jax or Obe will try it," Ben explained. "He's invented a new sport. Shaft diving."

Ean's imagination went into overdrive.

"He usually starts from the top outside the control room," Ben told him. "He dives into the shaft head first. The gravitational field accelerates him downwards, so by the time he is crossing the turnover point he is going at some speed. Then the field in the opposite direction slows him down so he only has a manageable amount of momentum when reaches the near-zero gee area at the bottom of the shaft. Then he reverses the process."

Ean had been coping until Ben said that Rae was trying the same manoeuvre tail to nose as he was doing nose to tail. Nose to tail there were an extra three levels where Rae had time to work out how to shed any extra momentum before impact. When he was travelling tail to nose, the top of the shaft was outside the control room.

"You haven't been up to the control room during the last three days," Ben pointed out. "Vic rigged a net across the top of the shaft but Rae is using it to ricochet himself back down so Vic's going to replace it with some padding."

Ean scowled to illustrate his displeasure, even though he was relieved that Vic had been paying attention. Did everyone other than him know what had been going on?

"He only does it when you're out of the way," Ben reminded him. "In fact, he waits until you and Tre are fucking."

Ean felt his cheeks beginning to burn again. "Maybe Vic could make Rae a helmet and some pads for his elbows and knees," he suggested, determined not to think about how much Rae could hear and probably smell.

"It will only make him take more risks," Ben pointed out. "It sounds crazy, but I think he is pretty cautious. It just does not seem that way because he's capable of so much more than any purebred. It's beyond me why any hybrid engineer would allow a hybrid with that much potential out of their control. He would be worth a fortune."

Ean flinched. He knew that Ben was not advocating buying and selling hybrids but the reality was that it happened. For reasons Ean could never understand, even people who condemned slavery for purebreds accepted it for hybrids.

Successful hybrid engineers made their fortunes breeding and raising hybrids for sale. The only ones who ended up among the corridor rats were dysfunctional ones that were released rather than destroyed.

Not hybrids like Rae.

"He's with us now," Ben pointed out, squeezing Ean's hand to comfort him. "He's safe. He has a future. A spacer is a spacer. Even being a hybrid doesn't change that."

Ean smiled; trust Ben to know when he was dwelling on how unfair life could be.

Then Art's voice cut between them. "Yes, even puppies like Rae can have a place in the Willow's crew."

Ben pulled away, trying to make distance between him and Ean before Art saw they were touching. Ean sighed, knowing it was too late. Art would only make a comment like that if he had seen.

"We take all types," Art added, looked directly at Ean, which confirmed that he was out to punish Ben for demonstrating affection for another.

Ben flinched and Ean resisted the urge to retort. It was an old game and one he had learnt not to play. At some point Ben had let slip that Ean's mother had been a whore. It had not been Ben's secret to share but Ean did not blame him; Ben had been in love and, at the time, it had never occurred to Ben that Art would use the information as a weapon.

The problem was that Ben could not forget that he had betrayed Ean's trust, so the weapon still had its edge, even after three standards.

Usually it ended there. Ben would scuttle away, mortified by the memory of what he had done to his friend. Art would give a triumphant look that was meant to remind Ean that he, Art, was paramount in Ben's affections.

As if there was any doubt of that.

However, today, the familiar pattern was broken by Tre, who appeared directly behind Art's left shoulder.

"Art," he menaced in a voice that sent a shiver of fear down Ean's spine, even though it was not directed at him.

There was a small noise from Ben; a hitch in his breathing that was almost a whimper. The blood left Art's face so quickly that it looked grey; Ean would not have been surprised if Art had wet himself.

"Tre," Ean chided gently.

Tre stepped back and smiled. "What's for breakfast? Where are those youngsters? Still asleep?"

"It's early," Ean reminded him.

"I'll wake Obe," Ben offered and left, dragging Art away before he could recover and start blustering.

Ean stood, intending to head towards the coffee machine.

"Let's wait and have Jax make us tea," Tre suggested, sitting down and tugging Ean onto his lap.

"That would be nice," Ean agreed. "Not in the galley, Tre," he added as Tre deposited a trail of small kisses down his neck. He slipped off Tre's lap and sat back on his chair. "You didn't have to be so mean to Art."

Tre looked away. "I am fed up with it; his insecurities and acts of petty cruelty. He is privileged to be a member of this crew and beyond lucky to have the love of a man like Ben. It's about time he started acting that way."

Ean was surprised but pleased. Normally Tre pretended not to notice crew dynamics, never mind commenting on them.

"Unless he changes he will have to go," Tre added.

Ean's heart sank. "Ben would go with him," he whispered.

"I know," Tre acknowledged. "That's why we all put up with it." His gaze came back to Ean's face and he smiled. "It's time to see if he is capable of behaving better."

Ean did not know what to make of that, so he told Tre about Rae's new sport instead. It worked. Tre was most amused; he even laughed.

"Clever little tyke, waiting for us to be busy fucking," he acknowledged.

"Ben told me because he was worried that Obe or Jax would try it."

The smile vanished from Tre's face. "You'll make sure they don't?" he queried.

Ean nodded. "This morning," he promised.

Jax had been sure that they were in trouble; Rae for diving down the shaft and him for not telling anyone. Instead Ean was talking about doing a proper risk assessment. He looked over at Obe, who did not seem surprised.

"Is there anything wrong, Jax?" Ean asked.

"You are going to let us do it?" Jax asked.

"No, I am going to let Rae do it," Ean replied. He studied Jax for a few moments, obviously reconsidering. "If we can work out a way of it being no more dangerous for you and Obe than it is for Rae, then you can do it too."

"I don't want to," Obe insisted. "I'm not completely insane."

They started by surveying the shaft and ended by writing two lists. The first included the things Rae had to do before he could go diving. They were mostly to do with making sure no one else entered the shaft while he was hurtling up or down it.

Jax looked over at Rae, wondering if he would enjoy diving so much now it was condoned rather than clandestine.

The second list was everything Jax would have to agree to before Ean would allow him to try it. It included putting nets across the ends of the shaft and padding various projections they had identified during the survey.

Worse, he would have to wear a helmet and a neck protector as well as elbow and knee pads. He would feel like a little child; the urge to argue was so great he could taste it.

"Jax?" Ean queried. "What will it be? You agree to the safety precautions or you promise not to try it."

Rae and Obe were looking at him. Jax could tell that Obe expected him to back out. He couldn't tell what Rae thought, other than he was interested in what Jax was going to do.

Then he spotted Tre leaning on the doorjamb. Jax swallowed. If he backed out, Tre might think he was a coward. He couldn't promise and then try it without the equipment; a man never broke his word.

He looked Ean in the eye. "I do not think all the safety precautions are necessary but I will agree to them."

Ean nodded. "I will look through the store cupboards and see if I can find what you need. If not, Vic and I will work out how to make it."

He turned to Rae. "Rae, no diving until you have sorted out the notices and the barriers. Jax can help you with them this afternoon."

Rae tried his usual nod but Ean held out for more. "Notices and barriers, got it," he replied.

"Good. Now, Obe, you go and practise your piloting using the simulator. You could check if Ben has time to help you."

Practising piloting sounded interesting; Jax wondered what Ean had in mind for him and Rae.

"We are going to discuss how spacecraft travel through space," Ean informed them.

Jax's heart sank; his father had insisted that his tutor prioritise mathematics and physics. He imagined the time it would take for Rae to understand even the most basic explanation and prepared himself to be bored.

Ean got up, went to a drawer and returned with a box. He sat down, opened the box and brought out what looked like a large piece of silk fabric, a ball of string, scissors, a piece of chalk and a pen.

He shook the fabric out so that it spread across the whole table. On it were embroidered a sparse scatter of stars in gold thread. Close to each was a small, black grommet.

"This is like space," Ean began. "People started out living on one planet close to one star." He put a ring of chalk around one of the small stars near the edge. "A space ship like the Willow can travel the width of my thumb in a standard. How long would it take for us to get from this star..." He pointed to the star he had picked out before. "...to that one?" He indicated a star at the opposite edge of the fabric, giving Jax the chalk to mark it.

Jax was intrigued. He made a ring around the star and helped Rae stretch the string between the two points, cut that length off with the scissors and then fold it into eight."

"It's twenty thumb widths," Rae decided, measuring the folded string. He checked the number of strands of string. "That's one hundred and sixty thumb widths."

Ean looked as relieved as Jax felt that Rae could do arithmetic.

"So how long?" Ean encouraged.

"One hundred and sixty standards. Too long."

"Yes," Ean agreed. "Luckily for us, space only looks flat. It's actually folded up in a very precise way."

Jax watched as Ean carefully folded the fabric. Every time he made a fold be brought two of the black grommets together and clipped them together; Jax realised that Ean was going to use them to talk about holes and gates.

"One piece of space may actually be touching many others," Ean continued, "but that does not help us because we can only see the bit we are in.

"What does help us is that there are little tunnels between the layers." He held up the fabric and peered through the hole in a pair of grommets that had been clipped together. "We call them holes. There aren't many but they are important because we can slip through them."

He pushed the folded fabric towards Rae. "Thread the string through the holes," he instructed, "between the same two stars."

One chalk-marked star was on top and the other on the bottom. It took a bit of time to find the path through but Jax could see that was a good thing; you had to travel across normal space to get from one hole to the next.

"Mark off the distance," Ean told them, giving Rae the pen.

They pulled the string as taut as it would go without puckering up the 'normal space' into the 'wrong folding pattern' and marked the point where it entered the top hole and emerged from the bottom.

Once the string was drawn out, Rae measured between the two ink marks. "Six thumb widths," he announced. "Six standards. It would be boring but you could do it."

"And how many holes did you use?" Ean asked.

Rae considered. "Maybe ten."

Ean nodded and then unfolded the fabric again, levering apart the pairs of grommets.

When he spread out the fabric Jax realise that there were twenty stars, twenty holes that had come together to make ten pairs.

"We go through the holes," Ean emphasised. "We go through this one and come out here. Then we travel to this one, go through and come out here."

Jax watched, fascinated, as Ean demonstrated how, in normal space, they seemed to be jumping from one part of space to another.

A child of five would be able to follow Ean's explanation; none of his tutors had been anywhere near as good.

"We call them jumps," Ean told Rae. "We use holes to jump across space. That's what we are going to do this afternoon. We are going to arrive at a hole and jump through it."

Rae stared at the fabric for a moment, twitched his whiskers and then looked at Ean. "What's a gate?" he asked.

Having got holes established, gates were easy. Holes had to be opened to get through them. Gates kept them open.

It was so simple that Jax felt slightly light-headed; all that mathematics, physics and hideously complicated explanations had been replaced by a piece of fabric and some grommets.

Jax wondered if Ean had come up with the explanation himself or heard it from someone else.

After lunch, he and Rae cleared away and then settled down to make the notices Rae needed in order to dive.

Jax wasn't looking forward to tackling the tricky issue of whether Rae could read and write. He had been hoping that Ean would clarify things but he merely showed them where the pens and paper were and left.

At least Rae was awake; now that he knew that he could always have a meal bar he had stopped eating so much that he fell asleep.

Rae picked out eleven sheets that were the luminous yellow colour used for warning notices across the ship.

It was a good start; there were eleven decks so they would need eleven notices.

"What do you want to write on them?" Jax asked.

Rae grimaced. "I'll have to write it eleven times," he complained.

"I could write them," Jax offered.

They settled on 'Danger Diving' and the no entry symbol. Rae drew the symbols and Jax wrote the words. Then they went to find Vic, who gave them eleven cords of exactly the correct length to go across the doorways and eleven plastic pouches that could be mounted on the wall to hold the notices and the cords when they were not being used.

There were already hooks at the right places on the doorframes.

They finished well before the jump. Ean had suggested that they sit on the couches in the crewroom for the jump. Ean was there, along with Vic and Obe. The captain, Ben and Art were in the control room. Tre and Cas were in the simulators.

Apparently they could be used as interfaces to control the guns.

Rae perked up at the mention of guns.

"Will there be baddies?" he asked.

Vic smiled but Ean frowned slightly. "Pirates do focus most of their attacks around gates," he admitted. "But this is a very well-used shipping lane so the risk is very low."

The intercom clicked. *"This is the captain. Jump in twenty seconds."* There was a pause. *"Five, four, three, two, one, jump."*

There was the momentary disorientation that Jax associated with jumping; it was like everything around him changed but so little that he couldn't sense it. He studied the others. Obe had gone pale and looked a bit sick; jumping affected some people that way.

Rae twitched his whiskers and frowned. "Was that it?"

Ean smiled and Jax realised that he had been worried that Rae might be the one in a thousand whose reaction was so bad that they could not space.

"Yes, that's it," Ean replied. He stood up. "I think it is time you boys started to learn to sew."

Jax almost groaned but managed to catch himself in time.

"Sewing?" Rae queried. "Is that fun?"

Vic snorted, Obe rolled his eyes but only Ean replied. "I like it. Maybe you will too."

Jax doubted that.

7

Rae had decided that purebreds were complicated. Hybrids were much simpler. Most hybrids were only interested in finding food without getting kicked.

He did understand Ean. Once he had worked out that Ean liked looking after people, everything else fit just fine. Ean liked looking after people like Rae liked eating or running and jumping. He was built that way.

Vic liked making things work, being looked after and doing things for people. The captain liked doing captainy things and was pleased when everything ran smoothly.

Obe didn't seem to know what he liked other than telling Jax and Rae what to do. Cas liked lying about, listening to music and stroking his rod or having it sucked by Obe.

Ben was a bit like Ean but he wanted Art to be pleased with him, which was never going to happen because Art was one of those people like the mean teacher in the orphanage and the woman who had run the clothing stall in the market. They wanted to show that they could hurt people. It made them feel big.

Tre was so complicated that Rae didn't know where to start.

So Rae had watched him. Tre liked Ean a lot. They fucked loads and they both enjoyed it, so Rae guessed it was a good thing. Most of the fucking Rae had seen before wasn't like that. Usually one person enjoyed it a lot more than the other. Often one of the people didn't enjoy it at all. Sometimes one of the people was only doing it because they were scared and thought they would get less hurt saying yes than no.

There had been times when they had said no but it hadn't made a difference.

But it wasn't like that with Tre and Ean. Ean liked it almost as much as he liked looking after people.

Then there was the way Tre looked at Rae. It was as if he wasn't seeing a cleaned-up corridor rat. He was seeing something more; someone faster and bigger and stronger and cleverer. Rae liked that. It made him want to be those things.

It was nothing like the way Tre looked at Jax.

It had taken Rae a long time to remember where he had seen a person look at another person that way. Then, one day, he remembered; the baker. The baker had always put out a basket of day-old bread for the corridor rats, even though he wasn't meant to. He was a big man with a big laugh and a big family. He had children and those children had children.

The way the baker had looked at his children and grandchildren was the way Tre looked at Jax.

Which might explain why Tre was not happy about Jax jumping down the shaft.

The way Rae saw it was that they were making Jax so worried about it that he would be all tense and then something would go wrong. Wearing a helmet would make Jax think about hitting his head and the neck brace told him he might break his neck. The nets and the padding at the ends of the shaft reminded him that he might crash into them.

Which he wouldn't, because the gravity-thingies only speeded you up as you went towards the airlock; they slowed you down once you had passed it.

Rae could see why Jax had decided to jump rather than dive. Jax wanted to be the same way up as he normally was, at least for the first bit. It also made sense to jump from outside the crewroom rather than outside the control room, because he'd speed up less.

"Keep your legs together and your arms in," Tre told Jax for the third time. "Like the cliff divers."

That last bit was new; Rae wondered what a 'cliff' was.

Jax seemed to understand because he nodded.

Then Jax made a little jump with his feet together and vanished down the shaft. There was a whoop that Rae guessed meant that he was enjoying it. Both Rae and Tre rushed to the edge and looked down.

Jax was already past the midpoint and slowing down. They watched as he came back up and then went back down again and again. Each time he went less high and less low. Finally he slowed down enough to grab the ladder.

Then he was climbing up past them. "I'm going to try from outside the control room."

"No!" Tre ordered in a voice that made every hair on Rae's body stand on end. It worked on Jax too, because he stopped. "You'll try it a few more times from here first," Tre told him.

Jax came back down and stepped off the ladder to join them.

"If you jump from the control room, there is a chance you will have enough momentum to overshoot the lower gravitational field and continue down," Tre reminded him. "It will be very different. Get used to this first."

Rae wondered what 'momentum' was. It was a word Jax and Tre used a lot when they talked about things that were moving.

After another five jumps from the outside of the crewroom Tre agreed that Jax could try from outside the control room as long as he waited until Tre was down at the engine room level, so he could be there if anything went wrong.

It didn't. It was the same but further, faster and more often.

Ten more goes and Jax was ready to stop. He climbed up the ladder to where Rae was outside the control room and took off his helmet.

He smelt different. Rae guessed it was because he had been excited and perhaps a bit scared.

"We'll need to remove the notices," Jax reminded him.

"I'll start from the bottom," Rae replied and dived down the shaft.

He built up speed as he hurtled towards the airlock and then began slowing down after he had passed it. He waited until he came to a stop and grabbed the ladder before he could be pulled back towards the nose. Then he started climbing up, or down, depending how you looked at it.

Tre was still at the bottom of the shaft outside the engine room. He looked at Rae in the way people did when they wanted to know what was happening.

"We're stopping," Rae told him. He unhooked the cord and tucked the cord and the notice into the pouch they had stuck on the wall.

Tre smelt relieved.

Once the bottom notice was gone Rae had to use the ladder; that was one of the rules that Ean had made. As he reached each deck he stepped off the ladder and took down the notice. When he reached crewroom level, Jax was waiting for him.

"I've done this one and the one outside the control room," he told Rae.

So Rae had done nine and Jax had done two; Jax was slower but not that much slower.

Sometimes Jax did that. He acted like even doing a smaller share of the work was a big thing. Rae hadn't worked out why.

"Meal bar and a drink?" Jax proposed.

Rae nodded.

No one was in the galley so they helped themselves to meal bars, three for Rae and one for Jax, and poured themselves a cup of berry-flavoured water from the coolbox.

They had settled down at the table to eat them when Art came in from the corridor, heading towards the coffee machine.

As soon as he saw them he changed course and sat down at the table.

"Make coffee," he ordered, looking at Jax.

Rae tensed. If Ean or Tre or Vic or the captain had been there, Art would have said please and used Jax's name. They weren't so he didn't.

Jax didn't respond immediately. Instead he finished chewing his mouthful, swallowed and took a sip of his drink. Only then, when Art was about to get cross, did he stand up.

"It would be a pleasure," he said, which was a lie and only made Art crosser. "Is that just for you or for more than one?"

"For me," Art confirmed.

Every time this happened, it got worse. Jax made the coffee slower and was more polite while not meaning it. Even so, Art didn't choose to make the coffee himself, which would have been quicker, or ask Rae to do it.

This time Jax used a cup that went on a saucer and put both on one of Ean's small, round trays. He walked across the galley as if he was carrying something precious and placed it on the table by Art's right hand.

"Think you're too good for us do you?" Art asked. His hand shot out and grabbed a fistful of Jax's shirt.

Rae didn't think; he just reacted. He was hovering with his bared teeth a handbreadth from Art's throat; growling.

Art began to say something but then he focused on Rae's teeth. Rae was used to that; the moment someone realised just how inhuman they were.

"Stop, Rae," Jax said softly. "I'm not in danger. Art wasn't going to hurt me. We're all on the same crew."

Rae wasn't sure that Art understood that. He stopped snarling but did not step back.

Then Art's grip on Jax's shirt loosened and it was over.

Only it wasn't quite over because someone was coming, too fast for a purebred. Then Tre was there, entering the galley, moving at normal speed.

"Go to your cabin, boys," he ordered.

Rae grabbed the third meal bar; Jax left his half-finished on the table. Tre watched them until they were in their cabin with the door closed.

Jax said nothing. Rae knew he was hoping that Rae would listen in.

"Did you see that?" Art was saying. "He's no more than an animal."

"You put your hands on Jax," Tre stated.

Art did not reply.

"Don't. Ever. Am I clear?"

There was another pause.

"Am I clear?" Tre repeated.

"You are clear."

"Good. Remember."

Jax was shaking his arm. "What are they saying?"

"Tre is telling Art off," Rae summarised. He listened again. "It's finished now."

Rae jumped up onto his bunk and lay down. He felt strange; tired. He didn't even want his third meal bar, so he stored it with the others under his pillow.

He had never defended another person before. Usually he ran. If he was cornered he attacked, but only to make an opening so he could run.

He guessed it was because Jax was his friend.

Rae wasn't sure how that had happened. Maybe Jax claiming him as his friend at the recruitment fair had made it true. Jax could touch Rae without Rae wanting to snap at him; Jax had even picked Rae up and carried him when he was asleep.

And it wasn't all one way. Jax didn't tense up when Rae came close like he did with other people.

Rae didn't understand it, but maybe that didn't matter.

It was good to have a friend, even when it made him do something scary, like almost attacking Art.

He curled up on his side and closed his eyes.

Jax heard it when Rae fell asleep; the slightly growly edge to his breathing, like very soft snoring.

There was no point in delaying; the more Jax thought about it the more tense he became.

Tre had signalled him as they had been leaving the galley. His fingers had said, "In the usual place. As soon as possible."

The usual place was hydroponics; almost everywhere else was packed with containers of nut butter.

He slipped quickly from the cabin, through the laundry and down the shaft they rarely used; the one outside the captain's cabin.

Tre was there, leaning on the storage cupboard where the mops and polishers were stored.

"Explain to me," he began in a soft voice that would not carry. "How could that situation in the galley have a constructive outcome?"

Jax felt himself flush.

"What would have happened if Rae had killed him?" Tre pressed.

Jax wanted to answer that Rae wouldn't, but the truth was that he was not sure. "I didn't expect Rae to interfere," he admitted.

Tre studied him for a moment and then gave one, short nod. "I accept that. You now know that Rae will attack someone who threatens you. As I will."

Jax's flush gave way into a cold sweat; he would never forget the vids of cyborg attacks his father had ordered his uncle to show him.

"This is who you are," Tre reminded him. "A careless word and a man will die. Your whims can, and will, destroy."

His parents had never spoken to him that way. They had used words like authority, power and responsibility. Then Jax thought of the vids; maybe his father had decided that images could be more powerful than words.

"Art is a petty bully but he has done nothing meriting a death sentence," Tre pointed out. "Also, you are meant to be behaving as an ordinary cabin boy who knows his place within the hierarchy of the crew. Describe the events in the galley that led up to Art putting his hands on you."

Jax did not need the expression on Tre's face to know how bad it sounded. Once he had finished, Tre studied him for what felt like minutes.

"So you behaved in a way you knew would antagonise a senior member of crew," Tre summarised. "How many times has this happened before?"

Jax thought of all the times Art had asked him to make coffee. "Five, maybe six."

"And you escalated the situation each time?"

"The last four times."

"Without considering the consequences?"

"Sí, señor."

"Do not call me sir and certainly not in our home tongue."

"Yes, Tre," Jax amended and then waited.

Finally Tre spoke. "You lack judgement. I shall give you the benefit of the doubt and put it down to your age. You are still a child. Let us hope you grow into your judgement before too many people die."

Inside, Jax squirmed, mortified by Tre's assessment.

"We are now going to discuss what would have happened if Rae had torn out Art's throat over the making of a cup of coffee."

It was horrible. Tre dragged him, step by step, through the likely consequences.

"So we agree that I would be faced with that choice," Tre summarised. "I could take you and Rae and leave the crew, or the blame could be pinned on Rae. Which should I do?"

The answer was obvious, as much as Jax hated it. Blaming Rae meant that they still had the ship with all its augmented systems.

"What should I do?" Tre insisted.

"Blame Rae," Jax whispered.

"And what would happen to him?"

"I don't know."

Tre leaned closer. "I know. Captain Mel would say we couldn't just let him go, because we were responsible for him. The discussion would go around and around. Ben would keep reminding us that Art had died. A man had been killed because he asked a cabin boy to make a cup of coffee. In the end, we would vote to take proper responsibility and kill him because he was too dangerous to live. And we would do it." He paused to allow the words to sink in. "Rae would be dead, ended, and whose fault would it have been?"

Jax's vision blurred. He could feel the tears running down his face. "Mine," he whispered.

"Yes," Tre agreed. "Yours."

Tre left him there, reminding him not to be late for supper.

Jax leaned forward to rub the tears from his face with the front of his shirt. Why now? He had not cried when his father had been murdered or when his mother had told him that he would never see her again.

Before he could straighten up, he caught sight of his reflection in the silvered floor. It was not a perfect mirror, but it was enough for him to see brown hair and unfamiliar, dark eyes.

Who was he? He had never asked himself that question before. He had always known he was Emanuel Rafael Jax Esteban of the clan Navaja, son of Joaquin Oro Sebastiano Socorro. He was heir to the leadership of one of the five historic spacer clans.

Who was this person looking back at him from the floor?

Tre observed through the crack in the door. He watched Jax weep before he stopped and wiped his face. The way the boy was standing with his head down was worrying.

He wondered if he had gone too far. It was so hard to look past the father and see the son. Oro had been incapable of caring about someone like Rae. Even those closest to him had been sacrificed for the good of the clan, or Oro's interpretation of it. Tre wondered if Jax knew about the two older brothers, their mothers and those mothers' families; probably not.

Maybe Jax was different. Perhaps he took after his uncle. Not his mother; Mya had been diamond-hard; obsidian-edged. She had made Oro look human.

Jax was pulling himself together. His shoulders went back and his chin came up. Despite the brown hair and dark eyes, he was a miniature copy of his father.

Of course he was; the embryo had been genetically engineered so that would be the case. Each leader of the Navaja clan had the same facial structure, build and posture as well as the same white-blond hair and bright green eyes.

Tre decided to get going before Jax realised he was still there. He moved swiftly and silently to the shaft. His body climbed the ladder automatically, leaving him free to think.

There was a bond between Jax and Rae. Tre did not understand why or how it had formed but there was no mistaking its presence.

Perhaps Jax was different. Or maybe him being eleven rather than fourteen meant he was still susceptible to influence; malleable.

Whatever, Tre would keep trying because, in the end, a leader like Oro was always toppled by a man like Gil.

8

They were all in a Meeting. This one, like most Meetings, was being held in the galley with them sitting around the table. Cabin boys were allowed to attend but not to vote. You had to be a cat to vote. Attendance was not compulsory and was dependent on them being silent and sitting still.

Jax had only meant to stay the first fifteen minutes or so. He knew how much Rae hated sitting still. Then Art and Ean had started arguing and Jax was too fascinated by the verbal battle to leave.

Why Art persisted in opposing Ean was beyond him. Ean had more authority and a greater level of support. Then there was the fact that everyone knew that Ean would back down if you could persuade him that you were right and he was wrong.

Art couldn't because he wasn't.

Then, to cap it all, Ean's determination and patience could wear down a block of granite.

This time it was about the marketing strategy they should use to sell some of the nut butter at their next port of call, a spacestation called Promise.

Art wanted to dock at the freight station, which had cheap berths, and sell a third of the nut butter to a wholesaler. They would get more for it than they had paid, because there had been a glut at Carrefour, and be quickly on their way.

Ean wanted to dock at Promise itself, where berths were much more expensive, and sell the nut butter directly to shopkeepers, stallholders and people who ran eateries. They would get a much higher price and, perhaps, they could create a demand. If they did, they could then sell the rest of the nut butter to a wholesaler at a good price.

Even a slim possibility of getting rid of all the nut butter made Ean's plan tempting.

Rae had started to comment on the smell less than two days out of Carrefour. They had put it down to the fact he was a hybrid; after all, Ean had opened one of the boxes and transferred the contents to sealed jars.

It wasn't like the scent of nut butter could be escaping from the containers; the boxes were made of impermeable material and the seals were excellent.

Then they had all started smelling it. Now, over a div out from Carrefour, the smell of nut oil had tainted everything; the air scrubbers could only do so much.

It had been Tre who had suggested that perhaps some of the boxes stored close to the gravity field generators had cracked. Trouble was, there was no way they could get through the tightly packed boxes to check.

It was almost another two divs to Mercy Station. The vote was seven in favour of Ean's plan and only one against; even Ben voted for it.

Art looked like he had been sucking limes.

Having seen Art defeated, Jax decided that it was time to rescue Rae. He caught Ean's eye and asked politely if they could leave.

"You could have left anytime," Jax pointed out once they were in the crewroom and the door to the galley was closed.

Rae twitched his whiskers and shrugged.

"What do you want to do?" Jax asked. "Go diving?"

"Floor polishing," Rae told him and set off towards hydroponics.

Jax told himself that trying to keep up with Rae was good for him. He had perfected sliding down the uprights of the ladder, using the inversion of the gravitational field to somersault outside the airlock and then climbing up to hydroponics.

When he got there Rae was finishing tying polishing clothes to his bare feet with the pieces of string he kept hidden at the back of one of the shelves. He wrapped the cloths so the toes on both feet and the ball of his right foot were left bare. That meant he could build up speed by running on this toes, slide and then use his right foot as a brake.

Jax guessed it would last until Ean realised that the floor was dangerously slippery due to the excessive amount of silicon polish they had used.

At the moment it was fine; he regularly complimented them on the excellent job they were doing keeping the floor clean.

His and Obe's techniques were less complicated. Jax would spread out a polishing cloth about one-third of the way along the floor. Then he would run barefoot and leap onto the cloth, riding it until the approaching wall gave him the option of jumping off or trying to control the collision.

Jax had had his fill of sliding, put his shoes back on and was watching Rae when the intercom clicked.

"This is Ean. Please could Jax and Rae come to the galley."

He signalled to Rae that he would set off and Rae nodded. Doubtless he would manage another couple of slides, unwrap his feet, hide the string, put on his shoes and still beat Jax to the galley.

Sure enough, he was there, grinning, when Jax stepped off the ladder; he must have used the other shaft.

Art stalked away without a look or a word for anyone as soon as the Meeting was over, still smarting over losing the vote. Ben cast Ean a worried look and followed.

"He should have just voted with Art," Cas muttered. "It isn't like it would have made a difference."

Ean sighed; Ben should have been standing up to Art for the last three standards.

"We've only got five days to prepare for this marketing strategy of yours," the captain pointed out. "I suggest we sort out the basics now."

"I'll call the boys," Ean decided. "I want them to be involved. Obe, can you make some tea?"

Once they were all at the table, they started by discussing how to distribute the samples and order forms.

"We need the containers to stack," Vic pointed out. "Then we can put them in backpacks."

"And to be disposable," the captain added. "We won't get them back."

"Stackable, disposable, cheap," Ean confirmed, starting a list. "I did think about using the empty nut butter containers but there won't be enough of them."

"Far, far too big," Tre pointed out. "They need to be small, so we can make a lot and give them out widely."

"About the size of a fancy box of sweeties," Cas volunteered.

Ean had been thinking about a small basket, but a box was much more sensible. Jax had a finger raised, asking for permission to speak.

"We could make a base, a lid and some dividers from plasti-card," he suggested. "Could we adapt the laser cutter we have in the workshop?"

Ean was beginning to wonder if there was a limit to the information that had been packed into Jax's head.

Vic looked thoughtful. "Can't see why not."

"We could print the order form on the plasticard before we make it up, while it's still flat," Obe added.

Five days later they had a berth rented in Promise and every surface in the galley was covered with shallow boxes, each a hand's length square and divided into four. Into each box went a small cake, a cookie, a heat-sealed pouch of Ben's savoury sauce and a sample of the nut butter itself. Once everything was in, the lid went on and they tied the box closed with coloured string.

The top surface had the order form and promised one of the recipes with each tub of nut butter purchased.

Finally each was filled, closed, tied and stacked with seven others on the side counters.

That done, Ean told Obe, Jax and Rae to sit down at the table.

"We are docking this evening and we will be walking the station tomorrow," he began. "A Traditional crew walks in a way that reinforces the crew's rep."

Obe rolled his eyes, which was fair enough since he had heard this lecture so many times before.

"Cats and cabin boys must behave in a specific way when off the ship," Ean continued. "You do not wander. You stay close to senior members of the crew. You do not speak to anyone without my permission. You do not make eye contact with strangers. This is not negotiable. To behave differently damages the rep of the crew. Do you understand, Jax?"

"Yes, Ean," Jax replied and Ean had no doubt that he did.

"Rae?"

For once Rae did not try to get away with a nod and a whisker-twitch. "Yes, Ean."

"Obe?"

"Of course, Ean," he answered in a tone that suggested that he was insulted to have been asked. "You know I do."

"Good. Now let's get supper on the table. It is going to be a busy evening."

Once supper had been eaten and cleared away, Ean sent the boys to their cabin early with strict instructions to go to sleep. Then he turned his attention to Cas, who was still at the table drinking coffee.

"I want you properly turned out tomorrow, Cas. Given that we are leaving at station's dawn, you might like to do most of the work this evening."

Cas blinked at him. "Art says there won't be any crews docked in Promise."

Ean sighed. "Cas, being smart isn't just about eyeing up the talent in other crews. Do you want to come with us tomorrow morning?"

Cas's gaze went to where Art and Ben were sitting in the crewroom. Neither of them was joining the next day's expedition; Art to illustrate his disapproval and Ben because Art still had not got over him voting with Ean.

"Cas?" Ean pressed.

"Yes, I want to come."

"Then do the bulk of the work tonight. Shower, sort your hair and lay out your clothes. We are not going to wait for you tomorrow morning and I will have enough to do getting Obe and the boys ready."

There was a pause. Ean knew how difficult it was for Cas at the moment. He was at the age to yearn for change and for love; at the moment the Willow offered him neither.

"Will you help me with my hair?" he asked.

It was not the response Ean had expected. He smiled. "Of course."

Ean lay out Rae's, Jax's, Obe's and his own clothes for the morning. By the time he had done that Cas had showered and dried his hair with the blowers.

Cas was one of those men whose hair grew really long, almost to his waist. Clean and groomed, it hung like a river of chestnut silk down his back.

Not that it usually looked that way; it was usually in sore need of a proper brush and the only reason Cas used a clip to fasten it as the nape of his neck was that Ean threw a fit if he saw it restrained with an elastic band.

Ean sprayed it with conditioner, brushed it out and plaited it loosely.

"Won't that make it all ripply?" Cas queried.

"Not if it is completely dry," Ean assured him. "Have you laid out your clothes?"

"Not yet but I will before I go to sleep."

Having sorted everyone else, Ean turned his attention to his own clothes and appearance. As well as looking good when the crew walked he would need to charm whatever official turned up to greet them once they had docked.

To Ean's surprise, Tre neither tried to sneak into the shower with him nor was waiting to ambush him as he emerged. Ean found him sitting at the table in the galley looking over Ean's planned route through the market.

"Maybe we should scout the station first," Tre suggested. "Give out the sample boxes the next day."

Ean scowled at him. "No. The cake and the cookie will be stale by then. If you had wanted an extra day built in, you should have said. Have you been monitoring the media feeds since we jumped into the system?"

Tre nodded.

"Is there any reason to be concerned?"

"No," Tre admitted.

Tre was silent for a while. Ean waited. He knew that Tre would raise another objection; he was worried about Jax being away from the safety of the ship.

After a few minutes it came. "Maybe you shouldn't take the boys."

Ean sighed. "Tre, taking the boys will give us more sales. Promise is a nice station. People settle there to raise their children. Also, it will do the boys good." He decided to leapfrog any other suggestions. "And, yes, of course I expect you to come but you'll have to work on not being too intimidating."

As expected, one of the Harbour Master's deputies appeared to greet them as soon as they docked. It was part of the residents' strategy for not allowing unsavoury elements any closer than the freight station.

The captain, Ean and Tre went down to the airlock. Tre would lurk out of sight, ready to react in the unlikely event of a threat.

"Captain Mel," the deputy acknowledged. "Spacer Ean."

Ean remembered dealing with the same man last time. He searched his memory. "Deputy Harbour Master Kinkaid," he replied.

The man smiled, pleased to be remembered; it was a good start. He brought out his tablet. "What is your business in Promise?" he asked.

"We have a cargo of nut butter that we intend to market directly to market stallholders and those who run eating establishments," Ean explained. "We have checked and none of your wholesalers currently offer this particular form of nut butter. If we create an ongoing demand, one of your importers could follow it up."

He proffered one of the sample boxes, which the man took "We will be giving these out tomorrow," Ean continued. "Please keep that one." He picked up the basket of nut butter cakes and cookies he had prepared. "And this is for you and your colleagues at the Harbour Master's office."

"Thank you, Spacer Ean. As always, the Willow is welcome." Deputy Kinkaid looked almost embarrassed as he handed over a sheet of plasticard. "Our regulations."

The captain took it. "We appreciate the civilised society the residents of Promise have created. I can assure you that we will do nothing to disrupt it."

"How many visitor's permits will you require?" Kinkaid asked, opening his satchel.

"Ten," Ean said firmly, handing over a one thousand credit Belmenth token before the Captain could finish reading the regulations and realise how much that would cost.

Kinkaid checked the token in his reader and printed a receipt before handing it over along with ten shiny badges. "These are only good for this side of the station. Please ensure that all members of your crew wear them where they can be seen."

Jax was up even before Ean sent Obe to knock on their door. They were going to get off the ship. It was only a spacestation, not a planet, but at least it was somewhere different that wasn't packed with containers of nut butter.

Hopefully Ean's marketing strategy would work and they would get rid of at least some of it.

They showered and dressed in the clothes Ean had put out for them; round-necked shirts, britches that tucked into their boots and short jackets. Jax recognised them as looser versions of a typical spacer outfit.

Ean looked them over as soon as they entered the galley. "Not bad," he pronounced. "Rae, your fur needs a proper brush."

"I tried," Rae complained.

Ean frowned. "Then you are going to have to let someone help you with it. Jax can try, but he probably doesn't have much experience so it will most likely hurt."

"Let Ean do it," Jax urged in a quiet voice.

Rae didn't look happy about it but he took off his jacket and sat down.

When Ean had finished, Rae's hair, or fur, looked so soft and fluffy that Jax wanted to touch it. It reminded him of a dandelion that had gone to seed.

"You next," Ean ordered, looking at Jax.

Jax was growing his hair out with the aim of it being spacer long. At the moment it just looked like short hair that needed cutting.

Ean put some stuff on it so it stayed in place when it was combed back from his face. Jax told himself it looked better and tried to ignore the little voice reminding him that putting stuff on his hair was girly.

Then someone utterly beautiful walked into the galley and most of Jax's mind stopped working.

He knew it was Cas but Cas didn't have huge, gorgeous eyes and pink, glossy lips. Cas rotated slowly on the spot, showing off long, shiny hair that fell down his back to his waist and a bottom…

Jax had never noticed anyone's bottom before.

"Will it do?" Cas asked.

Ean smiled. "Yes, Cas, it's perfect."

"Maybe a tad too much eye paint for first thing in the morning," Vic suggested, who must have walked in after Cas.

"Nonsense," Ean interjected.

"But I am certain the ex-spacer stallholders and bartenders of Promise will appreciate it," Vic continued. He ruffled Jax hair. "Cas cleans up well, doesn't he?"

Normally Jax would shy away before anyone other than Rae could touch him. This time he had been too busy staring at Cas.

Vic ruffling his hair had broken the spell. Jax realised that Ean was smiling at him rather than Cas and that Rae was looking at him as if he had something weird on his face.

He smoothed his hair and paid great attention to a mark on the tabletop.

Ben, Art and the captain were staying aboard; the rest of them were heading out. They packed the sample boxes into back-packs for the adults to carry. Then it was down to the airlock, a quick lecture from Tre about staying close and they were off.

Promise had not been one of the spacestations Jax had studied but from what Vic and Ean had said it was a typical two-faced design; disc shaped with an array of gravitational field generators sandwiched between the occupied levels.

Like the ship but on a vastly greater scale.

Everyone took a huge lungful of station's air as soon as they were through the ship's airlock. It was so good not to smell nut butter.

The pressurised docking bay seemed identical to the one in Carrefour but, unlike Carrefour, the docks and the surrounding spacer quarter were small; most of the traffic went to the freight station. Before long they were in one of the markets Ean had identified.

Jax looked about. Top of Ean's list had been bakeries.

"This way," Rae announced. "I can smell the dough." He shot forward.

"Rae!" Ean called. "Stay close."

Rae slowed down and waited for them.

The bakery was behind a baked goods shop, which made sense. The ovens would have to be permanent fixtures so you might as well have a shop attached.

As they approached, Ean began issuing instructions. "Obe, Jax and Rae, stand looking in the window. Jax and Obe, I want you looking at the food as if you want to eat it. Rae, no drooling.

Cas, you are with me."

They stood looking in with Tre and Vic behind them. Jax wished he could hear but he could see Ean speaking to a middle-aged woman who didn't seem that pleased to see him.

He must have been asking to see the baker because a tall skinny man wearing an apron with his sleeves rolled up appeared.

"Score," Vic muttered.

"Earring," Tre explained.

Jax spotted two studs in the baker's ear.

Ean spoke to the baker for a while and then Cas walked out of the shop, got a sample box from Vic and went back in again.

Obe raised a hand and spoke behind it. "Never take the sample box in with you. It's too pushy and this way Cas gets to show off his butt."

Five minutes later Ean and Cas emerged with a completed order form and a bag of freebies. Ean proffered the bag to each of them in turn.

"One only," he instructed. "And don't forget to smile and wave."

Jax picked a cookie and thanked the baker through the window. He smiled back.

His wife didn't look too happy though.

Jax was impressed. Ean's strategy was brilliant. Within an amazingly short time they had given out all the sample boxes and found an eatery at which to have breakfast.

The food was interesting but not as tasty as Ean made.

There wasn't anyone else in the eatery, so Ean gave him, Rae and Obe permission to talk. Obe prattled on about stuff he had seen in the market that he was hoping Ean would buy. Jax listened with half an ear and studied Rae, who was watching the stallholders and their customers through the window.

"What do you think?" Jax asked.

"Don't like it," Rae muttered, turning his attention back to his plate.

"Why not?" Jax asked, surprised. To his eyes Promise seemed particularly nice.

"No hybrids. No corridor rats. No poor people. No beggars. No mess," Rae pointed out. "What do they do? Throw them out with the trash?"

Jax didn't know the answer, but Tre answered for him. "They don't let them in. You have to buy your residency and pay a deposit on top. If you go bankrupt, the deposit is used to pay your passage somewhere else."

Rae considered. "What if a hybrid had enough credit to buy a place and for the deposit-thingy? Would they let him in?" He looked back out the window. "I haven't seen even one."

"I don't know," Tre admitted.

Jax doubted it. Hybrids were probably banned from Promise like they were at home.

He stared at the scene beyond the window.

Now Promise didn't seem quite so nice.

9

Tre spent a few moments scouting out the bar before entering.

Diverting the Willow to Mercy Station and seeking out Loy was a risk. Too many people knew of the connection between them. They could be watching Loy, waiting to see if he would make an appearance.

Or they could already have offered Loy something he could not resist, like the life of a loved one.

However, the other risk was greater; Tre had seen what happened when a cyborg lost control.

The bar had been Loy's choice and it was typical of him; so classy that it barely qualified as a spacer haunt. It was place for spacers who had moved on but did not like to admit it.

It was almost empty, which was not surprising as it was barely mid-morning. There were two men in one corner discussing business, a Belmenth credit card reader between them.

Tre claimed another corner; one from which he could watch all the exits.

Tre was early. Loy was usually on time, occasionally late. Tre ordered tea and used the time to review the situation.

Rae was definitely an asset. Since getting rid of the nut butter at Promise, Tre had been able to reinstate the gym and start training him. He was, as Tre had anticipated, phenomenally fast and abnormally strong. He also made good decisions, even under pressure. Tre was impressed.

Then there was the connection between him and Jax. While Oro or Mya would have seen it as a weakness, Tre regarded it as a strength. He wanted Jax to relate to people; to care. Only then would he inspire loyalty in his followers rather than fear.

He was pulled back to the present by Loy entering. He looked no older than he had six standards before when they had last met or indeed ten standards before that.

It was one of the many advantages of age retard.

As he approached Tre took the small bottle of pills from the inside pocket of his jacket and placed them on the table. Loy's gaze went straight to them, as Tre had known it would. No one with Loy's expertise would fail to recognise forgetting pills.

"Like that is it?" Loy asked.

"A choice," Tre stated. "I need a check-up. It can be just that. Or it can be that and a discussion. One outcome of the discussion is the pills."

Loy did not answer. Instead he asked the bartender to bring coffee for two. "You're paying," he added.

They served real coffee in Mercy Station.

It was good; not perfect but a thousand times better than the substitutes Tre had been drinking. It brought back memories of Kalakmul, as Loy had known it would.

"Maybe my situation is such that a discussion is tempting," Loy admitted.

Tre was intrigued. Last time he had been here Loy had talked as if he had found his place. He had been in a relationship. His research into prosthetic limbs had been promising.

"There has been a breakthrough in regeneration techniques," Loy explained. "Now it's all about that and nanobot technology."

Tre nodded. He wondered about the relationship but would never ask. "You could go back to your main specialism," he pointed out. Cyborg engineers earned a fortune.

Loy studied him and shook his head. "No, not after you."

Tre was surprised that Loy would admit it. Loy had been able to cope with the notion that the men who became cyborgs sacrificed everything. It was as if they died and their bodies became the cyborg. Tre had been different. He had refused to yield; stubbornly clinging to his personality and memories.

Loy had never made another cyborg. It was that, as much as anything else, that had led Tre to consider the risk or recruiting him.

Loy finished the last of his coffee.

"I heard about Gil."

Tre noted that Loy referred to Gil, not Oro. He tapped the cap of the pill bottle, warning Loy that they were crossing the line.

Loy nodded, confirming he understood. "I am surprised that you have not returned to Kalakmul."

This was it. After this there were only three options; Loy ended up as part of the team, dosed with forgetting pills or dead. "I am not sworn to Gil or to Oro," he pointed out.

Loy's eyes lit up. "You have the boy."

It was too much. Tre's targeting systems activated and his processor began providing helpful advice about killing techniques. He shut his eyes, which sometimes helped.

Even with his eyes closed he could detect Loy's fear.

"By the Lady, Tre," Loy complained. "Maybe you do need that check-up. Why don't we go and do that and then find somewhere to talk."

Tre re-measured and re-balanced the risks. Loy's mind had gone directly to Jax. He already knew too much. The pills were not an option. Either Loy joined the crew or Tre killed him.

"Fine," he agreed.

They went to his office, which was in one of the medical centres that catered for spacers. The receptionist's desk was unoccupied and there was no sign of a nurse or assistant.

"I moved all my appointments and gave them today and tomorrow off," Loy explained. "You only ever contact me when you need a check-up."

As always, Loy was utterly professional and irritatingly thorough.

"Can't find the slightest thing wrong with you," he pronounced after more than a hundred minutes of scanning, probing, testing and analysing.

In a way it was bad news; it implied that the automatic activations were justified.

"Have you arranged for somewhere for us to have this discussion?" Loy asked.

Tre nodded. He had safe houses all over this sector of Known Space; one of them was in Mercy Station.

Tre had to retrieve the location from his data crystal array; he had only been there once. It was the tiniest of one-room apartments and, despite the automated cleaning systems, the way it looked and smelt was consistent with its not being opened in over a decade.

Tre activated the control systems, turned up the air purifier and checked the storage lockers for what he would need. Meanwhile Loy made himself comfortable on the couch.

"If everything is working correctly, why do my cyborg systems keep activating?" Tre asked.

Loy frowned. "Perhaps you are super-sensitive to any threat to the boy," he suggested.

"His name is Jax."

"Jax. Is he like his father?"

Tre considered. "Maybe. Maybe not. I don't want to discuss him unless I know your level of commitment."

Loy looked him directly in the eyes. "Come on, Tre. We're already past that point and we both know it. Either I'm in or I'm dead."

"You don't seem angry about it," Tre observed.

Loy shrugged. "When you deal with men like Oro you know there will be a price to pay, even if it is decades later. I'm lucky it's you and not a clean-up squad tidying up loose ends. Where have you got him? In a Trad crew?"

Tre nodded.

"Then you had better tell me about them so I can charm them into recruiting me."

Ean had not expected Tre to call and say he wished to bring a guest for supper. There was a big difference between 'a contact who might know about hybrids' and someone trustworthy enough to let onto the ship.

However, he was too busy rushing around getting everything and everyone ready to spend time analysing Tre's motivation.

They made it; just. The meal was in the serving dishes and the crew properly turned out when the captain brought the guest in with Tre following.

He was medium height, dark-haired and well, if conservatively, dressed. Ean guessed his age as in his mid thirties, which was young for a fully qualified medico.

"This is Ean, our queen," Captain Mel began. "Ean, this is Medico Loy."

Ean extended a hand only to have it taken, bowed over and lightly kissed.

"I am honoured that you should receive me as a crew guest, Spacer Ean," the stranger declared in a voice that was definitely worth hearing.

Loy wanted onto the crew and was making no effort to hide it. Indeed he was charming; him and that sexy voice of his.

His eyes were nice too.

He was obviously an experienced spacer who knew exactly how to behave with a Traditional crew. He ignored the boys and Obe, flirted with Cas and Ean but respected Ben's lovering. He went out of his way to give compliments about the ship and the food.

Above all, he was a medico. How many crews as small as theirs had one of those? At the moment all they had was a decent medical kit, a dia-doc and a tank.

He had brought real coffee as a gift. Tre made a pot after the boys and Obe had been sent to bed.

Ean had never had real coffee before. It was very different from what they usually drank. At first sip he was not sure if he liked it but by the end of the second cup he was completely converted.

"I will be blunt," Loy admitted. "This is the perfect time for me. I have been considering moving on but none of the opportunities that have presented themselves have appealed. This…" He gestured to encompass the ship and then smiled at Ean. "This is very appealing indeed."

Tre went with him when he left, presumably to gauge his reaction. As soon as he had gone, Obe cracked open the door from the crewroom and peered through.

"Come on then," Ean encouraged. "Are the boys asleep?"

"They are in their cabin with the door shut," Obe replied, coming in and sliding the door shut behind him. "Are we going to recruit him?"

Vic frowned. "I am struggling to understand why he wants to buy in."

"Maybe he wants to get away from an ex-lover?" Cas suggested.

"But why us?" Vic persisted. "We are so small. A medico can write his own terms. Any crew would want him."

"Perhaps his connection to Tre goes back a long way," the captain suggested.

There was silence. Ean imagined a young Tre with a younger Loy; it was certainly a possibility.

"I like him," Art stated.

Everyone looked at him. Art never said he liked anyone other than Ben.

Ben smiled. "I liked him too."

"He seemed pleasant and would be interesting to have around," Vic admitted. "He can probably afford to buy a healthy share. We could use some of the credit to upgrade the infirmary and maybe some of the other systems."

"With a fully qualified medico aboard we could carry pods," Art pointed out.

Ean wondered if that was why Art was so keen on Loy joining. Podded passengers were the ultimate cargo; low volume with a high profit margin. A crew with as good a rep as the Willow's could slot in between the passenger liners, which most people could not afford, and crews who might decide to sell their cargo to an organ dealer or a slaver.

The captain stood up. "I shall turn in. We shall discuss the matter further tomorrow. By then we will know if Medico Loy intends to take matters further."

Ean watched the captain walk away and then beckoned Obe to him. "Why don't you run after the captain and ask if he needs anything."

Obe looked blank for a moment and then caught on. "Do you think so? It isn't one of his usual days."

"I think so, but as it isn't one of his usual days it is up to you."

Obe smiled. "I don't mind," he confirmed and trotted after the captain.

Vic chuckled. "Obe really is a sweetie." He sighed. "Somehow I can't see Jax or Rae adapting so well to that side of shipboard life."

"Those teeth," Art observed with a shudder.

For once Ean agreed with Art. It would be a brave man, or a foolish one, who was willing to put his rod in Rae's mouth.

The Willow deviated from Tradition in one way; they treated their cats differently. Ean had looked through the ship's log and he knew it was Captain Mel who had changed things. Cats catted, but they only used their fingers or gave blow jobs. Once a cat was sixteen, he could choose to offer his other hole but not before then.

Over the standards Ean had come to realise how unusual that was. Most crews used both their cat's holes from the day the lad was recruited. It was the deal; a better future in return for three standards of not being able to say no.

Ean was glad the Willow was different; in his eyes it was too close to prostitution.

"Jax will be pretty enough," Cas pointed out. "He's a cutie."

Ean could not see Tre being too happy about Jax catting. At least they had two standards before they had to face that particular problem

His eyes strayed to the chronometer, wondering if Tre would be back soon.

Tre had been impressed; Loy had made a real effort. Maybe it was because he was convinced that Tre would kill him if the crew refused to have him.

On their way back to the safe house, Loy was unusually chatty; Tre put it down to relief that the crew was better than Loy had expected.

"Ean's a gem," Loy pointed out. "You do know that?"

"I know that," Tre had replied.

"No ring on his finger," Loy observed.

Tre had tried not to bristle but Loy knew him too well.

"Maybe not Ean then. Ben is taken. Cas is pretty enough but he's so young."

"Feel free to try and charm Ben away from Art, you will be doing us all a favour."

Loy's eyebrows went up. "So life on the Willow isn't as idyllic as it seems?"

"No crew is perfect," Tre reminded him.

"Too true. So what next?"

Tre decided to be blunt. Nine-tenths of him trusted Loy. The other tenth was painting scenarios in which Loy was playing a role and there was someone after Jax lurking around every corner.

"You stay at the apartment until I come to get you tomorrow."

"Drugged," Loy checked.

"Sedated," Tre confirmed. "In the unlikely event you manage to wake up before I arrive, I would not recommend moving about."

"Motion triggered security system?"

Tre nodded.

"What about everything else? I have a business, employees, patients, an apartment, belongings."

"We'll sort that out tomorrow. You won't be going anywhere alone for a while. Not until I decide it is safe."

Once they were in the apartment, Loy got ready to be sedated while Tre prepared a hypospray.

"You haven't asked me what I thought of the boy," Loy observed.

"Jax," Tre corrected. "You could not form a proper opinion without speaking to him."

"And a hybrid?"

"Needs must. He has enormous potential as a future body-guard. You ready?"

Loy lay down on the bed and Tre pressed a hypospray to his neck.

The sedative took effect immediately. Tre draped a cover over Loy and sat down on the chair.

He was still not absolutely sure that he was doing the right thing. Loy knew so much about him and too much about Jax. Could he protect their secrets or would he drop clue after clue? Would Ean be able to resist interrogating him? If not, would Loy be able to resist Ean's charm? Tre doubted it.

There was an alternative. The check-up had established that nothing was wrong with his cyborg systems. He could load Loy into the stasis pod each safe house contained and tell the others that Loy had changed his mind.

Only then they would not have a medico. What if Jax was injured?

No, this was the best way forward. He would have to trust Loy.

He set the security system, locked up and headed back to the Willow.

Ean was sitting at the galley table with the wide-eyed look of someone who had encountered real coffee for the first time.

"You the only one up?" Tre asked, kissing him on the temple.

Ean nodded.

"So what did they think of him?" Tre asked, claiming the chair next to Ean's.

"You first," Ean insisted.

"He wants in," Tre replied. "Let's talk through the details tomorrow when the others are about."

Ean nodded. "Good idea." He stood up. "Bed?"

Tre pulled Ean into his lap. "No one's about. We could fuck on the galley table. It's standards since we did that."

Ean kissed him but pulled away. "No, Tre. The queen of the crew does not fuck on the galley table. It sets a bad example."

Tre supposed he was right. "Bathroom?"

"Bathroom," Ean agreed, taking his hand and leading the way.

✳ ✳ ✳

Jax woke up before Rae, which was unusual. He lay in his bunk and thought about the evening before. He wondered what had happened after they had been sent to bed.

He had wanted Rae to listen but Rae had been too tired. Anyway, Rae wasn't that good at following complicated conversations.

Tre hadn't told him much about Loy; just that he was someone they could trust.

Suddenly Rae's face was there, upside down, with whiskers twitching and a disbelieving look on his face.

"Yes, I know it is early," Jax confirmed. "I was thinking about Medico Loy. What did you think of him?"

Rae swung down onto Jax's bunk. "Smelt fine," he declared.

Jax decided that was good.

"He wants to fuck Ean," Rae added.

That was less welcome.

"And Ben and Cas and he thought Vic had nice hands," Rae continued.

Was Rae saying Medico Loy was a sex-addict?

"Most adult purebreds are like that," Rae explained. "Water, food, warmth, sex. They think about whichever one they aren't getting."

"Aren't hybrids the same?" Jax asked.

"Depends. There was an old dog hybrid. All he thought about was that his master wasn't there. He didn't care about water or food. He died."

"Where had his master gone?" Jax asked, imagining he had been killed or something.

"Was still where he had always been. With a new, younger dog hybrid. Kicked the old one out."

Jax was shocked.

Rae shrugged. "Just saying that sometimes hybrids are built to care about other things than water or food or warmth or sex. Like their master. Or killing. Or running. Or doing boring things perfectly. Or sometimes they only care about sex. Depends why they were built."

Jax wondered why Rae had been built and by whom.

"Let's go find out what happened," Rae suggested and was gone into the shower.

After breakfast they closed the door to the crewroom, the captain joined them and they had a Meeting. Tre told them what Medico Loy wanted, which no one thought was unreasonable.

Of course it wasn't, because Medico Loy was joining the crew to be part of Jax's team in the future.

Apparently he wanted to do some research so he would be turning the room next to the infirmary into a laboratory.

Jax guessed that was a cover so he could bring in equipment that a ship's infirmary wouldn't normally have, like a high spec synthesiser and maybe nanobot technology.

Then the crew voted on whether they should offer Medico Loy the chance to buy in and the vote was eight for, zero against, which was good.

After that things happened really quickly, so much so that Ean commented on how swiftly the situation had moved on and Jax wondered why Tre thought that getting Loy onto the ship was so urgent.

Then, within another day, they were off with a cargo of podded people who had received treatment and wanted to go home.

Loy had been on the ship five days before he said anything that suggested that he knew who Jax was. They were checking the pods, which their contract with the medical centre in Mercy Station said they had to do twice a day. Ean had suggested that Jax go with Loy and learn about what a proper check involved.

They had checked the first four when Loy said, "Is Rae far enough away?"

Jax's heart beat faster. "Yes, he's in one of the simulators on the crewroom level."

"When will you tell him who you are?"

"When Tre says it's safe," Jax replied cautiously.

"You know what Tre is?"

Jax didn't like that. Tre wasn't a 'what'; he was a 'who'. "He is the man standing in my father's place," he replied.

"He's a cyborg," Loy stated.

Jax hadn't been sure that Loy had known. It made sense that he did. The simplest medical tests would distinguish between a cyborg and an ordinary human. "I know."

"That does not worry you?"

Jax thought of the vids his uncle had shown him. "No," he lied. "My father chose Tre to stand in his place. He held me as a newborn and took the oath. I trust him utterly."

Loy stared at him and then nodded. "Maybe Tre is right. Maybe you are different."

Different from whom? From the other people Loy had served? From his father?

"When the time comes, I will swear to you," Loy added.

Jax looked this man, this stranger, in the eye and replied. "When the time comes, I will decide if you are worthy to do so."

10

Kip's mind was at its most disorganised at the interface of sleep and wakefulness. Or at least he thought it was. Perhaps it was even more chaotic when he was asleep.

"Kipawa Wheeler! Are you up yet? Do I have to come in there?"

It was his Ma. From the tone of her voice she had been calling him for some time.

"No Ma!" he yelled, rolling out of bed and into the bathroom linked to his bedroom.

He locked the door behind him, a sensible precaution if his mother was as agitated as she sounded. Sure enough, he heard her enter his room and begin the familiar monologue about the state of it.

He tuned it out; otherwise he might get annoyed that she was invading his space again when she had said she wouldn't.

Allowing his Ma to irritate him never got him anywhere.

Instead he turned on the shower so that his Ma would think he was in it, closed the lid of the toilet pan, sat on it and began sorting out his head.

He clustered intersecting lines of thought, grouped related clusters together and then thrust each group into a corner that he partitioned away.

It was a familiar process. Soon all that was left was Kipawa Wheeler, a clever but lazy schoolboy who was the bane of his mother's life.

A quick shower, an even shorter spell with the blowers and he unlocked the door. Steeling himself, he opened it and went back into his bedroom.

She had gone, which was a relief. Listening, he could hear her in the kitchen. He sniffed the air and detected the aroma of his favourite breakfast.

On the bed were the clothes she had picked out for him to wear. Usually he left them where they were and pulled others from the closet; being overdressed at school drew extra attention he could do without.

This time she had picked casual pants and one of his favourite tops, so he put them on. Then he dragged a comb through his hair and headed towards the kitchen.

His father was eating his breakfast while pretending not to read the tablet on the table. Pa had doing stuff without Ma realising down to a fine art.

"Son."

"Pa," Kip replied, sitting down in his usual place.

A plate of food was placed in front of him.

"Thanks, Ma," he acknowledged and was surprised to receive a kiss on the top of his head. He looked up and was rewarded by a smile.

"Nice clothes," his father pointed out as his mother went back to the sink to clean up the pan before she sat down.

Kip understood. He was wearing the clothes his Ma had laid out for him. Of course he hadn't done it to please her; he had done it because she had finally chosen something he was willing to wear. Doubtless his Pa had interfered, patiently wearing his Ma down until she accepted that her son did not want to dress like a boy visiting his grandmother.

"Good day planned?" his Pa asked, which was code for 'Have you thought about your day and identified the points where the risk is high?'.

"Yep," Kip replied which meant 'Yes, I have been over it and the only worry is the new mathematics teacher who is far too interested in me'.

His mother sat down on the third chair with her small bowl of breakfast cereal. "Are you doing anything interesting after school?" she asked.

The real answer to that was 'Yes, of course I am because that's when I get to live my real life' but Kip replied, "Just a chess match."

School was necessary because, on Darrenden, youngsters of fourteen went to school. Kip couldn't say he had never learnt anything at school, there had been the odd titbit of knowledge or flash of insight, but they were few and far between.

No, school was about establishing the public persona of Kipawa Wheeler.

The day went smoothly until he got to math. The way Mr Costello's eyes lit up when he entered the room was definitely disturbing.

It could just be a teacher's interest in a student who was highly talented in his subject. Or it could be that Mr Costello was the latest in a string of people who had wanted to find out if Kip was more than he seemed.

As soon as he sat down, Mr Costello came over. "Good morning, Kip."

He was the only teacher who called him that. To the others he was Kipawa, or Kipawa Wheeler, or Wheeler; it depended on how annoyed they were with him. "Good morning, Mr Costello."

"I want you to try these," Mr Costello said, giving him a tablet. "After all, we don't want you wasting lesson time on problems you can already do."

"Sure, Mr Costello," Kip replied.

As soon as Mr Costello walked away, Kip turned over the tablet and put it face down on the desk. If there was a camera it was likely to be front facing.

Then he allowed himself to use one of the parallel paths in his head, so he could think about how to fool Mr Costello while behaving normally.

He got his stuff out of his bag and listened to the boy next to him, making appropriate noises in the correct places. Meanwhile, he rehearsed the rules he and his Pa had worked out: tackle the problems one by one; never read ahead; make absolutely sure you analyse each question carefully.

His answers had to be consistent with someone who was very talented at conventional mathematics; no more, no less.

He waited until the rest of the class was pretending to listen to Mr Costello and turned over the tablet.

Facing him was the first question in the cognitive ability test set by the Institute of Psychology on Centre I.

It was a relief. It meant that Mr Costello had not been sent by Centre because Kip had taken the test, or variants of it, five times. The most likely explanation was that Mr Costello wanted to be known for identifying a typed-genius and Kip was the most promising candidate he had found.

Kip put up his hand and waited. Mr Costello immediately set a problem for the class to work on and came over.

"What is it, Kip?"

"I've done this test before, Mr Costello," Kip explained. "Under controlled conditions in the Principal's office."

Mr Costello's face fell; either he was disappointed or a really good actor.

"Do you want me to do it again?" Kip pushed.

Mr Costello took the tablet away from him. "No." He walked to his desk and swapped the tablet for another. "Try these."

It was some undergraduate level problems that he would need to use matrices to solve; the kind of thing Kip enjoyed doing.

At the end of the lesson Mr Costello asked him to stay behind. He studied Kip's answers.

"When did you learn about three-dimensional matrices?" he asked.

"Pa and I talk lots about math," Kip replied.

There was a pause. "Your father is Professor Azizi Wheeler?" Mr Costello sounded crestfallen. "The Chief Lecturer at the university?"

Kip couldn't believe that Mr Costello hadn't made the connection before. He shook his head. "Pa hasn't worked for the university for ages. He got fed up with the politics. He works at home now."

His father had given up work when Kip was two, when he had realised that it would be a full time job keeping the Centralite psychologists away from his son.

Nothing interesting or unusual happened for the rest of the morning. Kip had his midmeal in the canteen, sitting with a group who liked the same kind of music he did.

It made the small talk easier.

Then he went and played his chess match; being in the school chess team meant he wasn't expected to take part in any competitive sports.

He made sure he took over two minutes for each move. At least he could win the match quickly with a documented strategy so he didn't have to worry about not using a move no one else would think of.

Then he was off home. He called as he opened the front door; he always did when he arrived home early, ever since he had caught his Ma and his Pa at it in the kitchen.

Kip guessed it was good they still liked each other after so many standards but he could have done without the evidence being indelibly stamped into his memory.

"I'm home, Pa!"

"Kip," his father acknowledged from the living room, which was a bit odd; he was normally in his study. "Come and sit down."

That wasn't good. Pa didn't usually sound so serious. Kip hung up his coat, dropped his bag and went to sit on the sofa.

"I got notification today that we're going to have a visit from a tax official. Should I be worried?"

Kip didn't know. He wasn't sure what tax officials did other than calculate the amount of tax people did or didn't pay. He was sure his Pa and his Ma paid all their taxes.

"Let me put the question another way. Have you been doing anything that might attract the attention of the Tax Office?"

Kip was pretty sure he had hidden everything too carefully for any investigator to find. "No, Pa."

"Good. It's probably just a standard visit because I am self-employed." His Pa stood up. "Do you want a snack?"

After a sandwich and a glass of orange juice, Pa went to his office and Kip to his room. First he lay down on his bed for a bit so that he could sort out his head.

He took down the partitions one by one and checked what had been happening. Some of the clusters of paths had linked to others in interesting ways. Others hadn't. He decided what he was going to work on and parcelled the rest away.

Then he got up and opened his desk.

One good thing about his Pa working from home was that they had excellent communication channels. Kip used them in four ways: a way typical of any schoolboy of fourteen, the way his Ma thought he used them, the way his Pa thought he used them and the way only he could use them.

It helped a great deal that Kip could make it, apparently undetected, through every security system he had encountered.

His biggest breakthrough had been building his own high speed data transfer network linking four institutions that had data links directly to the gate.

The gate in the Darrenden system had a light speed data relay; it was Kip's door to the universe beyond.

He had thought of how to build the network when he was five, inspired by a workman coming to the house to upgrade their data link. It had then taken him another two standards to get himself into a position where he could start doing it.

The trick was to build it in bits. He would hack into a service company's systems and create a job, usually a repair.

Of course he also had to create a person to pay for it and that virtual identity had to have enough credit to settle the bill. Earning credit had held him back for a bit; Pa wouldn't approve of him stealing.

Then he had discovered the stock market. After that credit was never a problem.

His network had been built in four hundred and twenty-two parts. On the way he had created three hundred and eighty-seven identities and sixteen small companies, each of which existed in all the appropriate databases and had all the necessary documentation, including bank accounts.

He had linked the university, Planetary Security, the stock market and the Stellar Exchange just before his ninth birthday.

Hacking the light speed data relay in the gate without being detected had taken another three standards, which had been fine because until he did it he could use his virtual identities to send and receive information through the normal channels.

Normal channels could be monitored, so he had to get good at codes and encryption. By the time he hacked the light speed data relay he had a really neat system for sending two encoded messages that decoded each other at the other end.

Once he had hacked the data relay in the gate, Kip was able to surf the data streams from relay to relay along the main shipping lanes. He soon confirmed what he had already suspected; the world beyond the gate was much less regulated and policed than Darrenden. It was much, much easier to create virtual identities and companies out there.

Not that he had done much of that lately. He had been concentrating on data mining. It was exciting to encounter new information; he had exhausted every data bank on Darrenden by the time he was eight.

Spread across Known Space was more data that Kip could look through in a lifetime. However, he intended to try.

He was examining what one of his search algorithms had dug out of a library archive on a re-discovered planet when his alarm started pinging.

He reluctantly pushed up his visor, pulled out his earpieces and peeled off his control gloves; Ma would be home soon and she expected him to sit in the kitchen, help her make the evemeal and talk.

As his Pa said, it was the least Kip could do in return for the amazing job she did looking after him. Kip thought of it differently; it was the least he could do to make up for not being the normal child she had wanted.

She couldn't have another. On Darrenden breeding was tightly controlled. It was unheard of for a couple to be licensed for more than one child.

So as he shelled peas he told her about his lessons and the chess match. He even claimed to be interested in one of the girls in his Linguistics class when he wasn't. That way, at least for a handful of minutes, she could pretend he was the son she had dreamt of rather than a freak.

Next day Mr Costello started calling him Kipawa. Kip understood. Now he was just a student who was very good at math because he was the son of a man who was very good at math.

When he got home there was an unfamiliar one-man vehicle outside the house and Ma's bike was in the garage.

It had to be the tax official; Kip hadn't realised the official would be talking to his mother as well as his father.

It was a woman; neatly dressed in black and sitting on the sofa where she definitely didn't belong.

"Who is this?" she asked as he hung up his coat and his bag.

"This is our son, Kipawa," his mother answered. "Kip, this is Ms Ling."

Kip stood with his feet together and gave a small bow, as his mother would want him to. "Ms Ling."

"How polite," Ms Ling acknowledged. "And how lucky you are to have been granted a licence."

"We did not go through the lottery," his mother pointed out. "The licence was awarded on merit."

Kip suppressed a smile; he could rely on his Ma to give Ms Ling a very tough time.

"Go to your room, Kip," his father instructed.

His Pa hadn't told him to shut the door, which meant he wanted Kip to listen in case he noticed something that Pa missed.

"As I was saying," Ms Ling began, obviously picking up where she had left off, "irregularities have been found."

"But not with our accounts or our affairs," his Ma interjected.

"No, Ms Wheeler," Ms Ling replied.

Kip imagined the look his Ma was giving Ms Ling.

"Mother Wheeler," amended Ms Ling. "After we could find no explanation for the irregularities, we decided to buy some of a typed-five genius's time to look for patterns."

That was bad; that was very, very bad. Kip was absolutely certain no governmental official could detect what he had been doing, but a typed-five was another matter. A typed-five would be able to find patterns that Kip himself had missed.

"The outcome of the analysis was that the irregularities were most likely the work of a single person living on Darrenden. The consensus is that only eight people on the planet would be capable of creating the irregularities. You, Prof… Father Wheeler, are one of those eight people."

"Ms Ling, I can assure you that I do not have the slightest idea of what irregularities you are referring to, never mind being responsible for them. Do you have any evidence linking me to these irregularities?"

Kip waited, his heart thumping.

"No, Father Wheeler, although there is a higher possibility that the irregularities originate in the capital than elsewhere on the planet."

"And how many of the other seven live in the capital?" Ma demanded.

"Five of them," Ms Ling admitted.

"You said that the irregularities were most likely the work of someone on the planet," Pa stated. "What is the probability that they originate off-planet?"

Kip waited. He knew, absolutely knew without the slightest doubt, that this was the crucial point.

"Thirty-seven per cent," Ms Ling admitted.

His relief was so great that his knees almost buckled. Ms Ling was on a fishing expedition, probably one born out of desperation. They had paid for a typed-five genius's time and he, or she, had only been able to tell them that there was less than a two-thirds probability that the 'irregularities' originated on the planet.

There was the sound of someone standing up, followed by two others. His Pa spoke first.

"Ms Ling, I understand that you are only doing your job but I fear you are wasting your time speaking with me."

"Allow me to show you out," his Ma added.

There was the sound of the front door opening and closing. Then his father was standing in the doorway to his room looking at him.

Kip knew he was turning red and that there was nothing he could do to stop it.

Pa came into his room and traced a message with his finger on the shelf under the mirror. "Change nothing. Keep every pattern constant."

Kip understood. They would be looking for changes associated with Ms Ling's visit.

They didn't discuss it until the rest day. Then they took a picnic to the hills. He and his Pa went for a walk while his Ma set out the food.

"You have been doing stuff without telling me," Pa stated.

Kip couldn't meet his Pa's gaze but he nodded.

"For how long?"

"Nine standards," Kip admitted.

His Pa stopped walking. "Oh Kip, why? You know how dangerous it is."

Kip felt so ashamed. "Behaving normally is so boring," he confessed. He looked his father directly in the eyes. He pointed to his head. "I just can't keep it all in here. I have to do things. I haven't hurt one person, I promise. I just go looking for new information."

"Off-planet," Pa surmised. "And your scheme for getting to the information off-planet created these 'irregularities'."

Kip opened his mouth to reply only for his father to hold up a hand.

"Don't tell me, Kip. The less I know the less I'll have to lie if they get any further with their investigation. They are good at detecting lies."

He started walking again and Kip fell in beside him.

"I should have planned for it," Pa admitted. "Darrenden is a good place for you to hide but it isn't a good place for you to live. I should have taken a professorship at a university some-where else in the Borders, maybe even the Inner Fringe. Only your Ma…" He trailed off.

Kip knew how much his Ma loved Darrenden. Her family had lived on the planet forever; she could trace her ancestors back to the Founders.

"It's too late now," Pa continued. "Moving will raise suspi-cions. Hopefully you aren't on that list of theirs. Probably not, give the way Darrendenians think about children."

Kip chose not to mention that he hadn't been a child in the eyes of the law since he had turned fourteen.

"We have to think of a way of getting you off-planet," his father suggested. "Maybe a scholarship…"

Kip didn't hear any more. His mind had latched onto the problem. New lines of thought generated and divided. Parti-tions were ripped away and memories accessed so that new links could be made. Possibilities rose or fell until the best solution was thrust to the surface.

He reconnected to his surroundings.

"Kip?" Pa was saying. He looked anxious.

"Just thinking," Kip admitted. "I need to join a spacer crew, Pa."

His father looked at him. "You sure?"

Kip nodded. He was. No other solution had come close.

Pa sighed. "Your Ma isn't going to like that one little bit."

11

Ean's patience was wearing thin. He had to keep reminding himself that two divs was a short time, that recruiting Loy had been a good idea and that the crew dynamic would soon settle.

He would know that all was well when he could sleep past ship's dawn.

At least this morning he did not have to wriggle out of his bunk in a futile attempt not to wake Tre. Ean had gone to bed early, leaving Tre and Loy sharing a bottle of whisky in the galley.

Tre knew Ean's rules; Tre was not allowed near him when he had been drinking, even if the man did have an unnatural ability to imbibe alcohol without getting drunk.

At least there was no competition for the shower this early. Ean stood under the spray and tried to work out what was going wrong.

Loy was an excellent medico. He had given everyone other than Rae a check-up and there had been no complaints. Both Vic and the captain had commented on how expertly he had established the distinction between Medico Loy and Loy the crewmate.

It was Loy the crewmate rather than Medico Loy who had disrupted the dynamic.

It had all started when he had flirted with Ben. Now Art was always simmering on the edge of a jealous rage and Ben was doing a convincing imitation of a doormat. The situation was not improved by Cas having a crush on Loy. Cas spent most of each day trying to get Loy's attention, so he no longer had time for Obe, who was miserable.

Then, to top it all, Rae still had not had his check-up, which meant that Loy could not tell Ean if he could treat Rae if he was unwell or injured.

No, the situation could not go on like this; it was time Ean took action.

He finished showering, dried himself and dressed. Then he stalked over to Loy's bunk and pulled back the drapes as noisily as possible.

Loy blinked bleary eyes at him, woken by the sound or the sudden influx of cooler air.

"In the galley please, Medico Loy," Ean informed him. "As soon as is convenient."

They talked in the galley with the door closed. Or rather Ean talked and Loy listened.

"You want me to fuck someone, anyone, as long as it isn't Ben," Loy checked when Ean had finished.

Ean thought he had been clear. It was the way a Trad crew worked; Loy must know that. Anyone not off-limits was available. The captain was off-limits because he was the captain. The boys and Obe were too young. Art and Ben had exchanged love rings. "Given that Obe's blow jobs are obviously not a sufficient outlet for your libido, yes," he confirmed, trying not to sound too sharp.

Loy might have been pushed onto the back foot by Ean's lecture but from the amusement in his eyes he was making a swift recovery. "What about you?" he asked in his sexiest voice.

Ean sighed. "If that's what it takes." As queen, it was his responsibility to uphold Tradition; if Obe had to offer his mouth, Ean could hardly claim to be off-limits when he did not qualify.

Loy held up his hands. "I was joking. Tre would rip off my balls and feed them to me."

"Tre is not in a position to dictate who I take to my bed," Ean insisted. Tre knew the situation; no love ring, no exclusive relationship.

Loy just looked at him with a 'who are you trying to kid' expression and Ean felt himself flush. It was true; the only man he wanted in his bed was Tre. It had been that way since the day they had met and Ean did not see it changing any time soon.

"Cas would be delighted," Ean pointed out.

"He's very young," Loy complained.

Ean wondered, not for the first time, how old Loy was; certainly not as young as he looked. "Having an experienced partner is not a bad thing for a youngster."

Loy's eyes widened.

Some men really could not resist being a youngster's first. "Be gentle," Ean warned. He poured Loy another cup of tea. "And get Rae's check-up done."

Loy shook his head. "I can't force him, Ean. He has to trust me and he doesn't."

Ean sighed. "I'll talk to him again."

❀ ❀ ❀

Rae didn't know how Ean had got him to agree to the check-up. As soon as Rae had nodded his head Ean had escorted him out of the galley, along the corridor and into the infirmary.

Then Ean was gone, the door was shut and he was alone with Loy.

Loy talked to him for ages but Rae wasn't listening. He wanted to run away or, failing that, to snap at Loy. What he did not want to do was take off all his clothes. There was no way he was taking off his underpants.

Loy was running out of patience.

"Rae, I do not have a scanner. I cannot examine you with your clothes on."

Rae didn't know anything about scanners. He did know what happened when people saw him with no clothes on.

Loy retreated to the other side of the infirmary. Rae watched him warily as he sat down on a chair at a safe distance.

"Rae, everyone in the crew has had a check-up. Ean is particularly keen that you should have one. You have been avoiding having one for over a div. Do I have to call Ean on the intercom?"

The only thing worse than having one person there when he took his clothes off was having more than one person there when he took his clothes off. He shook his head.

"What's wrong?" Loy asked.

Rae could tell Loy was trying to be nice rather than getting cross. "I'm different," he admitted.

Loy smiled. "Yes, Rae. You are a hybrid."

Rae had known he wouldn't understand. He looked towards the door. He could easily escape now that Loy was further away.

Only next time Ean would be in the room with them and it would be worse.

There was a long-suffering sigh from the other side of the room.

"Rae, there is this thing called medical confidentiality," Loy told him. "Medicos don't blab. No one would trust them if they did."

"You won't tell anyone?" Rae checked.

Loy hesitated. "There are some things I would have to tell Ean about because Ean is the person who looks after you. He's like your parent."

In a way Rae was glad Loy hadn't said yes. Rae could think of things Loy should tell Ean. Hopefully his secret wasn't one of them.

He turned away from Loy and started taking his clothes off. Once he was down to his underpants he hesitated but took a deep breath and pushed them down.

It wasn't any bigger than it had been that morning in the shower. Like one of the boys in the orphanage had said, it was more like a clit than a rod. Rae hadn't known what a clit was but one of the older girls had obligingly shown him hers.

Rae's was bigger than that, or that was what Rae had told himself.

He reluctantly turned around. At least Loy didn't gasp or laugh or even stare too hard. Instead he started the examination.

It was weird being touched but Loy made it seem ordinary.

"As far as I can tell, you seem very healthy," Loy said once he had finished. "Now, do you want to talk about fact that your genitals aren't the same as a purebred boy's or not?"

Rae guessed that his genitals were his private bits. Before he knew it he had nodded.

Loy took a deep breath. "First of all, think about the fact that you were probably designed to be the way you are."

Rae thought about that for a moment. "Maybe that was the bit that was wrong. Maybe that's why they threw me away rather than keeping me."

Loy sat back. He smelt stressed.

"Rae, do you want to know what I found when I examined you?"

Rae nodded again.

"I think you have male bits and female bits but neither set have developed."

Rae was horrified. "I'm a girl?" He didn't want to be a girl. He had always been a boy.

"You may be both a boy and a girl," Loy explained.

If he was a girl he couldn't be a spacer. He would end up doing something girly. He didn't want to do something girly. "I am a boy," he insisted.

Loy smiled. "Yes, you are a boy. You are a boy with a few girl bits."

It sounded better put like that. "Can you get rid of the girly bits?" he asked.

"I don't know," Loy admitted. "I would have to do more tests. We definitely shouldn't rush into anything. Next time we are somewhere with a medical scanner we could rent time on it and give you a full scan. Then I'd have a better idea what you are like inside."

It sounded like a sensible plan. Rae nodded.

"There is something we can do now," Loy added.

Rae was willing to listen; Loy hadn't laughed at his tiny rod.

"Hybrid engineers often mark the hybrids they produce, usually with ink that shows up under ultraviolet light. If we could find a mark on you we may be able to find out if you were designed to be both a boy and a girl."

It was simple enough. Loy turned on the ultraviolet light and then turned off the normal lights. Rae couldn't see any marks on the parts of his skin he could see.

Then he turned around so that Loy could shine the light on his back and Loy gasped.

"What is it?" Rae asked, twisting about trying to see his back.

"Stand still," Loy ordered. "Mulligan's teats, that's amazing."

"What?"

"Stay still so I can get a decent image with the camera," Loy insisted.

Rae stared at the image on the screen. It showed him standing with his arms out. Over his back and spreading onto his neck, upper arms and bottom was a pattern.

It was like a bird's wings. He had seen birds in vids.

"That is some mark," Loy observed.

"It's beautiful," Rae whispered.

Tre stared at the image.

"That's a tattoo?" he asked, disbelievingly.

Loy shook his head. "No. You can't tattoo a child and expect all the elements of the image to stay in the right places as they grow. I don't know what it is."

"Markings?" Tre suggested. "Like on some cats?"

Loy shook his head. "If it's a pigment being produced by the cells, it's amazingly intricate. Look how symmetrical it is."

"So it isn't a hybrid engineer's mark?"

"A hybrid engineer who could get gene expression that perfect would make a fortune. He or she would be famous." Loy sighed. "Maybe in some isolated, Far Fringe sector." He shook his head. "No, it's probably been applied but in some way that means it keeps its shape over time. Nanobots would work."

He did not know what was worse, the thought of Rae having nanobots or him being designed by some incredibly talented but unknown hybrid engineer. Neither scenario was compatible with him living as a corridor rat in Carrefour.

"Anything else?" Tre asked.

Loy hesitated. "His physiology is less human than I expected. I need to put him through a full body scanner."

"Fair enough. Ean will be all for that if you suggest it. He's worried about you not being able to treat Rae if he gets hurt." Tre pulled his eyes away from the screen. He had other, more urgent, matters to deal with. "You got any ideas for getting the others to accept a cat that the crew doesn't need and most likely won't want?"

"Why do you want him?"

"He's clever; well beyond the normal range."

"You're hoping he'll operate like the advisor who worked for Oro? The one on contract from Alexandria?"

Tre nodded; it was close enough.

Loy shrugged. "You have my vote. You need three more. Can you deliver Ean?"

"Not for definite; not without telling him too much. Mel will be easier."

"Then you work on the captain and Ean. I'll work on Cas. How did you find out about the youngster?"

"You don't want to know," Tre admitted.

Tre decided it was time for a session in the gym. It was easier to think when his body was busy.

Persuading Ean would be difficult. The crew had only just begun to adapt to Jax and Rae when Loy had joined. The last div had been rocky. Ean was not going to want to introduce anyone else.

Only it couldn't wait. This would be his only chance to recruit someone who could substitute for a Alexandrian Advisor.

Also asking for Klennethon Darrent's advice and then ignoring it was beyond stupid.

It had seemed a good idea at the time, which had been during the divs between taking the oath and joining the Willow. Tre had been thinking about the clan's future, when Jax was clan leader, and had started to research alternatives to hiring an Advisor from the guild on Alexandria.

He had quickly learnt of Centre's system of classifying and acquiring geniuses.

Centre had agents, Central Civil Servants, scouring the Borders and the Fringe for children who showed typed-genius behaviours. Once they found them, they tested them. If they passed, they offered their families everything they wanted to hand them over.

If the parents refused, Centre turned to their communities. They started with bribes and then, if necessary, they moved on to threats.

The child always ended up in the Institute of Psychology on Centre I.

Tre knew why his interest had been caught. The same system, on a much smaller scale, happened on Kalakmul. His mother had not wanted to give him up but his uncle had been too interested in garnering the Navaja clan leader's favour.

So all the typed-geniuses were on Centre I. There was only one exception; Klennethon Darrent , the typed-five genius who had escaped Centre's clutches.

He had done it by becoming one of those who had hunted him. Joining the Central Civil Service and serving a ten standards term had earned him citizenship. Becoming a Citizen of Centre put him beyond the clutches of the Centralite Psychologists forever.

Then he had left Centre and, according to their rules, there was nothing his fellow Centralites could do to stop him.

That had been ninety standards ago. Since then Klennethon Darrent had built up a colossal fortune and a rep that rivalled those of the five great spacer clans.

To Tre's surprise, he had discovered that Klennethon Darrent was occasionally available for hire. Unfortunately he did not work for the type of payment that Tre could afford.

However, Klennethon Darrent was also known to answer questions if they caught his attention.

So Tre had submitted his question and, to his astonishment, he had been granted an audience.

It had been in a private suite in the most exclusive restaurant in Tarrasade. Before the meeting Tre had been subjected to a lecture from Klennethon Darrent's personal assistant. The man had explained that, no matter how fast or skilled Tre considered himself to be, he would be dead within a second if he compromised Klennethon Darrent's personal safety.

As Tre had entertained no intention of harming Klennethon Darrent, he merely stated that he understood. He had not, for a moment, believed that Klennethon Darrent's guards could take a cyborg down within a second.

Then he had entered the room and seen the box on which Klennethon Darrent's left hand rested; an electromagnetic pulse generator.

Klennethon Darrent had known he was a cyborg.

It also meant that Klennethon Darrent would not hesitate to burn out all the electronic circuits in at least this level of Tarrasade. There would be no communications and no control circuits; life support systems would fail.

Tre had forced his attention from the box to the man. Klennethon Darrent might be over a hundred but his age retard was holding well. His sculpted features and perfect skin made him look no more than thirty.

"Tre who serves the clan Navaja," Klennethon Darrent had acknowledged, which removed any possibility that Tre's cover was intact.

"Citizen Darrent," Tre had replied, taking the chair indicated.

"I liked your question," Klennethon Darrent had told him in a casual tone; as if his hand was not on a box that could kill thousands. "Please do me the favour of repeating it."

"Do any typed-geniuses avoid Centre's attention?"

"My answer is technically no because they are not typed-geniuses until they have Centre's attention and have been tested and classified. I shall modify your question. Do individuals who have the potential to be typed-geniuses, perhaps even display typed-genius behaviours, avoid Centre's attention? My answer is I do not know but it is a possibility. I shall think on it. My assistant will show you out."

And that had been that. Tre had left Tarrasade, put thoughts of typed-geniuses to the back of his mind and joined the Willow.

Then, two standards ago, when over nine standards had passed since the meeting, he had received a message saying, "Watch Darrenden for those wishing to space," and signed 'KD'.

Since then Tre had checked whenever they were in a system with a Stellar Exchange. This time, at Mercy Station, there it had been; a seemingly ordinary advertisement from a family looking for a suitable crew for their son.

Which was why the Willow was now delivering pods to the spacestation in the Darrenden system.

Tre had replied as soon as he had finished reading the advertisement. Hopefully the family would recognise the Willow's rep and would be willing to wait for the right crew. Otherwise Tre would have to chase down the successful crew and challenge them for their cat.

Explaining that to Ean would be even more difficult than persuading him that he wanted Kipawa Wheeler as their next cat.

To Ean's relief Rae had finally allowed Loy to examine him. Better still, he had not been as traumatised by the process as his reluctance had suggested he might be.

In fact he was sitting at the galley table next to Jax putting away meal bars as if nothing out of the ordinary had happened.

Ean found himself focusing on Rae's sleeve, which was looking suspiciously short. He tried not to think about the work sewing another full set of clothes involved; it was good that Rae was catching up on the growth he had missed when food was short.

"Did Loy find anything interesting?" Jax asked, which was an unexpected bonus; Ean had decided not to ask.

Rae stopped chewing for a moment, twitched his whiskers and looked suspicious.

"Like your teeth and your whiskers and your ears and your hair and your toes," Jax elaborated. "Interesting stuff like that."

Thinking about it, Rae's toes were unusually long.

"I have a mark on my back," Rae admitted. "It only shows under a black light."

It was probably a marker's mark. Ean was not sure what he thought about that. The last thing he wanted was someone having a claim to Rae.

"Can I see?" Jax asked.

"Loy took a picture." Rae was gone and then was back within moments with a tablet. He thrust it towards Jax.

"Wow," Jax exclaimed, his eyes widening. "It's like an eagle."

It was amazing. Ean had been expecting some tattooed numbers, not a glorious, glowing set of wings.

"What's that?" Tre asked from over Ean's shoulder.

Ean jumped; he really should be used to how silently Tre moved by now.

"Rae's got an invisible eagle on his back," Jax answered.

"What's an eagle?" Rae asked.

"It's a type of bird," Tre replied.

"Shame it isn't visible all the time," Jax pointed out.

Tre shook his head. "It being invisible most of the time is like Rae himself; there is far more about him than meets the eye."

Ean saw Rae's response, the way his shoulders went back, his chin came up and his whiskers arched; it was times like this when he remembered why he was with Tre rather than someone more ordinary who would put a love-ring on his finger.

"I need to talk to Ean about something," Tre added. "I shall have to steal him away unless you two boys have somewhere else you could be."

That was strange. Usually their private conversations were in the bathroom before or after fucking.

Jax decided that they should go to the gym, which was good; even Rae could not listen across that many levels.

Once they had gone, Ean looked at Tre and waited.

"I did something unwise eleven standards ago," Tre began.

Ean's mind flooded with possibilities. He even considered that Tre was about to admit that Jax was his son but that would have been thirteen standards ago, not eleven.

"I asked Klennethon Darrent a question," Tre continued.

Ean had heard of Klennethon Darrent. What spacer hadn't? Bring yourself to the attention of someone that powerful was unwise; it was also very unlike Tre. "Why?"

Tre shook his head. "I don't think I ever considered the consequences if he chose to answer it. Anyway, he did. He said he did not know the answer but he would think on it."

Ean held his breath. There had to be more to it than that.

"He has sent me an answer."

"Now? Eleven standards later?"

"Yes, he directed me to this." Tre placed an object on the table.

Ean recognised a data crystal wafer in its holder. He watched as Tre reached for the tablet Rae had left on the table and pushed the data wafer holder into the slot at the side.

The image of an adolescent's face filled the screen. He had dark, almost black, hair, one lock of which curled down onto his forehead. His eyes slanted up at the outer corners and his lips, especially the bottom one, were unusually full.

Either his neck was skinny or his head was rather large, Ean was not sure which. Maybe it was a bit of both.

The image began speaking. "*My name is Kipawa Wheeler. I am fourteen and I want to space. I am looking for a place in a Traditional crew.*" The image shifted, showing that it had been edited. "*I'm good at math and solving problems. I know stuff about circuits and electronics and communications.*" There was another edit. "*My grandfather spaced. Grandpappy has told me about being part of a crew and about catting.*" He suddenly looked directly at the camera and Ean's heart was suddenly in his throat at the depth in the dark eyes; such ancient eyes in so young a face. *"Darrenden isn't for me. I need to be out there, not in here."*

"There is the usual other stuff on the wafer," Tre added helpfully.

It suddenly sunk in what Tre meant.

"Another cat?" Ean queried, horrified at the mere thought of it.

"Ean, Klennethon Darrent has directed my attention to this youngster."

Ean swallowed what he had been about to say. Saying no to Klennethon Darrent was more than unwise. On the other hand, he knew Tre was manipulating him and he did not appreciate it. "What was your question?" he demanded. "What did you ask Klennethon Darrent eleven standards ago?"

Tre did not answer.

Ean flicked the tablet onto standby. "Not this time, Tre. You tell me or I will oppose recruiting him and another crew can have him."

"Please, Ean," Tre asked.

In a way that made it worse. Tre never pleaded for anything other than a fuck and that was always in fun.

"The question, Tre," he insisted.

"I asked if geniuses hid from Centre," Tre admitted.

Centre? First Klennethon Darrent and now Centre? And what

had Tre been doing asking about geniuses?

"Centre looks for highly intelligent children throughout the Borders and the Fringe," Tre explained. "When they find them they take them away from their families and take them back to Centre. Klennethon Darrent was one of those children. I think he has spotted this youngster and wants to stop the same thing happening to him. He is hoping that Centre won't be able to find him if he is spacing."

Ean was about to punch holes in Tre's pathetic excuse for an explanation when he remembered the youngster's eyes. He reached for the tablet and activated it. Kipawa Wheeler looked out at him from the screen.

"You think he needs somewhere to hide?" Ean asked.

"Yes," Tre answered.

"What about Centre? Won't they be angry if they find out we are hiding him?"

"No, because we will just be a crew who recruited a cat. Nothing on that wafer suggests he is any more than a boy of fourteen who is good at math. And we will have done what Klennethon Darrent wanted."

More importantly, they would not have gone against Klennethon Darrent's wishes. Ean looked back at the tablet.

"Attracting Klennethon Darrent's attention by asking him a question was foolish," Ean pointed out.

"I told you it was unwise," Tre agreed.

"This is why we took the contract for carrying pods to the Darrenden system?"

Tre nodded and Ean wondered if Klennethon Darrent had played a part in that too.

"I suppose it would not do any harm to have a look at him," Ean conceded.

Tre smiled in that way that made Ean's toes curl. "Thank you," he murmured.

Ean sighed; perhaps saying no to Tre was, indeed, beyond him.

12

Kip hid in the cupboard-sized bathroom and wished he could get far enough away that he couldn't hear his Ma yelling at his Pa.

There was a tap on the door. "You in there, Kiplet?"

It was his grandfather. Kip almost told him to go away before remembering that Grandpappy probably needed to pee.

He didn't. He wanted to talk. Kip wished he had stayed locked in the bathroom.

The last four divs had been awful. Very few youngsters from Darrenden chose to space and there were safeguards to check that they understood what they were getting themselves into.

Kip had been interviewed by officials from Education and from Welfare. So had his parents and each time his Ma came out more upset than she had gone in.

Which took some doing; Kip had thought she couldn't get more upset than that day at the picnic when Pa had finally got her to listen and understand.

"Jen, if Centre hears about him he will spend the rest of his life as a lab rat in the Institute of Psychology on Centre I," his father had pointed out for the third time.

"We wouldn't let them and the government wouldn't make us," Ma argued.

"It is Centre, Jen," his father repeated patiently.

That had been when Ma had started crying.

When they had finally got past the government officials, things had settled down a bit. Grandpappy had helped a lot by talking to Ma. They had made the equivalent of a would-be cat's 'tape' and sent it to all of the agencies that had a decent rep.

Fifty-eight crews had registered an interest, which was a lot more than Kip had expected. His Pa suggested it was because Kip was educated and was good at math.

His Grandpappy, when Ma wasn't about, explained it was because Kip was a virgin.

Kip could have done without hearing that.

They had whittled it down to seven crews, three of which could make it to the spacestation for the same six day window. Once that was settled, Pa had booked their places on the rocket and an apartment on the station.

Kip told himself he would replace all that credit once he was well away from Darrenden.

Then, four days ago, they had met representatives of the first crew; five senior crew members from a ship called the Loretta. They had a crew style; black and gold jackets, black mesh undershirts, skin tight black pants and high black boots.

They looked good but Kip knew he would look ridiculous dressed like that.

The queen was very thin, with long blond hair, painted nails and lots of makeup. He had looked at Kip as if he was something they were considering buying. At first he had looked very unimpressed but had become more interested when Pa had mentioned Kip's education and skills.

Then Pa and Grandpappy had started asking questions. The spacers' replies hadn't been answers, just collections of statements vaguely related to the question. At first Kip thought they were arrogant. Then, to his shock, he had realised that they were stupid.

Kip was used to being with people who didn't think like he did; no one did. He was not used to being with people who made his classmates at school seem like geniuses.

The discussion back at the apartment had been a new low. His Grandpappy had insisted that, as far as crews went, the Loretta's was impressive. His Pa had tried to be positive. His Ma, who had been silent throughout the encounter, would only stop crying to yell at his Pa.

Kip had said nothing. He had been imagining living with people who couldn't string three thoughts or two sentences together. It had suddenly hit home how much he was going to miss his Pa.

The second crew, the Savannah's, had been worse. They had all had turned up, including their current cat. That might have been a good thing but, as Grandpappy had put it, they believed in dressing to display their assets.

Kip hadn't followed much of what was said. He'd been trying not to look at the two who were making out in the corner.

Then the crew enforcer, a huge man whose muscle development had to be artificially enhanced, had started flirting with Kip and Grandpappy had decided to end the meeting before Ma did something awful.

Back at the apartment Ma had only yelled rather than cried. Kip had hid in his room and contemplated a future on the Loretta. There was no way his Ma would let him join the Savannah.

The third, the crew of the Nimbus, had been a little better and was now the front-runner. The queen had actually expressed interest in Kip's welfare. Two of the crew, the navigator and the captain, had put together logical answers to Pa's questions. They had dressed in a way that his Ma described as exotic rather than indecent.

Kip kept telling himself that the Nimbus would be a lot better than the Savannah or the Loretta.

Now there was only one left, the crew that had been added to the list after they had booked the apartment.

"This is the one," his Grandpappy told him once he had Kip sitting on the bed and was seated opposite him.

Kip hoped so.

"The Willow is an ancient crew. It is Trad to its core. Its rep is impeccable. Kiplet, you need to make an effort with this one, not sit there and act as if your mind is a thousand parsecs away."

Kip opened his mouth to complain that he had been trying but then shut it again. His Grandpappy was probably right. He usually was. "What should I do?"

"Be yourself," his Grandpappy advised, which did not help because Kip was never himself with anyone, not even his Pa.

He wasn't even sure if he was himself when he was alone.

Once Grandpappy had gone, Kip thought more about what he had said and decided the best thing would be to try to appear normal, like he did when he went to school. When the morning of the meeting arrived he partitioned off most of his mind and hoped that he could adapt behaviours he had used before to the new situation.

The queen of the Willow had suggested an initial meeting in one of the bars where spacers did their business during the day.

Only two of the tables were occupied and the men sitting at one of them stood as they entered. Kip guessed it was the crew of the Willow and they were being polite.

"This looks a bit more hopeful," his Ma murmured.

There were four of them. They would have looked exotic four days ago but now Kip could see that they were formally dressed.

The youngest took the lead. "I am Ean. I am queen of the Willow. This is Captain Mel, Enforcer Tre and Medico Loy."

They had a medico; that would please his Ma.

"I am Grandfather Wheeler," Grandpappy replied. "This is Father and Mother Wheeler. This is Kipawa, my grandson."

Ean gestured that they should all sit down. The three males were related, there was no missing that, and Ean could see some of the woman in the youngster's face.

The way they introduced themselves emphasised how important family ties were to Darrendenians. That, along with the fact that the woman looked downright unwell, convinced Ean that Tre had been telling the truth. They would never have allowed the boy to space if there had been another option.

Kipawa Wheeler was not very impressive. As the vid had suggested, his head was too big and his neck was too skinny. He wasn't fat but his body looked soft, as if he did very little exercise.

Ean's gaze strayed to the father, who was really quite handsome; perhaps the boy's looks would improve with age.

Ean ordered tea, which won him a look of approval from the woman.

"Let me tell you about the Willow's attitude to the youngsters we take on," Ean began as he poured tea into eight cups. "Our objective is to take every boy from where he is when he joins to having all the skills and attitudes he needs to be a successful spacer. For a youngster like Kipawa we will have three or perhaps four standards to achieve that objective. For a boy we take on as a cabin boy we have a few standards longer." He paused, offering an opportunity for someone else to speak.

"How many youngsters do you have in the crew at the moment?" the woman asked.

"We have three. We have two cabin boys, who are a couple of standards younger than Kipawa and a cat who is about a standard older. Each one is different." Ean tried to think of something else that might convince this woman that they would look after her son. "I catted on the Willow, as did two other members of the crew. We see the Willow as our home." He almost said that the crew of the Willow was his family but stopped himself in time. The last think she would want to hear was that they intended to replace her in Kipawa's affections.

The captain picked up where Ean had left off.

"Maybe Kipawa would like to tell us why he wants to space," he suggested.

Ean wondered what the youngster would say; not that he was on the run from Centre.

"I want to see other places," he began nervously. "I like the idea of seeing people who do things differently to the way we do things on Darrenden. I don't find school interesting and if I stay on Darrenden it will be school for another four standards and then university for another four. If I were spacing, imagine all the places I could have visited and things I could have seen during those eight standards."

It wasn't a bad answer. Ean was convinced there was at least some truth in it.

"Grandpappy spaced," the youngster added. "He has told me lots about it and I think it would be a challenge that would make me a more rounded person."

The more rounded person part was codswallop but the rest was interesting. Ean looked at the old man.

"I catted on the Morning Star and was crew on the Madeline and the White Star," the old man told them. "I was pushing forty when I returned to Darrenden. Spacing was good to me. It made me a better man. It also gave me the funds I needed to apply for a parenting licence so I could raise Azizi here." He gestured towards his son. "Academic study suited Azizi but it does nothing for Kip. Maybe he takes after me and spacing will suit him better."

While the old man was speaking, Ean saw the youngster's parents exchanging looks. After a short silence, Azizi Wheeler gave the family's decision.

"We would like to progress to the next stage."

Ean went through the formality of looking to each of the others before speaking. "The rest of the crew are on the promenade. I thought we would go there and introduce Kipawa to them."

Jax had been keeping an eye out for Ean and the others. He hoped they would have this would-be cat, Kipawa Wheeler, with them.

If it were up to Tre they would have. Tre wanted Kipawa Wheeler as an advisor, which was weird because, in Jax's experience, advisors were old, not fourteen.

The rest of the crew were not so convinced about recruiting another cat. The Meeting where they had discussed it had quickly degenerated into an argument.

It had been so bad that the captain had sent Jax and Rae to their cabin.

Rae hadn't been able to tell Jax everything that had been said but they knew the vote had been split five-four. The shock had been that Vic and Obe had sided with Art and Ben while Cas had voted the same way as Loy.

Five-four was a majority so they were here, on the spacestation that stood between the planet Darrenden and its gate. Ean had explained that very few boys from Darrenden decided to space so there wasn't a recruiting fair and none of the agencies had an office there. Instead the crews who wanted the boys spoke directly with the families.

After they had docked the ship they had come here, to the promenade. Apparently this whole area, with its viewing ports and benches, was set aside for people to enjoy themselves.

Not that there was much going on. There was the occasional person walking along and an old couple sitting looking out at the stars.

Ean had not missed the way Rae's eyes lit up when he saw all the open space. He had spent the next five minutes explaining to Rae why he could not run or jump but had to spend the time being good and sticking close to Vic or another senior member of the crew.

Every bit of Rae had looked disappointed, especially his whiskers. Jax had found himself wishing that he could take Rae somewhere where he could really run, like the beach or the grasslands.

Then the captain, Loy, Ean and Tre had gone off to meet with Kipawa Wheeler's family.

Rae nudged him. Sure enough, they were coming and they had three adults and an adolescent with them. He didn't look like much. He was skinny and weak-looking. His neck didn't look strong enough to hold up his head.

"You three sit down there and wait to be introduced," Vic told him, Rae and Obe. "Best behaviour," he reminded them.

Jax sat between Rae and Obe.

"Don't know why he wants to space," Obe complained as soon as Vic had moved away. "Look, he's got a mum and a dad. He's even got a granddad."

Jax wondered about Obe's background; spacers did not ask and Obe had never mentioned any family.

Then Ean was in front of them and they were standing up.

"We do not usually introduce our cabin boys and cats to strangers, but we will make an exception this time. This is Obe, our cat, and Jax and Rae, our cabin boys. Perhaps Kipawa would like to socialise with them while we talk."

"Kip, you could buy Rae, Jax and Obe a sundae," the younger of the two men, probably Kipawa Wheeler's father, suggested.

Ean nodded so the four of them headed towards a stand selling what looked like ice cream in small plasticard pots. Tre followed them but kept his distance.

"I'm Kip," Kipawa Wheeler began. "Only my mother and teachers call me Kipawa."

"Jax," Jax replied and frowned at Obe.

"Obe." Somehow Obe managed to make his own name sound grumpy.

"Rae," Rae added and started to sniff the air. He was either deciding if Kip smelt right or what flavour ice cream he wanted.

They did look nice; twelve different colours each in its own container. Jax could see Rae's eyes darting from one to the other, trying to make his mind up about which one to try.

"You may only be in the Darrenden system this once," Kip pointed out. "You really ought to try a Gargantuan Assemble-Your-Own Mega Sundae."

Rae's whiskers twitched. "What's that?"

It turned out to be a sample of everything on the cart with the pots arranged on a big platter according to whether it was ice cream, sauce or toppings. They each had a bigger pot to mix together what they wanted and a long spoon.

Obe carried the platter to one of the round tables. Normally Rae volunteered to do any carrying but he was too excited.

Jax spooned some of three different flavours into his pot and poured in some berry sauce. He noticed that Kip only took one scoop of a plain ice cream, probably vanilla, and added some chocolate sprinkles.

Obe glanced at Rae and loaded his pot to the brim.

Then Rae put the first spoonful of ice cream into his mouth. He looked as if he had never tasted anything so good. Once he had swallowed it he gave three yips of delight and dug in.

Jax hoped that Ean wasn't watching because it wasn't pretty.

Kip didn't seem in the least fazed, even when Rae forgot to hide his teeth like he usually tried to do.

"Enforcer Tre followed us because he is responsible for your safety?" Kip queried. "Another spacer crew might try to steal you?"

Jax tensed for a moment and then realised that Kip was referring to all three of them, not just him.

"Yes. You too if you have turned down any other crews."

"Two," Kip admitted. "We told the third that we were thinking about it." His brows puckered and he looked anxious. "Would a Trad crew steal a boy from his family? I thought they only stole them from other crews."

Jax had heard stories but he wasn't sure if they were true or whether it had been Trad crews.

"They wouldn't dare in a system like Darrenden," Obe replied. "The authorities would arrest them before they got through the gate. Probably charge them with kidnapping and confiscate their ship." He scraped the remnants from his pot and looked at the debris on the table, as if calculating the risk of coming between Rae and the remaining ice cream.

"There is no better crew than the Willow," Jax assured Kip. "And Tre can protect you from anyone."

"Ean is the best queen ever," Obe added.

Even Rae paused long enough for a nod and a whisker-twitch.

Kip thought it was going well. Ma had relaxed a lot as soon as she had seen the other three boys.

Pa sending him off with them had been unexpected but Kip told himself he could do it. It was all about staying in the top layer of the mind and maintaining the same laid-back persona he used at school.

Having Rae to watch helped. Kip had never met a hybrid before. It was interesting. Bubbles of thoughts floated up from deeper layers of his mind and popped, spilling their contents into the layer Kip was accessing.

Based on his teeth, Rae was some form of canine–human hybrid. He was highly functional, which was only true of one in ten of hybrids allowed to mature and less than one in a thousand of the embryos produced.

It didn't look like he had ever tried ice cream. Kip had made up the Gargantuan Assemble-Your-Own Mega Sundae on the spot and, luckily, the stallholder had gone along with it.

Kip hoped it hadn't been a mistake; could one person eat that much ice cream without being sick?

It appeared so. They made their way back to the adults with the enforcer, Tre, trailing behind. Ean was deep in conversation with Kip's mother while Pa and Grandpappy talked to the rest of the crew.

They were sent to sit on one of the benches. Rae was blinking owlishly and looked like he might fall asleep on Jax's shoulder.

"It happens when he eats too much," Obe explained.

Information about human and canine physiology bubbled up. Kip tried to ignore it.

"What music do you like?" Obe asked.

Kip was relieved. He could do small talk about music. He and Obe ended up sharing Kip's headphones and listening to Darrenden's latest musical sensation.

Then it was over. The Willow's crew was going back to their ship while Kip would be returning to the apartment with Grandpappy, Pa and Ma.

"We will exchange messages tomorrow morning," Pa explained. "Giving our final decisions."

They watched the crew walk away. Vic was carrying Rae, who was asleep with his head on the big man's shoulder.

"He ate too much ice cream," Kip explained. "He'd never had any before."

"I'm not convinced he's twelve," his Ma observed.

"He's a hybrid," Grandpappy pointed out. "Anyway, Lady knows what kind of life he had in front of him before they took him in." He looked directly at Ma. "Jennifer, you could look for a century and not find a better crew than that."

Ma didn't say so, but Kip could see she agreed.

"They may decide not to take him," Pa cautioned. "Captain Mel hinted that some of the crew thought they already have too many youngsters."

Ma bristled. "Kip is definitely good enough for their crew."

"Yes, Jen," Pa replied. "That's why they're here even though they weren't looking for a cat."

Kip's mind focused. Why were they here if they weren't looking for a cat? Suddenly he was deep in his mind at the middle of a web of fast-evolving thoughts.

Before he could decide where they were leading he was reconnected with reality by someone shaking his arm and whispering urgently in his ear. "Kip! Kip!"

It was his Pa.

"Good thing he didn't do that while they were here." It was his Grandpappy.

"Just thinking," Kip said, trying to ignore his thoughts about the Willow's crew in favour of seeing, hearing and putting one foot in front of the other.

Once they were back at the apartment Grandpappy suggested they should contact the previously front-running crew and politely say that Kip would not be joining.

They all agreed. If the Willow did not offer they would go back to Darrenden and consider alternatives; perhaps one of the spacer academies.

Kip knew that a spacer academy was nowhere near as good as a crew; he would be too exposed. "May I go and lie down for a bit?" he asked.

His Pa smiled at him. "You do that. Then, when you're ready, we can talk about you joining the Willow."

Kip lay on the bed, shut his eyes and took down the partitions one by one.

Why would a crew that did not want or need a cat be considering him?

Thought clusters appeared, all about Jax.

Why was he focusing on Jax?

His first hypothesis was that a crew that had Jax would not need to recruit the Kip described in the application tape. Jax was obviously clever and well-educated. He had looked fit, which Kip wasn't. Obe and Rae had followed when Jax led.

No one in their right mind would follow Kip.

The pieces did not fit. He tried modifying the question. Why would a crew that had Jax want him?

Most of the confusion vanished. For reasons Kip did not understand, it was a much better question. He decided to try partitioning away the parts of his mind that were thinking about Jax so that he could see if there was anything else.

There, out at an edge, was a thought he was shying away from. Kip forced himself to focus on it.

Could they know what he was?

He felt sick. If they knew what he was they could sell him to Centre for a fortune.

Only that didn't fit. They could sell Rae for a lot of credit and they hadn't done that. Also, they were a Trad crew so they would follow the spacer code, which condemned the buying or selling of any human.

Kip groaned. He didn't have enough information. His mind was trying to make links but too many of the links had nowhere to go and all those loose ends were casting about his mind like whips.

"Kipawa, are you all right in there?" It was his Ma.

"I'm fine, Ma," he called back but it was too late, she was pushing open the door.

He struggled to put his mind into some kind of order; it helped that he had partitioned away the parts thinking about Jax.

She sat down on the bed and took his hand.

"Kip," she whispered.

Weirdly it helped. He felt calmer.

"I liked Ean," she admitted. "At first I thought he was too young but I don't think he is. He cares for every member of his crew and he loves those boys, all of them, even Cas."

Kip hadn't focused much on Cas. He had been older. He had been wearing a knife, so he was a full-blown spacer. Now Kip thought about it, he remembered that Cas had pretty hair.

"I think he would love you too," his Ma continued. "Are you still sure that joining a Traditional crew is better than going to one of the spacer academies, or us moving to another system, or risking carrying on like we have been?"

Kip knew how much his Ma wanted every extra div he could give her. If it had been a viable option, he would have stayed on Darrenden longer.

The authorities investigating the 'irregularities' had made that impossible.

"Joining a spacer crew is safest," he confirmed, which was true. It was just this crew that he was worried about.

"Then I think this crew is for you," Ma told him. "And I know that your father and your grandfather agree. That boy, Jax, he might even be your friend. He seemed very bright and Ean says he plays chess."

Kip doubted that Jax would appreciate being annihilated at chess. "I liked Rae," he admitted. "He's different, like me." He had an interesting thought. "And probably, to Rae, I'm no weirder than any other purebred."

His Ma leaned over and kissed his forehead. "You are my Kipawa and I love you."

Which was one of the few things in the universe that Kip believed to be absolutely true.

Kip made up his mind. His Ma's instincts were impeccable. If she trusted Ean then there was no better crew for him to go to. He would worry about the rest later.

"If they offer, I want to accept," he told her.

His Ma managed a smile for him, even though he could tell that she wanted to cry. "Good. Let's go tell your father and your grandfather."

13

Rae had discovered that he didn't like it when the crew recruited people. Jax said it was because Rae was part canine and some canines, like the coyotes on Jax's home planet, lived in packs. The crew had become Rae's pack and the new person didn't feel like part of the pack.

It was more complicated than that. Rae had tried explaining to Jax but he didn't have the words to do it. When Loy had arrived, the pack had changed. It had smelled, sounded and moved differently. Rae hadn't liked that.

To Rae's relief, Kip didn't make such a big difference. Jax said it was because Kip was young and had joined the pack as a junior member, while Loy was older and had slotted in much higher up. Instead of it taking Rae two divs to feel comfortable, like after Loy joined, it had only taken one.

It helped that Kip was nice. He did things for people. He had bought them ice cream. He played board games with Jax and pretended to just beat him so Jax didn't feel too bad about losing. He had mended Obe's music player. He had persuaded Loy to use the new synthesiser to make Rae some body wash that didn't stink.

He had even checked all the speakers across the ship and stopped them making horrid, high pitched noises that only Rae could hear.

Also, like Rae himself, Kip was different. The way Rae thought about it, two people who were so different had something in common.

Kip could think more quickly than other people. Rae could tell. It was most obvious when he was playing chess or Go with Jax. He would decide which piece to move within a second of Jax touching his piece to move it. Sometimes he had decided long before that.

The really interesting bit was that Kip would then wait ages before actually moving one of his chess pieces or Go stones. It was like Rae not moving so fast that he scared people or trying to keep his teeth hidden by his lips when he ate.

Kip was pretending to think more slowly. Rae wondered if it was because other people found thinking so fast scary; like teeth.

Rae didn't like hearing people cry. He never had. It made him feel all squirmy inside and he had to stop himself whimpering. It made him feel even worse when it was someone he liked.

Kip cried a lot. He cried quietly in the head and he cried more noisily in the shower. Rae guessed he thought that the sound of the water would cover it.

Trouble was, Kip was really good at keeping it a secret. The Kip everyone got to see didn't look like he cried every time he went into the head or the shower.

He didn't even smell sad most of the time, just in the early mornings and when he was about to go hide in the head.

Since no one else could hear and smell like Rae, everyone else thought that Kip was doing just fine. That meant it was up to Rae to do something about it.

He started by being there and hoping that Kip would say something. It didn't work. Kip acted as if everything was just fine.

He thought about saying something but he didn't know where to start. Rae wasn't too good with words.

So he decided to talk to Jax about it. He waited until they were scrubbing the galley floor. For some reason they talked best as they cleaned.

As they scrubbed, Rae planned what to say. He didn't want to mention the crying, because that was Kip's secret.

"Do you think Kip is unhappy?" he asked, as an opener.

Jax stopped scrubbing, sat back on his heels and scowled at him. "No," he barked. Then he went back to cleaning the floor.

Rae had to stop himself cowering; he didn't like it when Jax was cross with him. Maybe he had picked a bad time, although Jax had smelt fine.

He thought about trying again, maybe later, but decided against it. Rather than risk making Jax cross again, he would say something to Ean, even though it felt like telling tales.

Rae had a sure-fire way of getting Ean's attention; pushing his food around his plate rather than eating it. Next morning he woke up extra early and listened to check that Ean was on his own in the galley. Then he slipped out of his bunk quietly, so as not to wake Jax.

As soon as he appeared, Ean started making him breakfast like Rae had known he would. A bit of food-pushing and Ean was sitting next to him with a concerned look on his face.

"What's wrong, Rae?"

"Kip," Rae replied.

Ean frowned. "What about Kip? Has he been mean to you?"

Rae wondered sometimes about the way purebreds' minds worked. Kip was nice, so he wouldn't be mean. Rae had teeth, so even mean people thought twice about being mean to him.

He decided not to ask a question like he had with Jax. "Kip isn't happy," he stated. "He wakes up sad."

Ean opened his mouth and then shut it again. Rae had noticed he did that when his thoughts were catching up. He waited for Ean's mouth to open for the second time. "Thank you, Rae."

Rae nodded and turned his attention to his food.

Kip missed his Pa and his Ma. He missed Grandpappy. He missed his home, especially his room. He even missed school.

It had been over a div and it wasn't getting any better.

Each morning he woke up to Ean calling his name. He would stumble into the shower, lock the door, turn on the faucet, sit in the corner under the spray and cry enough of the misery away to function.

He would then prepare for the day like he had prepared for school. There was one extra step; at the start he would sweep the misery out of the top later of his mind. Then he would erect partitions, walling away all the corners and the deeper layers.

It left him living in only the surface of his mind; the part that was really, really good at pretending.

He had developed the Kip who had gone to school into the Kip who catted on the Willow. The new Kip was poor at cleaning, terrible at laundry and hated his sessions in the gym. He was good at assisting Vic and not too bad at helping whoever was cooking. He talked about music with Obe, played chess or Go with Jax and solved problems that Rae would otherwise put up with.

Occasionally a bubble of misery would rise up from the lower layers. Kip had got better at knowing when one was on its way. He would escape into a head and sit there, waiting for it. Once it had arrived he would cry for a bit before sweeping the emotions into a corner and partitioning them away.

Then, one morning, it was different. Instead of waking to the sound of Ean calling him, he was woken by a hand on his arm. For a split second he thought it was his Pa.

Only it wasn't. The disappointment crushed him, leaving him broken in a pool of misery.

Kip started to cry.

* * *

After Rae had said that Kip woke up sad, Ean decided he ought to check for himself. Instead of calling for him to get up, Ean went to Kip's bunk and shook him gently.

He had not been sure what he expected but it was not a look of raw longing followed by such heart-breaking disappointment. He watched as Kip's face and then his body crumpled into sobs.

Ean had grown up surrounded by damaged and broken people, some of whom were barely sane and a few of whom were not. Only once or twice had he seen anyone as wretched as Kip at that moment. Experience told him that words would not get through, so he gathered the boy to him and held him so that he would know that he was not alone and that someone cared.

Kip did not fight him. Instead he clung. Ean hugged him, patted his back and was rewarded by a barely audible, "I miss my Pa."

Then Kip twisted away from him, rolled out of his bunk and headed for the shower.

Fifteen minutes later a completely normal Kip entered the galley, behaving in exactly the same way as he did every morning. There was no trace of the abject misery Ean had witnessed; not even a fleeting glance acknowledging what had occurred.

It was definitely not normal. Once everyone was settled into the usual morning chores, Ean went to find Tre.

He was in the gym exercising. Ean hopped up and sat on one of the empty packing cases; a reminder that the room was technically a storage hold.

"I can listen and move," Tre assured him.

Ean told him about what had happened. "It isn't normal, Tre," he concluded. "It was like seeing two completely separate people."

Tre stopped what he was doing and draped a towel around his neck to absorb the sweat. "Well he isn't normal. We know that."

It turned out that what Ean had thought when Tre had said 'genius' and what Tre had meant were very different concepts. Kip was not just cleverer than most people. If you had a billion people, one thousand million people, only one would be as clever as Kip.

"But he seems so ordinary," Ean complained, still not sure if he believed what Tre had told him. "Just a clever, well-educated youngster whose mother has coddled him."

"Well he isn't and what you saw this morning is part of that," Tre pointed out. "He is pretending to be ordinary. It's what he has learnt to do in order to hide from Centre."

"Can we tell him we know he is hiding from Centre?" Ean asked.

Tre shook his head. "Not a good idea. We know he doesn't trust us yet. He might panic. Lady knows what he's capable of doing if he thinks he's backed into a corner. However he behaved afterwards, he knows you saw him cry. Use that and go carefully."

Then he went back to doing push-ups, which was a clear signal that the conversation was over.

Ean made his way slowly back to the galley. Eight divs ago day-to-day life on the Willow had been pleasant if a little boring. He had been thinking that he didn't have enough to do since Cas had got his knife and Obe was growing up.

Now he had three additional youngsters to care for and none of them was exactly normal. Rae was a super-functional hybrid of unknown origin with a glowing pair of wings on his back. Kip was a mega-genius with Centre looking for him.

As for Jax, Ean still didn't know what a spacer boy from that privileged a background was doing on the Willow. However, he was positive Tre had something to do with it.

He sighed. His priority today was Kip. Mega-genius or not, Kip was suffering from homesickness and that was something Ean had tackled before.

✳ ✳ ✳

As the morning progressed Kip began hoping that Ean wouldn't mention the crying, even though Ean was about as likely to ignore it as his Ma would be.

Then, mid afternoon, Kip realised that they were the only two in the galley. They were sitting together at the table cutting up vegetables. The doors to the crewroom and the corridor were shut.

This was it; Kip knew it was.

"Everyone is different, Kip," Ean began. "We know we have to be flexible. Is there anything we could do to make you a little bit happier?"

Kip was about to declare that he was fine but the genuine concern in Ean's eyes stopped him. He thought about what he missed most. Ean couldn't give him his Pa or his Ma or his Grandpappy, but maybe the equivalent of his room was a possibility. "Maybe a bit of space that was just mine?" he asked cautiously. "Just enough for a desk and a chair?"

Ean nodded. "And what about a hundred minutes of your own each day? Not time when you were expected to socialise with Obe or the boys, but time when you could be completely alone if that was what you wanted."

That was far more than Kip would have dared ask for. "Thanks, Ean, I would like that a lot."

Ean smiled and went back to chopping a bell pepper. "It is natural to be homesick, Kip. Maybe you should let us help you deal with it rather than pretending you are fine. Have you written home yet?"

They had neither docked anywhere nor been in a system where the gate had a light speed data relay. Kip had intended to send a message as soon as he could.

"I don't mean just an 'I am fine, how are you' message," Ean explained. "What has happened that would interest your mother, or your father, or your grandfather? You could be putting stuff together. Like a diary or a journal. You could send your mother a picture of that shirt you made."

The shirt had been for Rae and it had only been after Rae had put it on that Kip had understood just how bad it was. One sleeve was longer than the other, the neck was stretched out of shape and the seams were all puckered.

Everyone had laughed and Obe had taken a picture.

Ean was right. Ma would love that. Pa would like to know what he had been doing with Vic. Grandpappy would like hearing about everyday life on the Willow.

To Kip's surprise, thinking about them helped.

As soon as they had the stew cooking, Ean took him to see a space that might work. It was one of the triangular cupboards that had been partitioned off larger rooms to make the rooms more usable shapes.

"One of the simulators is through that wall," Ean told him. "So it should be easy to make any connections you need. Do you want any help with it, or would you like to fit it out yourself?"

Kip was already imagining it. "I would enjoy doing it myself, Ean. Thank you."

Ean smiled again. "Why don't you start it now? You can have the time before supper."

Kip knew exactly where to begin. He went to find Vic and soon had a tablet showing wiring diagrams for the crewroom and control room levels, reels of cable, connectors and a tool kit.

He then fetched the larger of the two lockboxes he had brought from home. Inside were his processors, his data crystals, his interfaces, the diagnostic tools he had built and his selection of specialist connectors.

It didn't take him long to work out that the simulator was not wired as indicated in the diagram. That was good in at least two ways; more non-standard wiring would be less obvious and two-thirds of what he required was already there.

He set an alarm, because not turning up for supper would be bad, and settled down to work.

Ean watched Kip for a while, expecting him to come and ask for a chair or a desk. Instead he seemed more interested in getting the wiring right. Ean decided to leave him alone and worry about Obe.

No cat before Kip had ever been given his own space; Obe would be perfectly justified in thinking it unfair.

He was hanging out in hydroponics with Jax and Rae, pretending to be tending the plants. Ean stepped carefully over the threshold, mindful of the slippery floor.

All three of them were dutifully picking fruit; Rae had obviously given them ample warning of Ean's arrival.

Obe looked a bit anxious as they made their way back to the galley. Ean hoped he hadn't been up to anything more serious than sliding across the floor of hydroponics.

Ean made them tea and then told him about Kip and the cupboard.

"This is something Kip needs," Ean explained. "However, it is a privilege a cat normally does not have and, as Kip has not earned it, I want to give you something equivalent."

Obe frowned. "I don't want to sit on my own in a cupboard."

Ean stopped himself rolling his eyes. "I understand that Obe, that's why I said 'equivalent'. Think about it. What do you like doing?" He stopped himself continuing, 'other than being with Cas, who now has no time for you'. "There is no rush," he added. "Take a few days to think about it."

"I'll think about it," Obe agreed, obviously keen to escape being the sole focus of Ean's attention.

Once he had gone, Ean pulled out the draft of the next div's duty rosters; the least he could do was think of duties that Cas and Obe could do together.

He was just finishing when he realised that Tre was directly behind him; moments later lips were investigating his neck.

"How did it go with Kip?" he murmured rather than his usual suggestion of where they could go and what they could do.

"We talked about the ways to tackle homesickness," Ean replied. "I asked him if there was anything he was missing we could provide and he said he wanted some space of his own, so I have given him the corner cupboard in the room next to the simulator." He gestured towards the simulator he meant, the one next to the infirmary. "He's in there now modifying the wiring."

Tre immediately lost interest in Ean's neck and headed for the corridor. "I'll just go and see how he is getting on," he explained.

Ean watched him go. First he was interested in Jax, then in Rae and now in Kip. He was definitely up to something.

Once he had the wall panel off, Kip had discovered that the simulator had direct connections to all the ship's systems, even the transmitter and receiver. It was easy to piggyback a connection in a way that wasn't too obvious, using connectors that would give false readings for all the meters people used to detect circuits.

After that he replaced the panel and started building a control and data management system, only to be interrupted by a knock at the door.

Kip guessed that it would be Ean. He pulled a box lid over what he was building and called, "Come in."

It was Tre, which was unexpected. He leaned on the doorjamb and looked down at Kip, who was sitting on the floor.

"You are allowed a chair and a work surface," he pointed out. "Maybe some shelves or lockers."

Kip felt himself flush. "Thank you."

"I came to say that you can book time on the simulator." He gestured with his thumb to the room next door. "Since Rae arrived, I've set them up so that each person can save their own settings."

"Thank you," Kip repeated. He wouldn't dare use the simulator for anything interesting until he understood exactly how it worked and could control what went into its memory.

"Good," Tre acknowledged. For a moment Kip thought he might ask a question but instead he stepped backwards and slid the door shut.

By supper time Kip had constructed a system he was happy with, connected eight of his data crystals in a two cubed array and run a diagnostic of the simulator in the room next door.

It was no ordinary simulator. Kip liked simulators; they were the ultimate interface. He had considered building his own until he had realised that someone might query how he had paid for so many high-spec components.

The simulator next door was stuffed with top-of-the-range components. Even more interestingly, it had been customised by someone who knew what he or she was doing.

Why did the Willow have a simulator that had cost half the value of the ship?

Before he could think more about it, his alarm sounded. He put what he had constructed into his lockbox and carried it back to the locker next to his bunk. Tre was right; he would need some storage in his...Kip hadn't decided what to call it yet; it was too small to be a room but people didn't sit in cupboards.

After supper, prompted by Ean, Kip took Obe, Jax and Rae to see his cupboard. He felt silly doing it but Ean wouldn't have suggested it unless he thought it was important.

Obe glanced through the door and said that he couldn't see why Kip wanted it. Jax had a longer look and said nothing. Rae went inside and sniffed all the corners. Then he turned to Kip and grinned.

"It's your den," he announced.

Den sounded a lot better than cupboard.

Rae hoped that Kip would be happier now he had a den. Over the next few days he listened when Kip was in the shower or the head. Each day he cried less and there were fewer times when he suddenly smelt sad.

Then the day arrived when Kip didn't cry. Rae was pleased; it felt good to have helped someone, especially someone nice like Kip.

"Kip's happier now he has a den like we do," he told Jax as they scrubbed the galley floor.

Jax gave a nice laugh, the one that told Rae he had found something funny. "We have a cabin, not a den."

Rae liked making Jax laugh but he hadn't done it on purpose this time. Couldn't it be a den as well as a cabin?

Then Jax was looking at him. "It can be our den if you want it to be."

Rae liked it when Jax did that; when he guessed what Rae was feeling and said something to make him feel better.

They finished scrubbing and moved on to rinsing. As Obe said, Ean wanted the floor clean enough to eat off, which didn't make sense because they had a table and plates.

"I like Kip," he told Jax as they were pouring the not-very-dirty water into the recycling tank.

Jax frowned at him. "How much?" he demanded.

Rae felt suddenly wary. Jax sounded, looked and even smelt a bit cross. Even so, he had asked a question and Rae had to answer. "A lot?" he suggested.

"More than anyone else?" Jax pushed.

Rae thought about it. He liked Vic and Ean and Jax and Kip. He kind of liked Tre but was still a bit scared of him. "No," he decided.

Jax suddenly looked and smelt fine. "Good," he replied in a not-cross voice and went to get the mops.

Rae was a bit confused. Was it good that he liked Kip or good that he didn't like Kip best or both? He thought again about what Jax had said.

"I like you more than I like Kip," he added, which was true.

Jax handed Rae a mop and smiled at him. "Good. I like you too, Rae. You are my friend."

The smile made Rae feel good. "Can we be friends with Kip too?" he asked. "I think Kip might need friends."

Jax considered. "I don't see why not." He reached over and stroked Rae's fur. "You will always be my first friend."

Rae resisted the urge to push up into Jax's hand. He thought back to the other children at the orphanage. "Best friends?" he proposed.

Jax smiled again. "Best friends," he agreed.

14

Nine days ago Tre had still been congratulating himself on acquiring a genius who might be able to substitute for an Alexandrian Advisor.

Then Ean had given Kip the cupboard.

It had started with the wiring. Both Ean and Vic had told him that Kip had modified the wiring and there was a new light fitting and power point in the cupboard. Tre had tested the circuits and confirmed those modifications.

Kip had even dutifully entered them into the ship's wiring diagram.

Only why had Kip put the power point on the wall shared with the simulator? The job would take half the time if he had put it on the other wall.

So Tre had taken off the wall panel.

It had taken him a while to find the other new wires. If he hadn't been convinced they were there he would have missed them. He still remembered connecting his meter and confirming that they weren't there, even though his eyes were telling him they were.

He had stared at the seemingly innocuous connectors. As far as he knew, such things didn't exist.

Their positioning meant Kip understood how the simulator worked. Not how a simulator worked, although that would be impressive, but how this particular, highly customised, simulator worked.

Yet he had said nothing.

Then Kip had modified every speaker on the ship so that it didn't produce unwanted noise in Rae's audio range. Tre had disassembled one and examined the component Kip had added. It definitely did what Kip had said it did. It also appeared to have a number of other capacities, none of which Tre understood.

In all likelihood Kip could sit in his cupboard and access every system in the ship.

Tre was beginning to understand why Centre gathered up all the typed-geniuses and locked them away.

It had been that night, the one after Tre had disassembled the speaker, when he had woken up in a cold sweat. He had been dreaming of Klennethon Darrent only, this time, instead of his hand hovering over an electromagnetic pulse generator, he was laughing.

As Tre lay there it sank in that he was not dealing with one typed-genius, he was dealing with two. Klennethon Darrent had needed somewhere to hide Kip and he had found it. What better place could there be than the place Tre had been preparing for the last eleven standards? What better protector could there be than a cyborg?

What was Tre going to do about the cuckoo in the nest he had prepared for Jax?

Kip was much happier. He still had spells of homesickness but they weren't as bad. He had yet to sort out his head properly but he had stopped sweeping his emotions into corners and partitioning them away.

Cut off from the data streams, he had been occupying himself with investigating the ship. As he had suspected, the simulators weren't the only disproportionately expensive pieces of equipment onboard.

The detectors had five times the range and twice the sensitivity of those carried by most small trading ships. The manoeuvring rockets were uncommonly powerful and had fuel to operate for three times the usual duration. The guns met the spec for those of a courier carrying the sensitive information or the escort for a luxury liner.

They were controlled from those eye-wateringly expensive simulators.

Then there was all the equipment Medico Loy had installed into the infirmary. He said that it was from the medical practice that he had run in Mercy Station but that didn't make sense because it was all brand new. Also, medical equipment aside, Kip was struggling to wrap his mind around how Loy's vague descriptions of his research related to a top-of-the-range synthesiser and one of the best nanobot production rigs on the market.

To top it all, the escape pods were fitted with stealth technology. Who wanted survival pods that no one could find?

Next on his list to investigate was the shielding but they were closing on their next port of call and Kip was more interested in any opportunities for data mining.

He had checked the Kellard system in the catalogue he had stored on one of his data crystals. To his disappointment there was no light speed data relay in either of the gates. He wouldn't be able to hack into the data streams. There was, however, a branch of the Stellar Exchange, which meant that there would be information to be had if only he could get it onto the ship.

He couldn't have it delivered as a data wafer and say it was from his family because it was too soon for him to be receiving couriered items from Darrenden. He didn't dare use a direct data link; he was worried that one of the crew would notice.

No, he would have to resort to a data trickle.

How much information he could get would depend on the other data flowing to and from the ship. If the communication systems were active, he could sneak more in.

He managed to finish setting it up before he had to be in the galley for one of Ean's educational discussions.

Kip would have been second to last but Rae shot past him and took the seat next to Jax.

"Kellard is a mining system," Ean began. "It has no habitable planets. What do you anticipate about the system?"

Kip did not have to anticipate; he knew from looking it up in the catalogue.

"Obe?" Ean insisted when none of them volunteered.

"Nothing but mines, miners and people selling stuff to miners," Obe replied. "It'll be rough. You'll make us stay on the ship."

"Quite," Ean acknowledged. "Jax, anything to add?"

This could be interesting; almost every time Jax opened his mouth Kip found himself comparing a spacer education with the Darrendenian version.

"The system isn't in a main shipping lane, so it will be mined out and then abandoned," Jax began. "Even the gates will be sold." He paused and considered. "Systems like this are often owned by a single company but this one probably isn't because there are gates. It is often cheaper for a company to use mother ships with Mulligan drives than to pay the Gaters to install gates."

Kip saw Rae's whiskers twitch but so had Ean. "Kip, fill us in on mother ships and Mulligan drives."

"A Mulligan drive is like a mobile gate," Kip explained, being careful to start with the basics. "A ship with a Mulligan drive can jump through an ungated hole. Mulligan drives cost a lot, about half the cost of a gate. Mother ships are huge ships with a Mulligan drive that carry masses of cargo, including other ships, through ungated holes."

He paused but Ean gestured that he should continue, so he did. "There's this bit inside the Mulligan drive that opens the hole. It's the same technology as inside a gate." Ean's expression suggested he was hoping for more. "Only the Gaters know how to make the special bit. The Gaters are a very long-established group. They pre-date the founding of Centre."

As Kip finished, he was aware that Tre was leaning on the doorjamb between the galley and the crewroom. Either Kip had not noticed him before or he had not been there.

"Thank you, Kip," Ean acknowledged. "I did not know that the Gaters were such an ancient group."

Kip liked that Ean was happy to admit he didn't know stuff; lots of adults struggled with that.

"Why didn't Centre try to take the secret of the gates away from the Gaters?" Obe asked.

Tre stopped merely listening and joined in. "They can switch off the gates. And all the Mulligan drives. Each system would become isolated. You remember Ean's explanation of how systems that seem close together are actually a lifetime's travel apart?"

Kip didn't but Obe, Jax and Rae nodded.

"The six systems that make up Centre are many, many lifetimes' travel apart. No, the threat of closing the holes means that no one even goes looking for the Gaters. You express an interest in buying a gate or a Mulligan drive and they find you."

There was silence. Kip filled the time by designing a model to determine how long humans could survive in a particular isolated system.

"Kip hasn't heard Ean's explanation of how space is made up," Obe pointed out.

Ean flushed slightly, which recaptured Kip's attention. "I am sure…" he began.

"I'll do it," Rae said, jumping up and going to a drawer. He paused with his hand on the handle, looking back at Ean.

"Good idea," Tre encouraged, sitting down at the table. "Let's see if you can remember it, Rae. Jax can help you if you get stuck."

Kip saw that Rae still waited for Ean's nod before opening the drawer and removing a neatly folded square of material and some string.

What happened next was fascinating. Rae sat at the table and became a miniature version of Ean. It was perfect: the gestures; the intonation; the questions; everything.

At first everyone smiled and Kip saw Ean's look warning Obe not to laugh. Then, gradually, everyone's amusement gave way to astonishment.

Rae's version of the explanation, which was an impressively effective one, was perfect. Kip could see that it would only work if the cloth was folded in a certain way. He studied Ean watching every movement of Rae's hands.

When Rae finished, Ean started applauding, followed by Obe and Jax. Even Tre joined in so Kip did as well.

"That was wonderful, Rae," Ean praised. "How did you remember it so well after only once?"

"It was interesting," Rae admitted.

So it appeared that Rae had an eidetic memory if something interested him enough to trigger it.

Kip found that very interesting indeed. He added it to his lengthening list of intriguing things about Rae.

Ean decided that Rae's performance was a suitable highlight to end on. Obe, Jax and Rae were quickly out the door before Ean came up with something for them to do. Kip decided to head back to his den and check everything he needed for the data trickle was in place; he wanted it to start downloading data as soon as they jumped.

"Kip?" Ean asked.

Kip stopped and turned back.

"There is a Stellar Exchange in Kellard," Ean told him. "I could dispatch a tape to your parents."

Kip was about to say that a priority electronic message would be much quicker but he stopped himself in time; crews like the Willow's couldn't afford priority electronic messages.

"Thank you, Ean," Kip acknowledged. "I'll prepare one."

This jump looked like it was going to be like all the others since Darrenden. Kip wished he could be in his den or the control room or a simulator. Instead he had to sit in the crewroom with Ean, Obe, Jax and Rae.

They had just settled down when the alarms started and the room was flooded again and again with red light. Ean, Obe, Jax and Rae were moving. Kip knew he should be moving too but his head was too full of multiplying possibilities to remember what he was meant to be doing.

Then the alarm quietened and the captain's voice came over the intercom. "*This is the captain. We have a level 2 emergency with possible level 3 implications.*"

Level 2 was a possible breach and level 3 was hostile action. Kip's mind started supplying possible scenarios.

"Kip!" Ean shouted. "Suit! Now!"

Where were the suits in the crewroom? He couldn't remember. He tried to focus on what the others were doing. Obe had a locker open and was handing out suits.

He should probably go over there and get one.

In the end Obe brought the suit to him and Ean all but dressed him in it. Then Ean went over to the intercom.

"This is Ean in the crewroom. Obe, Kip, Jax and Rae are with me."

The alarm fell silent and the red light stopped flashing.

"*This is the captain. That was almost four minutes, Ean.*"

Kip realised that it had been a drill.

Ean gave Kip a look and then reactivated the intercom. "This is Ean. I realise. We will discuss it later."

Ean made them stay in their suits until after the jump. Then they had to replace the suits they had used with fresh ones from the store and put the ones they had been wearing into the sanitiser.

"You can run the checks on them later and put them in the store," Ean told them. "Kip, galley please. You three can go down and check that hydroponics is in a fit state for when we dock at the station and swap to the station's gravitational field."

Ean closed both doors before coming and sitting with Kip at the table.

"Kip, there are many situations on board a ship where you would be dead within four minutes. Do you understand that?"

Kip did; his mind had been full of them. "Yes, Ean."

"When the alarms sound, you get into a suit. There should be two thoughts in your head. Get into my suit. Make sure everyone else is in their suits. No other thoughts. All other thoughts can, must, wait." Ean sighed. "I am going to get Tre to work with you one-to-one on this."

"Thank you, Ean," Kip replied, meaning it.

Ean sighed. "I don't think you will be thanking me when Tre has finished with you. Off you go. I'll speak with Tre once we are clear of the gate."

Kip made his way to his den, trying to think through what had just happened. Why hadn't Ean been angry? Why had he assumed that Kip had too many thoughts in his head? It wasn't as if he had asked.

He decided not to dwell on it. Instead he would go and monitor what was happening with his data trickle.

Far more data had come through than he had anticipated. For a moment he thought that he had set up the parameters of the trickle wrongly. Then he realised that there had been a huge amount of data flowing to and from the ship, starting as soon as they had entered the system.

Someone on board had a premier subscription to the Stellar Exchange. The first data package had included their new digest and a snapshot of their database of publically available information. After that a large number of priority electronic messages had been sent and received.

Kip was split. Making silent, invisible copies of the downloaded news digest and the snapshot was a lot easier than getting them via a data trickle. On the other hand, a ship like the Willow wasn't meant to have the funds for a premier subscription to the Stellar Exchange or for numerous priority electronic messages.

Just like it wasn't meant to have all the equipment it had.

He was about to turn his attention to getting a priority electronic message sent to his Pa via the data trickle when a thought bubbled up from one of the deeper layers of his mind.

He checked. Only a tiny percentage of the data had been transmitted or received via the communications console in the control room. That fraction consisted of the standard messages like security checks and checking docking arrangements. The most exotic was an exchange with the supplier buying their cargo.

The rest of it went to one of the simulators instead; the one Tre had been occupying.

Kip's mind shifted as information deep in his mind aligned and new links were made. He was about to risk disassembling a few of the partitions and checking what was happening when there was a knock on the door.

"You in there, Kip?"

It was Tre. Kip yanked off his goggles and earpieces, gathered up all the other equipment, thrust everything into a locker, shut the door and locked it. Then he opened the door.

"Ean says you did badly in the drill," Tre stated. "How badly?"

Kip flushed. "Obe brought me my suit and Ean helped me get into it."

"And it still took almost four minutes?"

Kip nodded.

"Follow me," Tre instructed, heading for the shaft.

They didn't go to the gym as Kip expected, or rather they didn't go to the gym where Kip trained. Instead they went onto one of the levels closer to the gravitational field generators, where Kip weighed much more than the usual amount. Worse, the gravitational field varied. Within a few steps he could feel as if a load had been dropped on his shoulders or had been yanked away. It made even walking difficult.

Kip wondered what Tre was planning. He felt weak and exposed. He wanted his Pa.

They went into a large room. There were floor to ceiling piles of packing cases that divided the space like thick pillars. Tre switched off the lights, revealing fluorescent paint on the floor. The fluorescence illuminated the whole room with an eerie blue-green glow.

"The glowing parts are where the gravitational field is much higher. About five gee. What will happen if you enter one?"

"I'll be crushed," Kip whispered.

"Exactly," Tre replied. "Of course, as you probably know, the gravitational field at this distance from the generators has interesting patterns."

Kip did; it was a consequence of there being different fields overlapping.

"Here, the gravitational field intensity is much greater at the floor than the ceiling, so you can also avoid the five gee areas by doing this."

Kip watched as Tre ran and leapt. He caught something close to the ceiling and swung across the painted area before dropping to the other side.

"Do you think you can do that?" Tre asked.

Kip hadn't thought any purebred human could do that, not at high gee. He certainly couldn't; he could hardly stand. He wasn't sure what was scarier, the thought of being squashed by a five gee gravitational field or Tre himself.

"Well?" Tre demanded.

"No," Kip replied. His voice came out as a high-pitched squeak.

Tre smiled at him. It wasn't a nice smile. "I didn't think so. So you had better remember the pattern of fluorescent paint on the floor. You have ten seconds."

Kip stared at him. He was serious.

Kip grabbed his panic, thrust it into a corner of his mind and slammed down a partition. Then he studied the pattern.

Then the lights came on and the pattern vanished.

"A target on one of the walls will light up," Tre told him. "You will run to it, avoiding the high gee areas. If you don't run, I'll pick you up and throw you at it. Do you understand?"

Kip nodded; he did not trust himself to speak.

"Good. The exercise ends when you manage to hit a target before it goes out."

The first target lit up and Kip struggled towards it. He was trying to run but his body was so heavy and his muscles too weak. He had only got two-thirds of the way there when the target went out and another appeared on the opposite wall.

He turned around and started back the other way.

Each time he was weaker and covered less of the convoluted path to the target. Tears of frustration and exhaustion began leaking from his eyes. When the fifth target went out and the sixth lit up, he headed for Tre instead.

"Throw me," he requested. "It's the only way I'll ever make it."

Tre reached for him and Kip braced himself.

Only instead of being lifted and thrown he was gathered close and hugged. It helped. Kip felt safer and less scared.

"Well done," Tre told him. "Well done for remembering the pattern, well done for trying and well done for working out the solution even though you were frightened." He pushed Kip to arms' length and looked him in the eye. "Whatever you did to clear your mind, so you could learn the pattern, that's what you need to do when the alarms sound. Getting into your suit is much more important than learning that pattern. Do you understand?"

Kip did. He nodded.

"Good. Now, do you trust me to throw you or to decide not to throw you?"

Kip considered. He could lie or he could be honest and he did not know which was the safer. He imagined Tre's reaction if he thought Kip was lying to him. "Neither," he replied cautiously. "I don't trust you," he clarified. Kip didn't really trust anyone other than his Pa.

"But you came to me," Tre pointed out.

"It was the only way to end it," Kip admitted.

"Exactly," Tre agreed. "Sometimes you haven't got a better choice. Do you know who I am, Kip?"

Kip guessed that the answer wasn't 'Tre'. He shook his head.

"I am your protector. I will keep you safe. I will keep you hidden."

Kip had been beginning to feel a bit better until Tre used the word 'hidden'. Now he felt sick. Did Tre know? He wanted to ask but he didn't know if he could bear to hear the answer.

"Now would be a good time, Kip," Tre hinted.

"What do you know about me?" Kip asked, not wanting to give any extra information away.

"At least one person in your family, probably your father, believes you are a typed-genius. You parents have been hiding you from Centre since you were a baby. However, your behaviour has brought you to another's notice. That other person also wishes to hide you from Centre and has given me the job of doing it."

Even though Kip had known it was coming, it was a shock. Tre knew his secret. So did the person who had sent him.

Probably Ean did too. Ean had not been surprised or angry that Kip had mucked up the drill. He had given Kip his den when cats were never given their own space.

Tre pulled him close again and gave him another hug. It felt good. It reminded Kip of his Pa.

"This is a gym I have designed to train Rae," Tre told him. "All the areas three gee and above are blocked by the packing cases. The fluorescent painted areas are between two and three gee."

Suddenly the room was a lot less scary. "Rae is amazing." Kip observed.

"Yes he is," Tre agreed.

Kip had a sudden thought. "Are you hiding him too?"

Tre smiled. "Not deliberately. Rae found us rather than us finding him. Kip, you and I will need to talk about some rules."

Kip understood rules; they were things he had to work around. He nodded.

"Not now," Tre clarified. "Now you need to shower, eat and get some rest.

Tre had spent days trying to decide what to do.

The safest choice was to give up on any notion of Kip as an asset, stick him in a pod and ship him to Klennethon Darrent. Unfortunately that option was at odds with a crew's commitment to their cat, might irritate Klennethon Darrent and would mean being banned from Ean's bunk for divs, perhaps permanently.

The most dangerous path was the one he had been on. Kip was getting up to Lady knew what. Any one of the things Kip had done might endanger Jax; Tre had no way of knowing.

No, Tre needed a middle way, ideally one that reduced the risk and did not involve telling Kip about Jax.

Then Tre had realised that he could pretend that the nest had been built for the cuckoo. He would tell Kip that his job was to hide and protect him. It would explain the elaborate simulators and any other modifications Kip had found.

Decision made, Tre had to work out when to have the conversation and what he should say to make Kip look to him for protection.

So when Ean had come to him to discuss Kip's behaviour during the drill, Tre had decided to seize the opportunity. It was an excuse to push Kip far from his comfort zone, reminding him that he was too weak, young and inexperienced to survive without a protector.

Someone who could stand in his father's place.

It had gone well. Kip had been frightened but not terrified. He had turned to Tre for help. He had accepted comfort. He had not panicked when Tre told him that another two people knew his secret.

He had even agreed that they needed rules.

As they climbed down and then up to the crewroom, Tre congratulated himself on a job well done.

15

Jax wished he hadn't looked at the calendar. It wasn't as if it mattered what day it was when you were in space. There were no seasons, no weather, no days of obligation and no public holidays.

Even if the crew knew, there wouldn't be a celebration. When a person decided to space they left their old life behind them. A spacer celebrated the anniversary of the day he got his knife. That was a long way away for Jax; at least another three standards, maybe longer.

No, tomorrow wasn't his twelfth birth anniversary; it was just another day.

Ean had picked today to pierce Kip's ears. The ceremony was scheduled for early evening. According to Obe, Ean would make a fuss of him all afternoon and the food at supper would be special. Jax told himself it was good timing; that today being different would distract him from what would not be happening tomorrow.

Thinking about it, Jax was surprised Kip's ears hadn't been pierced when he first joined the crew. After all, he was fourteen. Instead there had been a two div 'probationary period'.

Jax hadn't known that cats had probationary periods. He was pretty sure they didn't in most crews. According to the ex-spacers at home, a crew would spot a cat, recruit him and then have a party where they 'all tried out both his holes'.

Jax had a much better idea of what that involved now. Cas and Loy were much less discreet than Tre and Ean or Art and Ben. Loy appeared to like 'trying out Cas's holes' in the infirmary and the laboratory as well as in Cas's bunk with the drapes closed.

It wasn't the kind of thing you could forget once you had seen it. Sometimes, often at inopportune times, Jax would find himself thinking about the way Cas had looked and then his rod would get stiff. Problem was, when it happened Rae would look at him as if he knew. Maybe he did. Perhaps it made Jax smell different. Jax had tried thinking about other stuff to make his rod go soft again. Scary stuff worked best, like how he had felt when his mother was telling him that his life had changed forever.

Obe had told him and Rae that Ean was very strict about what Obe called 'sex-stuff'. No one was allowed to do anything with a cabin boy. Apparently a member of the crew, Von, had been forced to buy out for just looking at Obe wrongly when Obe had been twelve.

Cats, of course, catted. As Jax's father had told him, a cat was an essential part of a Trad crew. Cats 'relieved potential sexual tension within the crew'. On the Willow that meant that Obe gave blow jobs to the Captain and to Vic, who didn't have partners.

Jax tried not to think about that much because imagining Obe doing to the captain or Vic what he had seen Cas do to Loy was plain weird.

Officially all the senior crew could call on Obe. Ean ran it on a rota system. There were eight senior members of crew, so there was an eight day rotation. Tre, Ean, Art and Ben, as far as Jax knew, had never used their days. When Cas had started to go with Loy they had both stopped too.

Obe had been upset about Cas ever since.

As soon as lunch was over, the three of them had been dispatched down to hydroponics so that Ean could concentrate on Kip. The plants never reacted well to being changed between ship's and station's gravity, like when the ship had been docked at Kellard. They were shedding lots of leaves and needed more attention. Obe and Jax were checking them over while Rae swept up the leaves.

"So Kip will have to suck rod?" Rae checked.

Jax tried not to flinch at how blunt Rae was about 'sex-stuff'. He talked about it like it was just the same as eating or sleeping.

Obe nodded. "He'll go with the captain this evening."

"But no arse fucking?"

Jax could feel himself going red. He knew it was just Rae's way, but If Jax had used words like that at home his mother would have sent to his room until his father could deal with him.

"No," Obe confirmed. "The way Ean runs the Willow, cats' rear holes are their own. He doesn't like a cat offering it to anyone before he is sixteen." Obe looked conspiratorial. "According to Cas, who heard it from Ben, Ean offered his to Tre when he was younger than that."

"Did he take it?" Rae asked, which was good because Jax wanted to know that too.

"Not sure," Obe admitted, which was a bit of a disappointment. "Cas thinks Tre must have wife somewhere and maybe children. He thinks that's the only possible explanation for why he hasn't given Ean a love ring."

Jax hadn't been ready for the change of subject. He almost declared that Tre didn't have a wife and children but stopped himself in time.

"It's just a bit of metal," Rae declared.

"No it isn't," Obe insisted.

"It isn't the ring that's important," Jax explained. "It's the promises it represents."

Rae stopped sweeping and twitched his whiskers. "Like a deal?"

Jax shook his head. "Not quite. In a deal it's 'if you do this, I'll do that' in a promise it's more 'I'll do this' and you try and do it whatever."

Rae resumed sweeping while Obe prattled on about love rings. Jax found himself wondering about Tre and Ean. Did Tre love Ean at all? Was Ean just another part of Tre's cover?

It wouldn't matter so much if Ean didn't love Tre but he did, Jax was sure of it.

"Is us being best friends a promise?" Rae asked in a quiet voice from only a pace away.

Jax realised that Obe had stopped talking and gone over to one of the storage cupboards. He looked back and was caught by Rae's eyes.

Ten divs ago eyes with no visible whites had been strange. Now they were just Rae. Jax noticed, not for the first time, the golden flecks in Rae's chocolate brown irises. "For me it was a promise," he replied.

Rae smiled, which always reminded Jax of the sun coming out from behind a cloud. "Me too."

Ean had thought about suggesting they put off piercing Kip's ears for longer. It wasn't like Obe was overworked. He only had two people to look after and neither of them was particularly demanding.

Then Ben had asked him when they were going to do it and Ean realised that delaying would only serve to draw attention to how odd Kip actually was.

He was undeniably strange. The more time Ean spent with him, the more he could see it. Like now; it was like Ean was dealing with a hologram and the real Kip was in his cupboard.

"Would you like studs or rings?" Ean asked, displaying their small selection of earrings. He had hoped that Kip's grandfather would give him earrings for Kip, maybe even his own first pair, but it had not happened.

Kip just looked at them and said nothing.

"Maybe these rings?" Ean suggested, pointing at a nice gold pair.

"Yes," Kip agreed. "Thank you," he added.

Ean sighed. "Kip, look at me." He looked into Kip's dark eyes. It did not help. It was as if there was a sheet of thick glass between them. Even so, Ean had to try. "How do you feel about this? About becoming a cat? About going with the captain this evening?"

"You said he would tell me what to do," Kip checked.

"Yes," Ean confirmed. He could not quite put his finger on what was wrong. "Kip, has anyone ever touched you sexually?"

Kip did not even blush. He just shook his head. "On Darrenden the age of consent for any sexual activity is sixteen."

"Not even mucking about?" Ean checked. "Maybe with friends?"

Kip looked away. "No."

Ean wanted to kick himself; Kip probably had never had friends. He almost left it there but he knew he was still missing something. "Do you touch yourself?" he asked.

Kip looked back and at him and there was a look of total incomprehension on his face before understanding dawned. "No. I never wanted to."

Ean hoped he managed to stop his reaction showing in his face.

As soon as Kip went to shower and change, Ean went to find the captain and tried to explain his misgivings.

"You're fussing, Ean," Captain Mel told him. "I understand. He's been very protected. He has no experience. I'm not new to this."

Ean had one more go. "I don't think he's interested in sex."

The captain laughed. "He's fourteen, Ean. Of course he's interested in sex."

✳ ✳ ✳

Kip hated being the centre of attention. He hadn't been put through anything like this since his eighth birth anniversary when his Ma had arranged a party and invited his classmates.

Afterwards his Pa had sat her down and made her see that she was torturing him.

He told himself it could be worse. Loy put anaesthetic on his earlobes so the needle didn't hurt. Being hugged wasn't so bad. Both Ben and Ean kissed him but it was on his cheek like his Ma. Supper included foods Kip particularly liked and pudding was one of Ean's special apple crumbles.

After supper he wasn't allowed to help clean up. Instead Obe dragged him into the crewroom.

"You need to clean your teeth," Obe told him. "And use mouth-wash."

He was still there when Kip came out of the head.

"The captain will tell you exactly what to do," Obe assured him. "Listen carefully. Don't be worried. Ean, Ben, Cas and I all had our first times with the captain. He's really kind."

Kip was reassured by that. If he could learn to iron and fold clothes to Ean's impossibly high standards, he could do this.

Only he couldn't. The first bit went well. They played a card game called cribbage that Kip had heard of but never tried. Then the captain went to sit in his big chair and summoned Kip forward to kneel down between his legs.

There were a few minutes when Kip thought it might work. After that the captain's rod refused to stand up and Kip touching it just made it worse.

They played more cribbage instead and then the captain sent him off to bed.

Kip went to his den. He put in his earpieces and set them so they blocked out any noise from his surroundings. Once his goggles were in place he could lose himself in his data and not think about why the captain's rod had stood up for Ben and Ean and Cas and Obe but not for him.

Ean sat in his usual place in the crewroom and pretended to read while watching for Kip. As time went on, he started to relax. If Kip was still in the captain's cabin then it couldn't be going that badly.

Then Tre came and sat beside him.

"Kip's in his cupboard," Tre told him quietly. "He's been there a while."

Ean's heart sank. He started to stand up but Tre's hand on his arm stopped him.

"Wait. Think about what you are going to say. It might be better to let it go tonight and talk to him tomorrow. Maybe in the morning Mel will drop a hint about what went wrong."

So Ean waited until it was almost midnight and then went to knock on Kip's door. When he did not open Ean spoke a warning and then cracked the door open.

Kip was utterly lost in his virtual world. Ean studied him. Maybe that was the only place Kip could be happy.

No, Ean refused to believe that. There were times when Kip seemed fine. Not today, Ean had to admit that, but when he was with Rae and Jax or helping Vic.

Ean had to put a hand on Kip's knee to get his attention. Kip slowly pulled out his earpieces and pushed up his goggles.

This time Kip was present; the look in his eyes reminded Ean of the expression of the boy in the vid Tre had showed him.

"Bedtime, Kip," Ean told him.

Kip started to stash his equipment in one of the lockers.

Ean's instincts agreed with Tre. This was not the time to press. He settled for an open-ended offer. "Anytime you want to talk,

Kip, I am here for you."

Kip nodded but said nothing.

Sleep eluded Ean and when it finally arrived it did not last. He was up before ship's dawn. He showered in a vain attempt to drive away the weariness and then went to the galley.

As Tre had suggested, it was not long before the captain arrived. He shut the door to the corridor behind him and then crossed the galley to the crewroom door and closed that as well. He looked tired; Ean doubted he had slept.

"Coffee?" Ean offered, already out of his seat and on his way towards the counter.

"Yes please," the captain replied in a voice that sounded as weary as he looked.

Once they were settled at the table, the captain began. "I am sorry, Ean, but in my defence it was strange."

Ean was surprised at how upset he sounded. What had happened?

"Are you sure he's not been abused or anything?" the captain added.

Alarm bells started sounding in Ean's head. Surely if it had been that bad the captain would have sought him out immediately. Was going to have to ask what had happened? He didn't know if he could. On the other hand, how could he help Kip if he didn't?

The captain looked embarrassed and cleared his throat. "I couldn't get it up," he admitted.

Ean tried to stop his relief showing in his face. Of course the captain was upset; as far as Ean knew, he had never had any problems with that. "Well we know it isn't you," Ean assured him.

The captain relaxed a little. He sipped his coffee.

"It was strange," he repeated. "He was willing to try but it was like…" He stopped and thought before trying again. "It was like trying to have sex with someone you shouldn't. Like a little kid. Or your sister."

It helped. It opened a way forward that would salve the captain's wounded ego and give Kip more time. "He isn't ready," Ean declared. "Despite his age, he's not mature enough. You felt that."

As Ean had anticipated, the captain was happy to go with that. "Yes, that would make sense. He needs to grow up a bit. You have a word with him and I'll back up what you tell him." He stood up and picked up his coffee, obviously intending to take it back to his cabin.

Ean would have preferred it to be the other way around but he accepted that this was not a situation the captain found comfortable.

He arranged to have Kip alone after breakfast. Kip sat with his shoulders hunched and his eyes fixed on the tabletop.

"I want to apologise," Ean began.

Kip glanced at him, obviously surprised.

"I shouldn't have sent you to the captain after what you had told me yesterday. You aren't ready. Different boys grow up differently. You aren't ready for sexual intimacy yet. When you tried with the captain, he instinctively knew that. He reacted as he would towards a child."

Kip's gaze was back on the tabletop.

"Kip?" Ean queried. "Are you listening? Do you understand what I am saying?" He waited.

After too much silence, Kip finally responded. "It wasn't because I'm weird and ugly?"

Ean did not hesitate. He gathered Kip close and hugged him.

"You are not ugly. You just have to grow into yourself and then you'll be as handsome as your father."

Kip did not resist the hug. On the contrary, he relaxed into it; Ean resolved to hug him more often.

"I am weird," he insisted.

"Weird and sexually attractive are by no means incompatible," he insisted, stroking Kip's back to reassure him. Ean knew that to be true; the men frequenting the whorehouse had paid much more for weird. "Weird just means different, Kip. There is nothing wrong with being different."

Jax was woken by Rae shaking him.

"Obe wants to come in. Do we let him in?"

Jax considered. He didn't want Obe thinking he could come into their cabin. It was their space. "No." He checked the time. "We'll go to the laundry."

Within a few minutes the three of them were in the laundry, still in their sleep shorts.

"Can't see why you won't let me into your cabin," Obe complained. "I always used to let Cas in."

"It's our den now," Jax replied. "What's up?"

"Kip didn't stay with the captain. The captain sent him away. That never happens."

Rae looked worried. Jax could see he was anxious about Kip.

"We should never have taken him on," Obe added. "It was a split vote. You should never recruit someone on a split vote. Last night, I heard Art talking about swapping him."

Jax didn't want that. Kip was meant to be part of his team. "Rubbish. It would be dishonourable to agree with his parents that we would take him on and then swap him. The captain and Ean would never allow it. Neither would Tre. Neither should you."

Obe flushed. "I was only telling you what Art said."

"Art should keep such thoughts to himself," Jax insisted. "We don't even know what happened." He cast about for a mundane explanation. "Maybe Kip had eaten too much apple crumble and felt sick."

Obe thought about that for a moment and then laughed.

"Yeah, you can't suck rod if you are throwing up."

Jax did not want that image in his head and, based on Rae's expression, he agreed.

"I didn't think you minded Kip," Jax pointed out. "He fixed your music player. You said it was much better than it was when it was new."

Obe grimaced. "I know. He's just odd."

Rae twitched his whiskers. "I'm odd."

"You're a hybrid," Obe pointed out.

Jax decided to go with his best guess. "So he isn't like Cas."

Obe flushed and Jax congratulated himself for having hit the nail on the head.

"No one is like Cas," Jax insisted. "Cas is Cas. Kip is Kip."

Obe sighed. "I guess so."

"You shouldn't listen to Art," Jax added. "He's only interested in Art."

"Art gave Ben a love ring," Obe pointed out.

Jax rolled his eyes. Obe and his obsession with love rings.

Then Rae began impersonating Cas offering Obe a love ring and Obe swooning. Next Obe was chasing Rae around the laundry and out the door into the corridor.

Jax went through the other door, through the crewroom and back into his cabin. Rae would soon get fed up of running slowly enough for Obe to chase him.

He looked at himself in the mirror. Brown eyes looked back. His hair had grown out wavy. Jax thought it looked a bit girly but various people, including Cas, had said how nice it looked.

Today he was twelve. A standard ago he had been celebrating his eleventh birth anniversary and expecting three more such celebrations before joining the Willow.

Instead his father and mother were gone, his uncle had usurped his father's place and he was hiding.

He knew he should miss his father and mother more. Kip had hated being separated from his parents and that wasn't forever. They were still there, on Darrenden. He could send them tapes and visit them in the future.

Kip's parents weren't dead like Jax's were.

The door opened and Rae dashed through into the shower, grabbing a pair of underpants and a towel on the way. Jax moved towards the door to block Obe's entrance.

"He's in the shower," Jax announced, sliding the door shut. "You'll have to see him at breakfast."

Only Cas was at breakfast so Obe didn't want to bring it up in case Rae repeated his impersonations.

Kip didn't look good, he stared at his plate and only ate a few mouthfuls. Jax wondered if he was unwell. It was more likely that he thought he had failed. Maybe he had heard the gossip about swapping him.

After breakfast Ean sent Jax and Rae to clean the lower corridors. They knew what that meant; Ean wanted Rae far enough away not to be able to hear. When they were summoned back Kip looked a lot better.

The rest of the morning went normally, mostly cleaning stuff that didn't really need cleaning until it was time for Jax's one-to-one training session with Tre.

He found himself wondering if Tre had remembered what day it was.

Jax enjoyed his sessions with Tre. Tre emphasised hand-to-hand combat and knife fighting. As long as Jax concentrated and worked hard there was lots of praise.

He had wondered if he deserved the praise. After all, he was nowhere near as good as Rae. Then he had spied on one of Tre's sessions with Obe and been reassured that, for a purebred, he was pretty good.

At the end of the session Tre summoned him over rather than sending him off to the shower. He laid a hand on Jax's shoulder.

"Twelve standards ago you were put in my arms," he said quietly. "It was the proudest day of my life."

It felt as if someone had reached into Jax's chest and touched his heart. It was like having his Papá praise him, only better because Jax hadn't had to do anything to make Tre proud. Just being himself, even as a newborn baby, had been enough.

Tre reached into his pocket and brought something out. "I was given these, to give to you when you are old enough to have your ears pierced." He opened his hand.

On the palm sat two ear studs. Jax recognised the motif that decorated them. It was the same as on the ear studs his father had worn.

"I want you to have them and keep them until they are needed. Hold out your hand."

Jax did so and Tre spilled the ear studs into it. "Thank you," Jax whispered.

Tre gently squeezed his shoulder. "I am proud of you, Jax. You are a credit to your clan. Now off you go."

Jax felt warm; wanted. As he climbed the ladder to the crewroom, he decided that, despite everything that had happened, his new life was good. There was no better crew to be in than the Willow's, especially with Ean looking after them. He now had a team of three: Tre, Loy and Kip. Tre, the man standing in his father's place, was proud of him.

And, top of the list, he had a best friend: Rae.

16

Supper was over, the debris had been cleared away and Jax and Rae had been sent to their cabin. Tre sat back in his chair nursing the small cup of real coffee that Loy had made him. He did not tilt his chair back or ask Obe to pour him a whisky because Ean was still at the table.

It had been a restful four divs between Kellard and Mercy. Jax and Rae were doing well. Art had been almost pleasant; maybe Loy being with Cas had changed the crew dynamic to something he could live with. Kip had agreed to a few simple rules; don't tell anyone anything and don't make changes to the ship without asking Tre first.

Neither the captain nor Vic had made a big deal of Kip being useless at catting.

They would jump into the Mercy system tomorrow. A day after that they would reach the station, deliver the pods they were carrying and get Rae scanned. Then, hopefully, they would have some time off the ship before picking up the next load of pods.

Maybe he could persuade Ean to go clubbing.

"Cards?" Art suggested.

Tre sighed. Art liked cards and was good at them. Tre could beat him but only using his processor. Given that he had promised himself not to do that, because it risked discovery, he had to put up with Art winning.

"Can I play?" Kip asked.

Tre perked up; this could be fun.

"No," Ean replied. "They bet so it's gambling."

"We use counters," Tre reminded him. "And Kip's a cat, not a cabin boy. He's old enough for cards." He played his ace. "We could close the door to the crewroom and ask the captain to join us. You know how much Mel likes playing cards."

Ean hesitated and Tre considered smiling but decided against it; it would be too much.

"Please, Ean," Loy added in that voice that sounded like silk and velvet.

"Very well," Ean conceded. "No feeding Kip or Obe alcohol." He turned to Ben. "Are you staying?"

Ben smiled but, to Tre, it looked a bit sad. "No, I'm with you."

They were soon set up. Obe went to ask the captain if he wanted to play, Vic got the whisky out and Art produced the cards and the counters.

"Credit a counter?" Art checked.

Tre automatically checked the door. It was firmly shut.

"Maybe not with Kip playing," the captain replied; Obe only ever spectated.

Tre was about to say he would cover Kip's losses but Kip spoke first.

"My Pa gave me some before I left." He checked the stacks of counters in front of him. "I'm good for a hundred credits."

"Your 'Pa'," Art sneered.

"That's what we call our fathers on Darrenden," Kip replied. His tone was mild but Tre wondered if Art wouldn't regret the comment later.

They were playing Courts, a game Art had introduced when he had joined the crew. It was a good game because it was complicated enough to remain interesting when you were losing and no one got knocked out of a hand early unless they chose to lay it down.

What made Courts different was that it was played with a big pack that had ten suits rather than the usual five. Half the pack was laid out face up on the table. The other half was divided between the players' hands and a reserve stack. Each round you had the option of buying one of the cards that was face up and swapping a card out of your hand for the one that was at the top of the stack.

The best hand after four rounds won. You could bet at any time but, in practice, all the betting happened after everyone had built their final hand.

Tre noticed that Kip made absolutely sure he knew the rules before the game started.

Tre could not resist using his processor to follow what Kip was doing. That way he could anticipate Art's reactions and enjoy them more thoroughly.

Kip was using probability theory to calculate odds. Every time a card was claimed or swapped, he recalculated them. He only bet when there was a seventy per cent chance that his hand was better than anyone else's.

It took Art ages to realise that Kip knew what he was doing and it was not beginner's luck. The most amusing part was watching Art's futile efforts to tempt Kip into betting on hands that had a less than seventy per cent chance of winning. Second best was when Art tried to bluff.

Watching Art wriggle on the end of Kip's hook was most entertaining.

Slowly and steadily, all the counters gravitated towards Kip. Finally, as Kip cleaned Art out, Vic spoke.

"You really should have looked through Kip's application more carefully."

Art was still watching Kip pull the last pot towards him. He looked up and scowled. "What?"

"The optional background part where he stated that his Pa was a mathematician specialising in games theory," Vic informed him.

Tre bit back a laugh but then Loy started and everyone but Art and Kip followed. Art scowled at Kip, who did not seem particularly bothered.

"We'll say we were playing for counters," Kip proposed, as if he gave up more than five hundred credits' worth of winnings every day.

Tre stopped laughing. A spacer always kept his word and paid his debts.

"Don't you dare insult me, you ugly, useless excuse for a cat," Art bit out, his every word dripping with malice.

Kip was suddenly very still and any remaining laughter died away. Tre wondered if Art had lost his temper; usually he was careful to stay on the right side of the line he had just crossed.

"Art, that's enough," the captain warned.

Art stood up. "No, I am fed up with it. First we get a dog and now we have a scrawny kid who is so ugly that no one's rod will stand up for him."

Tre revised his opinion. Art knew exactly what he was doing. He seemed more triumphant than angry.

Captain Mel stood. "That is enough, Navigator Art. This is the Willow. We treasure our cabin boys and our cats. In our care they grow into fine men and outstanding spacers. It is who we are. If you do not concur you are at liberty to request a buy out."

Art grabbed his cup from the table and threw back the whisky it contained. He looked from the captain to Tre and then back at the captain. "I intend to. Tomorrow. Ben and I are leaving when we dock at Mercy Station."

There was a long silence that Cas broke.

"Ben won't go with you," he insisted.

Art smirked. "He will. He is telling Ean now."

Tre's gaze went to the closed door. He wanted to grab Art by the back of the neck and slam his head into the table. How dare he smile when Ean was receiving news that would break his heart?

Ean's heart had sunk when Ben took his hands. He could tell from Ben's expression what was coming. Knowing it had been inevitable for a long time didn't help.

Ben drew him over to Ean's bunk and they sat on the edge. "We've talked about it a lot," Ben began. "Looking forward, it's the best thing for us."

Ean doubted that it was best for Ben. He shut his eyes. Until the words arrived he could pretend it wasn't true.

Ben leaned forward until their foreheads were touching. "We're going to buy out," he confirmed.

It was worse than Ean had anticipated. He hadn't known how much that last shred of hope had meant to him. He wanted to scream. He wanted to throw himself at Ben and beg him not to leave. He wanted to rush into the galley and bury his knife in Art's gut for stealing Ben away.

This was not meant to happen. They were going to grow old together and end up running some hostelry in a place like Promise. They would snuggle together in Ben's bunk and talk about it. Ean would argue for a planet and Ben for a spacestation. The spacestation won out because then they could receive more visits from the men who had been boys on the Willow.

"We're going to look for another Trad crew," Ben continued. "Who knows, maybe we will be able to find one where the queen will be retiring in a few standards."

Ben had always said he did not want to queen a crew, that he had been happy as pilot, but that had been before Art. Art wasn't attracted by the isolation of being a captain or by the sheer hard work of being a queen. Whoever shared the queen's bunk had power without responsibility.

Ean had to say something before he thought any more about what was happening and became too upset to speak. "I will miss you terribly," he admitted. "I love you, Ben. You are my closest friend. Nothing can change that."

Ben looked as if Ean had hit him. "I know. I love you too but it isn't working and it's getting worse. Recruiting Kip was a step too far. At least Jax and Rae were suitable."

As Ben talked, Ean realised that things were going to happen horribly quickly. Art was insisting that Mercy Station was a good place to look for a crew. He and Ben were going to leave even if they didn't have another ship to go to.

"You could wait," Ean suggested, trying not to plead. "What about Minunderville? Or even Tarrasade? We could head that way next."

Ben shook his head. "Mercy Station is better. Injured spacers often decide to retire, so there is a good supply of crews looking." He sighed. "Also, there are no casinos there. Art's never got hold of the idea that in a casino the house always wins."

Ean imagined Art gambling away Ben's share from the Willow. Part of him wished Art would, because that might persuade Ben to leave him. Ben could return to the Willow; Ean would give him what he needed to buy back in.

"You won't make it difficult for us?" Ben asked. "Please tell me you won't make the Meeting even worse than it has to be."

"I won't," Ean heard himself promise.

Ean allowed Ben to persuade him to lie down. Ben lay down beside him and pulled the drapes closed, safe in the knowledge that Art was more interested in winning at cards than checking up on them. Ean did not snuggle close; it would just make the next few days even harder.

They stayed like that until there was an outbreak of laughter in the galley, followed by shouting; first Art and then the captain. With the door shut it was impossible to make out the words but it did not sound good.

Ben was out of Ean's bunk like the alarms had gone off.

Sure enough the door slid open and Art stalked out of the galley. Ben hurried towards him. Ean watched through a gap between the drapes and saw Art grab Ben by the arm and drag him in the direction of Ben's bunk.

The rough sex was one of the many aspects of Ben and Art's relationship that Ean hated.

He heard Tre's step and a familiar hand pulled one of the drapes to one side.

"Kip won and Art was cruel to him," Tre stated.

Ean knew Tre was distracting him from the noises coming from Ben's bunk. It worked. He headed for the galley. Already he was beginning to think how much better it would be for Kip and for Rae without Art around.

Tre could be fiendishly clever.

Kip was sitting at the table with an impressive stack of chips in front of him, flanked by Vic and the captain with Loy and Cas opposite and Obe lurking anxiously near one of the counters. The way they were looking at Ean said, "It was about the catting and he wants to run away to his cupboard and hide," as clearly as if they had spoken.

"Ean," the captain acknowledged, standing up. "I'll be off then." He laid a hand on Kip's shoulder. "Well played, Kip. Remember, Art's a sore loser and he picked those words to hurt you, not because they are true."

Kip did not look up.

Ean took the vacated seat and put an arm around Kip's bony shoulders; the boy really was too thin.

Kip did not stiffen so Ean pulled him closer and kissed the top of his head.

"I'll make cocoa," Cas volunteered, making eye contact with Ean.

Ean gave a slight nod. Slipping some sleepdrug into Kip's cocoa would stop Art's words going around and around in his head while he was trying to get to sleep. By morning, it would not seem so bad.

Vic leaned down, trying to get Kip to make eye contact. "He's a bully, Kip. You and Rae are each worth ten of him."

Ean bristled, wondering what Art had said about Rae. Kip's gaze finally came off the tabletop as he glanced at Vic's face.

"We only put up with him because of Ben," Vic continued. "You need to listen to the people who care for you, not him."

Kip considered for a moment and then, to Ean's relief, nodded.

The cocoa tasted good.

"Thanks, Cas," Kip acknowledged.

Cas smiled at him. "No sweat. Art really is a self-centred prick. Try to ignore him."

"Cas," Ean chided, but he didn't sound like he meant it.

Kip knew they were right about Art but it didn't stop Art's words being true. He was ugly and he couldn't cat because no one found him attractive. Even so, the rest of the crew did care about him. The captain had stood up for him, Vic had said nice things and Cas had made cocoa. Tre, who was usually so cold and scary, had gone to get Ean.

And, like Ma had said he would, Ean loved him.

Ben was crazy to give up his crew, his family, for a man like Art. Kip took another sip of cocoa. Maybe it was a good thing not to be interested in sex if it led to doing stupid things like that. He looked sideways at Ean. Did he know? Had Ben told him?

Kip wasn't going to mention it.

He started to feel strange. It was like the different layers of his mind were moving relative to each other. He stared into his cup and decided to put it down on the table before he dropped it.

Only the tabletop wasn't where he thought it was. Luckily Ean caught the cup before it went over.

"How much did you give him, Cas?" Ean asked.

"Two-thirds, like you should for a young adolescent," Cas replied.

They had given him something?

"It's just some sleepdrug, Kip," Ean assured him.

"Let me look at him," Loy suggested coming around the table. "Maybe he is super-sensitive to it."

Kip was more interested in the weird things that were happening in his head than Loy taking his pulse and looking into his eyes.

"Put him to bed, he'll be fine by morning," Loy reassured them.

Given that he could not put a cup down on the table, Kip was pretty sure that walking would be beyond him. Luckily he didn't have to because Ean carried him to bed like his Pa used to when he was little.

Ean stripped him down to his underpants, tucked him into his bunk and kissed him on the forehead.

"Go to sleep, Kip. I'll check on you later."

Kip grabbed at his arm. He missed but Ean sat on the edge of the bunk rather than leaving.

"Kip?" he queried.

Kip thought about how he made his voice work. "Thank you, Ean."

Ean smiled. "You are welcome, Kip."

That had not been quite what he wanted to say. Kip had another go. "Thank you for loving me."

Ean's eyes softened. He kissed Kip's forehead again. "Do you want me to stay until you are asleep?"

Kip decided that he would like that very much.

Next morning was better but not good. He could make his body do what it should but none of the different parts of his mind were lined up right.

Kip hadn't reordered his mind properly in a long time, not since before joining the crew. He had only done sections and he had shied away from taking down the partitions he had put up when he had been so homesick. He was frightened of the emotions he might find behind them.

Now he didn't have a choice and doing it would take a while; experience told him that the longer he put it off the more time the sorting out took. He would need a quiet place to do it where he could be guaranteed not to be disturbed.

When Tre left the galley, after breakfast, Kip ran after him. Tre stopped and turned around as he approached.

"I don't think I've ever seen you run without me telling you to," Tre observed, obviously amused. "And, to my surprise, it's towards me rather than away."

Kip flushed. It was true. He avoided speaking with Tre whenever possible. He checked that there was no one about and made a gesture towards his temple. "I need to sort out my head and it won't wait any longer. The sleepdrug has made it ten times worse."

Tre studied him, obviously intrigued.

Kip shifted uncomfortably on the spot. "Today?" he asked hopefully.

"Not this morning. Art's called a Meeting.

Kip tried not to think about sitting though a Meeting with his mind in such a mess. "After the Meeting?"

Tre studied him for a bit longer and then nodded. "What do you need and for how long?"

"Somewhere quiet where no one will bother me. It may take a while; it's difficult to know in advance."

"What about one of the simulators?"

Kip thought that was an excellent idea; people would leave him alone and he would be isolated from his surroundings. "That would be great."

"I'll sort it with Ean and make sure the one next to your cupboard is available. Now get back and see if Ean has any chores for you before the Meeting."

There wasn't anything to do other than helping to clear away breakfast. Within a short time they were all sitting around the table and the Meeting had begun.

Kip had expected this Meeting to be like the others. He usually stayed quiet, listened and voted whichever way Ean did.

This one was different. There was only the one agenda item; Art and Ben buying out. Ean looked pale and said nothing. It reminded Kip of the way his Ma had looked after she had accepted that he was going to space.

No one argued. It was as if they had all decided that it was inevitable that Ben and Art were leaving. The only issue was the notice, which was far short of the div that the spacer code specified. Art wanted the value of their shares within a day of docking in the form of Belmenth credit tokens.

"It's a lot of credit," the captain pointed out. "A twelve stand-ards' share for Ben, a three standards' share for you and the five standards' share you bought in with. That's a twenty standards' share."

Kip wondered how many shares there were and what each one was worth. He knew their value varied depending on the success of the ship.

"Loy could buy them," Art stated. "Or Tre."

Kip was wondering why he had specified those two when he felt a bubble forming deep down in his mind. Even knowing it was on its way was a bad sign; it must be huge.

When it arrived it popped, spilling its contents across the surface of Kip's mind and swamping any thoughts related to what was happening around him. It was a mixture of memories; mostly snippets of Art commenting about Tre or Loy having more funds than spacers usually did.

"You all right, Kip?" Loy whispered, which drew Ean's attention and annoyed Art.

Kip managed a nod.

The next bubble was triggered by Art staring at Jax and the third by Art not arguing when Vic suggested that they would be rushing the calculation of the ship's worth, so it might not be accurate.

That one was a doozy; an estimate of the ship's true worth, including detail of the calculation.

Luckily the Meeting was short. Art and Ben were buying out. They had agreed what twenty standards' share came to in credits, which included valuing the Willow as a standard 14-hex-eight-6 despite it being obvious to anyone, even Art, that it was worth more than that.

The captain had agreed to ensure that the payout was made within a day of them docking at Mercy Station.

As soon as the Meeting was over, Kip escaped into the simulator. He had to get his head sorted before one of the big bubbles arrived when he was doing something other than sitting in a chair.

He searched through the recreational programmes and found a sim of some woods. It wasn't perfect but it reminded him of walking with his Pa so it relaxed him.

Then he started to take down the partitions in his mind one by one.

There wasn't any way of telling what was behind a partition.

Sometimes the released thoughts just seeped away to find places in one of the other layers.

Occasionally Kip found the emotions that he had walled away; homesickness, panic, loneliness, fear and feelings that Kip didn't know how to label. Experiencing them out of context was strange, but separated from the situations that had caused them they had less impact and passed more quickly.

Then there were the times when he took down a partition and loads had been happening behind it. The lines of thought would shoot across this mind as soon as they were free. They whipped about, sparking off new thoughts until the loose end was caught in a link and finally settled into one place.

To Kip's surprise those lines of thought were mostly about Jax.

It was exhausting but he made himself finish. Finally he lay there, surrounded by the sights and sounds of the simulated woods, too tired to think.

Kip slept.

Tre had been amazed that Kip took up his suggestion to use one of the simulators. Simulators were loaded with detectors and monitors so that they could tailor the simulation to the occupant. Tre would have a unique opportunity to observe a typed-genius.

It was very educational. Given his heart rate, respiration rate and stress levels, Tre wasn't surprised that Kip fell asleep when whatever he had been doing was finished.

As for the electrical patterns in his brain, Tre had never seen anything like it.

It was a reminder that Kip was far more than the shy, clever, immature, exercise-adverse youngster Tre got to see every day.

Tre checked; Kip was still asleep and it looked like he would remain so for some time. Tre linked his internal alarm to the simulator and set it to warn him when Kip woke. Then he went to check on Ean.

Ean was with Ben packing small transit crates. It was so like Ean to help rather than sulking or arguing against a decision that had been made. Tre leaned on one of the door-jambs and watched for a few moments before deciding not to interrupt.

Cas, Obe, Jax and Rae had gathered in the galley. Rae looked at him as he approached and twitched his whiskers.

Tre did not have Jax or Ean's skill at interpreting whisker twitching. He looked to Jax.

"Where's Kip?" Jax supplied.

"In one of the simulators," Tre answered.

"We were talking about how we could make Ean feel better," Cas informed him.

"It will take time," Tre replied. "Doing what you are meant to be doing without being asked would probably help."

The boys took the hint and left. Cas went back to preparing lunch. Tre made them some tea.

"I didn't think it would come to this," Cas admitted. "I thought that Ben would choose us when Art finally gave him an ultimatum."

Tre shook his head. "Different humans are wired in different ways. For some, the mate gets priority over the family group. For others, the group wins out. It's that kind of variety in humans, along with their adaptability, that makes the species so successful."

Cas smiled. "And here I was thinking about love."

"What's love other than an expression of a certain mix of survival instincts?"

Cas's smile vanished. "Sometimes I feel sorry for Ean. In your way, you're no better than Art."

Tre did not argue. He was, as Cas had said, no better than Art. In truth he was worse. At least Art had fought for a future with Ben. Tre would abandon Ean within a heartbeat if his mission required it.

His alarm pinged; Kip was awake.

By the time he got there, Kip was up to something. Tre tried to follow what was happening but it was impossible. There were hints. Kip had definitely accessed the ship's log and the data crystal array that Tre knew he owned.

Suddenly, the screen Tre was using went blank. An encrypted message appeared that proceeded to decode in front of him.

Art knows about Jax. He is intending to sell the information.

His cyborg systems activated, suggesting a variety of ways of eliminating Art. Tre shut his eyes and thought about anything other than killing. At least he had not classified Kip as a target. By the time he managed to calm himself enough to risk opening his eyes the message on the screen had changed.

You can enter information. I have set up a secure system.

Tre wanted to go to the simulator, pull Kip out of it and interrogate him but he stopped himself. Neither Klennethon Darrent nor Ean would be pleased if he lost control and snapped Kip's scrawny neck.

Also, Kip's 'secure system' would be a lot more effective than whispering, especially given Rae's phenomenal hearing.

Instead he dug out an interface that would allow him to input text and entered his reply.

What about Jax? He watched it encrypt and vanish.

Kip's reply was immediate. **This is his hiding place, not mine. You are his protector.**

Tre stared at the screen. How much did Kip know? The message vanished and another appeared.

I currently estimate that there is a seventeen per cent chance that Art has a conspirator outside the crew. He may have sent messages via the Stellar Exchanges on Darrenden or Kellard or even before that. I cannot check until we jump into Mercy.

It felt surreal. How in Known Space had Kip come up with seventeen per cent? How could anyone, never mind a youngster of fourteen who had never left his home planet before, have a way of checking whether Art had been sending messages via the Stellar Exchange?

Maybe the sleepdrug had scrambled his typed-genius brain.

Only maybe not; Art's desire to make a sudden getaway was suspicious. If there was a conspirator, Tre had to know who. **Can you find out the content of the message if he did?**

The answer was immediate. **Only if it is an electronic message. Not a tape. It takes a flesh and blood operative to intercept a tape.**

Kip could hack the Stellar Exchange? And what in Known Space was an operative that wasn't a flesh and blood person?

Tre found himself wondering, not for the first time, what Kip had got up to on Darrenden to attract Klennethon Darrent's attention. However, he did not have time to be speculating about Kip. They were jumping today and docking tomorrow.

Another message appeared. **What are you going to do about Art?**

Tre entered his reply. **Leave Art to me.** He checked his chronometer. It was almost lunchtime. After that they would be jumping and then, hopefully, Kip could investigate whether Art had a conspirator before they docked tomorrow.

Thinking about conspirators raised an ugly thought. **What about Ben?**

The screen renewed without delay. **Ben does not know.**

Kip's answer fitted with what Tre believed; Ben did not have a treacherous bone in his body. However, he did have bad judgement; he had fallen in love with the wrong man.

17

When Kip had woken it had taken him a moment to remember where he was and why he was surrounded by birdsong and trees. Then he had remembered that he was in the simulator so that he could sort out his head. He focused. His mind was ordered, layer upon layer of undivided inner landscape, and there, laid out where he could not miss it, was a new certainty.

Jax was special. This crew had been prepared to hide him. Tre was his protector. Only later had someone decided that Tre could hide two youngsters as easily as one.

Around that certainty orbited his suspicions about Art. Kip activated one of the simulator's interfaces and dived into the ship's log, establishing a timeline. Immediately some of the uncertainties clarified. He checked some facts against his data crystal array and then went looking for Art's personal files. There were none originating within the last ten divs.

Alongside the ground Art had given during the Meeting and them leaving despite having no crew lined up, it was enough. Kip was sure.

Art knew about Jax and intended to sell the information.

Kip had known that Tre would monitor him in the simulator. To his surprise it had not bothered him; as scary as Tre was, Kip saw him as a protector rather than a threat.

He checked. Tre was still connected; Kip had wondered if he had been there all the time, even when he had been asleep.

He sent the first message on impulse. Then Tre had taken up his invitation to reply and Kip had discovered that communicating with text was far easier than face to face.

It felt strange being open with anyone other than his Pa. Kip told himself that Tre already knew what he was and probably had a shrewd idea of what he could do.

It was going well. Tre seemed to be accepting what Kip was saying. He wanted Kip to investigate whether Art had been communicating with anyone.

Then those words had appeared. **Leave Art to me.**

Kip's mind had momentarily frozen. When it began working again there was a new certainty; Tre would kill Art without the slightest qualm.

So when Tre had asked about Ben, Kip had lied. There was an eight per cent possibility that Ben knew but Kip wasn't going to tell Tre that. He wasn't going to 'leave Ben to Tre' on odds of less than one in twelve.

He waited, breath bated, for Tre's reply. When it came it was not what Kip expected.

Lunchtime. Do not be late.

And then Tre deactivated the connection.

Before climbing out of the simulator, Kip prepared his mind for interacting with others. He wasn't sure if he had got it right; he should have paid more attention to how school-Kip had changed into Willow-Kip over the last six divs.

It would have to do.

During lunch, Kip focused on Jax. It was easier than looking at Ean, whose pale, pinched face reminded him of his Ma, and a great deal easier than looking at Art, who might be going to die because of what he had told Tre.

There was undeniably something special about Jax. He was one of the pivots around which others turned. Even now, when he was seated neither at the head nor the foot of the table, people looked to him.

Kip wasn't sure if it was cause or effect. Was that what made Jax special or did it happen because people already knew?

Who was he? Spacer; Kip was sure about that. Rich; the modifications to the Willow had not come cheap. From a planet rather than a spacestation; he knew too much about landscape and weather. Bilingual; there was something about his intonation.

His imagination strayed into fantasy. Fantasy-Jax would be from one of the five ancient spacer clans, hiding because some evil, power-mad passed-over relative had seized the leadership. He was the heir, raised to lead, which explained why Obe followed him despite being three standards older and even Kip had experienced the occasional urge to fall into step behind him. Tre, as his protector, would be a mega-warrior, maybe a hybrid who had undergone surgery to conceal his true nature, which would explain why he could jump so high at two gee.

Kip knew the reality would prove to be much more mundane. There were many spacer clans whose leading families were rich enough to provide a customised ship so that their sons could space in relative safety.

He was pulled from his fantasy by hearing his name spoken by Tre.

"…Kip for this afternoon?"

Ean managed a smile for Kip. "That won't be a problem. That means that you will have responsibility for Kip when we jump. Are you all right with that, Kip?"

Kip nodded. "Yes, Ean." He hoped he hadn't agreed to anything physical but it would serve him right for not listening.

It wasn't. It was him in one simulator and Tre in the other. Tre gave him permission to use the simulator as a communications interface and asked him to get ready to investigate any messages that Art had sent or received since Jax had joined the crew. He finished with a warning.

Make sure that you do not expose us to danger without realising it.

Kip knew the answer to that. **I won't expose us at all.**

Kip prepared to hack the Stellar Exchange and constructed a series of search algorithms for after they had jumped and he had access to the data streams. As well as ferreting out any messages Art had sent or received, he wanted to identify Jax.

Meanwhile, Tre was busy protecting the ship on her way to and from the gate. If there was going to be an attack it would be there.

Being in a simulator for the jump was a lot better than sitting on a couch in the crewroom. Kip took full advantage of the simulator's access to all the external detectors.

The trick was to take the gate without decelerating, everyone knew that. Changing velocity wasted time as well as subjecting the ship to forces that aged components and inconvenienced occupants. A good pilot calculated velocity and trajectory so that a ship arrived precisely on time and went through the gate without the slightest correction.

Kip knew that Ben was good because they had made many jumps over the last six divs and, except for drills, each one had gone without a hitch.

Watching the jump live was a disappointment; they were travelling too fast to see the gate. Kip shrugged. Later he would slow down the recording he had made and view it microsecond by microsecond.

Not now because now that they had entered Mercy system he had other things to do. He had to be alert for any incoming or outgoing messages while hacking the light speed data relay in the other gate and sliding unnoticed through the Stellar Exchange's security systems.

It wasn't a challenge but it was fun.

There was a limit to what he could achieve before supper; even data couldn't travel faster than the speed of light. The first packets of data should arrive while they were eating so Kip hoped that he could sneak off to his cupboard later that evening to check.

Kip decided what Tre needed to know, sent him a report, ordered his mind and went to supper.

Tre had set aside thoughts of Art as they approached the gate. Gates were by far the most dangerous part of any route; they were the only places ships had to be.

On less frequented routes there was the danger of pirates. Not here. All the holes leading to the Mercy system, gated or not, were patrolled. It made the gate fees high but it was necessary; Mercy Station was the only supplier of high tech medical services in this sector.

No, Tre was not worried about pirates.

What worried him most was a Navaja battleship demanding they hand over Jax. Second on the list was some opportunist from another clan declaring that the Willow was the Navaja flagship because she had the leader of the clan aboard, whereupon they would have a battle on their hands with no way of winning it. Third was a smash and grab attack where a specialised attack craft damaged their shell so badly that they had no choice but to take to the escape pods and then another vessel picked them up under the guise of a rescue mission.

The list ran longer, but those were the top three.

If Art had a conspirator outside the crew, the probability of any of those doubled or even trebled.

None of them happened. They approached the gate on time, transmitted the code to confirm they had purchased the slot and jumped. There were no ships other than the patrollers lurking on either side of the gate.

As soon as they were through, Kip started to transmit. Not that Tre would have recognised it as a transmission unless he had been expecting it. It was masquerading as the type of electromagnetic noise you got from a faulty transmitter.

By the Lady the boy was good.

Tre decided to leave Kip doing what Kip did best while he concentrated on how to resolve the problem with the least possible fallout.

Most of the feasible solutions involved Loy so the sooner they discussed it the better.

He was not sure how Loy would react. The Loy he had known had been a medico and a scientist. Tre had not been sure how he would adapt to a life of subterfuge.

Loy seemed to relish it, particularly when it involved allowing a starry-eyed youngster like Cas persist with his misconception that Loy was in his thirties. However, he might feel very differently about being involved in disposing of Art and Ben.

Tre checked the chronometer. If he finished up quickly he should be able to catch Loy before supper and arrange a meeting once Rae was in bed.

He was about to ask Kip what he had been doing when a report arrived. It outlined what Kip had done and gave a schedule for eliminating the possibilities he was investigating.

Tre was impressed. He sent Kip a reminder not to be late for supper and went to find Loy.

He was in his laboratory, tidying up. They arranged to meet in the gym on the hydroponics level.

Then Tre went to the galley and managed to persuade Ean to sit with him in the crewroom while Obe, Kip, Jax and Rae got the food onto the table. While there Tre established that he wanted to fit in a light training session that evening as he had not found time for one during the day.

Ean did not even warn him about the dangers of exercising on a full stomach, which was an indication of how upset he was.

Supper was quieter than usual but not as tense as lunch had been. The captain did his best to keep the conversation going, ably assisted by Loy. Art had enough sense to keep his mouth shut. Everyone's manners were perfect, even Rae's.

Tre excused himself as soon as the pudding bowls had been cleared. This time Ean did catch his hand and make him promise not to push himself too hard.

Loy was right; Ean was a gem and Tre knew he did not deserve him.

He had been exercising for forty minutes when Loy turned up with a whisky bottle and two cups. Tre stopped, draped a towel around his neck and activated his long-range hearing. The last thing he wanted was Art eavesdropping on them; things would get messy and mess was always difficult to explain.

"We've got a problem," Tre admitted.

Loy poured two shots and waited.

Tre hated saying it out loud but he forced himself. "Art knows about Jax."

Loy knocked back his shot. "Ben?"

"No."

"So you've got a problem and a day to solve it," Loy observed.

Tre looked at him and sipped his whisky.

Loy corrected himself. "We've got a problem and a day to solve it." He poured himself another shot and drank it. "This could be a way of weaning Ben off Art."

"Only by telling him about Jax," Tre pointed out. "Also Art will lie and Ben will believe him over me. We would have to involve Ean."

"You don't want Ean to know," Loy stated.

"I don't want Ean to know," Tre confirmed. "I certainly don't want Ben to know." He thought about telling Loy about Kip's involvement and decided against it.

Loy sighed. "I am uncomfortable with the idea of killing Ben."

Tre had expected that; even he was uncomfortable with it and he was no medico.

"I am not even sure about killing Art before he actually does anything," Loy continued.

Tre could kill Art without turning a hair; the man did not understand honour. "Letting him do something is too risky," he pointed out.

Loy poured a third shot, drank it and considered.

"We could drug them both, dispose of Art and then pretend that Art has run off with Ben's credit as well as his own," he suggested.

It was tempting but lies should be believable. Unlikely lies led to questions. "Art would not do that. In his way he loves Ben. He'll have convinced himself that he is doing this to give them a better future together."

There was silence. Tre finished his drink and Loy poured them another; his fourth, Tre's second.

Tre sipped his drink, savouring its quality. He was having problems thinking past the neat solution; dead men did not talk. On the other hand, the inability to talk could prove inconvenient; there was that seventeen per cent chance of a conspirator outside the crew.

Loy emptied his cup and turned it between his fingers. "Stash them somewhere until the information loses its value. Then we can tell Ben what Art was planning to do and he can make his own mind up."

At least the first part of that was an excellent idea. "We'll need a second pod for the safe house," Tre pointed out.

"I thought you had one there," Loy admitted. "How close did I come to spending the next decade in it?"

Tre shrugged, finished off his drink and accepted a refill. "Not a decade," he replied. "I would have needed another check-up."

Loy studied him for a moment and then chose to laugh.

Tre smiled in return.

Loy started on Ben as soon as they returned to the crewroom. Tre went into the galley and sat with Ean. It was easy to listen to Loy and Ben's conversation through the open doorway, particularly using his processor to pick out their voices.

What Loy was saying made perfect sense. He had lived in Mercy Station for over a decade; of course he knew about renting an apartment to live in, where they could stash their stuff and which were the best bars to visit when they went looking for a crew.

By the time Loy had finished, it would seem the most natural thing in Known Space that Loy and Tre would accompany them off the ship and help them settle in.

Even Ean looked happier. "It's kind of Loy to give Ben advice," he whispered to Tre. "And I want to thank both of you for agreeing to buy more shares. Otherwise we would have had to sell equipment or borrow against the ship."

Tre felt a slight pang of guilt but ignored it. "We want Ben to be safe," he replied. At least it wasn't a lie. "What's the plan so far?" he asked.

"Ben and Art spend tomorrow getting ready to leave, including renting somewhere to stay. Then, the morning after we dock, you, Loy and the captain will accompany them to the local branch of the Belmenth bank to sort out the share transfer."

Tre did not want Art and Ben back aboard once they had left; unplanned interactions could disrupt the plan. "You realise that once the transfer is done, they are no longer crew?"

Ean's head went down and Tre knew he was blinking back tears. "I know," he whispered. His chin came back up. "Then they will come back to the docking bay and pick up their stuff. Maybe Ben will let me go to the apartment and help him settle in."

That would not do at all. Tre stroked Ean's arm. "Perhaps saying goodbye on the ship would be better," he suggested, resolving to check that Loy was giving Ben similar advice. "Let Ben build a home for him and Art, even if it is only a temporary one."

Ean thought about it and nodded.

Even so, Tre decided not to take any chances. What was needed was a well-timed and extremely messy leak that would require Vic and Ean's full attention.

Supper over, Kip helped clear the table and then escaped to his den. Normally Ean would stop him, insisting that the crew should socialise in the crewroom.

Not today; this evening Ean was too upset to notice.

The first packets of information from the Stellar Exchange at Mercy Station had arrived, including a snapshot of their news archive.

Kip put that to one side and concentrated on tracking down any messages Art had sent or received.

There were two groups of messages: electronic and other. Under 'electronic' there were two thousand three hundred and sixty-eight possibilities but a few minutes' work established none of them were relevant. Under 'other' there was a list of the tapes and data wafers that had been sent or received while the Willow had been docked at Mercy Station ten divs before.

Kip set up a programme to examine the address of each and allocate it to a group according to the probability that it was associated with Art.

Then he encrypted another report for Tre, sent it and turned his attention to the news archive.

It took him six minutes and forty-two seconds. He stared at the image of the blond-haired, green-eyed boy. He did not have to run any facial recognition software; it was unmistakeably Jax.

The Navaja clan; Kip's fantasy had crash landed in reality.

Could Jax have been kidnapped as the bulletin stated? Could Art be the hero, trying to get away so that he could contact Jax's family? Had Kip's intervention prevented a rescue?

Possibilities exploded in Kip's mind, fuelled by excitement and fear. He ran after one and then another, this way and that, until he realised that he had to exert some control.

He posed a question: was Jax the victim of a kidnapping?

The more he thought about it the less likely it seemed. Jax neither behaved like someone held against his will nor someone who had been conditioned. A quick check revealed that most commentators considered his parents' deaths suspicious and his maternal uncle's claim on the clan leadership unfounded.

No, it made much more sense if Tre was hiding him from his uncle.

A little more digging confirmed that the Navaja clan sent its boys into space at fourteen. No male child was exempt, particularly not the son of the clan leader; having a successful career as a spacer was a prerequisite for inheriting the clan leadership.

Clan leaders kept their sons safe by placing them incognito in carefully prepared crews.

So Tre must have been preparing the Willow for Emanuel Rafael, whom they knew as Jax, only for the hiding place to be needed early.

He was about to prepare some search algorithms to find out everything he could about the Navaja clan when there was a knock on the door.

"Come in," he called, pushing up his goggles and pulling out his earpieces.

It was Ean. "Bedtime, Kip."

Kip quickly closed all his programmes and stored his equipment in one of the lockers. When he turned back, Ean was still there.

"How are you feeling?" Ean asked. "Are you over the effects of the sleepdrug?"

"I'm fine now," Kip assured him. It felt wrong that Ean should be checking up on him when Ean was the one who was upset. "I'm sorry Ben is leaving." The words came out rushed and sounded all wrong.

Ean smiled at him. "Thank you, Kip, that is sweet of you." He moved away from the doorway and Kip followed.

Ean waited so that they would be walking side by side back to the crewroom. "Did you train today?" he asked.

Kip shook his head.

"You must tomorrow," Ean told him. "Even if Tre is not available to make you." He touched Kip's arm. "To be a spacer you need to be able to fight."

Kip imagined himself in a one-to-one knife fight; it wasn't a good thought.

"It's not about challenges, Kip," Ean explained. "Hopefully you will always be in a crew and never have to fight solo. It's about defending yourself and your crew from those who do not follow the code. One parry might save a crewmate's life. One blow might buy you the time for a better fighter to arrive to defend you."

Ean's version made much more sense than Tre telling him he had to be able to hold his own in a knife fight. "I'll try," he promised.

"I know you will," Ean replied. They had reached the crewroom. Ean kissed Kip on the forehead. "Sleep well, Kip."

Kip lay in his bunk, thinking. Until today, life on the Willow hadn't been shaping up to be any less boring than life on Darrenden. In fact, on balance, it was probably worse. He hadn't found anything as interesting as talking to his Pa or having daily access to the data streams.

Now all that had changed. Instead of hiding on the edges, trying not to be noticed, he was in the middle of something amazing. Jax was the missing heir to the Navaja clan. It was like being plunged into a drama only it was real.

He had used his talent for something useful by warning Tre about Art. What was even better, Tre had listened to him.

True, there were scary bits like what Tre would decide to do to Art. On the other hand, selling out your crewmate was definitely against the spacer code; Art probably deserved whatever he got.

Kip tried not to think too much about Ben. Maybe Tre would come up with a solution that got rid of Art but meant that Ben would stay. Ean would like that.

Tomorrow he would send out a new set of search algorithms and start learning everything there was to know about the Navaja clan.

Then he could come up with a plan for Jax to reclaim his heritage.

18

Ean had known the mess was bad as soon as Vic suggested he come to the storage hold and look for himself. The floor, ceiling, walls and, worst, the pods, were coated with a film of oil. The leak had obviously started some time ago, when the gravitational field at this level had been in the opposite direction and near zero. Swapping between the ship's and the spacestation's gravitation field had just spread the oil further.

"They are coming to pick up the pods later this morning," Vic reminded him.

Ean had not forgotten. They could not give over pods coated with oil. It was unprofessional and there was a chance they would lose their approval rating. "Has Loy checked them?"

"They are fine," Vic assured him. "It takes more than a bit of dirt to make a pod malfunction."

"Have you stopped the leak? Is the damage serious?"

"No more oil is leaking and the damage should be easy to put right. Looks like a gasket gave up when we were decelerating."

They were going to have to get organised to get the pods clean in time, especially given that the captain, Tre and Loy have to go to with Art and Ben to the bank.

In a way it was good, because it gave Ean something to concentrate on other than Ben leaving. Running about organising the clean-up was better than a long, tearful goodbye.

Yesterday, as the ship travelled from the gate to the dock, had been a special day. The two of them had spent it talking as they packed, creating memories that they could cherish.

Art had shown uncharacteristic sensitivity. He had stayed well out of the way, even to the extent of not saying a word when Ben spent the night in Ean's bunk. Ean had snuggled close and tried not to imagine Art listening in to check that they didn't get up to anything.

As if Ben would break any promise, never mind the one his love ring represented.

A last hug at the airlock and Ben was walking away. Ean watched, knowing that Ben would stop, turn and smile before leaving the docking bay. When it happened, he was ready to smile and wave in return.

Then it was into his overalls and down to join Vic and the boys in the storage hold. As he entered Obe danced up to him. He was holding a bottle with a spray attachment in one hand and a cloth in the other.

"Look, Ean, it's like magic," he announced. He sprayed the wall near the doorjamb, waited a few seconds and then gave a single wipe.

Where the cloth had been was completely oil-free.

"Kip used Loy's synthesiser. You treat the cloth with one chemical and then spray the oil with the other. It makes all the oil stick to the cloth."

Vic was smiling. "Lady knows how he thought of it."

"Is it safe for the pods?"

Vic put a reassuring hand on his shoulder. "Ean, I keep telling you. Pods are everything-proof."

It certainly made the cleaning quicker, as did Rae's ability to climb anything and therefore reach even the most inaccessible places. Even so, they were only half done by the time Ben and Art were due back at the docking bay to pick up their stuff.

Ean was not sure what to do. As goodbyes went it had been a good one and he did not want to spoil it. On the other hand, he did not want Ben thinking he was avoiding him.

His problem was solved by the captain appearing in the doorway. Ean hurried over.

"Ben and Loy went ahead to the apartment while Art and Tre came back for the crates," the captain explained. "They are going to hire one of the wheeled trolleys." He dropped his voice. "It's easier on you and Ben. Also Tre wants to be back before the team from the medical centre turn up for the pods. You know what he's like about outsiders being near the ship."

Ean did. The captain was right, it was better this way. He watched as the captain talked to Cas and the boys about the excellent job they were doing. Obe repeated his demonstration and the captain complimented Kip, who turned pink. Then the captain left and the rest of them went back to cleaning.

Finally it was done. The storage hold, the racks and the pods were spotless. All the oil had stuck to the cleaning clothes, which, for the moment, were in two large laundry bags.

Apparently, according to Kip, they could reclaim the oil.

They decided to put the laundry bags in a storage crate for now, in case any of the oil leached out, and returned to the galley for refreshments.

Ean settled at the table to review the schedule for the rest of the day. They had only booked the docking bay for a day; in just after midnight and out just before. It saved a lot in docking fees but time was tight.

Cas made tea, Obe diluted fruit concentrate, Jax fetched the cups and Rae found cookies.

Everything was on the table before Kip had worked out what was happening but no one minded. Kip had done his part by halving, maybe quartering, the time they had to spend mopping up the oil.

Ean found himself studying them rather than the tablet in front of them. He was so proud of them.

"What's the plan?" Vic asked.

Ean pulled himself together. "I think we are back on schedule. The team from the medical centre will arrive in..." He checked the chronometer. "...eighty minutes to pick up the pods and deliver the next batch. This afternoon Rae is due to get scanned and I don't see why we all shouldn't go. There aren't that many places where it is safe to walk as a crew, we should make the most of it."

Vic and Cas started suggesting places they should go but Ean's attention was caught by Jax and Rae. Rae had stopped eating and Jax was trying to find out why. Ean waited. Jax could be persistent; if anyone could find out what was bothering Rae, he could.

"Rae doesn't want people there when he gets scanned," Jax announced.

Rae looked half-cross, half-embarrassed.

"We'll wait outside," Ean promised. "Just you and Loy and the scanner. Like your check-up. Afterwards we'll all go and have a treat."

"Ice cream?" Rae asked hopefully.

"Something sweet like ice cream," Ean assured him; he could not remember seeing any ice cream vendors in Mercy Station.

Rae went back to his meal bar, finished it and started on his cookie.

Tre and Loy were back before the people from the medical centre arrived, which was good because the pickup team always reacted well to seeing a medico.

Then, after the old pods had gone and the new ones installed in the racking, it was time for lunch.

Ean was determined not to dwell on those who were missing from the table. Instead he talked about his idea for an outing and, to his surprise, even Tre had reacted well to the idea.

"He wants you distracted," Loy informed him in a low voice.

"So you won't think so much about Ben."

Ean felt himself flush. Tre could be surprisingly sweet sometimes. "What was the apartment like?"

"Small," Loy admitted.

Ben had told him that he did not want to waste funds on an expensive apartment.

"Perfectly adequate," Loy added. "Ben and Art will be safe there until it is time for them to move on."

Ean would have asked more but he could see Tre's eyes on him. "Good," he confirmed.

It was a bit of a rush to get everyone ready and the ship properly sealed before they had to leave but they managed it. Tre had sorted out a new walking order. He went first with Loy, followed by Cas. Next were the four youngsters and Ean with the captain and Vic at the back.

The Willow's crew walked smartly rather than strutted; confident and proud but not seeking a confrontation.

Having Loy with them made everything much easier because he knew Mercy Station so well. They were soon at the Medical Centre where Loy had booked the scanner.

"Is this where you worked?" Cas asked as they entered.

It was a question that Ean would have liked to ask but could not. However, Cas, as Loy's lover, had a little more latitude.

"No," Loy replied. "It was easier to book a slot here."

Ean wondered if that was the case or whether Loy did not want his old life and his new life overlapping.

There was a waiting room but it was small; Ean guessed that most people were accompanied by one or two people, not nine. The receptionist looked flustered, as if she would like to ask them to wait elsewhere but did not dare.

Ean took pity on her and suggested that everyone other than Rae and Loy should wait in the corridor.

The scan was over unexpectedly quickly; they had only just found a place where eight people could stand when Loy and Rae rejoined them.

"It was about getting the images," Loy explained, tucking the data wafer away into the inside pocket of his jacket. "I'll look through them back on the ship." He smiled at Rae. "Rae made it easy by lying very still."

"Treat time then," Ean announced.

Loy took them to an eatery that specialised in fancy cakes and served real coffee. Ean tried not to think about the prices; maybe Loy would take it into his head to foot the bill. Otherwise the budget would be taking a hit and they would not be buying luxuries like apples in the market.

It was only when they had crossed the threshold that Ean realised how posh the place was. The tables and chairs were elegant but they looked horribly breakable, as did the crockery.

He checked the people at the other tables; there wasn't a spacer among them.

He half expected to be asked to leave but Mercy was a spacer station and they were a Trad crew.

He need not have worried, the owner greeted Loy by name and the waiter was friendly. Loy ordered a dozen different small cakes and Ean cut each into four so that people could try more than one.

Then they had a few more of the ones that Rae liked best.

Rae sat between Jax and Kip. He was obviously enjoying himself but Ean doubted that the treat came up to the standard of a Gargantuan Mega Sundae.

Loy paid the bill, to Ean's relief.

Once they had finished indulging they made a quick tour of the food market, picking up some apples and a few other favourites before heading back to the ship.

Mercy Station never felt crowded. Away from the medical centres, the shops and the markets the wide, well-kept corridors were almost deserted at this time of day. There was just the occasional trolley, moving goods, and a very few crews.

It was a consequence of the way most crews operated. When docked, mornings were for business and evenings were for clubbing. Afternoons were for preparing to go on the razzle or resting, depending what had happened the night before.

So a crew lurking at an intersection was suspicious. There were four men and one cat. Ean could not spot the captain; perhaps he was not with them or maybe they did not have one.

Each of the four men looked tough enough to be an enforcer but one of them was huge. As for the boy, no decent crew would allow their cat to dress like that. Even so, he couldn't be a floozy; he was too young. Ean was struggling to believe he was even fourteen.

They did not slow as they approached the intersection; to do so would be to invite trouble.

"Stay close," Ean warned the youngsters in a low voice. "Remember, if we stay within the code we are protected. If we go outside it, we lose our advantage."

For a moment he thought they would pass by without incident, but then one of the other crew, not the biggest, stepped out into their path.

It was a challenge.

Ean felt the usual mixture of excitement, fear and confidence. Challenges were part of spacer life. They dealt with them. It was why Tre trained so assiduously.

This one seemed typical of the type that was more of scam than a challenge. A crew with a big, effective enforcer challenged any crew that obviously cared for their cat. When the conditions for the challenge were negotiated, they chose to fight until someone yielded, rather than death, and stated that they would settle for alternative reparations. When their enforcer won, they would agree to being paid off rather than claiming the defeated crew's cat. The going rate was two or three thousand credits.

Tre had won seven such challenges over the last nine standards. The first two had been for Ean back when he had been cat.

There had been only one in the last three standards; Tre's reputation had spread.

Ean made sure that everyone other than Tre, Vic and the captain were on the same side of the corridor with their backs to the wall. He kept Kip to his left, because Kip was the least experienced, and Rae on his right, in case Ean had to grab him.

Their job was to stay well out of the way until Tre had done his thing.

"We are the crew of the Saber and we are challenging for the boy," the man in the middle of the corridor announced. He pointed directly at Jax. "The pretty one with the wavy brown hair," he clarified.

Rae growled. When Ean looked down he was snarling, displaying his canines. Ean tried to hush him but to no avail. Luckily Jax put a hand on Rae's arm and whispered something that had more effect.

The huge guy on the Saber's crew laughed. It was loud, echoing along the corridor, but, more shockingly, in his open mouth Ean could see long, curved canines.

He was a hybrid.

"I like the little one," he declared. "Can we challenge for him once we get the pretty one?"

Ean's gut twisted; this did not seem like the other challenges.

Vic stepped forward to act as negotiator.

"We are the crew of the Willow. You cannot have the boy. We choose an enforcer to enforcer challenge. Our enforcer is Tre." Tre took a step forward to confirm his identity. "To death or yield?" Vic asked.

The hybrid struck his chest. "To death. Always to the death."

"To death," their negotiator confirmed. "Our enforcer is Garth."

The huge hybrid stepped forward. He exuded confidence and he was so big, much larger than Vic. If his strength to mass ratio was anything like Rae's, Tre might lose.

This was no scam. They wanted Jax. Ean wondered what they did with the cats and cabin boys they won. Did they use them, like the painted little hussy they had with them, or did they sell them on?

Ean remembered the queens fighting over Jax in Carrefour; a boy like him was worth a lot.

"Venue?" their negotiator queried.

The choices were where they were or the Killing Square. Moving the challenge to the Killing Square was a legitimate delaying tactic. Vic looked to Tre, who pointed to the floor.

"Here," Vic confirmed. "Reparations?"

Ean's heart was thumping in his chest. Maybe, just maybe, they were after credit. The only thing worse than Tre dying was Tre dying and them having to give Jax over.

"Our cat," their negotiator stated. "No alternatives offered or accepted. We offer the option of unarmed combat."

Ean looked at the huge hybrid, imagined Tre crushed in a bear hug and thanked the Lady that a spacer always had the option of his knife.

With a knife Tre had a chance.

"Standard knives," Vic confirmed.

The Saber's enforcer made a big show of taking off his jacket and handing it to the cat to hold. His upper body was now bare, displaying his broad, deep chest and massive arms.

He appeared to be in magnificent condition, which he confirmed by jumping up and down on the spot and then indulging in a flurry of practice blows against an imaginary opponent.

By the Lady he moved well; maybe not as fast as Rae but inhumanly quick.

Tre was handing his jacket to Cas. In comparison with the hybrid, he looked puny and ordinary.

Ean felt sick. It was one of the certainties of his life that Tre would never lose a challenge. It was as if a void was opening up under his feet.

No, he refused to think about what was about to happen or how little of his life could be left once it was over.

Tre walked to his position, ten paces from the centre of the intersection. Ean tensed. Tre always started standing in the corridor where the rest of his crew were, so that they could watch his back. This time he chose to stand in the empty corridor across to their right.

The hybrid had no choice but to take up the position opposite Tre, twenty paces from him, in the empty corridor to Ean's left.

With no referee, both crews counted down.

"Ten, nine, eight, seven..." Both men drew their knives. "...six, five, four, three, two, one, attack."

Tre shot forward. He had passed the midpoint of the intersection before the hybrid took his first step. He leapt, sailed over the hybrid's shoulder, pushed off the wall with his feet, twisted, landed on the hybrid's back and punched his knife through his ear canal into his brain.

Ean was not sure he believed what he had seen.

Tre jumped clear as the huge hybrid toppled and fell, dead, to the ground. He leaned down, grabbed the handle of his knife and yanked it free.

The hybrid's head bounced against the floor.

Ean watched as Tre wiped his blade on the hybrid's pants, returned it to its scabbard and stood up.

Everyone stood still, as if frozen, and then someone in the other crew was moving. It was their cat, who was walking towards them.

"I'll be going with you, then," he announced brightly. His voice was high and clear, confirming what Ean suspected about his age.

Their negotiator pulled himself together. "Take him," he confirmed.

"We don't want him," Tre growled.

Ean stiffened. Did they have a choice? As far as he knew, the conditions of the challenge did not give them another option.

Tre moved threateningly towards the small figure who, incredibly, did not pause even for a moment.

"There is no way I am staying with them," he declared, his gaze flicking from one face to another as he approached and finally settling on the captain's. "Have you any idea of how many enemies they have? Now that Garth's gone, they'll be lucky to make it back to their ship."

Tre closed the gap between them with a few long strides and blocked the youngster's path.

This time the boy had no option other than to stop. His chin went up and he looked directly into Tre's eyes.

"It's the way it works," he insisted. "I'm your cat now."

Ean wondered if he understood the concept of fear, never mind felt it.

"Enforcer Tre," the captain warned. "The boy is correct. He is our responsibility now."

Tre stepped to one side but Ean could see how reluctant he was to do so. Not that Ean himself was keen on the idea of such a youngster in their crew.

He was about Jax's height but Ean hoped he was older. He was slight, with a feminine look that was enhanced by artificially long eyelashes and brightly painted, exaggerated lips. His clothes were tight and had gaps that were positioned to attract the eye: a shoulder, a knee, bared midriff, slim neck and delicate wrists.

His hair was dyed blond but his eyes were brown.

You could not look at him without knowing what those four men, and perhaps others, had done to him. The boy's childhood had gone, obliterated by the men who had used him. Ean wished he had been there to stop it but he had not. Common sense told him that there was no turning back time. This youngster did not belong on the Willow.

The remains of the other crew were gathering about the hybrid's body, debating what to do with it. The mere suggestion that they were considering abandoning a crewmate's body made Ean want to throw up.

"What's your name, lad?" the captain asked.

"Noe," the boy replied.

"We should move on," Loy suggested.

"I agree," the captain confirmed. "Enforcer Tre, lead the way. Noe, this is our queen, Ean. You will walk beside him."

Ean knew that he should say something to the boy but he could not bring himself to do so. He felt numb. He concentrated on walking.

It was not far to their docking bay. He stood, motionless, as Vic entered the code that acted as their key for the day. As soon as they were through and the door was shut behind them, Tre turned to him.

"Ean, get the young ones and Cas onto the ship. Vic go with them would you?"

Ean frowned. What was going on? Why was Tre sending them ahead? Was he worried about comeback from the Saber's crew? If he was, surely they would be better off with everyone aboard.

Vic started towards the ship and Ean gestured to the boy, Noe, that he should follow.

"Not him," Tre stated. "He stays out here."

There was something very wrong here. Ean searched Tre's face. It was like looking into the eyes of a stranger. They were utterly cold.

"Are you going to kill me?" Noe asked as if death was something he faced on a daily basis.

The boy's words and a gasp from Obe reconnected Ean to reality. Kip was so pale his lips were grey. Rae was too still. Obe was holding Cas's hand and Cas was letting him.

Only Jax looked as he usually did, which in itself was not normal.

"No," Ean stated. "You are safe with us." He turned to Cas. "Cas, take Obe, Kip, Jax and Rae onto the ship. Vic, please will you unlock the ship for them."

As soon as they had moved away he turned on Tre. "What is this about?" he demanded.

"We choose who goes onto our ship," Tre stated.

It was true but the spacer code was clear; they did not have another option. Tre was being utterly unreasonable. The captain was correct, like it or not, Noe was their responsibility now.

"Tre and I will find some other crew who will take him," Loy suggested. "If we clean him up a bit and get him some decent clothes it shouldn't be a problem."

"I am clean," the boy objected shrilly. "And I don't want to go to another crew." He looked at Tre. "You won." He turned to Ean. "I belong to your crew now."

Ean crouched down so that they were eye to eye. "Maybe you would be better off with another crew," he suggested quietly. "We are very Traditional. You are not used to that."

The boy had no problem looking him in the eye. "I'll adapt. I am very adaptable," he whispered. For the first time Ean could detect uncertainty in the boy's face and words.

"Noe…" he began.

Then any pleading was gone, as if Ean had been tested and had failed. "No," Noe declared loudly. "I won't agree to it." His chin came up. "So if you get rid of me you'll be like the Saber. They got rid of the cats they won."

The Willow was better than that. They had won, Noe was theirs. Not that Ean was going to convince Tre of that; he had obviously taken against the boy. Ean stood up and looked towards the ship. The others had not got far; they had stopped and were listening.

Sometimes it was not about choosing. Sometimes it was about fulfilling your responsibilities.

"I call a Meeting," he announced.

"Ean," Tre hissed.

"I call a Meeting," Ean repeated. "There is one item. Do we fulfil our responsibilities under the spacer code and accept Noe as a member of the Willow's crew? Or do we get rid of him against his will? The proposal is that Noe had been our cat since the moment our enforcer won the challenge. I vote for."

"Against," Tre stated. "The Saber's crew was involved in the acquisition of cats for sale. This means that they are not a spacer crew but slavers masquerading as spacers. Therefore the challenge was invalid and we are not required to take their cat. It is only because we have honour that we will find the boy an appropriate crew, even if it means paying a fee."

Ean scowled. It was nonsense. They had accepted the challenge, therefore it was valid.

"Against," Loy agreed and had the audacity to look at Cas as if he expected Cas to vote with him.

"Against," Cas agreed. Ean would have to have a word with him about thinking for himself later.

"Against," Obe echoed.

"For," the captain insisted. "I do not accept Tre's argument. According to the code, we should accept him."

"For," Vic added. "We accepted the challenge, so we accept its consequences."

It was down to Kip. If he voted against or abstained, the proposal would be defeated. If he voted for the proposal it would be carried because the captain had the casting vote.

Kip did not even seem to be present. He was standing there motionless, his eyes unfocused.

"Kip?" the captain encouraged.

"Let him think," Tre argued. He appeared confident that Kip would either vote against or abstain.

Ean's heart was thumping. If he lost, Tre would whip Noe away before they had time to reconsider.

Kip's eyes focused. "For," he stated.

"What?" Tre queried in disbelief.

"For," Kip repeated. "Your reasons for not wanting Noe to join the crew are invalid."

The captain nodded. "The vote is equally split so I have the casting vote. As I voted for the proposal, it is passed. Welcome to the crew, Noe."

Ean saw how Noe sidled up to Kip and took his arm as they walked towards the ship. Kip seemed surprised to be touched and turned his head to look down at Noe's face.

There was no missing the way Noe was batting his eyelashes at him, even if Kip appeared oblivious to its meaning.

"We'll regret this," Tre stated from about a pace behind him.

Ean jumped. After all these standards, he should be accustomed to how silently Tre moved.

"You don't understand," Tre added. "The boy is dangerous."

Ean turned and scowled at him. "What do you mean?" he asked, keeping his voice low.

Tre seemed on the edge of saying something but then shook his head. "What's done is done."

Ean was fed up with all the secrets. "Tre, if you want my support you have to trust me. It is as simple as that."

Then he walked away, towards the ship, trying not to think about ways in which Noe could endanger his crew.

19

Jax hadn't been bothered by any of it; not the Saber's challenge, the combat, the disagreement between Tre and Ean or the split vote.

Climbing up the ladder behind Noe was a different matter. Jax had an unforgettable view of extremely tight pants with strategically placed rips.

Noe did not wear underpants.

Noe was not a suitable cat for the Willow. He was the personification of everything Jax's mother had disapproved of about spacers and spacing. Even worse, Tre suspected he was a plant.

Jax knew because Tre had suggested foisting Noe off on another crew. They had won. Noe was theirs. The spacer code was clear. The only explanation was that Tre considered Noe a threat to Jax's safety.

Noe might only look like an underage cat who had been misused by an unprincipled crew. Starting age retard early could arrest puberty. He could be a highly trained agent in his mid twenties or even older. He might even be an assassin.

Jax wasn't sure what would happen next. Noe was on the ship.

As far as Ean and the others were concerned, he was just a cat who had been with a bad crew.

Rae and Ean had climbed up before him and were waiting in the corridor.

"Do you want us to send to the Saber for your things?" Ean asked as Noe stepped off the ladder.

"No point," Noe replied bluntly. "I carry everything I care about on me."

There couldn't be much of it because Noe's ripped pants and mesh top wouldn't hide anything. Perhaps he hid stuff in the heels of his boots or, if he was a plant, maybe he had a secret compartment built into his torso somewhere.

He was wearing a very short jacket; it was conceivable that he could have a pocket in that.

Ean's smile was looking a bit strained. He began walking towards the galley, beckoning Noe to follow.

"And how old are you, Noe?" he asked as they moved away.

Obe had climbed up behind Jax. "I hope he's under fourteen," he whispered. "Then he'll be in with you and Rae."

Rae whimpered. Jax was horrified. Whatever Noe was, Jax didn't want to share their den with him.

"I don't know how old I am," Noe answered.

Was that suspicious or not? On balance Jax decided not; Rae didn't know his own age.

Ean put the groceries he had been carrying on the galley table before taking Noe into the crewroom and sliding the door shut behind them.

Jax checked where everyone was. Rae was beside him, as always. The captain was heading for his cabin. Cas and Obe were in the galley unpacking the groceries. Kip had vanished, probably into his cupboard. Tre and Loy were a few paces away.

Vic was still at the airlock, securing the ship.

Tre turned to Rae. "Rae, I need the smaller of the two blue boxes from the rack in the gym. Can you get it for me?"

Jax suspected the assortment of boxes only existed so that Tre had an excuse to get Rae out of hearing range. Rae nodded and vanished back down the shaft.

Tre turned to Loy. "As soon as Ean has him in the shower, I want you to talk to Ean about giving him a check-up. Lay it on thick. Mention pubic lice. Ean has a thing about pubic lice. Then see if there is anything odd about his physiology and find an excuse to tank him."

Loy paused before answering, as if considering the practicalities of Tre's plan. "What of he refuses to be tanked?" he asked. "Like he refused to go to another crew."

Tre scowled. "Do your best. Jax, with me."

Loy went into the galley to listen for the shower. Jax followed Tre into the empty room where Kip had his cupboard. As soon as they were inside and the door was shut, Tre crouched down so that they were eye to eye.

"Noe is most probably what he seems to be. My role as your protector makes me cautious. Tell me if anything out of place occurs. Now go, I must speak to Kip."

"Does Kip know?" Jax asked. A few days ago he wouldn't have thought of asking the question but Tre had been asking for Kip's time and now he was cross with him for voting with Ean.

Tre hesitated but answered. "He knows that the Willow is your hiding place and I am your protector. No more. Go, Jax. Rae will be back soon. Tell him to put the box in the control room."

Tre was at the door to Kip's cupboard before Jax had left the room. Jax went to the door to the corridor and cracked it open. From where he was he could watch for Rae and eavesdrop on what Tre was saying to Kip.

"Out you come," Tre began. Jax could not resist moving his position briefly so that he could see. Tre had pulled Kip out of his cupboard and was holding his upper arm.

Kip looked truly frightened. Jax ducked back to the doorway. He didn't want Tre to spot him and he mustn't miss Rae.

"Why vote with Ean?" Tre asked. "Surely you understood it was about more than the spacer code."

"The probability of Noe being a plant is vanishingly low," Kip replied. "I had checked all the ships that were docked. The Saber was not a candidate for Art's contact or for any other clandestine activity."

Jax's opinion of Kip shifted; the only people Jax had ever heard speak like that were his father's intelligence analysts. Also, why would they be looking for Art's contact?

"They could be in deep cover," Tre insisted. "Or they could be what they seem but Noe could be a professional spy or assassin."

"It is so unlikely that it did not outweigh our obligations under the spacer code or consideration of Noe's well-being," Kip argued.

Jax noticed that Kip's fear of Tre did not stop him from speaking his mind.

"Noe's well-being should not have even been a consideration," Tre hissed.

"A crew like the Willow's would take the cat. Not taking him draws attention. Also, foisting him onto another crew bordered on dishonourable conduct. It was not worth the potential damage to the Willow's reputation."

"It was not a risk worth taking," Tre stated.

"It was the smaller risk," Kip countered. "I will show you the calculations."

There was a sound like a snort from Tre. "As if you couldn't make the math show anything you want. Send me a report reflecting the new situation."

That sounded like they were finishing. Jax slipped through the gap and closed the door behind him. There, at the top of the shaft, was Rae. He was holding a small blue box and Jax had no idea of how long he had been there.

Rae's whiskers twitched; it was the 'what's going on' twitch.

Jax hurried towards him. "Tre told me to tell you to take the box to the control room."

Rae was looking over Jax's shoulder so Jax was not surprised when Tre's voice came from along the corridor.

"Thank you, Jax, but I am here now. Rae?"

Rae went over to Tre and handed him the box.

"I'll be in the control room," Tre told them. "We need to keep our eyes on the time; we have to be undocked and away by midnight. Go down and check that hydroponics is all set for another gravitational field inversion. Then go and have a quick look around the rest of the lower levels to see that there isn't anything loose. Be back in good time for supper."

They headed for hydroponics. This time Rae didn't dash ahead or pretend to stay behind and then overtake Jax using another route. He just followed Jax down.

Jax didn't know what to do. All his training told him not to tell Rae but Rae was his best friend. Kip knew and Kip was barely a friend at all.

Loy knew. Jax didn't even know what he thought of Loy.

He decided. Tre was going to be angry but Jax knew it was the right thing to do.

He waited until they reached hydroponics. Everything looked fine. They had prepared thoroughly for the inversion that had happened when they had docked. There was no reason to believe anything would be amiss.

"Rae, do you know why Tre didn't want Noe on the ship?" Jax began.

Rae considered and then shook his head.

Jax wished he had waited and thought more about the words to use. "Tre is worried that Noe is not what he seems. He is worried that Noe is a spy or an assassin."

Rae growled and Jax suddenly imagined Noe lying on the floor with his throat torn out.

"He probably isn't," he added hastily. He remembered what Kip had said. "He almost certainly isn't. It's just Tre being over-cautious." He took a deep breath and went for it. "My family is important. If someone knew who my family was they might try to kidnap me or even kill me. Tre has made sure that this crew is a safe place for me to space. He does that by vetting those who join the crew." It was the simplest version; what would have been the whole truth if Jax's world had not shattered.

Rae's whiskers twitched. "He accepted me."

Jax knew what to say to that. "He chose you, Rae. He trusts you to protect me. He knows that you will be beside me even when he is not because you are my best friend."

Rae smiled. "Best friends."

Jax felt much better and smiled back. "Best friends," he confirmed.

Rae felt good. Jax had shared one of his secrets. Better, Jax had told Rae that Tre trusted him, even if he sent him to get boxes just to get rid of him.

He and Jax were best friends. Best friends told each other secrets.

They finished checking the hydroponics level and decided to go up rather than down. Jax liked going to the places that were usually out of bounds for him; the high gravity gym and the no-go areas of the storage holds where ship's gravity was a body-crushing six gee.

Also, as Jax said, Vic would probably do the lowest four levels like he usually did.

Sure enough, as soon as Vic heard them in the shaft, he called up that he had checked the engine room and the three levels above it.

"I don't want to share our den with Noe," Jax admitted as they hung out in the level closest to the ship's gravitational field generators, looking for loose things that weren't there.

Neither did Rae. He hadn't even before he knew Noe might be a threat to Jax. "I'll tell Ean he smells wrong and makes me feel snarly," Rae suggested.

"That's a good idea," Jax confirmed. "Does he?"

"He reeks of the hybrid," Rae admitted. "And smells of the other three men. It's because they all fuck him."

Jax stopped; he had gone a funny colour. "All of them?"

Rae didn't want to upset Jax. Jax could be weird about sex-stuff. "Not any more," he pointed out. "It was probably better than the stuff they did to the other cats they won. They probably sold them to whorehouses or slavers." Rae thought about it. "Or organ harvesters or even Snuffers."

It didn't work. Instead of making Jax feel better about Noe being fucked, he went even paler and smelt like he might throw up.

"Snuffers?" he whispered. "Are they real?"

As far as Rae knew they were. When Snuffers couldn't get a victim any other way, they would pick up a corridor rat. The word would go out and everyone would be extra careful but next morning someone would be gone; always male and always purebred.

"Are they?" Jax repeated.

Rae nodded. "I think so," he added, because that might make Jax feel better.

Jax took a couple of deep breaths and flexed his shoulders, like he always did when he was stopping himself thinking about something scary.

Rae decided to help by changing the subject. "Does Kip know?" he asked. "About your family?"

It worked. Jax looked a bit worried but he didn't smell upset. "I didn't tell him but, yes, he knows."

Kip was clever so he had probably worked it out.

"What did the scan show?" Jax asked.

Rae knew they were just talking but he couldn't stop himself tensing. "Don't know yet."

"Maybe it will be more neat stuff like your teeth and the eagle on your back," Jax suggested.

Girl-bits weren't neat. "What's the time?" Rae asked.

Jax checked the chronometer. "If we went back now we could volunteer to help," he suggested.

Rae thought that was a good idea; he headed for the ladder.

Ean was sitting at the galley table while Cas finished cooking the supper. Rae could only smell where Noe had been rather than where he was. He looked at Ean and twitched his whiskers.

"Noe's previous crew didn't look after him properly," Ean explained. "Loy has decided that he should have three days in the tank." He sighed. "Maybe it's not such a bad thing. It will give us more time to prepare for him properly."

Rae wondered if Ean was thinking about putting a third bunk in their den. "I don't want to share with him," he blurted out.

Ean frowned for a moment before pulling Rae close and stroking his head fur. "Don't worry. Your den is safe."

Rae managed to stop himself shying away or going stiff. It was just the way Ean was. He even hugged Jax occasionally. "Jax's den too," he pointed out.

Ean smiled at Jax who was helping Obe set the table. "The den the two of you share," he agreed. "No, on balance, I've decided we will treat Noe as if he is fourteen, so he can have a bunk in the main crewroom."

"Is he fourteen?" Jax asked.

"Loy thinks he could be fourteen," Ean replied. "Now, let's get this delicious meal Cas has cooked for us onto the table."

After supper Ean stopped Kip escaping into his den by suggesting that he and Jax play a game. Usually Rae curled up next to Jax and watched. This time Loy beckoned him over and suggested that they go and look at the scan.

Rae thought about saying no. He was tired. Then he glanced over to where Jax was setting up the chess set. Now might be a good time.

They went to the infirmary. In one corner was the tank with Noe in it. Rae went over and looked while Loy started up his equipment.

The green regen gel made him look a funny colour. Even so, Rae could see lots of bruises and scars. Even though Noe was small and skinny, his rod was bigger than Rae's. Rae sighed.

"We're ready," Loy announced.

Rae went over. It was odd. He didn't want to know but he couldn't bear not knowing.

Loy said the images showed his insides but Rae had seen people's insides and they didn't look like that. Then Loy started to explain what the grey shapes were and it made a bit more sense. He pointed out Rae's brain and his heart and his lungs before talking a bit about his guts.

Then Loy hesitated and smelt a bit stressed. Rae knew they

were going onto the boy-bits and the girl-bits.

"Rae, do you realise that hybrids are infertile?"

Rae had no idea what 'infertile' meant.

Loy sighed and tried again. "Purebred humans can make babies. Hybrids can't. Hybrids have to be made in a laboratory and grown in a gestator."

Now some of the insults people had thrown at him made more sense.

"So hybrids' testes and ovaries are about producing hormones rather than gametes."

Rae didn't get any of that.

After another two goes they agreed that Loy would keep it really simple and Rae would do some studying so that he could understand what Loy was trying to tell him.

"You have a rod not a clit," Loy began. "We know that because boys pee through their rods and girl don't pee through their clits."

Rae hadn't known that. It made him feel a lot better. Boys had rods; girls had clits.

"Now your balls. You can move them, yes?"

Rae nodded. He could pull them up or he could let them hang. If he was cold or scared they went up on their own.

"Most purebred humans can't do that but a few can. Right, so those are your boy-bits, as you call them. Then there are your girl-bits."

Rae braced himself.

"There's a hole in front of your anus. It leads to a passage, a vagina."

Girls had another hole, Rae knew that. "A slot?"

Loy nodded. "You have probably never noticed because the opening is very small at the moment." He started rotating the image and pointing stuff out. "Here is a vestigial womb. That's a womb that is too undeveloped to work. And here and here are your ovaries."

He had a full set of girl-bits. Rae stared at the grey shapes.

"The good news is that you haven't started puberty yet, so none of your bits have started to develop. We should be able to influence which develop and which don't."

"Stop the girly bits working?" Rae checked.

"If that's what you want. We will need to start by testing your hormone levels."

Rae nodded, the sooner they started the better. Otherwise he might get jugs. He really, really didn't want jugs.

After Loy had taken some blood, Rae went to find Jax. He had finished the game, or rather Kip had.

"I think Kip could play with just pawns and beat me," Jax admitted.

Rae knew that the pawns were the little pieces that couldn't do much. "Kip is clever."

Jax sighed. "Yes, Kip is clever like you are fast."

"You are faster than Kip and cleverer than me," Rae pointed out.

Jax reached out and stroked the fur on his head. "Thank you, Rae."

Rae couldn't resist pushing up against Jax's hand just a little.

"Where were you?" Jax asked.

"With Loy," Rae admitted.

"Did you look at the scan?" Jax asked. "Was there anything interesting?"

Rae shook his head. "Grey shapes."

Jax looked disappointed and Rae resisted the urge to tell him more. Jax liked boys, not girls. It was better to wait until he was definitely a boy with a few girl bits that had never worked and didn't matter.

Before Jax could ask any more questions, Ean came over. They both knew what that meant.

"Time for bed, you two," Ean told them. "Remember that we are undocking in forty minutes, so be ready for the switch over." He paused and looked at them.

"Make sure everything is secured," Jax supplied. "And the faucets are off."

"And the drains plugged and the head sealed," Rae added.

"Good," Ean acknowledged.

They washed up and changed into their sleepshorts before checking over the den. They were ready well before the intercom clicked.

"This is Cas. We are undocking. Prepare for variation in the gravitational field."

It was odd to hear Cas's voice rather than Ben's, but Rae didn't waste time thinking about that. This was the fun bit.

It was even better than usual because Cas wasn't as skilled as Ben had been at keeping the Willow aligned with the spacestation's gravitational field, so everything tilted this way and then that; at one point the wall where the bunks were attached became the floor.

Then Rae felt this weight becoming less and less until he could launch himself across the room, jackknifing so that he landed feet first on a wall or the ceiling.

Jax was practising tumbling head over heels when the intercom clicked again.

"This is Cas. The ship's gravitational field generators will be switched on in ten seconds from my mark. Mark, nine, eight…"

Rae snagged Jax and pulled them both into the gap between the two bunks. He didn't ask permission because Jax would insist on doing it himself and there was a chance he would be too slow.

"…three, two, one, switch."

They dropped onto Jax's mattress.

"I would have been fine," Jax complained.

Rae didn't answer. Instead he disentangled himself from Jax and climbed up to his bunk. Sure enough there was a knock at their door; it would be Ean checking on them.

"Yes?" Jax called.

Ean slid the door partly open and peered through the gap. "You two all right?"

"We're fine," Jax answered while Rae settled for a twitch of his whiskers.

"Sleep well," Ean replied and closed the door.

Rae was about to burrow under his covers when Jax spoke.

"Do you want to talk?"

That meant that Jax wanted to talk. Rae grabbed the cover that Ean had made for him and swung himself down into Jax's bunk. Jax moved over a bit and Rae took up his usual position: between Jax and the wall; wrapped in the fluffy cover; breathing in Jax's scent.

"We're going to do great things," Jax told him.

"Have adventures," Rae added.

"Including having adventures," Jax conceded. "You and me and Kip and maybe some of the others. We'll be a team."

"A crew?" Rae checked.

"Like a crew but maybe we won't always be on a ship. Sometimes we might be in a spacestation or even on a planet. You'd like being on a planet, Rae. You'll be able to run and run because there aren't any walls. You'll be able to jump as high as you want because there isn't a ceiling."

Rae wasn't sure about being somewhere with no walls and no ceiling but both Jax and Kip insisted that he would like it. "Will Ean be there?"

Jax hesitated for a moment. "We'll visit him lots," he decided. "We'll tell him about our adventures and he'll feed us apple crumble."

Rae was never sure how much of what Jax said was just dreams. There again, Rae's dream had been joining a Trad crew and he was here, on the Willow.

He remembered what Jax had said about his family being important. Jax had never mentioned family before. Rae wondered if he had a Ma and a Pa like Kip did.

He had decided to ask what kind of adventures they would have but the thought kept slipping away. They were in their den that smelt just right, he was warm, the cover was soft and Jax was close.

Rae fell asleep to the sound of Jax's voice.

20

Tre took a few deep breaths. It was his own fault. Ten days ago he had challenged Kip to explain why he was convinced that Noe was not a plant.

When Kip had requested a session with them both in the simulators, Tre had anticipated another of their encoded exchanges. He had not expected to be surrounded by a multicoloured tangle of lines.

After a few minutes he realised that the underlying shape was familiar; a topological map of this sector of Known Space. Then it clicked. The ribbon-like lines were ship's paths. How in Known Space had Kip obtained so much information about so many ships?

At least Kip was in the other simulator, waiting for Tre's questions. Tre began with the most obvious.

What do the colours mean?

A string of characters appeared and decoded. **They are colour-coded according to the likelihood that they are looking for the heir to the Navaja clan.**

Tre's heart missed a beat. Strangely, his augmented systems did not activate; Kip must have been identified as an irreplaceable asset that had to be protected. **How long have you known?**

As soon as we jumped into the Mercy system and I could interrogate the Stellar Exchange data archive. It is easy once you realise that Jax is from a prominent spacer family.

Tre had known that. Jax had to be kept hidden because once he became the focus of attention, exposure was inevitable. His attention went back to the diagram.

Explain the colours.

I used the spectrum. Violet is negligible risk. Orange is that they are actively seeking Jax. Red is that their movements or communications suggest that they are on our trail.

There was no red but a fair amount of orange. Tre wondered if they were Navaja ships. He would check later.

He reached out with a finger and touched one of the virtual ribbons. All the evidence that had led Kip to believe that ship was at that place at that time appeared. A twist took him into the layer upon layer of calculations that had led to the colour allocation.

It was astonishing. The Navaja intelligence system had been developed for centuries but it was utterly inadequate when compared with what Kip had created within ten days.

Tre posed his next question. **What about the Saber?**

All the ribbons but one blue one vanished.

It is blue because of the challenge. Before the challenge it would have been violet. This shows the Saber's movements over the last five standards. Evidence suggests that they picked up Noe nine divs ago, from a ship called the Otter that is known to favour underage cats.

Another ribbon appeared, this time in violet.

Tracking the Otter back, they probably acquired him on Jewel, which is renowned for its slave market. Given the timing, there were five planets that were raided for slaves. Noe's genetic makeup, physiology and isotope ratios are consistent with one of those planets; Idyll.

Various statistics popped up about Idyll. It was a low tech, agricultural society where large families were encouraged; the type of planet that attracted slavers.

One word appeared. **Satisfied?**

Tre still hesitated. There was still a slim possibility that Noe was a plant. He could have been swapped in for the real Noe either on Idyll or at any of the transition points: Idyll to Jewel; Jewel to Otter, Otter to Saber. The Otter or the Saber could be deep cover for one or more operatives.

Another message arrived and decoded.

I give up.

Then the simulation stopped running. Too late Tre remembered that Kip was only fourteen and had been raised on

Darrenden. Tre checked his interface; the other simulator was powering down.

He hurried to follow, risked being seen moving far too fast, and managed to intercept Kip before he could make it to the galley.

Tre put an arm around Kip's shoulders and guided him into the empty room that contained his cupboard.

Kip tried to twist away from him but Tre had no intention of allowing him to escape.

"Kip," Tre began.

"No!" Kip shouted.

It was a shock. Tre resisted the urge to clamp a hand over Kip's mouth and forced himself to step back. He needed Kip to calm down or Ean would hear.

"I don't want anything to do with you," Kip continued, thankfully at a more normal volume. "I tell you that Art is dangerous and you get rid of him. Ben too, even though he knew nothing. Now I show you Noe isn't dangerous and you ignore it. You're going to get rid of him anyway. Like you said, his well-being is not a consideration. Who will it be next? Obe? Vic? Ean?" He looked Tre directly in the eye. "The sooner you take Jax and go the better. From now on I'm just a cat who is useless at catting but good at math and mending stuff."

Tre did not know what to do. His instincts and experience told him to treat Kip like any other youngster of fourteen. Logic was telling him that this was a typed-genius and he had absolutely no idea how to handle him.

Sometimes it was better to play for time. "We'll talk later, Kip," he suggested. "What you did was incredible. I didn't think it was possible for you give me a definitive answer. You did."

Kip did blush a little at the praise but then he scowled. "But you are going to ignore it."

"I haven't said that," Tre reminded him. "Why don't you have some time in your den? Or you could use the simulator."

Kip nodded and slouched away towards his cupboard.

As soon as the door to the cupboard closed, Tre brought his fist down on the nearest surface. The metal gave, leaving a dent. Tre stared at it; at least it was an unwanted table in an empty room.

He headed for the gym, intent on an intense workout. Only, once he had got there, some whisky seemed more appropriate.

Several drinks later he had decided that it could be worse. The situation was not irredeemable. Balanced against losing Kip's cooperation, the risk Noe represented was insignificant.

Tre set off to find Loy.

As he approached the infirmary he heard raised voices; two people arguing. He activated his augmented hearing and compensated for the muffling effect of the closed door. One was Loy. The other was Ean.

"You said three days, Medico Loy. It has been ten. Ten! Unless you can tell me, now, exactly what is wrong with Noe, I am going to go to the captain with my concerns."

Tre flinched. He had rarely heard Ean so angry.

"Are you questioning my medical judgement?" Loy demanded.

"I don't think this has anything to do with medicine. Tre didn't want Noe as part of the crew. This is part of his scheme to get his own way. Don't think that I haven't noticed you softening me up. You are getting ready to tell me that Noe has some condition that can only be treated by specialists and that we have to let him go for his own good."

It was exactly the tactic that Tre and Loy had been discussing.

"Ean..." Loy began.

"Don't even try it," Ean warned. "I'm not letting him go without getting an independent medical opinion. So unless you want to set up a situation where I prove that you are lying, tell Tre that it won't wash. And if Noe isn't out of the tank tomorrow I am calling a Meeting."

The door to the infirmary slid open and Ean stormed out before Tre had time to slip away. Ean stabbed a finger at him.

"You have stepped over the line. Your behaviour is unacceptable. I am ashamed to have you as a crewmate."

Tre took one step towards him. "It's all a misunderstanding, Ean."

"Don't you dare, Enforcer Tre. Don't you dare suggest it is all in my imagination. Think yourself lucky I am not going to give you an opening to deny it because if you lie to me it is over between us."

He tried again. "Ean..."

Ean's eyes hardened. "You've been drinking," he accused in a low voice. "Stay away from me."

Tre had no choice but to step to one side. Ean swept past him, into the galley and on into the crewroom.

Cas and Obe were in the galley. Tre wondered where Jax and Rae were. Hopefully in hydroponics. Up the other end of the corridor was the captain, who must have come out of his cabin to see what was amiss.

Tre stepped through the open door to the infirmary and slid the door shut behind him.

Loy was sitting at his desk with his head in his hands. As soon as he realised Tre was there he turned on him.

"I told you it wouldn't work." He sighed. "Are you sure Noe is a plant?"

"No," Tre admitted. "Kip has managed to trace his origins back to a planet that was raided by slavers. It is highly unlikely that he is anything other than he seems."

Loy stared at him in disbelief. "I've lost Ean's good opinion for nothing? You need to sort this out, Tre. Do you want my advice?"

Tre did not but he knew it was pointless to say so.

"Tell him. If you don't, it's all going to fall apart."

Tell Ean? Tre wanted to; he had been resisting the urge to tell him for the last fourteen divs.

"Tre, the situation has changed," Loy pushed. "I know. Kip knows. Does the captain know?"

Tre sighed. "I think he might."

"And I am guessing that Rae knows because Jax will have told him by now," Loy pointed out.

Tre walked the long way from the infirmary towards the galley. Loy was right. Ean was no Cas or Ben. He would not support his lover no matter what the situation. Ean was better than that. He was……Ean.

He cut through the closet directly into the crewroom. He could hear that Ean was in his bunk. Tre could tell that he had been crying from the tiny catch in his breathing.

He approached quietly but not silently. "Ean?"

"Go away," Ean replied.

Tre pushed apart the drapes. "No, we need to talk. I have to tell you something."

Ean scowled at him. "It better not be any more crap, Tre."

At least he had permission. Tre toed off his shoes, climbed onto the bunk and closed the drapes. They sat opposite each other, crossed-legged, knees almost touching.

Tre took a deep breath. "Twelve standards ago a man put his newborn son into my arms and I took an oath. I swore to protect that child. I dedicated my life to him."

Ean gave one slow nod. "Jax."

"Jax," Tre confirmed.

"Why do you think Noe is a danger to Jax?" Ean asked.

Trust Ean to go to the heart of the matter. "We were trapped into a situation where we had to take him; a situation not of our choice or of our making. He seems harmless. It is a classic manoeuvre for getting a plant onto a ship."

"Jax is important enough to merit that level of attention?"

Tre settled for a nod.

"A prominent spacer clan," Ean observed. "That makes sense. Does the captain know?"

"Maybe," Tre admitted. "Probably."

Ean scowled again. "We will have a Meeting. We tell everyone that Jax is from a prominent spacer clan and that you chose the Willow to be the crew where he would space. No more. We ask everyone not to ask more questions because that will expose Jax and the rest of us to more risk. We then discuss Noe and we vote."

It sounded so simple when Ean said it. Tre considered. Now that Art was gone, there was no one in the crew that he could not trust with that level of information.

"Yes," he agreed.

Ean managed a smile. "Good. Now you go and speak with Jax and I will round everyone else up."

"Now?"

"Now," Ean confirmed.

Jax was with Cas, Obe and Rae in the galley. He looked anxious. They all did.

"Can I have a word in private, Jax?" Tre asked.

Jax hesitated, which was not a good sign; usually he was eager to go with Tre whenever offered the opportunity. Then he gave Rae's arm a reassuring pat and stood up.

They went up to the control room. Jax sat in the pilot's chair and Tre took the navigator's.

"It's time to tell the crew some of our story," Tre began and then paused, wanting to judge Jax's response.

Jax nodded. "I think everyone knows at least some of it," he suggested. "How much?"

"Just that you are from a prominent spacer clan and that the Willow was selected as the Trad crew for you to space in."

"I think even Obe may have worked that out," Jax admitted.

Tre found himself smiling. "But acknowledging it makes it possible to discuss some matters openly."

"Noe."

"Noe," Tre confirmed. "Kip is convinced he is nothing more than he seems. He's collected evidence to support that position over the last ten days. He believes that getting rid of Noe is a greater risk than keeping him."

Jax was silent for a few moments and then he nodded. "It would be uncharacteristic behaviour for a Trad crew with a rep like the Willow's. Instead of an attempt to plant an agent, it could be a test. If we do not take Noe, we identify ourselves."

Tre had not seen it that way. He had been too focused on Jax's safety. Probably Kip had; doubtless it was one of the many scenarios he had factored into his calculations. "I shall probably go with Kip's recommendation," he admitted.

Jax surprised him with a smile. "Is Kip an analyst or an advisor?"

Tre had no idea what Kip was. "Both, I suspect," he admitted. "Do you need some time with Rae before the Meeting?"

Jax shook his head. "I have told him that much. It didn't seem right that Kip knew and he didn't."

Once they were all sitting around the galley table, the captain chose to begin.

"Eleven standards ago Tre contacted the Willow and stated that he wished to buy in to the crew. Initially I did not think it was anything out of the ordinary. Our enforcer was past his peak and we had received a number of enquiries from individuals who were looking for a Traditional crew.

"Vic will remember that as soon as we met Tre it was apparent that he outclassed any of the others. We were quick to recruit him and delighted that he could afford so many shares." The captain paused and took a deep breath before continuing.

"As you know, the Willow has a second log that is for the captain's eyes only. I knew that individuals of Tre's quality had joined the Willow as enforcer on eight other occasions and I knew where each of those eight recruitments had led."

Tre had never asked Mel what he had thought; asking questions opened the door to having to answer them.

"So I want you to know that this is part of the Willow's tradition. Tre?"

It had been kind of Mel to set the context. This was it. Tre glanced towards Ean, who nodded.

"Spacer clans want their sons to be spacers," Tre began and was not surprised when everyone's eyes went to Jax. "Spacers start as cats. They earn their knives. They are part of a crew. They travel. They trade. They live by the code. They may die by it.

"Being the son of any prominent family, spacer or otherwise, makes that individual a target to those for whom the code is meaningless. Yet to be a spacer a man must space. This is their solution. An exemplary crew with an impeccable rep; Trad to its core. Us."

Obe lifted a finger and Tre decided to let him speak.

"So you chose us? To be with Jax?"

Tre managed to stop himself smiling. "Yes, Obe."

"But Noe isn't good enough?" Obe suggested.

Ean was opening his mouth to object when Vic spoke. "We don't know enough about Noe to judge his quality. That isn't the issue. The issue is whether he's a plant."

Obe's eyes and mouth were circular. "Wow," he breathed. "An assassin?"

"No," Loy stated. "There are much easier ways of killing a person once his location has been confirmed." He looked Tre in the eye. "I have examined Noe thoroughly. I can find no evidence he is anything other than he seems."

Tre felt rather than saw Kip's eyes on him. "Kip and I have been investigating the Saber's recent history. We also can find no evidence that Noe is a plant."

"But you wouldn't have chosen him," Obe pointed out.

"That is irrelevant," Tre replied before Ean, the captain or Vic could answer. "We are a Trad crew. We accepted the conditions of the challenge. Unless we have evidence that the challenge was invalid, we must follow the code."

"So we are keeping Noe," Cas checked.

"We vote," the captain decided.

This time it was eight for, none against. Tre had thought he would resent having to vote in favour, he was only doing it to appease Ean and Kip, but it felt right. You stood by the code and, almost always, it supported you.

His crew would help him watch Noe.

After the vote, the captain fixed Obe with a stern look and reminded everyone that spacers did not ask other spacers questions about their backgrounds.

"Will we be detanking Noe this afternoon?" Cas asked.

"No," Loy replied. "I have been taking full advantage of the delay to treat him. He's had a hard life. The earliest would be tomorrow and, to be honest, another three days would let me complete some of the treatments I have started." He looked a bit sheepish. "I confess I thought he would like to wake up with nice hair and skin and nails, so I have included some cosmetic treatments."

Everyone's eyes went to Ean, who was known to disapprove of such treatments.

"It is difficult to have nice hair and nails without a healthy diet," Ean conceded. "And we do know that Noe cares about his appearance. I cannot see a problem with three extra days."

By the time they finished, it was approaching suppertime. The captain invited Vic to have a drink with him in his cabin while Ean suggested that Loy and Tre sit in the shared area of the crewroom.

Tre knew Ean wanted to make sure that he did not have any more whisky but he did not mind. It was enjoyable listening to Ean with Cas and the youngsters in the galley.

"I expect Obe is close to exploding with all the questions he wants to ask," Loy observed.

Tre had to smile.

"It was the correct way to go," Loy assured him.

"I know," Tre agreed.

"Have you a plan for when someone locates him?" Loy asked.

Most of Tre's ideas were based on Jax's whereabouts not being made public until he had his knife and could claim the leadership. There were the safe houses, but that was not a plan, merely a fallback position. He shook his head.

"Maybe you and Kip should be working on that. Jax too," Loy suggested.

Tre nodded but turned away, uncomfortable talking about such things where Rae and perhaps others could hear. He was about to suggest to Loy that he hold his tongue when Ean summoned them into the galley.

Now that the dispute had been settled, the atmosphere at the table reminded Tre of before Art had joined. It was pleasant; restful. Hopefully, adding Noe would not change that.

Afterwards they played cards. Obe chose a game they all could play and they had fun, even though, in the end, the inevitable happened and Kip won.

Once their game was over, Tre found himself alone with Ean. Jax and Rae had gone to bed. Obe was with Vic and Kip was with the captain. Loy and Cas had claimed the bathroom.

Ean offered to make cocoa but, rather than replying, Tre pulled Ean into his lap.

"It was nice this evening," Tre admitted. "Thank you for forcing the issue so we could sort it out."

Ean relaxed against him in a way that promised a pleasant night together. "I think of you with that tiny baby in your hands, of the oath you took, and everything fits."

Tre understood the unspoken message. Ean was saying that he understood why Tre had never, would never, offer him a love ring.

"Is it true?" Ean asked. "What you said to Obe? That you chose us?"

There was something in Ean's tone that reminded Tre of that youngster that the madam had offered him a decade before. He cupped Ean's jaw with his hand and ran the ball of his thumb across his lips.

"Vic had spotted you, when he was there as a customer."

Ean nodded. "I remember him. Everyone was excited because he was a spacer and we didn't get many spacers being so far from the spaceport. Also he was handsome and he said nice things about the brothel."

Tre smiled to himself. Describing Vic as handsome was a bit of a stretch but on a planet like Nova Tremaine being whole, healthy and fit would have made him stand out.

"I didn't realise he had noticed me," Ean admitted.

"Well he had," Tre insisted. Thinking back, it might not have been that. Maybe the whore Vic had been with had spoken out on Ean's behalf. Whatever, the next day Tre had accompanied Vic on his second visit.

The madam had misunderstood when Tre had asked to meet the youngster. Ean had been pulled out of the attic where he had been living, bathed, perfumed, dressed in clothes that left nothing to the imagination and pushed into the room where Tre was waiting.

He still had not looked like a whore.

Once Ean had got over his fear, which had lasted only until Tre had convinced him he was not going to be raped, they had talked. Within a few minutes, Tre had agreed with Vic that the lad was worth consideration. After that visit, Tre had not been able get Ean out of his head and by the time they had recruited him Tre had begun to think that Ean could be the one; a queen for the crew he was building.

"The queen is the heart of the crew," Tre stated. "I wanted that exemplary crew to bring Jax into. All his ideas about spacers will be set by the time he spends in this crew."

"You always thought that I would be queen? Even then?"

Tre nodded. "I hoped so." He kissed Ean gently on the lips. "You have fulfilled my every hope whilst you exceeded all my expectations. A perfect queen for my exemplary crew. Someone I can trust Jax to without the slightest doubt entering my mind."

Ean smiled and flushed with pleasure.

It was only words, not a love ring, but it was all that Tre could offer.

21

Ean studied the small figure sitting across the galley table. Noe looked healthy, which was good. However, Ean wished Loy had restricted himself to mending all the damage Noe had accumulated over the standards.

There was a small possibility that Noe's hair was naturally golden brown and would have grown two-thirds of the way down his back on its own. After all, Cas's was naturally chestnut and grew longer than that. Skin did come that flawless and teeth could be that pearly white.

However, the eyelashes had to be enhanced.

Ean sighed. Perhaps Loy had felt guilty about keeping Noe in the tank.

At least Noe no longer looked like a cheap whore; he definitely looked expensive.

Noe was delighted. Ean kept catching him looking at himself in any reflective surface.

"Did you make these clothes for me?" Noe asked cautiously, as if he was worried that Ean would want something in return.

Ean nodded. He had taken even more care than usual with them, hoping that by making them nicer he would tempt Noe away from ripped pants and mesh tops.

"Thank you," Noe replied but he sounded reluctant, as if did not want to feel beholden. He examined one of the hems. "You are very skilled." He looked at Ean. "I can make clothes. I can cook too."

"Good," Ean acknowledged, pleased that Noe was making an effort to mention skills he would appreciate. "Noe, I suspect that life on the Saber was very different than the life we lead on the Willow. We are a very Traditional crew."

"You mean about who fucks who?" Noe queried immediately.

Ean tried not to flinch. He was used to boys being shy, not brazen. "Among other things, yes." He explained their conventions.

By the time Ean had finished, Noe was staring at him in disbelief. "No touching the youngest two and you want me to restrict myself to hand jobs and blow jobs because you think I am under sixteen?" he checked.

"I am sure you are under sixteen," Ean stated firmly. "I am not convinced that you are even fourteen but that is at least a possibility."

"I understand the rule," Noe admitted. His chin went up. "I even accept that it is good to protect youngsters." He shook his head and laughed. "You do realise that it is ridiculous to apply it to me? I have been fucked for standards. I like it."

Ean was not convinced by the laugh; it only made him more certain that he was doing the right thing. "Blow jobs and hand jobs only," he insisted.

Noe sniffed. "Fine. Is anyone else other than the cabin boys off limits?"

"None of the regular partners have exchanged love rings," Ean replied. "However, only Engineer Vic and Captain Mel take up the offer of places on the cats' lists."

"So I can have a go at the enforcer?" Noe asked with a gleam in his eye,

Ean forced himself not to bristle. "He does not wear a love ring," he repeated.

"Yours then," Noe observed. "And the yummy medico?"

Ean imagined Cas weeping; his heart broken. "Is in a relationship with Cas."

"The one with the gorgeous hair?"

"That's the one," Ean confirmed.

"Got it," Noe replied. He smiled. "Who is going to show me around the ship then?"

"I have asked Vic to do the honours," Ean told him.

Noe perked up. "Engineer Vic who is on the cats' lists?"

Ean frowned at him. "Yes, Engineer Vic who is on the cats' lists for blow jobs and hand jobs only."

Vic looked stunned when he and Noe returned to the galley after Noe's tour. Ean took pity on him, poured him a cup of tea and took Noe off to the fabric store. Noe's eyes lit up when Ean said he could pick out some lengths to make up into garments, confirming Ean's suspicion that he really liked clothes.

Ean was relieved that he liked anything other than fucking.

Vic was still there, at the table, when Ean returned. "That bad?" Ean asked. "Or should it be that good?"

"Both," Vic admitted. "I think I would have had to knock him out to keep his hands out of my pants. His technique is…" Vic trailed off and he took a gulp of his tea.

Ean might have said more but Noe appeared at the open doorway to the corridor with two folded pieces of cloth.

"Can I have these?" he asked.

They were two lengths of shot silk that had probably been bought at the same time decades before. Ean had forgotten they were there. He fingered one of the two. The fabric had some body and texture, so was not entirely inappropriate for everyday clothes.

"For now you can have one of them," he began.

Noe smiled and looked from one to the other, settling on the one that was blue when angled in one direction and golden when tilted the other way.

"But I want to see a few garments made in more ordinary fabrics first," Ean added. "Show me that you have the skill to make the most of the silk."

"Fair enough," Noe agreed and disappeared in the direction of the fabric store.

Vic waited until he was out of earshot. "He's……different."

Ean poured another cup of tea. "It will be fine. We specialise in different."

Kip had been pleased that Tre had reconsidered about Noe. The problem was, there would be other Noes. Maybe not individuals joining the crew but other situations where Tre put Jax's safety above other people's lives.

It wasn't that Kip did not value his crewmates' lives above those of strangers; he did. It was a matter of degree. He did not want people eliminated just on the off chance they were a threat.

The problem was that Tre was never going to see it that way. He had taken an oath to protect Jax.

Looking up the Navaja clan had not helped. The clan had a reputation for ruthless self-interest and Joaquin Oro Sebastiano Socorro, Jax's father, had been known to bend the spacer code as far as he could without breaking it.

As far as Kip could see, if you entered an airtight agreement with the Navaja clan you could trust them to keep it. If there were loopholes, the clan would not hesitate for a moment to exploit them. Interacting with them without an agreement was plain stupid; most of the people who did that ended up either robbed blind or dead.

Kip was not stupid.

He had decided to go around Tre and approach Jax directly. If Kip could get a grip on what type of leader Jax intended to be, he would feel more comfortable helping him. Long term, Kip would need one of those airtight agreements and, at the moment, he had nowhere near enough information to concoct one.

He waited for Rae to be training with Tre and intercepted Jax in the corridor outside the laundry.

"I need to discuss something with you," he stated.

Jax replied with a look. That was how it was with Jax; there was always this pause before he spoke, when you knew he was thinking but you did not know about what. During that pause Kip's head was always full of all Jax's possible replies, some of which might lead to futures that could be scary.

However, on balance, Kip thought it was a good thing; a leader who thought before he acted was better than one who didn't.

The reply when it came was not one of the front runners in Kip's head. "Without Rae?"

"I'm happy to talk in front of Rae," Kip confirmed, "but I may know stuff that Rae does not know. Stuff you may wish to tell him rather than him hearing it from me."

The look that engendered was definitely cold and more than a bit scary. Kip waited.

"You know stuff?"

Kip sighed. This was proving to be even more difficult than he had thought; Jax was as reluctant to give up his secrets as Kip himself.

"Tre asked me to provide evidence that Noe was not a plant. I had to ask questions and look for answers to do that."

That only got a pause followed by a nod. Kip considered giving up and walking away. Then he remembered how boring it had been before he had reconnected to the data streams. Tre had accepted that Kip was more effective if the Willow spent some time in systems with light speed data relays. If Kip chose not to help, Jax was safer away from the main shipping lanes.

Also, it had been challenging to answer Tre's question about Noe. Kip liked a challenge. He decided to try a more direct approach.

"Jax, I want to keep my crew safe, including you. Trouble is, Tre is willing to do almost anything to keep you safe and, well, I'm not. I have limits. If someone gave Tre a choice of saving a planet and its billions of inhabitants or saving you, he'd pick you."

This time Jax opened his mouth as if to retort but then he closed it again.

"Not if it were Kalakmul of course," Kip added. "And probably not if it were one of the planets under Navaja protection. Any other planet." He watched the colour drain from Jax's face. Perhaps a more direct approach had not been such a good idea.

"How much has Tre told you?" Jax croaked, only it was more of a squeak than a croak.

"Nothing," Kip replied. "What I know, I worked out or researched."

Jax's colour had returned; Kip was impressed at how quickly he had recovered. "And Tre is happy with that?" he asked.

Happy was definitely not the word Kip would use. "He sees me as an asset. Isn't acquiring high value, potentially dangerous assets a characteristic of Navaja leadership?"

Talking to Kip was reminding Jax of the time when his father had shown him a wild pony and told him to ride it.

Even at age ten, Jax had been an excellent rider. He had helped break colts. He had expected riding the wild pony to be similar. It hadn't been. Jax had been lucky not to break his neck or have his skull kicked in.

He had learnt from the experience. Some situations were far more hazardous than they first appeared and sometimes apparent similarities masked significant differences.

Could this situation be as risky as his instincts were suggesting? Could someone as physically weak as Kip be dangerous?

Kip gaze slipped away. His face was settling into the mild expression that Jax suspected Kip used as camouflage; like Rae's smile and Tre's laid-back demeanour.

After Jax had been thrown for the third time, his trainer had pointed out that two broken limbs, or even death, was not the worst possible outcome. Refusing to approach the pony and being considered by his father to be a coward would have been much worse.

Letting Kip walk away would be like not trying to ride the pony.

"Yes, acquiring high value but dangerous assets is a character-istic of Navaja leadership," Jax confirmed.

Kip turned back. "Sometimes a leader has to negotiate use of an asset rather than being able to control it," he suggested.

Jax knew that was true. His father had not controlled the Alexandrian Advisor; instead he had been forced to operate within the conditions of the contract.

"I will never swear to you, Jax," Kip added.

It was difficult not to be angry and Jax was definitely offended. "Why not?" he asked.

"Many reasons," Kip replied. "One being that I would break my oath and you would be obliged to kill me."

Jax bristled; oath-breaking was not something to joke about. On the other hand, perhaps Kip wasn't being flippant. "Why would you break it?"

For a moment Kip's eyes unfocused. Then it was back; that intense gaze from those dark, deep eyes. "I do not see the universe the way you do." He shuddered. "I want to help you, Jax. You are my crewmate. You and Rae are the closest I have to friends. But it would not be an oath. It would be a contract; an agreement with limits. I could say no when I cannot live with the consequences of yes. If necessary, I could walk away."

Kip was reaching out to him; Jax was sure of that. He hated understanding so little of the situation but he knew he should not reject Kip's advances. He chose his next words carefully.

"I need time to think through what you have said. As you say, you see things differently to me." That sounded too cold so Jax cast about for a way to soften it. "It took me a while to understand whisker twitches. It may take a while for me to interpret Kip-speak."

It worked; Kip smiled. "No rush," he confirmed. Then he stepped around Jax and ambled away.

Jax watched him until Kip rounded the corner, probably heading towards his cupboard. Then he continued his original journey towards the simulator to practise piloting.

Only once inside he found himself thinking about what Kip had said, what it might mean and why talking to Kip had reminded him of the wild pony.

He considered talking to Tre about it but then decided against it. Kip did not trust Tre and Jax could understand that. Tre's vow was about protecting Jax, not anyone else, not even Kip or Ean.

No, he would deal with Kip by himself, like he had ridden the pony.

Kip did not expect Jax to seek him out that afternoon. Jax had said that he would need time and Kip had expected that to be a day or so, maybe longer.

Instead he was suggesting that the three of them, Rae included, find somewhere to talk in private.

"Ean's asked Obe to spend this part of the afternoon with Noe," Jax explained, "and Noe wants to spend it picking out stuff from the stores and maybe sewing."

Kip did not ask how Jax knew; Jax always seemed to know what was going on. "Where should we go?" he asked.

"Hydroponics," Jax decided.

Getting to hydroponics followed its usual pattern. Jax set off at a run while Rae leaned nonchalantly against the wall. As soon as Jax was out of sight, Rae shot off in the direction of the other shaft.

Kip followed Jax as his usual pace, which meant that the other two had been there for a considerable time when he arrived. As soon as Kip appeared, Jax stopped larking about with Rae and sat down. Rae then sat down, making two sides of a triangle.

Kip joined them, making the third.

"I thought that we would begin by saying a bit of why we joined the crew of the Willow," Jax proposed. "I'll start. I was always going to join the Willow but I joined much earlier than planned because..." He hesitated. "...my father was murdered and my mother sent me into hiding before his murderer could reach me." He paused and inhaled deeply. "She stayed behind so that I could get away," he stated in calm, measured tone.

Kip had known at least part of that but it did not look like Rae had. His whiskers were drooping and his eyes were wide with sorrow. As for Jax, Kip marvelled that he could speak of it without breaking down. Kip imagined his Pa being killed; it would be like having his heart torn out of his chest.

"Rae?" Jax encouraged.

Kip made himself concentrate on his surroundings rather than what was happening in his head; Rae rarely said more than a few words.

"It was my dream," Rae began, "but no one wanted a hybrid." He smiled; the type of smile that made Kip want to smile back. "Then Jax said I was his friend and that made Tre look at me. He tested me and decided I was worth having."

So what was between them had started by Jax claiming Rae as his friend; that explained a lot.

"Kip?" Jax urged.

Kip had decided to stick to facts, at least some of them.

"I had to leave Darrenden. Joining a Trad crew was the best way." Kip knew that was not enough. "Once people know what I can do, they will try to control my life. I was careless on Darrenden. I left too many traces of what I can do. The authorities had started to look for the person who could do those things."

Rae's whiskers twitched. He looked to Jax.

"Kip is clever like you are fast," Jax began.

There was another, subtly different, twitch.

"If people know how clever he is they will trap him. They will make him work on the problems they want solving rather than the ones he chooses to solve."

Kip was impressed; that was exactly it.

Rae nodded. "Like an owned hybrid," he suggested. "Or a slave."

"Owned hybrids are slaves," Kip insisted; he and Rae had disagreed about that before.

There was a small disbelieving noise from Rae.

Jax glanced from Rae to Kip and then back to Rae.

"I agree with Kip," he announced. "Hybrids are people."

Kip noticed that Rae did not argue with Jax. Instead he stared at him with those huge, brown eyes. They had gold flecks, arranged in rows radiating from the pupils; Kip had never noticed them before.

Jax pulled out a small, stand-alone tablet. "That can be the first statement for our agreement, Kip. People include both hybrids and purebreds." He entered it and held it out so that they both could see the screen.

"I have another," Kip suggested. "People should not be owned."

Jax spoke as he entered the words. "People should not be owned or treated as if they are owned."

Kip decided not to point out that Jax had inflated the statement so that it clashed with the way previous Navaja clan leaders had behaved. He might have done it deliberately or perhaps he did not know that much about his father's or grandfather's practices.

Jax put the tablet away again. "I think that was a good start," he stated. "Now I think we should tell each other a secret."

Kip was definitely not sure about that. Rae did not look too certain either.

"It can be something small," Jax amended quickly. "Maybe something two of us know but the other doesn't. I'll start. I am a standard younger than I said I was when I joined, so I'm still twelve, not thirteen."

Kip had known that; Jax's birth date was on record.

Jax was looking at him. Kip did not know what to choose. His whole life was made up of secrets. He decided to go for something that Jax might know. "Tre told me that someone knows about me. That person suggested to Tre that I should join the Willow and not another ship. I don't know who that person is."

Jax's eyes lit up. "A secret that you don't know the answer too. That's neat." He turned to Rae, who was looking downright uncomfortable.

Kip wondered what secret he did not want to share.

"Rae, I don't expect Kip knows about your wings," Jax suggested.

Rae perked up. Kip wondered what Jax meant. Rae had wings?

"We could go to the high gravity gym and you could show him."

Kip didn't want to go anywhere near that place, not after the last time, but he did want to see Rae's wings.

It turned out that Jax knew a path where the gravitational field was never more than one-and-a-quarter gee. The variation in gravitational field strength still made Kip feel a bit sick but it wasn't too bad.

Once they were there Rae took off his shirt and Jax switched the lighting from normal visual range to ultraviolet.

Then Rae turned around and it was amazing.

"Push your pants down and spread your arms," Jax instructed.

Rae pushed his pants down at the back and extended his arms. "It's my maker's mark," he explained.

"Only no maker we know of uses that mark," Jax added.

Kip's mind was buzzing with all the ways such a mark could be made. "Have you always had it?" he asked.

Rae pulled up his pants and put on his shirt. "I don't know. I didn't know I had it until Loy looked for my maker's mark with a black light."

"It's beautiful," Jax said, sounding more than a little wistful. He switched lights.

"Yes it is," Kip agreed. "But Rae is beautiful in lots of ways."

Rae twitched his whiskers and Jax frowned.

"His eyes," Kip pointed out. "With the different shades of brown and those gold flecks arranged like sunrays."

Jax nodded. "And your fur has so many colours in it and it's so soft."

"And your whiskers," Kip added.

"And your teeth," Jax insisted. "Your teeth are really neat."

Kip wasn't quite so sure about the teeth. "I like your pointy ears."

Rae was blushing, which was sweet. "Stop teasing," he complained.

Jax walked to him and put an arm around Rae's shoulders. "We're not. You are going to grow up into a handsome hunk of proud hybridness."

Then Jax reminded them that it was time for them to make an appearance before Ean summoned them to help with supper. When they arrived in the galley, Obe was showing Noe how to set the table.

"Kip, could you get these into serving dishes?" Ean asked, indicating some of the cooking pots.

"Yes, Ean," Kip replied. He still did not know why Ean, like his Ma, never wanted the cooking pots on the table but he knew better than to argue.

The meal was, as always, delicious. It was half over before Kip thought about Noe, which probably meant that he was fitting in just fine.

Once they had finished dessert the senior members of the crew settled down in the shared area. In the galley Kip cleared, Obe packed the dish cleaner, Jax cleaned the surfaces and Rae showed Noe where everything was put away.

Through the open doorway Kip heard the captain inviting Vic to his cabin for a game of chess. Loy and Tre were arguing about who should have the bathroom given that no one had booked it. In the end they spun a coin and Tre won.

Tre and Ean disappeared into the bathroom while Loy and Cas vanished; Kip had no idea where they went when the bathroom was unavailable.

Jax proposed that the five of them play trumps and Rae was seated at the galley table before anyone could suggest that they sit in the shared area.

Kip guessed Rae could hear everything through the door to the bathroom; being in the galley might mean the sounds were more muffled.

"How long have Tre and Ean been a couple?" Noe asked in an offhand tone as Jax dealt.

"Since Ean got his knife," Obe confirmed. "Seven standards ago."

"No rings though," Noe observed with a smile that Kip wasn't sure matched his voice. "What about Loy and Cas?"

"That's much more recent," Jax replied. He glanced at Noe. "I expect Ean explained the crew rules."

Noe offered Jax a much more genuine smile. "In detail. You little ones are off limits."

Even Kip could not miss that Jax did not like being referred to as a 'little one'.

"And we three are only meant to use our fingers..." He waggled his fingers. "...and our tongues."

Kip watched, transfixed, as Noe's tongue extended from between his open lips and rotated lazily in a circle.

Jax blushed slightly.

"Not that young then," Noe observed, which turned Jax from pink to red and evoked a growl from Rae.

Noe's gaze flicked to Rae and he nodded but Kip had no idea what the interaction meant.

They played two hands and then it was Noe's turn to gather up the cards. Kip watched him shuffle. It was quick and precise with all the cards perfectly aligned; Noe had played a lot of cards. He passed the pack back to Obe to cut and then on to Rae to deal.

"So Ean is genuine," Noe began. "A proper Trad queen who is focused on the welfare of his crew rather than himself."

"Yes," Kip answered. He might not have a clue what Noe was up to, but he was determined to defend Ean. "We're lucky to have him looking after us."

Noe smiled. "Then it looks like I have landed on my feet. An historic Trad crew with a great rep. A caring queen who can run the ship and makes great food. An enforcer who can take out a top-quality hybrid fighter with a single blow. You are quite a crew."

There was a short silence that Rae broke. "We are quite a crew," he pointed out. "You are part of this crew now."

For a moment Noe looked young. "I am, aren't I?"

Jax and Rae vanished into their cabin as soon as Rae heard the water draining from the tub. Sure enough, Ean appeared at the door of the galley a few minutes later wrapped in a robe with his hair loose.

"Everything all right with you youngsters?" he asked.

Kip nodded; Obe likewise. Noe looked a bit stunned. Thinking about it, Ean did look different with his hair down.

"Don't stay up too late," Ean warned them before Tre walked up beside him, snaked an arm around his waist and drew him away towards Ean's bunk.

Within a few minutes there were the familiar sounds; this time not muffled by the bathroom door.

"Do they fuck a lot?" Noe asked in a low voice.

Kip nodded; Ean and Tre did it more often that his Ma and Pa, which was saying something.

Kip did think about sneaking back to his den. Ean wouldn't know and he had done his bit socialising with the others. On the other hand, it had been quite a day and he was tired. He decided to turn in instead.

The last thing he expected was for Noe to climb up into his bunk and pull the drapes closed behind him. Kip pulled up his feet and hugged his knees, leaving the bottom half of the single bunk to Noe.

"What do you want?" Kip whispered, not wanting to attract Ean's attention.

Noe smiled. "I want to say thank you for voting yes in the docking bay. Otherwise I might never have made it onto the ship."

It took Kip a moment to understand. Then he noticed that Noe had his hair loose and was only wearing a pair of sleep-shorts that Ean must have made for Rae. Kip thought back to his disaster with the captain. "No," he stated sharply and then realised how rude he sounded. Thanks," he added.

Noe sat back on his heels and scowled at him. "What do you mean, 'no thanks'? Are you turning down a blow job?"

Kip studied the wall. "I'm not interested."

Noe laughed but it wasn't a nasty laugh. "Kip, I could make a wrinkled fossil who believes he's only turned on by breasts interested."

Kip looked back. Perhaps it wasn't such a bad idea. If he got some experience, maybe the captain's rod would stand up for him.

Ean had been drifting off to sleep when he heard it. He sat bolt upright. It sounded like Kip.

"Hush," Tre whispered.

Ean listened. It was Kip but he wasn't upset; rather the opposite. Given that Kip had never made any sounds even remotely like those he was uttering, Ean assumed that Noe was responsible.

"Kip and Noe?" he queried.

Tre wrapped him in a hug and pulled him back down. "Hush, Ean, you'll embarrass the boy." He stroked Ean's back. "It's just a blow job."

"You sure?"

"Quite sure. It'll be fine."

It was impossible not to listen. The noises escalated before dying away. Then Ean heard Kip say thank you, just like he did when someone passed him something at the table.

He started to laugh. He could not help it. He tried his best to stop it but a small snort escaped.

"You mustn't, Ean," Tre whispered.

Ean nodded, his lips clamped together, but his shoulders were shaking, which was a very bad sign.

Next thing he knew, Tre was out of the bunk and lifting him up. Ean complied, wrapping his arms around Tre's neck; it was a much better plan than Kip hearing him laughing.

Somehow Ean managed to hold it in until they were through the galley and well clear of the crewroom; inside one of the storage rooms with the door shut behind them. Then he threw his head back and let loose, laughing until his ribs ached and tears ran down his cheeks.

Tre spun him about before putting him down on a convenient storage chest. He waited until Ean finally managed to stop. "I like it when you laugh," he admitted.

Ean knew what Tre meant. There was a huge difference between the occasional chuckle and laughing uncontrollably. He wiped his eyes and studied Tre's face. For once he looked happy. "And I like it when you smile."

22

Rae hoped he understood what Loy was saying. He decided to check.

"So I'm a boy."

Loy gave a small shrug. "Your male characteristics are developing and your females ones are not." He pointed at the numbers and graphs on the screen, none of which made any sense to Rae. "Here are the results from your four blood tests, which were taken at intervals of one div." He fiddled with the controls. "The red ones are the male hormones."

The red numbers were going up, as were the red lines on the graph. Rae's whiskers twitched. "But you didn't do anything."

Loy shrugged again. Rae wished he wouldn't. Medicos should have a rule; no shrugging. "Either you were always going to be male or something has happened to trigger a male response."

Rae decided that he was always going to be a boy. It made more sense that way; he had never thought of himself as a girl.

"Your growth spurt won't stop for a while, probably standards," Loy told him. "Soon your male characteristics will start developing."

"My rod will get bigger?" Rae checked.

There was that shrug again. "I don't know, Rae. I don't know what is normal for you. I have got one piece of good news for you."

Rae thought being told he was a boy had been pretty good.

"Kip and I have managed to programme the dia-doc, the tank controller and the pod interfaces with Rae-specific settings. They will work for you now, like they work with the other members of the crew."

Rae knew that Ean had asked Loy to do that as soon as he had joined the crew. It must have been complicated if it had taken over a standard. "Thank you."

"I couldn't have done it without Kip," Loy admitted. "No matter how difficult the problem, he always comes up with a solution. It's just a matter of asking him the right question." He turned off the display, signalling that they had finished talking about the medical stuff, and glanced at the chronometer. "Isn't Ean holding a pre-briefing briefing for you youngsters?"

He nodded.

"I expect you are looking forward to visiting a planet," Loy added.

Rae decided not to answer; he was already late for Ean's pre-briefing briefing.

When Rae arrived in the galley everyone was already sitting around the table.

The surface had been covered with a cloth with pieces of plasticard fastened to it; Rae recognised one of Ean's teaching aids.

Ean looked at him. Rae twitched his whiskers, meaning, "I have been with Loy discussing hybrid stuff", and Ean nodded, meaning, "Yes, I remember and I'm not cross that you're late because I know how much Loy talks."

Noe was sitting next to Jax. Rae had noticed that he did that. Rae wasn't sure about Noe. It was like Noe was playing a game that Rae didn't understand.

It wasn't really a game between Noe and Rae, but between Noe and Jax. Jax's voice said he didn't like Noe but his body didn't agree. Jax's pupils got bigger and he smelt different when Noe pushed back his hair or moved in a certain way or smiled. He certainly noticed when Noe fluttered his long eyelashes.

Noe didn't smell different when Jax was close; Noe smelt exactly the same whoever he was with.

Rae made sure that he approached Jax from the left, where Noe was sitting. Otherwise Kip would move from his place on Jax's right. Would he have to growl? He's only had to growl once; that first time. Since then Noe had moved.

Sure enough Noe moved, leaving the chair next to Jax for Rae.

He sat down and peered at the table. It was a map. Given that they were dropping to a place called Excelsior, Rae guessed it was a 2D map of Excelsior.

His whiskers drooped; Rae struggled with 2D drawings of 3D objects.

Kip leaned forward to attract Rae's attention. "I've loaded a 3D version into the simulators," he whispered. "You can try it out later."

Ean frowned at Kip, warning him to be quiet, and then began talking. "We are going to be visiting the city of Excelsior where the Library of Janine is situated." He pointed to one of the plasticard sheets with printed details. "The library is in this complex here. These lines are contours; they join together points on the surface which are equal heights. When they are close together like this the land is sloping up or down. The complex is built on a hill. Kip?"

Kip switched on the projector and a picture appeared on the wall. It did not make much sense to Rae; grey shapes under what he guessed was sky.

"Excelsior does not get much spacer traffic," Ean continued. "The spaceport is small and there isn't a spacer quarter. The important thing about that is that the people we meet may not understand spacers or the spacer code. We will have to step carefully and think through each encounter. We will start off living on the ship and going into Excelsior during the day. Luckily we do not have to book a jump slot out of the system in advance because traffic is light. Any questions?"

Obe raised a finger and Ean nodded that he should speak. "Are we taking a cargo in?"

"In a way," Ean answered. "Kip?"

"They are only interested in one thing; information," Kip answered. "I have prepared a database. If they are interested in it, they will let me look stuff up in the library. If they aren't, they won't let me in."

That was why they were visiting his particular planet: Janine. Although Ean was determined to take Rae to visit a planet, he had not minded which one. Kip wanted to visit the library. He had tried to explain why, but Rae didn't think any of the crew had understood. They had just seen how his eyes lit up when he talked about going there. The vote had been nine for, zero against.

Rae hoped that the people in charge of the library would let Kip in. He looked at the map.

"What's this?" he asked, pointing to a large, featureless blob.

"It's a lake," Ean answered.

Rae looked to Jax.

"A huge basin filled with water," Jax explained. "Like a bathtub but massive."

Rae had yet to take a bath. He couldn't see why anyone would. Showers worked just fine for keeping clean. He looked at the 'lake' and compared it with the spaceport. It was much, much bigger.

Noe sighed. "I prefer ships, or even spacestations. Planets are dirty and they smell bad."

Rae glanced at him. The others all talked as if planets were wonderful.

"It is an experience everyone should have," Ean insisted. "Rae will make up his own mind."

Tre's security briefing followed a much more familiar pattern: don't get distracted; stay close; don't trust strangers. Apparently carrying weapons was illegal but spacers were allowed to carry their knives because they were a symbol rather than a weapon.

Rae didn't get why calling a weapon something else stopped it being a weapon.

Then the captain took over and they ran through the procedures for drop and lift. The captain, Vic and Cas would be in the control room. Tre would be in one of the simulators. The rest of them would be in the room next to the closet.

"On the Willow, we wear suits for drop and lift," the captain reminded them. "Rae, do you know why?"

Rae guessed he must have looked as if his attention was wandering. "Components may fail during drop or lift."

"Good. Why is that so? Obe?"

"We do things we don't usually do, like travelling through an atmosphere and high gee force on lift," Obe answered.

"Exactly," the captain confirmed.

They spent the rest of that day preparing. Most of it was everyday stuff, like making sure everything was secure, but they also had to sort out the acceleration chairs.

Vic and Cas would be with the captain in the control room and Tre would be in one of the simulators. The rest of them would be in acceleration chairs, which would be in the room next to the closet, with the escape pods.

As soon as they entered the room, Rae's gaze went to the wall where the escape pods were stored behind a panel. In another wall, an outer one, were three circular airlocks. Each airlock could take a pod end on or two people in suits if they lay on top of each other.

They had done drills about getting into pods and operating the airlocks but, to Rae's disappointment, they had always stopped short of shooting someone out into space.

Rae had not realised that the big packing cases at the other end of the room contained acceleration chairs.

Ean decided where each chair needed to be. They then unlocked each crate from its current position, moved it, locked it into the floor and connected the cables. Once the six crates were in place, they folded down the top and the sides, revealing the chairs in their gimbal mounts.

Rae pushed one, seeing how it could tip in any direction, like the simulators.

Next they had to set up each chair for the person who would be using it. Ean's, Loy's, Cas's, Obe's and Kip's were easy. Noe's and Jax's took a lot longer because they were so much smaller than the average spacer.

Rae looked at the last chair. Would it fit him?

When they finished sorting Noe's, Kip turned to Ean. "I'll have to take it apart and rebuild it to fit Rae."

Ean sighed. "The specs say it can be adapted to someone of Rae's height," he complained.

"It can," Kip admitted, "But it'll take ages and next time we'll have to do it all over again because he'll have grown so much. Ean, the simulator fits him perfectly."

Rae realised they must have talked about it before.

Ean sighed. "I'll speak to Tre."

Tre must have agreed because the sixth chair was packed away while Rae put his suit on so that he and Tre could calibrate the simulator.

"I wanted you with the others," Tre explained as they created a new setting and labelled it 'Rae suited'.

Rae understood what that meant. Drop and lift were potentially dangerous. Given that Tre had to be in one of the simulators, he had wanted Rae next to Jax.

He took it as a compliment; Tre trusted him to protect Jax.

Next morning they were up early. Breakfast was soon over; everyone other than Rae was being careful not to eat too much in case the variation in gee force made them throw up.

Once everyone was suited and checked, Tre escorted Rae to the simulator.

"Drop takes a long time," Tre reminded him. "Keep yourself busy," he advised.

Rae tried. He started by reviewing their trajectory, which had been worked out to minimise friction between the atmosphere and the outer skin of the Willow. Second he looked at the planet, but he and Jax had done that the previous day and there was nothing new to see. After that he studied Kip's 3D map of Excelsior, which made more sense than Ean's 2D version but still contained lots of shapes he didn't understand.

Then he looked through the vids Kip had found; the ones of Janine in general and Excelsior in particular. That was interesting until he found images of non-human animals. Rae wasn't sure what he felt about non-human animals, particularly canines like dogs and wolves.

He switched the vid off and brought up the diagram showing their trajectory; drop was less than one-tenth over.

Tre had not been kidding; drop took a long time. It was also very boring.

He decided to alternate between training sims and games. Every time he switched between the two he would check where they were.

Maybe it was good that he was in the simulator. Rae wasn't sure he would have coped in an acceleration chair with nothing to do.

About two-thirds through, Tre's voice came over the dedicated channel between the two simulators.

"Rae, you might want to watch the live feed."

One glance and Rae forgot about being bored. Some of the cameras showed a bright blue background streaked with white. Others showed a fast-moving, shimmering, flat expanse that suddenly gave way to greys and greens and browns.

Then, all at once, he understood: above him was sky; below him was land. They were travelling fast, nose fast, and Rae had to resist the urge to run.

"This is the captain. We are going to have to shed some velocity before landing."

They had to use the rockets and it was, as the captain had warned, rough. Rae concentrated on the images of the land, picking out trees and rock and areas of green that might be grass.

Then they were over more of the flat, shimmering surface and Rae guessed it was the lake Jax had told him about. Had the larger expanse been water too?

A final manoeuvre to put them tail down, the vibration of the legs being extended and they touched down.

"This is the captain. We are safely down. You may unbuckle."

Rae wondered what a buckle was and had one last glance at his surroundings through each camera as he powered down the simulator. He could see some other spacecraft and, between them, views of the lake, mountains and distant buildings.

He was beside Jax before Jax was out of his chair.

"What's it like?" Jax asked. He sounded and smelt excited, which was good, because they could be excited together.

Rae did not know what to say. "Big," he decided. "With lots of colours."

"Can we open the airlock?" Jax asked.

Ean smiled. "I imagine Tre is already doing so."

Rae tried to go slowly enough for Jax to keep up with him, at least until Jax told him to go ahead. Tre was at the airlock, running through the checks that were required before they could open the inner and outer airlock doors at the same time.

"It's different when it's real rather than an image," he warned. "You may take a while to get used to the open sky."

Tre waited until Jax was there and then opened both doors. Rae had intended to dash forward but was stopped by the inward draft of air.

Such smells; a few were familiar but most were entirely new. He took a deep breath and then crept forward and peered out.

It wasn't big, it was huge. Space was huge but space was empty. This was full of stuff. Upwards was the sky, which was bright blue.

"Don't look directly at the sun," Tre warned. "It will overload your retinas."

"Can we go outside?" Jax asked.

"No," Ean answered firmly, "I want you to wait until Tre, the captain and I are back from checking in with the authorities."

Rae looked out the open door and then back at Ean in disbelief.

"It's a safe planet," Tre pointed out. "Let Vic and the captain go. They can take Loy. A medico is always welcome. Meanwhile we can throw together a picnic and take the youngsters down to the lake."

Ean hesitated. Rae knew he considered it the queen's duty to meet the local officials.

"Very well," he agreed. "This once." He smiled. "You and Jax can wait here with Tre. It won't take long for Cas, Obe, Kip, Noe and I to pack a few baskets."

They watched the captain, Vic and Loy climb down the ladder and walk away. Then the two of them sat in the airlock, close to the outer edge. Rae's attention kept being caught by things that moved: clouds; waves; trees; birds.

Birds were best; Rae wished his wings were real, so that he could fly.

The picnic was soon ready. Tre went first. He clambered out of the airlock onto the ladder and climbed down. Jax was next. Rae followed. As he left the airlock he realised that the air outside was moving. He tensed, because moving air meant a leak.

"It's the wind," Obe called from within the ship, as if reading his mind. "Air moves on a planet. It's safe."

Rae guessed that Obe understood because he was also from a spacestation.

He paused at the top of the ladder. As well as all the new smells, there were strange sounds beyond the familiar hum from the ship.

"Come on, Rae," Jax called.

Climbing down the ladder he felt something warm on his back and the soft touch of the moving air in his fur and against his skin. Instead of jumping the last seven or eight rungs, he continued down and stepped tentatively onto the flat but rough grey surface,

"Concrete," Jax told him. "You pour it like a liquid, so it gives a flat surface when it sets. You need it to be flat to land the ship."

Rae looked at the ship towering about him. From this view point it was huge. Only Jax wasn't interested in the ship. He was heading in the direction of the lake.

"Jax!" Tre called.

Jax turned and reluctantly came back.

Once everyone was down the ladder, they walked towards the lake. Between the concrete slabs was short grass with lots of other plants mixed in with it. There were even tiny flowers.

Then, without having to cross a barrier, all the concrete was behind them and there was only a grassy slope leading down to the water. Rae was being bombarded with new smells, sounds and sights. It was making him feel lightheaded.

"You all right?" Jax asked.

Rae stared at him for a moment and then nodded.

"You should take your shoes off," Kip advised.

Rae glanced at Tre; Kip's ideas were sometimes less than practical.

Tre considered and then nodded.

Rae lifted his left foot to pull off his shoe. Then he put it down, intending to lift the other. Instead he just stood there, one shoe on and the other off.

The ground against his left sole felt weird. It wasn't smooth or uniformly rough. He could feel the tiny stems and leaves. He wiggled his toes, burrowing them through the carpet of plants to the ground beneath. What was it? Substrate? Growing medium? He remembered a word from lessons: soil?

"Rae?" Jax queried.

Rae realised that the others had stopped and were waiting for him. He pulled off his other shoe and resumed walking, relishing the sensation of living ground under the soles of his feet.

"The land speaks to you," Jax suggested.

Planets didn't speak but, weirdly, Rae understood. He nodded.

Jax looked out over the lake and then up at the mountains. "It speaks but, for me, it is not the language of home."

Rae had to think about that but he thought that he got it; Jax's home planet did not smell, sound and look like this one.

They walked a little further, to where the grass started to slope down towards the lake, and then sat down. Rae sat next to Jax, Kip with Noe and Obe with Cas. Tre did not sit; he lurked.

"You are very quiet," Jax observed.

Rae had too much to see, smell and hear to spare a thought for words. He settled for a nod and a whisker twitch.

He inhaled the air brought to him by the breeze and studied the others. Kip was sprawled on his back, eyes closed, enjoying the sun on his skin. Cas was on his front, looking out over the lake. Obe seemed less comfortable. He was wearing a cloth hat with a wide brim that he must have brought from the ship. Noe was picking flowers and doing something with them.

"What's Noe doing?" he asked.

"Making daisy chains," Jax replied.

Rae heard the disapproval in Jax's voice and responded with a whisker twitch.

Jax sighed. "It's something little girls do," he explained in a whisper that only Rae could hear.

Rae watched Noe link the flowers together by their stems, making circles that he put around his wrists and one of Kip's ankles.

Kip did not seem to mind. Rae had noticed that Kip wasn't as worried as Jax about 'girly' behaviours. Maybe Kip liked girls. Given the noises that occasionally came from Kip's bunk, he liked Noe.

Only Noe seemed to prefer Jax. Certainly he didn't try to get Kip to notice him the way he did with Jax. Rae imagined Noe with Jax in Jax's bunk and growled.

Tre was immediately on full alert, checking their surroundings.

"Rae?" Jax demanded.

Rae felt his skin warm with more than the sun. "I thought of something."

Tre settled and Jax looked at him. Rae wondered what he would say if Jax asked what he had been thinking. Could he tell the truth? Could he lie?

Only Jax did not ask. It was as if he knew Rae wouldn't want to answer.

Then the captain, Vic and Loy were back. Apparently there wasn't a harbourmaster. Instead they had registered with local security, who were called police.

"Their rules seem straightforward," the captain told them. "Usual stuff. No fighting, no stealing, no damaging property and treat their people with respect."

"An excellent choice for a vacation," Ean acknowledged. "Well done Kip."

Vic said they had passed a place that would be good for their picnic, so they moved. There were some benches, a table and a structure that jutted out into the lake and had a ladder going down into the water. Jax called it a pier. There was a small sign. Rae concentrated on the letters but Jax read the words out loud before Rae could work them out.

"Picnic and swimming site. No diving. No fishing. No nudity. Please take your rubbish home with you."

Rae had to ask Jax what 'nudity' meant and he explained that they would have to wear shorts when they went swimming. That was when Rae realised that by swimming Jax meant going into the water.

He couldn't see himself doing that any time soon.

Picnics, Rae decided, were fun. There was lots of food. Ean let everyone eat wearing only shorts, when in the ship he insisted they wore shirts and shoes as well. Kip had made them Rae-friendly sunblock that didn't stink. Rae let Jax rub some into his back and then did the same for Jax.

He liked the way Jax's skin felt; smooth and warm.

After a while even Tre began to relax.

Ean wouldn't let Jax and Kip go swimming just after they had eaten, so they played a game of catch on the bank. Rae remembered the lessons he had learned from playing with purebred children at the orphanage, so he didn't throw too hard or too accurately.

Running about was fun. Rae would have liked to run further but that would have meant leaving Jax.

Then, without warning, Jax ran down the pier and jumped into the water. The water closed over his head. He had vanished.

Rae had only one thought; Jax was missing and he had to find him. He accelerated, sprinting across the bank and onto the pier.

"Rae! No!" someone yelled; it was Tre.

Then Jax's head reappeared some distance away, only Rae was going too fast to stop; he had run out of pier and was over the lake.

He crashed through the surface of the water. It was shockingly cold. He was tumbling slowing; sinking downwards. The water pressed against his arms and legs, making it difficult to move. He couldn't see much. Sounds were weirdly low. Worst, he couldn't breathe.

He refused to panic. Which way was up? One way was lighter. He pushed with his arms and legs against the water, stopping his rotation. Then he pushed again, heading towards the light.

His head broke the surface. He could see Jax moving through the water towards him, propelling himself by kicking his legs and steering with his arms. Tre was crouched on the edge of the pier, looking down at him.

"Grab him before he goes under again!" Ean shouted.

Rae had no intention of going under again. If he pushed downwards against the water with his arms and legs he could keep his head above the water.

Tre smiled. "He's fine."

Rae wasn't sure if he would go that far.

He managed to navigate to the ladder and climb out. Jax followed behind.

"Next time, warn Rae that you are going to do something," Tre told Jax. He turned to Rae. "Rae, think before you act. If Jax had been in danger, what you did wouldn't have helped."

"Yes, Tre," they both replied.

Tre smiled again; he had obviously found the whole incident amusing. "I'll calm Ean down. Rae, if you want to go back into the water you should let Jax and Kip teach you how to swim."

Rae decided that swimming lessons could wait until another day, although watching others do it was interesting. There were lots of different techniques; Jax alone could swim three different ways.

Finally Ean decided that the picnic was over and they trekked back to the ship. Rae didn't want to admit it but he was tired;

there had been so many new things. He would be content to go to bed after supper.

Mealtime was usually quiet; Rae guessed that he wasn't the only one who was tired.

"Still think planets are dirty and smell bad?" Kip asked Noe.

Noe sniffed. "It does not smell bad," he conceded.

"And what did you think, Rae?" Ean asked.

Rae didn't hesitate. "Planets are fun."

23

Tre had chosen to set a fast pace as they climbed the steep, cobbled streets to the library. Kip was struggling to keep up and wondering if Tre would substitute the journey for a session in the gym. He doubted it.

Finally, thankfully, they arrived. The outer door was huge; constructed of wooden slabs bound with iron. Kip speculated about the choice of materials. Like those making up the cobbled streets and the stone buildings, it was as if they had been selected to reflect another time and perhaps another place. Or maybe it was not that. Perhaps here, in these mountains on this planet, those materials were the obvious choice.

"Are you going to knock?" Tre asked. "Or just stare at the door?"

Kip lifted the heavy, cast iron knocker and allowed it to drop onto the underlying plate. The sound was surprisingly loud.

A small shutter in the door slid open, revealing a grille and a pair of eyes.

"Yes?"

Kip had been thrown by the eyes, which were gooseberry green with vertical slits rather than circles for pupils. He pulled himself together. "I want to use the library. Please," he added as an afterthought.

The only answer was the shutter being closed and then silence.

"He or she is walking away," Tre told him. "I can hear footsteps."

Kip couldn't but he knew his listening skills were poor. He hoped that the doorkeeper had gone to fetch someone.

They waited. Finally Tre spoke. "Someone is coming."

The shutter was drawn back. The green, cat-like eyes looked out. "You can come in." His eyes flicked to Tre. "Not him."

"We are spacers," Tre replied. He gestured towards Kip. "He is our cat. He cannot go somewhere without being escorted by a member of his crew."

The shutter closed again without a response.

They waited again. This time there was no response after double the time.

"Do you think I should knock again?" Kip asked.

"No point," Tre replied. "Someone is coming."

After another wait the shutter was opened. Watery blue eyes in a wrinkled face appeared. "The boy can enter with a different escort," he told them. He looked at Tre. "Not you and not another like you. You know why." The shutter closed.

Kip looked at Tre. What did the man mean? What did he know about Tre and how?

"Back to the ship," Tre told him.

"But…" Kip trailed off. He really wanted to go inside. He was so close. Even so, he knew there was no point in arguing.

Halfway down the hill Kip decided to ask.

"Can I go back with someone else?"

Tre did not answer for another ten paces. Finally he spoke. "I'll talk to Ean."

Whatever Tre said to Ean, it made him angry. Within twenty minutes the whole crew, even the captain, were dressed neatly and walking up the hill.

Kip didn't like to think what the others thought about visiting a library rather than playing on the banks of the lake.

Ean knocked twice. When the shutter slid open, revealing the now familiar pair of cat-like eyes, he spoke immediately.

"My name is Ean. I am queen of the Willow. This is my crew. I wish to speak to the gentleman who spoke to a member of our crew earlier today."

Kip wasn't sure why Ean thought turning up mob-handed was a good idea but when Ean was annoyed it was best not to argue.

They waited. Finally the shutter opened and the owner of the watery blue eyes peered out.

Ean did not wait for him to speak. "My name is Ean. I am queen of the Willow. This is the Willow's crew. We wish to be admitted to your outer receiving room to discuss the circumstances under which our cat, Kip, might be able to use the library. We give you our word that we will behave honourably and appropriately."

To Kip's amazement, a person-sized door within one of the huge doors was opened by the cat hybrid. The blue-eyed man, who was very old and stooped, gestured them inside.

Both of them were wearing exactly the same shade of grey.

The cat hybrid hissed as Rae stepped through the door; Rae growled in return.

The old man chuckled. "Shame on you, Leo. I expect you to treat all visitors with respect."

They were shown to a medium sized room with a wooden floor, wooden chairs and wooden tables. As soon as they were all inside Ean had another go at a formal introduction; he was obviously trying to get the old man's name.

"My name is Ean," he repeated. "I am queen of the Willow. This is our captain, Mel, our engineer, Vic, our enforcer, Tre, our pilot, Cas, and our medico, Loy. These are the young-sters in our care, one of whom is Kip, who wishes to use your library."

"Not our library, we are merely its custodians," the old man replied. He paused. Ean waited expectantly. "I am Researcher Bernard," he told them. "This is Junior Assistant Researcher Leo. We are librarians. Does Kip wish to become a librarian?"

Kip's heart fell; he had been sure they allowed outsiders to use the library.

"Kip is entrusted into our care," Ean answered. "He will remain a member of this crew until he has gained his knife and is mature enough to take decisions for himself. We under-stood that it was possible to use the library without becoming a librarian. If it is not, we shall leave."

"I have information to offer," Kip added, risking a frown from Ean. He knew that he was not meant to speak; this was a formal negotiation, like a trade. On the other hand, cats were not usually named to outsiders and Ean had introduced him.

The old man studied him. Kip felt himself flushing but he looked back, making eye contact. Researcher Bernard nodded.

"We will consider what you have to offer," he confirmed. "You have made a good start. Throughout the library's recorded history, it has never been visited by a Traditional spacer crew. The occurrence of his event is, in itself, information of interest."

Kip had not considered that possibility; it explained why they had been admitted as a crew when Tre had been turned away.

Researcher Bernard continued, "Junior Assistant Researcher Leo will ask another librarian to select and bring an assortment of books for the other members of your crew to peruse while you and I discuss your other offerings."

Kip decided to show Researcher Bernard the structure of the database first. He reached into his pocket and brought out the equipment he had built; a pair of spectacles with built in earpieces that incorporated a data crystal wafer reader into one sidearm and a dedicated pre-programme processor into the other.

"You have to put them on," he hinted.

Researcher Bernard extended the side arms and put the spectacles on.

"You touch the button close to the right hand hinge to activate them," Kip added.

He watched the old man smile and then nod before, hopefully, becoming lost in the database Kip had constructed and populated.

Kip was proud of the technology in the lenses. When you wore them it was like you were looking at a screen that filled your field of view. His attention had been captured by the concept six standards ago, just after he had completed his network on Darrenden and had gained access to the light speed relay. It had been proposed by a young woman with no means of making her idea a reality.

So Kip had made it happen. Now there was a company producing the lenses. Kip, indirectly, owned three-fifths of it. The company was finally beginning to turn a profit but Kip doubted he would ever make back the credit he had poured into it. Even so, the lenses were really neat. He used them for his goggles and they had been the obvious choice for these spectacles.

Finally Researcher Bernard sighed and removed the spectacles.

"You built these yourself?" Researcher Bernard checked.

Kip nodded. "From commercially available components." Then he began thinking about all the parts that linked the components together. "Mostly," he clarified.

"And the design of the database?"

"Mine," Kip admitted.

"And what's in it?"

"I found it," Kip told him. "I like looking for data. You probably have all that information in the library already."

"Most of it," Researcher Bernard acknowledged. "How many pieces do you think we might not have?"

Kip flushed. "Three."

The old man chuckled. "Four. How old are you, Kip?"

"Fifteen," Kip replied.

Researcher Bernard studied him for a moment. "You can use the library in return for a promise."

Kip had not expected that. He waited.

"You have to promise to return here, to the library, before your fiftieth birthday," Researcher Bernard told him.

"Just return and visit?" Kip checked.

"Just return and visit," Researcher Bernard confirmed.

Kip thought he could do that and it felt right. He nodded.

Jax had always liked the smell and the feel of proper books with real, printed pages. Some of the books Leo brought had pages made from plant fibres and leather covers. One of them had handwritten text rather than print; every page was a work of art.

Rae was looking at a book of fairy tales. It was much more modern, with plastic pages, but the illustrations were colourful with dragons, sea serpents and other monsters. If it had been anyone else, Jax would have made a comment about how childish it was but Rae had missed out on so much when he was younger.

Often Jax wished he could turn back time and give Rae the childhood he deserved.

It looked like Researcher Bernard was impressed by Kip and was going to let him use the library. There was a brief discussion during which two things were decided; the captain would be Kip's escort and Kip would only visit the library in the mornings, so that he could do more active things, like swimming in the lake, in the afternoons.

Jax was sure that Kip would prefer to be in the library all day every day but Ean was never going to agree to that.

So Researcher Bernard, the captain and Kip left to go into the library proper and Leo escorted the rest of them to the outer door.

Once outside, Ean announced that they would take advantage of being in the middle of the town and so neatly dressed to look about. He gave Obe, Noe, Jax and Rae each a small purse containing some coins.

"This is local money. This amount would buy a good quality evening meal. If you see something you particularly want that is more than you have, you will have to speak with me about it. Remember, you can look today but leave the buying for another day."

They went in and out of a variety of small shops and spent time in one museum. Then Ean took them to what was referred to as a tea room, where they were served tea and buns stuffed with a variety of savoury fillings.

"We are here so that Kip can use the library," Ean confirmed once everyone but Rae had finished eating. "However, if we were looking for a trade, have we seen anything we should be considering?"

Jax opened his mouth to speak but Noe got there first. "The small, carved wooden ornaments in the fourth shop."

The way Ean smiled confirmed that Noe had made the perfect choice. Jax hurried to reconsider; he had not got past deciding on wooden artefacts.

"Why that particular supplier, Noe?" Ean asked.

Noe began ticking off points using his fingers. "Wood is rare on ships and in spacestations. Spacers appreciate handcrafted objects. Small, because spacers travel light and any precious ornaments should fit easily into the average lockbox."

Being outperformed by Noe was a shock. Jax was used to Kip outthinking him and Rae excelling at everything physical, but Noe?

"Why that shop rather than any of the others?" Ean asked.

The question was addressed at all of them but, again, Noe answered before Jax had even recalled what had made that shop different from the three before or the two after.

"The ornaments were smaller and more tactile," he replied. "Also Rae liked them more than the ones in the other shops."

Jax bristled. It was one thing for Noe to be keen on impressing Ean, but quite another for him to claim to know Rae's likes and dislikes. He glanced across and, to his surprise, caught Rae looking a little guilty.

Had Rae been confiding in Noe? Jax did not like any part of

that possibility, however unlikely it seemed.

Ean nodded. "Well observed, Noe. Given the storeowner's attitude, I don't think it is a member of his family who produces them. I shall make some enquiries. Perhaps we can identify the artisan and deal with him directly."

After their snack, Ean studied Rae, as if judging his tolerance for more shopping, and then decided that they should return to the ship. Once they were clear of the built up area, heading across open ground towards the spaceport, Rae started to run ahead and come back, as if he was attached to Jax by an elastic cord.

"He's desperate for some exercise," Tre observed. "The more he grows and the fitter he gets, the more he will need. I am going to ask Kip to design and build a treadmill for him."

Jax could see that was a good idea. He nodded, thinking of all the things Kip had done to make Rae's life easier: adapting the simulator; changing the speakers so they didn't produce ultrasonic noise and reformulating all the cleaning products so they didn't stink.

Now Noe was noticing what Rae liked. Jax felt a pang of guilt. Did he take Rae for granted?

"Don't underestimate Noe," Tre warned him.

Jax guessed Tre had seen him look in Noe's direction. "Do you still think he is a plant?" Jax asked in a low voice.

"No," Tre admitted. "It is not that. Consider what it takes to survive what he has been through and end up as a spacer on the Willow."

Jax did and shuddered. "Rather than a prostitute or a slave or a collection of organs or worse."

"Worse?" Tre queried.

"Snuffers," Jax whispered.

Tre raised his eyebrows.

"Rae," Jax admitted. "He talks about stuff like that as if it was normal."

"It probably was," Tre confirmed. "Rae thinks quickly, runs fast, has phenomenal reflexes and teeth. What do you think Noe has?"

"Eyelashes," Jax replied without thinking about it and felt himself flush.

Tre smiled. "His body," he agreed. "Also, according to Vic, some impressive skills."

Jax tried not to imagine Noe sucking rod.

"What else? Tre asked.

"He must be clever," Jax admitted. "Also able to manipulate people." He thought about what Noe had said at the tea shop. "Observant and good at making connections." He remembered Noe facing up to Tre. "Either he's fearless or he can hide his fear."

"More," Tre urged.

Jax tried to imagine surviving what Noe had been through. "He is probably brilliant at pretending," he added and was rewarded by a flash of approval. "He couldn't afford to have things he would not do, so…" He trailed off, unable to put his thoughts into words.

"If he is respecting boundaries it is because he chooses to do so," Tre finished for him. "Not because there are lines he will not cross."

It was a sobering thought.

Back on the Willow Ean sent them to change while he finished preparing the picnic that had been abandoned when Tre and Kip had returned unexpectedly.

Jax and Rae put on their swimming trunks and rubbed sunblock over their exposed skin. Then Rae did Jax's back before Jax did Rae's.

Rae's skin had been tanned by the sun, but on his back the colour was not even. Jax realised that the parts of his skin that glowed when illuminated by ultra violet light were paler.

"Your wings are showing," Jax told him.

Rae tried to look over his shoulder and failed but Jax promised to take a picture later.

Jax recapped the sunblock and threw it into his open backpack. Turning back to his bunk for the towel he had rolled up, he spotted a small pouch on his pillow.

"What's this?" he asked.

Rae twitched his whiskers. "For you," he admitted.

Jax picked up the pouch, carefully undid the tie and tipped the contents into his palm. He did not know what he had expected; maybe a tasty morsel or a joke. Not a tiny wooden bird that must have cost Rae every one of his coins.

He made himself concentrate on the gift rather than his guilt. "It's beautiful, Rae. Thank you. It reminds me of the hawks that soar through the skies of my home planet and it reminds me of you, because of your wings."

Rae's whiskers arched high with pleasure.

"I think it should stay here, where it will be safe," Jax suggested, placing it gently on the narrow shelf that was halfway between his bunk and Rae's.

There was a whisker twitch of assent.

Once outside, Tre took Rae to one side to practise sprints. Instead of going swimming, as he had planned, Jax sat and watched. Rae was amazingly fast.

"What's wrong?" a gentle voice asked.

Jax had not even realised that Ean had sat down beside him.

"Rae spent all his coins on a gift for me," Jax admitted.

"Is that surprising?" Ean asked. "After all, you are, by far, the most important person in his life."

Jax was not sure he wanted to hear that, particularly not from Ean. Rae loved Ean. Did Rae really love him that much more?

"Before you, Rae had never had anyone," Ean pointed out.

Jax shut his eyes, remembering. Ean had said, "Is that your friend?" He had replied, "Yes."

How could one little word have so many consequences?

"Jax?" Ean queried.

"I have commitments," Jax admitted.

Ean sighed.

Jax opened his eyes. At first he thought Ean was looking over at Rae but then Rae shot away and Ean's eyes did not follow him. He was watching Tre.

Tre, whose life belonged to Jax; Tre, whom Ean adored.

"Do your best and do not lie to him," Ean advised.

Jax nodded, wondering how often Tre had lied to Ean.

To Kip's surprise he did not resent it when the captain told him it was time for him to leave. The library was phenomenally well organised; finding relevant information had been easy.

Assimilating it was another matter.

They headed down the hill. The second time Kip stumbled, the captain caught his arm. "Stay connected to your surroundings," he ordered.

It was simpler said than done, but Kip tried. He separated off the top layer of his mind and made himself stay there, concentrating on putting one foot in front of the other and not walking into things.

As they left the main part of the town, Kip could see the banks of the lake and small figures that were almost certainly the other members of the crew.

"Another picnic," the captain observed. "You can go swimming."

Kip nodded, even though swimming while he was so distracted was probably a very bad idea.

Ean stood up and walked over as they approached. He greeted Kip with a hug.

"How did it go?"

Kip liked it when Ean hugged him; it reminded him of his Pa. "It was great," he confirmed. "I am looking forward to going back tomorrow," he added, in case Ean had any doubts about that.

Ean nodded. "You go and get changed. We'll be eating soon. Don't forget to use sunblock."

The captain opened up the ship so they could change clothes and fetch anything they needed. Part of Kip wanted to escape into his den, but the rest wanted sunlight and fresh air so he managed to be ready before the captain called him.

They joined the others and Noe volunteered to rub sunblock onto his back while the others finished setting out the picnic.

"Did you find anything interesting?" he asked.

"Loads," Kip replied, looking over to where Rae was hovering over the food, waiting for Ean to give him permission to dig in. Jax said something to him, Rae twisted about to reply and Kip caught sight of the two-tone pattern on his back.

"Do you know what that is?" Noe asked.

"Maybe," Kip replied, thinking about what he had discovered.

Kip hadn't expected his quick search based on the key words 'human-canine hybrid', 'maker's mark' and 'wings' to yield anything. To his surprise the results were unequivocal. A pair of glowing wings was the mark of a hybrid engineer called Bara.

Trouble was, Bara had lived and died before the founding of Centre, somewhere between twenty-five and thirty thousand standards ago.

24

Ean finished selecting the final image for his memory dodeca-hedron; a picture of their last picnic on the banks of the lake on the day they had lifted.

The empty storage dodecahedrons and their associated projec-tor had been a present from Ben standards ago. Ean turned the dodec in his fingers, touching the faces to the projector one by one and admiring each of the twelve images. It had been a fabulous vacation; even Ben's absence had not sullied it. He sighed. It already seemed much more than six days since they had lifted and begun heading towards the closest shipping lane.

He placed the newly filled dodec in its correct place, shut the box and activated the tablet he used for the ship's accounts.

There was no way selling the small wooden ornaments they had purchased would cover the cost of the vacation, particu-larly when they factored in the pods they had not carried. Ean added in the time it would take them to make it back to Mercy Station and sighed again.

"I could pay for the vacation," a voice offered from behind him.

Ean jumped; he had not heard Kip approaching. He smiled and almost said that it was sweet of Kip to offer. Then he remembered what Kip was. "You have your own credit?" he asked cautiously. "Separate from anything your parents gave you?"

Kip hesitated before nodding. "Making credit is easy," he admitted.

"Have you been gambling?" Ean asked. He had not had the 'dangers of gambling' talk with Kip; he had seemed too unworldly to need it.

"No. Pa told me not to," Kip replied. "He says that when you know as much math as we do it's like kicking puppies."

Not for the first time, Ean silently thanked Azizi and Jennifer Wheeler for being such excellent parents.

"I made a lot of it trading on stock markets," Kip continued. "I'm better at predicting market trends than most other people."

Ean recognised a massive understatement when he heard one. "It is good of you to offer, Kip, but we are fine."

Kip's brow puckered. "You would let me help before making some compromise that could hurt someone?"

Ean reached over and patted his arm. "Yes, I would let you help rather than make a bad decision."

Kip nodded and Ean went back to the accounts, only to realise that Kip was still there, lurking. He deactivated the tablet.

"What's wrong, Kip?" he asked, pulling out the adjacent chair to encourage Kip to sit down.

"There was lots of information in the library," Kip told him, taking the place Ean had offered.

Ean resisted the urge to point out that it was a library and waited.

"I found out stuff." Kip glanced sideways at Ean as if reluctant to tell him more but then he continued. "Stuff about hybrids with marks like Rae's. Stuff about Jax's clan."

Kip knew what clan Jax was from? Ean resisted the urge to ask.

"Should I tell them?" Kip asked. "Maybe they would prefer not to know. Or maybe they won't like knowing I know. What happens if I don't tell them now but I have to later? Will they resent me keeping secrets that are theirs more than mine?"

Trust Kip to make even the simplest situation complicated. "You could tell each of them separately that you found information and ask them if they want to know." Ean suggested.

Kip considered. "But…" He sighed. "You think that will work best?"

"It is what I would do," Ean assured him.

Ean watched Kip saunter off before reactivating the tablet. He sighed for a third time. He had always been proud of the way he had kept the budget balanced. Even after he had realised that Tre lied about how much he spent on equipment, Ean had still made sure the everyday trading paid for food, fuel, general maintenance and life support. Now that Kip and Jax were on board, Ean had a shrewd idea that any such pretence was over.

He turned the tablet off and stowed it in a drawer. Next on his list was finding out what Obe had been up to. There was definitely something. Ean knew that guilty look.

Kip always felt better after checking stuff with Ean. His advice was always based on what was right, like his Pa's. He started with Rae, because that situation was more complicated; Kip was pretty sure that Jax would want to know everything.

He waited until Jax was training, which was the only time the two of them were apart. That meant getting between Rae and the simulator so Kip waited in the doorway.

Rae just managed to stop in time. He gave a small scowl at being kept from the simulator and twitched his whiskers in the way that meant, "What's going on?"

"I need to talk with you," Kip explained. "Alone," he added.

Rae considered and then nodded.

They went into one of the empty rooms. Rae waited and Kip took a deep breath.

"I looked up your wings, your marker's mark, in the library."

Rae's brown and gold eyes studied him. Kip could swear the gold flecks were larger than they had been a few divs ago; now they had coalesced so that they were more like radiating streaks.

"Do you want to know what I found out?" Kip asked, trying to follow Ean's advice.

Rae considered and gave a short bark of assent.

"Your mark is associated with a hybrid engineer called Bara. Only he lived and died thousands of standards ago, so it doesn't make sense."

Rae frowned. "So he couldn't have made me?"

Kip's mind was immediately filled with all the ways that it would be possible. "You could have been in stasis," he suggested doubtfully. It didn't seem very likely. He didn't know any examples of people surviving over twenty thousand standards in stasis. Then again, an embryo might last that long because you could freeze an embryo.

"Or?" Rae prompted.

"It could be a false mark," Kip admitted. "Made by someone wanting to suggest you had been made by Bara. Bara is, like, the most famous hybrid engineer ever, so maybe someone wanted to suggest you were made by him."

"A scam?" Rae suggested.

"Maybe," Kip admitted. "It's more likely that it's a false mark than you were made over twenty thousand standards ago."

Rae nodded. He stepped towards the door, making it clear that he would prefer to be in the simulator rather than talking to Kip.

"You don't want to know more about Bara?" Kip checked.

"No," Rae replied and was gone.

Kip was a bit disappointed. Researching Bara had been interesting. Bara had been able to control epigenetic variation, which modern hybrid engineers could not. Epigenetic variation was what made so many hybrids develop wrongly, so getting a functional hybrid was a mixture of luck and the willingness to terminate the thousands of embryos that didn't turn out right. Bara had been able to produce perfect hybrids to order.

Perfect hybrids like Rae.

Kip shook his head. No, it was much more likely that a modern hybrid engineer had lucked out, ended up with Rae and then decided to add Bara's mark in hope that he could con someone into paying extra.

He checked the chronometer; another forty-three minutes until Jax finished his session with Tre and there might be a narrow window when Kip would be able to speak with him without Rae there. Kip set his alarm before deciding between indexing the information he had collected from the library and working on Rae's treadmill.

He really wanted to get into the data streams but they wouldn't reach a system with a light speed data relay for another ten days.

He had half a circuit of the corridor to decide because his new workshop was at one end of the empty room where his den was located. As he entered he chose the treadmill, because building something helped him think.

He was making good progress with one of the control units when the door opened. Kip looked up, half-expecting to see Rae with questions about Bara, but it was Noe. Kip went back to testing the control unit's circuits.

"What are you doing?" Noe asked.

Noe knew that he was designing and building a treadmill for Rae. He wouldn't be interested in the detail of one of the control units. Kip glanced over. Sure enough, Noe was perched on the edge of one of the tables in a way that Kip guessed was meant to be seductive.

"I don't want to give or receive a blow job right now," he answered. "Thank you if you were offering."

Noe scowled at him. "You are no fun sometimes, Kip."

"I thought you were concentrating on Obe," Kip pointed out. Blow jobs were distracting but he could talk to Noe and work at the same time.

"Obe is an idiot," Noe complained. "Ean's managed to get him to confess that we'd been fucking."

Kip hadn't known. They must have been doing it somewhere other than in the crewroom. He guessed that Obe would be the one in more trouble, just because he was over sixteen, even though it was obviously Noe's fault.

"Surprised?" Noe asked.

Kip thought about it. "No," he decided.

"Jealous?"

"No," Kip replied. The only thing about it that bothered him was that Ean might be upset.

Noe sighed. "I expect Ean will make Obe promise to stop." He hopped off the table and approached. "Maybe you'd like to take his place."

Kip wasn't sure he could resist Noe but he intended to try. "Ean would go ballistic," he warned. "And there is absolutely no way he would blame me."

Noe stopped a few paces from Kip's workbench. He shrugged. "So what? Ean's already furious."

"No, Ean's pretending to be furious," Kip explained. "There's a difference."

Noe considered and then sniffed. "You're right. You're one of his babies, like Jax and Rae."

Kip guessed Noe was saying it to rile him but it wouldn't work. "Ean promised my Ma he would look after me," he pointed out.

Noe went back to the table. This time he sat properly, to be comfortable rather than to display himself.

"You're different, Kip," he observed.

Kip had worked that out the first time he had met other children. He continued testing the circuits, wondering where Noe was going.

"Why?" Noe asked.

"My brain works differently to other people's," Kip admitted but, as he did so, he felt a bit sick.

"How?"

Kip found himself thinking about his Pa and how frightened he had been that Kip would reveal his secret. Trouble was, Noe would keep working on him. "I don't want to tell you," he replied. At least that was true.

Noe scowled. "Why not?"

"I don't trust you not to use what I tell you against me." Kip was surprised how hurt Noe looked. "It isn't personal. I don't trust anyone other than my Pa."

"Not even your Ma?" Noe asked.

Kip shut his eyes. He felt bad thinking it, never mind admitting it out loud, but it might make Noe give up. "No, not even my Ma," he managed. In his mind's eye he could see his Ma's wounded expression. He opened his eyes, hoping to dispel the image, only to discover that Noe was studying him.

Noe looked away. "Don't worry about it." His voice was different: thin; young. "I understand." He turned back to Kip and smiled, although his eyes were sad. "There isn't even one person I trust."

Jax had enjoyed the vacation. He had liked having sunlight on his skin and the wind in his hair. His skin had gone the same rich shade as it had at home. The only downside was that the sky had made him a bit homesick; it was the wrong blue.

Best had been watching Rae. Jax had been right; Rae had immediately adapted to life without walls and a ceiling. He had run like the wind and climbed like a spider monkey. He had learned to swim, although his technique was a bit basic.

Even now his skin was tanned, making his eyes look more gold than brown, and his head fur had been streaked the colour of ripe maize by the sun.

"Jax?" Tre queried.

Jax flushed. He had been going through his cooling down routine, when thinking about something other than training was usually permitted. "Yes, Tre?" he replied.

"You and I and Kip need to begin talking about a plan, maybe more than one. Perhaps Loy as well."

Jax agreed that was necessary. He must claim the leadership on his sixteenth birth anniversary. Anything else would make him look weak. That was just under three standards away but before then they would need to have built a position where the claim was realistic. "Not Loy," he decided.

Tre looked as if he would like to argue.

"Kip does not trust you, never mind Loy," Jax pointed out. "And I want Rae there."

"Rae won't understand," Tre warned.

"He understands far more than you think he does," Jax argued. Tre was always underestimating Rae. "What are you going to say to Ean to explain us spending time together?" he asked.

"I was going to suggest that it was medical training for you and Kip but without Loy that won't wash," Tre pointed out.

Jax made sure his expression did not change. He was not giving in. He was not comfortable with Loy and he was determined to give Rae the option of being present. "You will come up with something," he replied.

Tre left the gym before him, behaviour that indicated that he was annoyed or frustrated. Jax did not follow immediately; that might indicate that he was open to Tre's argument. Instead he began repeating the last phase of his cooling down routine.

He was halfway through when Kip appeared in the doorway, which was unexpected; Kip avoided the gym as much as possible.

"I need to speak with you," Kip began, as if that was not obvious.

"Without Rae?" Jax queried.

Kip gave a tiny huff through his nose. Jax had noticed it before; Kip did it when Jax said something that was too obvious to merit wasting words on it.

"You want to give me the choice of whether to tell Rae or not," Jax added.

Kip nodded. "I found out lots of stuff about your clan in the library. There's other stuff as well, from other sources. Do you want to know about it?"

Jax felt like huffing back; of course he wanted to know. "Yes," he replied. "What would be the best way for me to interact with it?"

Kip considered. "A database. That would be easier to search."

There had to be a lot of it if it needed to be organised as a database. "Can you write me a report picking out the parts that are most relevant to my current situation?" Jax asked.

Kip's eyebrows went up.

Jax scowled. It had been a question not an order. "Like a briefing," he added.

"I can do that," Kip agreed.

Jax's mind went to what Tre had been saying about needing to plan for when he was sixteen. "Did you find anything out in the library that would be useful in building a power base?"

Kip's gaze unfocused, indicating that he was thinking more deeply than he usually did with other people about. Jax waited patiently. Finally Kip spoke.

"Your clan has had agents all over Known Space for centuries. Given the distances involved and how slowly information travels, those agents had standing orders to act on their own initiative in the best interests of the clan."

It was not something Jax had thought about. He nodded that Kip should continue.

"There will be differences between what the clan thinks it owns and what it actually does own," Kip continued. "It's inevitable. Also, inheritance laws vary from system to system, so there are bound to be assets that you can take control of before you are sixteen, whether you are the recognised clan leader or not. It helps that you are your father's recognised heir and that your uncle is not and has never been your guardian." He paused and continued. "To find the correct ones, the ones your uncle will not know about, I will need to compare databases. I've checked. I can hack into the Navaja clan archives." He looked at Jax expectantly.

Jax scowled back. "What?"

"Do I have your permission?" Kip asked. "To hack the Navaja clan archive?"

Jax nodded. "Go ahead. What kind of assets are we talking about?" he asked.

Kip shrugged. "You know. Bank accounts. Shares in spacestations. Asteroids. Perhaps the odd planet."

"Planet?" Jax queried. How could anyone forget that they owned a planet?

"Planets aren't always worth a lot," Kip reminded him. Some are uninhabitable and mined out. Others are too far away from the shipping lanes." His eyes unfocused again and Jax made himself stay quiet. "You need a ship fitted with a Mulligan drive," he said finally.

Jax snorted. "As if I can afford one of those. Anyway, mother ships are so slow."

"Spacehopper ships aren't," Kip reminded him.

Spacehopper ships didn't carry freight or other ships; they were built to be as small as possible given that they had to carry a Mulligan drive and its shielding. Instead of paying for themselves by transporting freight and other ships, they paid for themselves by discovering new planets.

There weren't that many high quality planets left to discover; no one built spacehopper ships these days.

Jax went back to thinking about what Kip had said. "I won't be able to claim any assets in my own name," he pointed out. "It would give people a lead on where I am."

"No, but you want to be in a position to claim them," Kip told him. "The chance of you getting to your sixteenth birth anniversary without your whereabouts being discovered is currently about twenty-two per cent."

Jax went cold. No wonder Tre was insisting they needed a plan.

"So a spacehopper ship would be really useful," Kip added.

"Well we haven't got one or any prospect of getting one," Jax snapped and then pulled himself together. He mustn't dismiss Kip's ideas or Kip might choose not to share them. He tried to adjust his tone to be more positive and encouraging. "Maybe we should look into more realistic options first?"

✳ ✳ ✳

Tre had not been surprised when Jax had refused to go with his idea of passing off their planning meetings as medical training. In a way it was good that Jax was asserting himself, even if he reminded Tre of Oro when he did so.

What did surprise him was spotting Kip lurking, obviously waiting to speak to Jax. It was too tempting; Tre made sure he was out of sight before activating his processor and enhancing his hearing.

He learned a lot. Firstly, it was obvious that Jax and Kip had regular conversations about Jax's situation. Second, Jax was struggling not to imitate his father's attitude to his subordinates, even though Kip only owed him the service of a crewmate and friend. Third, Kip did not think small. While Tre had been wondering how far his reserves would stretch and if he could trust anyone other than Loy, Kip was thinking about acquiring planets and a spacehopper ship.

Tre was reminded that Centre searched Known Space for typed-geniuses and then locked them away. He thought of Klennethon Darrent; in a single lifetime the man had acquired more wealth and power than most clans.

Then he imagined Oro with a man like Klennethon Darrent at his command and shuddered.

He pushed the thought aside. What mattered was keeping Jax alive.

Jax and Kip had stopped talking and were coming out of the gym. Tre stayed still and quiet until he was certain that they were both climbing up the shaft. Then he shot over to the other ladder, smiling at himself for behaving like Rae.

He was in the shower before Jax entered the crewroom.

Once he was washed, dried and dressed, he searched for Ean and found him in the laundry. He was still fuming that Obe had given in to Noe. Tre listened, again, to how disappointed Ean was in Obe and how impossible Noe could be.

He did not comment; Ean would not want to hear that Tre thought Obe had done pretty well to resist as long as he had.

"Noe is probably over sixteen," he offered once Ean had run out of steam.

Ean scowled at him. "He is not. Loy says that his physiological age is twelve, maybe thirteen. We are already pushing it by saying he is fourteen."

"Kip traced him back to his home planet. He has a probable timeline. It includes considerable time being shipped as cargo by slavers."

Ean shook his head. "Time in stasis does not count. Tre, whatever Noe thinks, two standards as a cat on the Willow will do him good and being a cat on the Willow means blow jobs only, no fucking."

Tre managed not to sigh. "You are queen," he acknowledged. "Do you have time to discuss something else? About Jax?"

Ean listened carefully as Tre stumbled through a badly thought out argument to justify Jax, Kip, Rae and him having regular meetings. The more he said, the less convinced Ean looked. Finally he stuttered to a halt.

"Kip is helping you keep Jax safe," Ean checked.

Tre nodded.

"Jax has a right to know what decisions you are making about him and his future," Ean added.

"Yes," Tre confirmed.

"Why Rae?" Ean asked.

"Jax wants Rae included."

Ean considered for a moment and then nodded. "Fine."

"Fine? You don't want to know anything more?" Tre checked.

"I want to know much more," Ean admitted. "But it is Jax's business and up to him how much he wishes to tell me. As for Rae, he would follow Jax to the edge of Known Space and beyond so I think it is good that Jax wants to include him rather than keep secrets from him."

Tre did not miss the implied criticism. He wished there was something he could say, but he knew from experience that there was not.

Ean turned away and began sorting the clean clothes. "In a few standards' time Jax will move to a clan ship, taking Rae with him," he stated in a matter-of-fact voice. "You will go with him, along with Loy and probably Kip. I understand. It's inevitable."

Tre wanted to take Ean in his arms and hold him but he knew it was not fair to do so because Ean was absolutely correct. Ean would be left on the Willow, without Tre, without Ben and without three of the youngsters he had helped raise.

Ean put down the shirt he had been folding, one of Rae's, and turned around. "So we should make the most of every day we have together," he suggested.

"We should?" Tre queried, surprised by the unexpected turn in the conversation.

"Of course we should," Ean insisted.

Tre pulled Ean close. "By the Lady, I don't deserve you," he whispered. He loved this amazing man so much but he must never say it. The only thing worse than abandoning someone you loved was abandoning the person to whom you had confessed your love.

"No, you don't," Ean whispered in return.

25

Jax stared at the screen, blinking back tears. Over the last four divs he had come to hate the database that Kip had built and populated for him. He had not felt that way when Kip first gave it to him. At the beginning it had been exciting, like being faced with a succession of wrapped parcels, and Jax had opened each one eagerly.

Unfortunately the contents had often proved to be painful and occasionally devastating. Like finding out he had two dead half-brothers.

The younger of the two had been terminated at the age of seven. That was the word his father had used in the order; terminated. The boy's mother had been from Kalakmul. She and the whole of her family had been killed at the same time, to prevent any 'ill-conceived retaliation'.

Would Jax have been 'terminated' if he had refused to ride the wild pony?

The older of the two had made it to his equivalent of the Willow. There was a series of reports from his equivalent of Tre. The reports had started positive and upbeat but had become progressively shorter and more critical.

His Tre had killed him because his father, Jax's father, had ordered it. It had been made to look like an accident. This time the mother had been from another spacer clan, the Edgers, so she had been sent home with a large financial settlement.

Jax found himself looking at Tre. Would Tre have killed him if he had not come up to his father's expectations?

Once he knew about his brothers, the rest of it was less shocking. A man who would kill his own sons would not hesitate to slaughter strangers.

He shut the database; there was only so much he could take at one sitting. He set off to find company, any company; even Noe would do. Luckily there was no need to be so indiscriminate. Rae was on his treadmill. Jax loved watching Rae run.

Today Rae had the treadmill on his favourite setting, the one where it responded to him rather than him reacting to it. He would run at his usual astonishingly fast pace and then accelerate to his top speed for a few moments before slowing.

Suddenly, instead of slowing, Rae leapt off the treadmill, shed some of his momentum in a controlled collision with the wall and bounced back to land in a crouch at Jax's feet. He shook himself, showering Jax with drops of sweat.

"Rae!" Jax objected but he didn't really mind.

Rae dashed off towards the shower, pleased with himself for having managed to mark Jax with his scent. Once inside their den, Rae stripped off his clothes, underpants included. He was no longer so obsessed with no one catching a glimpse of his rod; it still wasn't large but it was respectable. He dived into the shower stall, turned the faucet and squirted body wash into his hand.

He liked touching his new body. Every div he was bigger and more muscular; he was already taller than Noe and catching up with Jax. His head fur was longer, better for flicking sweat at Jax, and there was the promise of body fur in interesting places. Best, his rod had started standing up and it felt really good when he stroked it.

It was all very, very male.

He rinsed himself and then the shower stall; Jax was fussy about stuff like that. A combination of the blowers and a towel meant that he wasted as little time as possible drying himself. Then it was fresh clothes on, used clothes into the hamper in the laundry and he was into the galley where, if he was lucky, Ean would prepare him a snack rather than him having to make do with meal bars.

As his sense of smell had suggested, Ean was cooking. Hopeful eyes and whiskers ensured a tasty pre-lunch snack.

"What have you planned for this afternoon?" Ean asked.

Rae wasn't sure why Ean was asking, because he must know already. Ever since they left Janine, four divs ago, Rae, Kip, Jax and Tre met to discuss clan-stuff every three days. Rae swallowed before replying.

"Usual."

"How do you think Jax is coping with those meetings?"

Rae sniffed the air and listened carefully. Jax was nowhere on this level, which was odd. He concentrated on Ean, who smelt a bit stressed. Ean must have had sent Jax away so he could ask Rae questions. "Meetings make him feel better. The information Kip gave him makes him sad."

"The information Kip found in the library?" Ean checked.

"And other places," Rae confirmed. He took a huge mouthful of food and gave Ean a look that meant, "I don't want to say more."

Ean sighed and turned back to the stove.

Kip had discovered that he enjoyed the challenge of explaining stuff to other people. Describing what was in his head never worked. Instead he would decide the most important points he had to convey and create a vehicle, like the ribbon diagram showing the ships' movement.

It was surprisingly difficult.

He expected their meeting this afternoon to follow the usual pattern. They started by looking at the ribbon diagram. Kip would display the ships' last known positions, based on when he had last been able to hack a light speed data relay, and then their most likely current positions.

It had been almost a div since they had been in a system with a data relay on one of the gates. Kip thought a div was too long but Tre disagreed. If it were up to Tre they would never be in a shipping lane that was busy enough to merit a data relay.

Tomorrow they would reach the next gate. Beyond was a system with a data relay. Kip would be able to update his model.

After discussing ships' movements, the next item on the agenda was always The Plan. The Plan was what Jax should do when he reached his sixteenth birth anniversary or he was located, whichever came sooner.

So far The Plan consisted of Jax declaring himself clan leader and then going into hiding. The thinking behind it was that enough Navaja ships would choose him over his uncle because he was the rightful heir. When, or if, he had enough ships, Jax would go up against his uncle.

Kip did not think that version of The Plan would work. As far as he could tell, Jax's uncle was a very competent leader who was doing an excellent job of running the clan. Given a choice between the usurper and a youngster with no experience who might have inherited his father's homicidal tendencies, Kip guessed that most crews would stay with what was working.

No, The Plan needed to be far better than that. Today, for the first time, Kip intended to propose an alternative.

They always met in the room that Kip had been using as his workshop, where he had built Rae's treadmill. Kip went there straight after lunch so that he could set up the projector and check through his presentation.

Tre arrived next, as always. "Anything I should know?" he asked.

It was a not a question that Kip could cope with; it was too open. Thoughts bubbled up from the lower layers of his mind, distracting him from his surroundings.

"Kip!" Tre demanded.

Kip swept the thoughts into a corner and partitioned them away.

"What are you planning to tell us?" Tre tried instead.

Before Kip could answer Rae shot into the room with Jax following.

Kip started with the familiar three-dimensional projection of the ribbon diagram and then cranked it forward to show the most likely current positions of the ships.

"As suggested at the last meeting, I've been analysing the orange ships in more detail," he began. "Those are the ones whose movements and communication patterns indicate that they could be searching for Jax. Taking away all the others…" The great majority of the ribbons vanished. "…there are twenty-three ships. As we have discussed before, the weird thing is that none of them are Navaja."

"None of them are overtly Navaja," Tre insisted.

It was a familiar argument. "Eighteen are definitely not Navaja," Kip continued, "because they openly display another clan's colours. These three groups of three are all Edger. These two pairs are Nova. Two of the singles are Xing and these three singles are Eunha, Crimson and Chielo. The five remaining are, at least overtly, free agents. As Tre suggested, some of them could be working for Navaja but we have no evidence of that. However, based on their communication patterns, I believe these two are rival investigative journalists."

Rae's whiskers twitched. "Why are the Edgers interested?"

Jax flinched. "The Navaja have recent history with the Edgers," he admitted. "There was an alliance that we ended."

Rae's whiskers demanded more but Jax chose not to see. Kip was not surprised. Four decades ago Jax's father had needed the alliance and he taken full advantage of it over the sixteen standards it had lasted. Then, when he no longer needed the Edgers, he had not hesitated to dispose of his son in order to take advantage of one of the exit clauses.

The Edgers had to suspect that the accident that killed Jax's brother was nothing of the sort. They could be out for revenge.

"And Nova?" Rae asked.

"Opportunist scavengers," Tre replied. "The only reason they are a clan is that they call themselves one."

Kip thought that was a bit harsh; Nova was almost as old as Navaja.

"But there is no indication that any of them know which ship I am on?" Jax checked.

Kip hesitated. "There is no evidence of it," he conceded. "The trios of Edger ships are definitely investigating Traditional crews." He brought up white ribbons showing fifty-eight of the three hundred and sixty-two registered Traditional ships, the Willow among them, and superimposed the paths of the nine Edger ships. "However, their methods are not efficient or effective."

"Thank the Lady they haven't got you working for them," Jax acknowledged.

Kip considered. "Even I would not be sure." He thought about it. "I could narrow it down to twenty-seven of these fifty-eight.

They all have crew who have connections to Navaja, like Tre and Loy. I assume that they were planted deliberately," he checked with Tre.

Tre gave the smallest nod. "It is standard practice. Otherwise it would be too easy to identify the crew the Navaja youngster had joined. Shall we move on to discussing The Plan?"

Kip was more than willing to go with the change of subject. This was it; time for his proposal.

He made eye contact with Jax. "I don't think you should hide."

There was silence. Rae's eyes widened and his whiskers arched. Tre's eyes narrowed, making him look downright scary.

"Explain," Jax demanded.

"Once you have your knife and are old enough to claim the leadership, hiding gets you nowhere. You'll waste all your resources on staying hidden. Then when you are finally found, which you will be, you will still be in a weak position.

"Instead you build your powerbase where the clans, even Navaja, are weakest. Tarrasade."

✳ ✳ ✳

Tre managed to bite back his initial response, which would have sent Kip scuttling off to hide in his cupboard. Going to Tarrasade was a ludicrous idea. The place was utterly corrupt; weighed down by residents who were loyal to no one but themselves and infested with media. Even the spacers who guarded it were barely worthy of the title; men who had given up their ships and merely clung to a shell of the code.

"Tarrasade is real?" Rae asked.

"Yes, it is a spacestation in the Inner Fringe," Jax answered. He was trying to sound sensible but Tre could see the way his eyes were shining and hear the excitement in his voice. He was not surprised. When he had been Jax's age Tarrasade had seemed more myth than reality: a place in songs and stories; the Jewel of the Fringe; favoured destination of heroes and lovers.

At least Kip did not look star-struck. On the contrary, his expression dared Tre to put his prejudices aside and consider the idea on its merits.

"Take us through it, Kip," Tre ordered. "Small steps. Leave nothing out."

As Kip worked through his explanation, Tre reluctantly and gradually conceded that the strategy had much to commend it. Jax could not wield Navaja power, so being located in the Inner Fringe, where all the clans were weakest, made sense. The media, which Tre so detested, could be an asset. Kip was suggesting that they would fall over themselves to turn Jax into a celebrity. As a celebrity, he would have a brief, bright, flare of influence that could be used as a springboard.

Tre only half-listened to Jax's questions and Kip's replies. He was thinking about the spacers with no crews and all those residents, a people without a leader. Powerbases were about more than territory and resources, the more supporters or even followers Jax had the better.

Jax and Kip had stopped talking, disturbed by Tre's silence.

"Why Tarrasade rather than another Inner Fringe location?" Tre asked. He was certain he knew the answer; Tarrasade had the most powerful media, the largest number of residents and it was the place the clans were weakest. If Kip's argument was valid, it was most valid for Tarrasade.

Kip smiled. "I think Jax might own a chunk of it."

What followed was terrifying.

Not Kip's explanation; that was straightforward enough. Navaja had agents all over the Fringe and had done so for over a thousand standards. There would have been times when detail of what they had done was lost before it was transferred to the clan's archive. Agents died. Ships carrying tapes were lost. Some archivists were more effective than others. It made perfect sense that the archived records on Kalakmul would be inaccurate.

No, it was what came next that shook the foundations of Tre's world. Kip had been comparing what Navaja thought it owned with what it actually owed. To do that, Kip had to be able to access databanks that everyone assumed were secure.

Databanks like the Navaja archive.

"So what part do I own?" Jax asked.

Tre had to review the last few minutes of the conversation using his processor; he had been thinking too much about what Kip could do to listen. Apparently someone had put up a part of Tarrasade as collateral for a loan from Navaja. The loan had not been paid, so the agent had claimed the property on behalf of the clan. Since then the agent in Tarrasade had transferred ownership every time an heir inherited.

"I couldn't find out which bit," Kip admitted. "The electronic record just refers to a hard copy, could be a tape or even a physical document, held in the Tarrasade records office. Any part would be good. Not only would it be worth a fortune, but owners have influence." Kip looked at Tre and this time his eyes were anxious rather than challenging.

Tre made himself concentrate on The Plan rather than Kip's potentially society-shattering abilities. "The idea of developing Tarrasade as Jax's powerbase has merit," he admitted.

Once Jax and Rae had left, Kip started putting away the projector. Tre lurked. Kip knew what that meant; he wanted to discuss something in more detail; probably whatever had been distracting him when Jax had been asking questions about Tarrasade. He waited.

"Is there any databank you can't access?" Tre asked finally.

Kip was surprised. He had thought that Tre had understood the extent of his hacking when he had first seen the ribbon diagram. "Loads," Kip replied. "The ones that don't have a physical link to an uplink to a light speed data relay are tricky. Some of them are impossible. The library on Janine was impossible. That's why I wanted to go there."

"You could…" Tre trailed off before starting again. "You could divert ships or empty bank accounts."

Kip did not understand why Tre should say such things. Was he suggesting that Kip should divert ships or empty accounts? Then he realised that it was probably a test. "You could knife loads of people. You don't because it's wrong and, anyway, people who do stuff like that are identified as killers and dealt with."

Tre nodded slowly. "So what rules have you set yourself?" he asked.

Kip had never tried to put it into words. "If the information can be accessed, if I am just speeding it up, that's fine. If I have permission, like from Jax to access the Navaja archive, that's fine too. I don't do stuff I think will hurt people, like stealing. If I'm not sure I think what my Pa would say or I check with Ean."

Tre smiled; a proper smile that reached his eyes. "Those sound like good rules," he confirmed. He put out a hand and gently squeezed Kip's shoulder; something that Kip recognised as a gesture of approval. "I'll need some time to get used to the idea that Tarrasade may be the place to be rather than somewhere to avoid."

Kip was delighted. He had guessed that Tre would dislike the Tarrasade idea but his initial reaction had been even more negative than Kip had anticipated. Tre let go of his shoulder and moved away, so Kip assumed that he was leaving and went back to packing away the projector.

"Could you empty a Belmenth bank account?" Tre asked.

Kip stopped what he was doing and went through what he knew about the Belmenth systems. "I wouldn't dare hack the Belmenth data system," he admitted. "They might detect me." After what had happened on Darrenden, Kip was wary of going near any organisation that stated that it had consulted with typed-geniuses. "I might be able to initiate genuine trans-actions with false demands, perhaps lots of bills that it looked like the account holder had agreed to pay. Only I wouldn't, because it would be stealing."

Tre nodded and continued on his way, leaving Kip thinking about all the ways that Belmenth bank accounts could be compromised. There were too many of them; that was why Kip kept most of his liquid funds in Belmenth credit tokens, the originals of which were deposited in various Stellar Exchanges across Known Space.

Next thing Kip knew Noe was at the door.

"You are meant to be helping Ean cook," he pointed out.

Kip checked his chronometer. It was true. The meeting had overrun and then he had talked to Tre and after that he had been distracted thinking about banks. He closed the lid of the projector box; he would put it away later.

Once he had apologised to Ean, he and Noe settled at the galley table to prepare the vegetables. Kip was chopping peppers while Noe had the trickier job of dissecting tomatoes into skins, juice, pips and neatly diced flesh.

"You are hopeless," Noe stated suddenly.

Kip looked at the neat piles of brightly-coloured pieces. They looked fine to him; all approximately the same size so that they would cook evenly.

"You haven't noticed," Noe added in a hurt voice.

Kip caught on. It was nothing to do with his competence as a cook's assistant. Noe had changed something about his appearance and Kip was meant to notice. It was one of the games Noe played and Kip was appallingly bad at it. He glanced over to Ean at the stove but Ean merely smiled.

Was it clothes? Kip was pretty sure that he had seen the top Noe was wearing before. What else could it be? His hair looked the same. He tried a general complement. "You always look nice, Noe."

Ean sighed and Noe sniffed. "You might like to work on that for when you have a lover," Noe pointed out.

Kip could not see that happening anytime soon, if ever. Who would want someone ugly and weird like him?

The smell of food was making Rae's stomach rumble. He and Jax were on laundry duty. As always, Jax did the tricky stuff, which was mainly ironing and folding, while Rae did everything else.

"Don't put that in with those!" Jax warned.

Rae looked at the top in his hand. It was one of Noe's. Thinking about it, it did feel a bit different.

"That's silk," Jax told him. "Put it in the basket over there."

Rae wadded the top into a tight ball and launched it at the indicated basket.

"Silk is made of protein rather than cellulose or an artificial polymer," Jax informed him. "So is wool."

Rae knew that and went back to loading the machine. He even knew that they put all the silk and wool stuff to one side and cleaned it using a different setting. It was just easier to stuff everything into the machine.

Jax sighed and Rae took some of the clothes out before Jax told him, yet again, that the machine cleaned best if you did not exceed the maximum load.

He hated doing laundry.

Once the machine was running, Rae settled to watch Jax fold the clean clothes and make a neat pile for each crew member. There was no point in offering to help because Jax would redo every garment he folded.

"Are we really going to Tarrasade?" he asked.

"Maybe," Jax answered. "It's just another spacestation, Rae."

Rae chose to overlook the fact that Jax was lying. His smell, his tone of his voice and the tension in his body told Rae that Jax was just as excited about Tarrasade as he was.

Jax did that a lot. Ean had explained; it was all about Jax trying to appear grown up and 'worldly'.

"Then why does it turn up so often in stories?" Rae asked.

Jax shrugged. "I'm not sure. It's very old; it was founded almost a thousand standards ago. All the other spacestations founded that long ago are long gone, destroyed or scrapped and the bits recycled." He stopped folding for a moment. "Also, people say it is beautiful but I can't see how; it's just a spacestation."

Rae might have asked another question but, at that moment, his stomach gave such a noisy rumble that even Jax could hear it.

"Go and get some meal bars," Jax suggested.

Rae hesitated; he didn't want to leave Jax but he was so hungry.

"Go!" Jax ordered.

Rae slipped through the door to the galley and headed for the jar of meal bars on the counter. Ean was at the stove. Kip and Noe were at the table cutting up vegetables.

"Sit down," Ean told him. "I'll make you something."

Rae hesitated; he had left Jax folding clothes. Then Ean began throwing ingredients into a pan and the smell of cooking food made a meal bar seem unappealing.

It wouldn't take long; he would eat extra quickly. He slipped into the seat opposite Kip, who smiled. Rae responded with a whisker twitch.

"Rae," Noe acknowledged.

"Noe," Rae replied. He always used words with Noe; just not many of them.

"Isn't Rae meant to notice?" Kip asked Noe.

Rae was much more interested in the pile of food Ean was tipping onto a plate than being drawn into a conversation between Kip and Noe.

"Rae only notices Jax," Noe pointed out, which was not true but Rae was not going to correct him.

At that moment Jax appeared in the doorway to the galley. He stood there, scowling at Rae. Rae jumped up. He felt awful; he should have least have told Jax what was happening.

"Sit down, Rae," Ean ordered, bring the plateful of food over. "It is my fault, Jax. Rae was just going to grab a meal bar before I tempted him. Why don't you make us all some tea?"

Jax had assumed that Rae had got distracted by an offer of food; he could smell that Ean was cooking. Sure enough, Rae was sitting at the table, fork in hand, his eyes fixed on the plate Ean was bringing over.

At least Rae was contrite, his whiskers were drooping, and Jax knew how hungry he had been from the noise his gut had been making. Rae was always ravenous these days; Loy said it was because he was growing so quickly.

Making tea was preferable to folding clothes. Jax made sure he patted Rae on the shoulder as he passed, confirming his forgiveness. Rae flashed him a smile, whiskers recovered, before attacking the pile of food Ean had put in front of him.

Ean, Noe and Kip's hands would be dirty from preparing food so Jax chose ordinary cups but still made the tea in the good pot so it would brew properly. Once he had poured the boiling water onto the leaves, he carried the tray bearing the cups and pot to the table and sat down.

Noe's eyes looked different. Instead of being surrounded by coloured shadows, there was an intricate pattern painted at the outer edges. Jax wondered if he had done it freehand or used some type of transfer.

"Nice pattern," he acknowledged, touching the side of his face, close to the eye.

Noe fluttered his eyelashes. "Why thank you, Jax." He glanced at Kip. "At least somebody noticed."

Kip just shrugged.

"I noticed," Ean pointed out, taking the seat closest to the tray and lifting the lid to check the brew.

Noe sniffed. Jax interpreted that to mean that Ean did not count; Noe was not out to attract Ean.

"Did Obe notice?" Jax asked.

"He has not seen it yet," Noe admitted. "I only did it after lunch." He sounded hopeful that Obe would rise to the challenge.

On balance, Jax didn't think that was very likely.

"Neither Kip nor Rae noticed," Ean informed him, pouring the first cup, which he put in front of Jax.

"Rae notices smells and sounds and movement more than visual stimuli," Jax pointed out. No one bothered to offer an excuse for Kip. There were times when Kip didn't notice a door was shut until after he had walked into it; he wasn't going to notice eye paint.

"It looks very nice, Noe," Ean added.

Jax had noticed that Ean went out of his way to encourage Noe to make himself attractive in ways that did not include exposed skin or lewd gestures.

Ean finished pouring and distributing the tea. Noe stopped chopping tomatoes, wiped his hands on a cloth and took a sip.

"There is an inhabited planet in the system we jump into tomorrow," he observed. "Couldn't we make a slight detour and drop?"

Ean sighed. "No chance, Noe. We are jumping in, crossing part of the outer system to another gate and jumping out. Even so, this is a good opportunity to review what we know about the Verdant system. Jax, why don't you start us off?"

Rae usually went first, but his mouth was full.

"It's called Verdant because the fourth planet used to be green," Jax began. "It was seeded with a standard ecology by a Centralite spacehopper, probably in the first or second wave of exploration."

Kip held up two fingers.

"Second wave," Jax added. "It was first colonised about ten thousand standards ago, over-exploited and abandoned; the usual story. Then, just over a thousand standards ago, this shipping lane was gated and suddenly the planet was worth inhabiting again."

"Very good, Jax. Noe?"

"Turned out Verdant was a crossroads," Noe continued. "There are loads of holes." He glanced at Kip who held up nine fingers and then folded down four of them. "Nine of them, five of which were worth gating. It no longer mattered that the system was mined out, because what counts is the traffic and the trade. As well as the planet, there are three spacestations."

"Excellent, Noe," Ean confirmed. "Kip? Just essentials," he added hastily.

Kip considered. "Two of the gates have light speed data relays. One of the spacestations is essentially a factory station. The other two are mixed. The planet produces more than it needs to support its population, which it exports. As it is such an important crossroads, the system is neutral territory for the clans. It has its own security forces that guard the gates, the spacestations and the planet." He paused and looked to Ean.

"Well judged, Kip," he confirmed.

"I still don't see why we can't visit the planet, or at least one of the spacestations," Noe complained.

"Rae?" Ean asked.

Jax checked and, sure enough, Rae's plate was empty; how he ate so quickly without being sick was beyond Jax.

"Time is credit," Rae stated in a voice that was suspicious like Ean's. "We are carrying pods so we have commitments."

Ean's brow puckered slightly and everyone else was careful not to laugh. Then Rae gave one of his best smiles and Ean smiled back.

"Very good, Rae," he confirmed.

Then Rae went to put his plate and fork in the dish cleaner, Jax drained his cup and the two of them headed back to the laundry. On their way through the crewroom they passed Obe heading in the opposite direction.

Rae caught Obe's attention with a movement and then tapped the outer corner of his eye with his fingertip.

Obe frowned and looked to Jax for an interpretation.

"You'll see," Jax whispered.

They waited just out of the line of sight. Obe caught on at once; as soon as Noe looked at him.

"Nice eye paint, Noe," Obe commented. "Not that you need it to make your eyes look pretty."

Jax smiled at Rae and Rae grinned back.

26

Kip had expected to have to take the jump into the Verdant system in the crewroom but then the captain asked for Obe to be in the control room. It had opened the way for Tre to suggest that Kip should be in the simulator, so that he could start collecting data as soon as possible.

Ean had not looked happy, Kip knew he preferred to have the cats and cabin boys with him, but he had agreed.

The jump went smoothly. The Willow did not decelerate or even make a correction. Kip guessed that the captain had piloted the ship rather than Cas.

As soon as they were clear of the gate, Kip sent his first coded transmission. To his surprise it did not transmit. Instead he received an error message. He immediately tried the backup transmitter only that wasn't working either.

That was strange; the odds of both transmitters malfunctioning must be low. He was partway through the calculation when the simulator's link to the intercom activated.

"This is Obe. Both transmitters are non-operational."

Kip thrust the incomplete calculation into a deeper layer of his mind.

"*This is the captain. Kip, please run a diagnostic and advise.*"

Kip activated his link. "This is Kip. Understood and will do."

Then there was a clunk. He was wondering what it could be when the alarms started.

He froze. What was he meant to do? Should he be getting out of the simulator and into his suit or should he be trying to find out what was happening?

Then the blare of the alarm dipped and there was a voice in his ear. "*Kip, this Tre on the sim to sim channel. Are you there?*"

Hearing Tre's voice calmed him. "I'm here," he replied.

"*I am sealing the simulator rooms. It will mean we can continue working. We may be under attack. Anything you can find out will be useful. Report to me directly over this channel.*"

"I understand," Kip acknowledged.

The transmitters were definitely not working; they must have been deliberately damaged. Kip assigned a lower layer of his mind to the task of finding an alternative way of transmitting and concentrated on incoming data from the detectors, including the cameras.

There were at least two ships, probably three, and there was a small foreign object stuck to the hull.

The alarm died away; three minutes had passed. Kip knew that outside the simulator the red light would still be flashing.

"This is the captain. We may be under attack. Suits and weapons. Report in."

He couldn't get into a suit without leaving the simulator. Did the captain know Tre had told him to stay in it? Would Ean be angry with him? Kip swept the thoughts to one side and partitioned them away. He needed to concentrate. The crew was beginning to report.

"This is Vic, I am in the engine room. Suited."

"This is Loy, I am in the infirmary. Suited."

There was a third ship and the foreign object on the hull was transmitting.

"This is Ean, I am in the crewroom with Jax, Rae and Noe. All suited."

The transmitter was mimicking their signature. "Kip to Tre," he reported. "They have stuck a transmitter on our hull. It is transmitting a distress call as if from us." Kip paused while the transmission finished and began again. "It is citing a drive malfunction."

The word 'drive' was barely past his lips when Tre reacted.

"Vic! Get away from the drive. Now!"

The Willow's guns fired; once, twice, three times. Then the whole ship shuddered and the camera images were moving quickly, as if the ship was spinning. For a split second Kip wondered why he wasn't feeling it but then the simulator synchronised with the ship and he was tumbling head over feet.

He mustn't throw up. It would be really bad to throw up.

"This is the captain."

How could he sound so calm?

"We have been hit near the tail of the ship. We are sealing the levels. All crew with the exception of the captain and Enforcer Tre are ordered to abandon ship. This overrides all other orders."

Abandon ship? He wasn't even in his suit. Could he get to a pod without one? What about his stuff?

"Kip, please acknowledge," the captain added.

Kip realised he had not even reported in. "This is Kip in simulator one. Orders understood. Vacating simulator."

Once he cracked the lid of the simulator open, Kip realised how difficult that was going to be. The ship was still tumbling. He lay there for a moment, uncertain what to do.

"This is the captain. Firing lateral rockets to correct pitch and roll. Brace yourselves."

Kip pulled the lid closed; if the simulator was operational it would smooth out the changes in angular momentum.

He lay in the simulator listening to the intermittent roar of the rockets. There had been no warning; no challenge. That made their attackers pirates, even if they were pretending to help a ship with a defective drive.

What would happen to them? Possibilities multiplied, filling his mind. None of them were good. He was cold. He had to fight the urge to curl up into a ball.

Most of the possibilities in his head vanished; it he stayed in the simulator there was over a two-thirds chance he would die.

The ship had stopped tumbling. Kip pushed open the lid and climbed out. He had to concentrate on getting into a suit: four steps across the room to the locker; open door; toe off his shoes; pull off his top; grab suit; put suit on.

He had done it. His suit was on. Next was a pod and the nearest was next door in his workshop.

Ean did not think about whys or maybes. All that mattered was getting into suits. He headed for the locker but Rae was ahead of him. Ean caught the first suit and threw it to Noe. The second went to Jax. The third he put on.

The four of them were suited before the alarm stopped. Ean went to the intercom and waited.

There was the familiar click. *"This is the captain. We are under attack. Suits and weapons. Report in."*

"This is Vic; I am in the engine room. Suited."

"This is Loy, I am in the infirmary. Suited."

Where was Kip? Why wasn't he reporting? Ean depressed the button. "This is Ean; I am in the crewroom with Jax, Rae and Noe. All suited."

The three of them were looking at him; their eyes were wide and between the flashes of red light their faces were pale.

Then Tre's voice came over the intercom, "*Vic! Get away from the drive. Now!*" Then the Willow's guns started firing.

Ean was about to warn the boys about possible impacts when the whole ship shook and the floor went from under him.

"Helmets!" he yelled, raising his own as he fell. His helmet hit the edge of a bunk and then he was thrown onto the ceiling; the ship was flipping nose over tail.

His finally managed to get a handhold. He looked about. Rae was holding one of the grab rails with one hand and Jax with the other. Noe was between two of the bunks.

The intercom clicked again. "*This is the captain. We have been hit near the tail of the ship. We are sealing the levels.*"

Ean tried not to think about Vic, who may not have got clear, or about Obe, Cas and the captain, who were now separated from him by blast doors.

The captain was continuing. "*All crew with the exception of Enforcer Tre are ordered to abandon ship. This overrides all other orders. Kip, please acknowledge.*"

Ean's heart speeded up. What orders? Why was Kip doing anything other than getting into a suit?

"*This is Kip in simulator one. Orders understood. Vacating simulator.*"

Kip was still in the simulator? If they survived this, Ean was going to have words with Tre.

"*This is the captain. Firing lateral rockets to correct pitch and roll. Brace yourselves.*"

Rae had Jax, so he was fine. Ean looked towards Noe. Determined brown eyes looked back at him, confirming that Noe intended to survive this as he had survived everything else life had thrown at him.

The rockets began firing.

There was no point trying to move until they were stable, so Ean took advantage of the time to think. They had to be after Jax. He activated his suit radio; Tre was bound to be monitoring all the channels.

He chose channel three. "Tre?"

"*Switch to channel five*," Tre told him.

There were only four channels marked on the dial. Ean turned the dial to the space above four. "Tre?"

"*You get Jax into a pod and launch it*," Tre told him. "*Soon as you can. All other decisions are up to you. I love you, Ean.*"

Ean's gut twisted. He had wanted to hear those words for so long but not now, not like this. "Will do, Tre. I love you," he added in a whisper but there was no reply.

The ship was almost stable; the rockets were on their final few, short bursts.

"As soon as the ship is stable, we will be heading for the pods," he reminded them.

"Can we get our stuff?" Noe asked.

Ean would need to get a laser pistol and he did not want them going ahead. "Twenty seconds," he told them. "I want you to count it out loud."

They ran; Jax and Rae towards their cabin and Noe towards his bunk. Ean headed for the panel that concealed the weapon's locker and inputted the code to unlock it. He thrust a laser pistol into each of the holsters on his suit, relocked the panel and shut the panel. As he turned, he could see Jax and Rae coming out of their cabin. Noe was already at the door of the crewroom, waiting for him.

"We are heading for the room next to the closet, that is where the pods are," Ean reminded them because people forgot stuff in a crisis. "You lead the way, Jax."

As they exited the galley, Loy joined them. Like them, his helmet was up but the faceplate open. He fell in at the back, beside Ean.

"We are going to pod and launch the boys," Ean said quietly.

"Good plan," Loy agreed.

"Maybe you should go and look for Kip," Ean suggested.

"No, it will be quicker with both of us," Loy replied.

By the time they entered the room next to the closet, Rae already had the wall panel open, exposing the three by three array of pods. He pulled out a pod from the lowest row, which was already on a trolley. He was looking expectantly at Jax, who was scowling back.

"You first, Jax," Ean confirmed. "Put down your helmet and unseal the access points on your suit."

"But…" Jax began.

"Now, Jax!" Ean ordered. "The longer you take, the more

dangerous it is for everyone else."

"You next, Noe," Loy said, pulling out the second of the lower pods and opening it.

Noe did not hesitate. He tossed his small backpack into the foot end of the pod before lowering his helmet, turning the five access points to open and hopping in.

"Thank you Loy, thank you Ean," he said as he lay down.

Ean blinked back tears as Loy lowered the lid and sealed the pod.

Meanwhile Jax had followed Noe's example and, behind him, Ean could hear Rae rolling out a third pod and taking it over to the airlock. Ean waited until Jax was lying down and kissed him on the forehead.

"Until we meet again," he said keeping his voice steady. "May the Lady be with you. Take care of Rae for me."

Jax managed a small nod and Ean shut the lid.

Rae was already in his pod and Loy was closing it.

"Wait" Ean called. He hurried over.

Loy nodded and went to open the airlocks.

Ean looked down into Rae's eyes with their starbursts of gold. "Look after him and yourself, Rae," he said. "I love you. We all do."

Rae twitched his whiskers in reply.

Ean fastened the lid. He opened the inner door of the airlock. At the other end, in the outer door, was a small viewing port. He peered through it, into the small circle of space beyond, but could see nothing.

Jax's pod was the first one ejected, as Tre had asked, follow closely by Rae's and then Noe's. They reset the airlocks and looked at each other.

"I am going to find Kip," Ean stated.

"I'll come with you," Loy replied. "Once we've launched Kip's pod, the two of us can persuade Tre that it is time to leave."

Ean managed a small smile; as if he could persuade Tre to do anything.

Tre acquired another target and fired. The three large ships were staying out of range and there were too many of the small fighters; no matter how many he took out there always seemed to be more. He was down to three guns; one of the lower turrets had been taken out when the drive had been hit and he had lost the nose turret to a direct hit soon afterwards.

He wished he had missiles.

At least keeping Kip in the simulator for those extra minutes had meant that he knew what was happening. The key piece of information had been the false message about the Willow's drive malfunctioning.

They intended to destroy the ship and pretend that the drive had blown up. They must have bribed the gunners at the gate to go along with deception.

He checked the feed from the radio receiver. There, buried in what looked like background noise, were the signals that told him that five pods had been launched, two from the control room and three from the crewroom level. The beacon in one of them had detected the transponder in Jax's brain, confirming Jax was inside.

It was time to go.

He set the simulator to mimic what he had been doing; picking off the small craft before they got close enough to damage the remaining guns. It would not be as effective as he was, but it would buy a little more time.

He refused to think about Ean and the others; all that mattered was Jax.

Then he was out of the simulator and unlocking the panel that no one else, not even Kip, knew was there. Behind it was his spacesuit; a spacesuit built for a cyborg.

Ean tried his suit radio first; if Kip did not answer he would have to decide whether to use the intercom or start looking.

"This is Ean. Kip, where are you?"

"I'm in my workshop getting a pod out," Kip answered.

Loy was already heading for the door. Ean ran past him. "Kip's in his workshop. We'll use the pods from there."

As he entered the room was Kip pushing an open pod into the airlock. It made Ean ridiculously proud to see Kip in his suit, trying his best to do what he had been taught; he had come a long way from the boy who had frozen when the alarms sounded.

Ean pulled him away, taking the opportunity to give him a hug. Meanwhile Loy pulled the pod back out onto its trolley.

"In you get," Ean ordered. "Have you unsealed your access points?"

Kip nodded and climbed in.

Ean kissed his forehead. "It will be fine, we will find you," he promised. Kip's mind would be full of possibilities, most of them horrific; a simple promise might give him something to hang on to.

He shut the lid and sealed the pod. Then, just as he was about to slide the pod forward into the airlock, he saw something cross the viewport of the outer door.

"There is someone out there," he stated.

Ean pulled the trolley away from the airlock and jumped in. Crawling to the other end, he pressed his helmet close to the viewport for the best possible view.

There were small, dark figures out there; lots of them. One of them accelerated and he saw the brief burst of a jet gun.

He felt sick. They had probably been on the other side as well. At this very moment, they would be picking up the pods carrying Rae, Jax and Noe. Then, from nowhere, there was a small face looking back at him, distorted by layers of transparent material. Ean caught a glimpse of eyes without whites, whiskers and long, pointed canines before he drew back.

"There are lots of people out there," he announced as he crawled backwards out of the airlock. "From their size they are hybrids. They're waiting for the pods."

Loy thought for a moment and then shrugged. "What other option do we have? As soon as they confirm they have Jax they will blow the ship up. Do you want to be aboard when they do that?"

Ean made himself think. Would they blow up the ship? Surely they would board it first? It did not feel right to be pushing Kip's pod into their hands. He turned his radio to channel five. "Tre?" he whispered.

There was no answer.

"Alive we have some value," Loy reminded him. He began pushing Kip's pod into the airlock.

Ean pulled it back. "No, we should try and think of something else." The Willow had fourteen levels. They couldn't have people waiting outside each one. There were ways through the blast doors. They could find another way out. He began opening Kip's pod.

Loy put a hand on his arm. "This is a mistake, Ean. You are endangering Kip's life."

There was something wrong. Loy's voice was too smooth; too

measured. Too late, he realised that Loy had opened the access point on the upper arm of his suit. He twisted away but not before he felt the needle bite into his flesh.

Ean staggered back and drew one of his laser pistols.

Loy was holding up his hands. "Think, Ean. I am doing this for your own good. It's better to be off the ship."

Ean knew Loy was lying. He tried to speak but his mouth would not cooperate. He brought the pistol up but his arm was becoming numb and moved too slowly.

Loy knocked it out of his hand. "Stop fighting it, Ean," he advised. He closed the distance between them and took Ean's second pistol. Then he slammed shut the lid of Kip's pod, slid it forward into the airlock and shut the inner door.

Ean made one last attempt to master his limbs but his lunge only ended up with him on the floor. He looked up and saw Loy turn the switch. Kip's pod was shot out into their attacker's arms.

"You next," Loy announced.

He tried to crawl away but Loy grabbed his ankle and pulled him back. "He doesn't love you," he stated.

Ean froze.

"He's incapable of love, or of any emotion," Loy continued. "He was before, but not since. He's not even human. How could he be? Now he's just a combination of flesh, metal and electronics; a machine. Oro destroyed him. The same way he destroyed anyone with enough spirit to oppose him."

Was he talking about Tre? Who was Oro? What did Loy mean?

Loy manhandled him into a sitting position, lifted his chin and kissed him gently on the lips. Then he pulled back and looked into Ean's eyes. "He's a cyborg, Ean. It was all just an act. He needed a queen for his perfect crew and, by the Lady, he chose well. You needed affection so he provided a show of it. He doesn't, can't, care. Look what he did to Ben."

Ben? What about Ben? Ean fought against the enveloping greyness but it was hopeless. Then he was falling down a shaft; away from the Loy's voice and into the darkness.

27

Kip had braced himself as Ean shut the pod. He immediately regretted his decision to reset the controls so that he could
control the pod from inside. If it had been on automatic, it
would have started putting him to sleep seconds after it was
closed.

Then the lid opened partway, which was weird. He almost sat
up but Loy's words made him hesitate.

"This is a mistake, Ean. You are endangering Kip's life."

Then there was an exclamation of disbelief from Ean and
sounds of a scuffle. What was happening?

Loy spoke again "Think, Ean. I am doing this for your own
good. It's better to be off the ship." There were more sounds,
including a grunt of pain and something hitting the floor.
"Stop fighting it, Ean," Loy ordered.

Kip had just decided to jump out when the lid was slammed
closed, hitting him on the head. He fell back, stunned. Then
the pod was moving forward and there was the thud of the
inner airlock closing.

He knew what came next and managed to make himself relax
as the pod was ejected.

The launcher thrust the pod beyond the gravitational field of the ship. Kip felt the force pulling him into the mattress lessen; a small push had him floating free until the tip of his nose and his knees touched the underside of the lid.

Kip knew exactly how the pod should behave. The calculations were easy. He should be travelling at a steady velocity away from the ship, not slowing abruptly, turning and accelerating in a new direction.

Someone had hold of his pod.

Luckily the pod was made to accommodate people much bulkier than Kip. There was a fair amount of wriggle space, easily enough for him to get a torch out of one outer pocket of his suit and his small toolkit out of another. Then he began disassembling the internal interface of the control panel. The pods had been chosen by Tre. They were bound to have capacities far beyond keeping someone alive.

When Kip had put on his suit he had intended to do exactly what Ean would have wanted him to do: unseal the simulator room; go into his workshop; get a pod out; go through the tricky procedure of getting into one and launching it singlehanded.

Only that took him past the door to this den and Kip hadn't been able to resist. A thirty-second detour and he had his data crystal array in a backpack and the outer pockets of his suit filled with tools.

The priority was making the pod look like it was set on automatic with Kip unconscious inside. Next was seeing if there were any detectors, or anything that could be used as a detector, on the outer surface. A camera would be good or, failing that, a microphone.

Kip set to work.

Tre had forgotten how long it took to get the suit on, never mind interfaced with his processor and enhanced senses. It did not help that he had not practised wearing it for close to fifteen standards.

Every second that passed, the situation would be changing. In desperation, he hardwired his helmet's display to the simulator so that he could monitor what was happening. Nine of the Willow's pods had been launched; one short. The likely explanation was that Vic had not survived the hit on the drive. Tre tried to ignore the pang of regret. He should only be thinking about Jax; he could not afford to be distracted.

Despite his success with the guns, there were still more than twenty of the small fighters out there; too many pairs of eyes. Being dressed in a super-spacesuit would make him an obvious target. However, he could not stay on the ship. They obviously intended to destroy it and there was a limit to the damage the suit it could withstand. He disconnected from the simulator and approached the door, intending to unseal it.

Only, beyond it, he could hear footsteps. Not heavy enough for an adult or even an adolescent. It reminded him how Rae had sounded when he had first joined the crew. He walked over to the simulator and used it to connect to the ship's systems.

The ship was swarming with small, suited figures. Tre could not make out if they were searching the ship or stripping it.

Then someone thumped on the door. He jumped, he could not help himself. There was chittering, which could be them talking, and then the unmistakable sound of someone cutting through the door.

He froze. Did he make a run for an airlock? There was no way he would not been seen and there were too many of them to be sure he could kill every witness.

Once they knew of his existence they would take precautions. Even a cyborg in a super-suit could not survive a direct hit from a big enough gun. Also whoever was after Jax obviously wanted him alive; otherwise they would have just destroyed the ship.

Their cutter was remarkably effective; he could see the metal distorting.

He made the decision; there was a better chance of getting to Jax if he remained undetected. He stepped into the recess where he had hidden the suit and closed the panel.

The outside of the pod proved to be depressingly short of detectors. All Kip could do was try to interpret the way the pod was moving. Given the number of changes in speed and direction, Kip guessed that the pod had been intercepted and towed to a ship.

As much as he wanted that ship to be the Willow, it didn't seem very likely.

The gas pressure and oxygen concentration outside the pod were rising, which was consistent with being in an airlock. There was no downward force, so if the ship had gravitational field generators they had entered where the field was negligibly low.

Two more changes in direction and, suddenly, Kip was dropping head first. He choked back a shriek; he thought the pod was soundproof but he couldn't be certain. He was wondering what would happen when the pod stopped when it did. He managed to brace himself against the sides of the pod to stop himself cracking his head on the end of the pod and, by luck, caught his backpack between his butt and the pod before it could fall further.

Then he was horizontal to the gravitational field of about one gee and discovering that a backpack containing a data crystal array wasn't the most comfortable thing to be lying on.

He stopped moving. He felt the pod being lifted up, moved sideways and put down.

After a while he risked wriggling the backpack out from under his thighs.

He had another go at finding something, anything, that would transfer information from the surface to the inside of the pod but it was hopeless; all the systems were designed to work in the other direction.

Other than controlling the internal environment, the only thing he could do from inside the pod was open it. In the end, Kip decided he had better do that before someone else did.

He made sure that the gas pressure was the same inside as outside, so there wouldn't be a hiss. Then he undid the catch, holding the lid closed in case it was sprung.

It wasn't. Kip cracked open the lid by the smallest amount, hoping to hear something.

Someone was shouting. "Don't you dare put a foot in here, you filthy little rats. Leave it on the trolley out there and get back to your own level where you belong."

Kip held his breath. There was a rhythmic squeaking, like a wheel that needed oiling.

"One, two, three, lift," the voice said, this time at a more normal volume. There was a double grunt and a thump. "Luck's twat, these pods are heavy," the same person complained.

Another person mumbled.

"I don't care how strong they are, I don't want those dirty rats in here." It was the first person again.

There was more mumbling.

"Don't be stupid," the first person replied. "It was a Trad ship, so of course there won't be any women aboard. Maybe some pretty boys. Not that they'll be pretty by the time we get a go at them." He laughed. "Who cares? As long as they have a hole to poke."

The other one joined in and Kip shivered; the mumbling one had a really scary laugh.

Another pod arrived and then another. Each time the loud one shouted at the 'filthy rats' and the two men would have a conversation, of which Kip could only hear one side.

It was enough. Kip knew beyond doubt that he had no wish to meet either of them. He spent the time deciding what their capturers would think if they found an empty pod. He did not want them looking for him.

After a while he worked it out. From the outside it had to read as if it had an unconscious person inside, like his did, but from the inside it should read as if it had been empty. That way it would seem like a decoy.

Then, finally, the conversation turned to something more interesting.

"That's the last one," the loud one stated. "Let's go take a break. Get some food."

There was a mumbled reply.

"It'll be fine. You worry too much," the loud one insisted. "There's no way we'll miss the commander coming this way. Not with all his hangers-on." His tone changed. "You could sniff some stuff," he wheedled.

Then they were gone. They even shut the door. Kip grabbed his backpack and was out of the pod before he could have second thoughts. He closed the lid behind him and ran to the next one along.

It was Rae and, of course, he was unconscious. Kip had not thought of that. He punched the button on the pod's control panel, so that it would give Rae a wake-up shot. Then he started resetting the pod so that it seemed like a decoy.

He resisted the urge to go to another pod. If it came to it, he could carry Rae. He couldn't carry two people.

He had just finished resetting the controls when Rae sat bolt upright. Then he was out of the pod and running about the room, sniffing each pod in turn. Kip guessed he was searching for Jax.

Kip checked the pod and found a backpack. He grabbed it and closed Rae's pod.

Rae was whimpering. Kip was going to suggest that they open a pod at random when Rae froze, his ears pricked and his whiskers arched.

"Someone's coming," he warned and shot across the room.

Kip lumbered after him. By the time he was half way there, Rae had yanked the cover off a service duct running under the floor.

"In," he ordered.

Kip didn't hesitate. He threw in both backpacks and jumped down, just managing to get out of the way as Rae followed him. Rae pulled the cover back into place and put a finger to his lips. Kip didn't need to be told. He made himself take small, quiet breaths and asked the Lady for it not to be a hybrid; he was sure he stank with fear.

Rae crouched in the duct, wishing he could hear more and smell anything other than Kip. He tuned out the sound of Kip's breathing and listened to the people entering the room and walking across the floor towards the pods. There were nine, maybe ten. From their footsteps they were all purebred men and most of them were heavy.

Luckily the service duct was illuminated, like the ones in the better maintained parts of Carrefour. There wasn't much light but it was enough for him to see Kip and hopefully Kip could see him.

Rae held up ten fingers and waggled a thumb, trying to tell Kip how many men there were.

Kip was concentrating on staying quiet and not breathing too hard but his eyes said he understood.

The people had stopped. Rae peered both ways. The duct seemed to run the length of the room, possibly into the corridor beyond. He signalled that Kip should stay where he was and Kip nodded. Then Rae crept forward until he was under where the pods were, which was also were the people's breathing was loudest. As he did so they started talking.

"So these are all the pods you retrieved?"

"Yes, commander."

"Only nine. How many in the crew?"

"Eleven, commander."

"Perhaps two were killed, commander."

"You should hope so, Mutt. Just as you should very much hope that the person we want is among those we retrieved. Doctor, will the occupants wake when the pods are opened?"

"Unlikely, commander. It is usual practice that there is a button in the pod that has to be pressed. I have a gaseous anaesthetic ready in case it is required. It is unlikely to clash with the drugs they have already received."

"Scar? Do you have anything to add?"

"No, commander."

"Very well. I shall go with your recommendation, doctor. Men, be ready to shoot but only do so if I give the order."

"Yes, commander!" a chorus of voices replied.

Rae made a note of the names of the people who had spoken: the commander, the doctor, Mutt and Scar. The commander was definitely the leader. Scar had sounded scary. Mutt had sounded and smelt scared. The doctor had sounded smug.

Then Rae heard the pods being opened one by one. He smelled Obe, Loy, Noe, Ean, Captain Mel, Cas and, finally, Jax. When he smelled Jax he wanted to burst through the floor to be beside him.

Only getting his head blown off was a really bad idea.

He made himself concentrate. There was no Tre, no Vic and the empty pods only smelt faintly of him and Kip.

"Only seven," the commander observed.

"Two decoys," Scar informed him.

"Mutt, tell your rats they have two more to find, four in all, and get over there to make sure they do it properly."

"Yes, commander." There were hurried footsteps followed by the sound of a door opening and closing. Some of the terrified stink faded.

Then there were other footsteps, slower and more measured, like someone was visiting each pod.

"None of them look like him," the commander stated.

"This one," the doctor informed him. "Although the hair and skin colour have been altered, the bone structure is correct."

There was a pause. "Yes. Good work, doctor. Scar, you understand what you have to do?"

"Deliver the boy to the client at the rendezvous on the planet."

Rae's heart began hammering. They were talking about Jax. They had to be talking about Jax.

"Untouched," Scar added and Rae froze. There had been something very, very bad in the way Scar had said 'untouched'.

"Yes, he is unexpectedly pretty," the commander observed. "You can take the other boy as a reward for your excellent service."

"Commander…" the doctor began.

"Yes, doctor?" the commander interrupted and Rae knew it was a warning rather than a question.

"It is not urgent," the doctor replied, sounding cowed rather than smug.

Then Scar and two of the men left and they took Jax with them. They took Noe too but Rae didn't have any caring to spare for Noe.

Rae listened to the sound of their footsteps as they receded. The duct led in that direction, so he followed, moving as silently as he could but determined not to lose Jax's trail.

Kip hadn't been able to hear all of the conversation. He had heard their leader, the one they called commander, and the man called Scar; their voices had carried. It had been enough to work out that Scar was taking Jax to a planet, which was most likely Verdant, to be delivered to someone. He was also taking 'the other boy' as 'a reward'.

Given how unboyish Obe looked these days, Kip guessed 'the other boy' was Noe.

By craning his neck Kip could see where Rae had been lying. He had gone. He had been there before Scar left with Jax but when Kip checked afterwards that part of the duct was empty.

He took a few slow, deep breaths to calm himself. Maybe Rae would come back.

He decided to concentrate on listening to any further conversation. There were fewer people now, which made it easier, and he decided to edge his way to where Rae had been lying to give him a better chance of hearing.

"Who is missing, doctor?" the commander asked.

There was a pause. "The enforcer, the one with the reputation as a fighter," the doctor answered. "Also the engineer and two of the cats. Perhaps the cats were with the engineer in the engine room."

"Good thing the Navaja brat wasn't," the commander observed. "Close the pods and post a guard on the door. I don't want any of these damaged until I am sure I have no need of them."

Kip's spirits lifted; maybe he could wake the others.

"I recommend guards inside as well, commander. It is possible that the pods are programmed to wake the occupants after a certain period of time within a breathable atmosphere."

Kip's mouth was suddenly dry. Would they make the connection and realise that the two empty pods could have had people in them when they came aboard? Even if they didn't, he wasn't going to be able to unpod the others with guards inside the room.

"A good point, doctor," the leader acknowledged. "We will have guards inside and out. You!"

"Yes, commander!" another man answered.

"Arrange it. I expect the merchandise to remain untouched. I am holding you personally responsible."

"Yes, commander!" the man repeated.

Then the commander and the doctor left.

Kip lay there. Rae didn't come back. Kip remembered Rae running off the end of the pier. Rae was never going to accept being separated from Jax; he would either make it onto the ship dropping to the planet or he would be caught trying.

If Rae was caught then they would make the connection, even if they hadn't yet, and start looking for him. He should move and find somewhere better to hide.

Then he would need to find their network.

Tre had never been so frustrated. Every fibre of his being was demanding that he burst out of his hiding place and slaughter everyone between him and Jax. Wearing the suit made it worse, because it boosted his adrenalin.

Common sense told him otherwise. He should wait.

He couldn't even check where Jax's pod was because that meant powering up the suit and he knew how noisy it was.

The little hybrids didn't seem to be in a hurry. He could hear them on the other side of the panel, disassembling his simulator. Surely the pretence that the ship had blown up killing all the crew wore a bit thin if they stripped it bare before it exploded?

Then, suddenly, the sounds of tools on metal ceased and there was an outburst of chittering.

Tre boosted his hearing to maximum, winced at the resulting cacophony of sound and instructed his processor to prioritise speech.

To his surprise it worked.

"Stop that!" a man was yelling. "I told you no stripping. I don't care how expensive the components are." The man's voice softened. "He's going to kill me, he's going to kill me." Then he was yelling again. "Have you found anyone? Just one? There are meant to be four. Four!"

One? Could that be Vic? Tre wondered if he was alive. Who in Known Space were the other two? Nine pods had left the ship and nine plus two made eleven.

There was a pause and some sounds that hinted at a radio exchange. Unfortunately his processor could make no sense of it. Then the man started yelling again.

"We go. Now. Three minutes and I am going to blow the ship. And, no, I am not just saying it. See this in my hand? It's the detonator. Three hundred and sixty, three hundred and fifty-nine, three hundred and fifty-eight, three hundred and fifty-seven…"

There was a lot of squeaking, chittering and running; then silence. Then Tre heard very human footsteps along the corridor and the unmistakable sound of one of the escape hatches being cycled.

It was time to go; out of the cupboard, through the simulator room and along the corridor to the shaft outside the captain's cabin. Someone had opened the blast doors, which was convenient. Tre dived down the shaft and, after he had crossed the turnover point, landed on the ladder. He climbed up towards the engine room.

Blood was splattered around the tail end of the shaft but there was no sign of a body. Satisfied that he had done everything he could for Vic, Tre headed for the nearest escape hatch.

It was closer to five minutes than three when the explosives were detonated, so he was well clear.

Tre watched the Willow, his home for the last twelve standards, the home Ean had built for them, being totally and utterly destroyed.